Tide & Scale

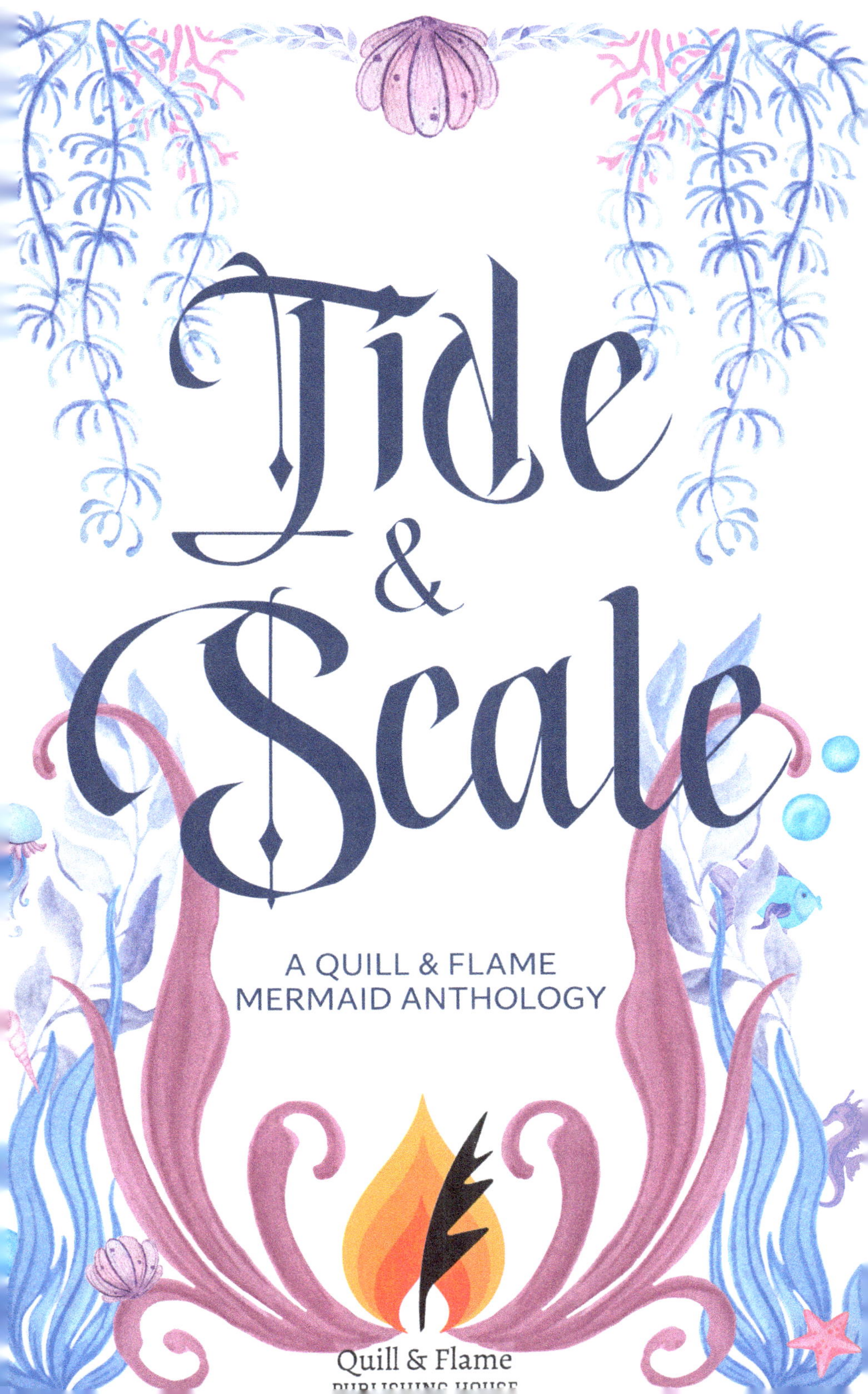

Tide & Scale
A QUILL & FLAME
MERMAID ANTHOLOGY
Quill & Flame
PUBLISHING HOUSE

For Beka Gremikova:
For Hannah Carter, my fellow mermaid, editor, and Aizawa Stan.
Thanks for agreeing to this off-the-cuff idea and journeying with
me into this grand open sea full of pirates, mermaids, sirens, and
monsters.

For Hannah Carter:
For Beka Gremikova, because without your hard work, fearless
edits, and extreme grace, this anthology would never be. I'm so
grateful to have you as my editing partner, my fellow Loid simp,
my sneaky Athelas, my stalwart Gus—and one of my best friends.
WE DID THE THING. Love you, *Baby Gorl*!

Art
Image 1: Angela Patera
Image 2: Kaitlyn Emery
Image 3: Meaghan Ward
Image 4: Meaghan Ward
Image 5: Maxine Monroe
Image 6: Kaylyn Davis

INTRODUCTION

To all fellow mermaids and pirates whose sense of adventure takes them onto the sea—welcome. Did you smell the salt air as you cracked open the spine of this book? We dearly hope so, because this anthology is not for any land-lubbers. This is for those of us whose spirits are made of brine and sea foam, who stand at the edge of the shoreline and wonder what might lurk beneath the undertow.

In these pages, you'll find many mystical and mysterious mers and monsters. As we started pulling this collection together, one question bubbled up in our minds: what makes mermaids so intriguing that they have such universal appeal? In all cultures, you can find mermaid lore and mermaid admirers. From *The Little Mermaid* to *H2O: Just Add Water*, *Splash* to *Ponyo*, we find these magnificent creatures in all mediums, across all continents, and throughout many centuries.

Perhaps part of their appeal is because they have such strong lore. There are many fascinating tales (pun intended) where we can learn more about mermaids.

Perhaps it is because longing seems to encapsulate so many mermaid stories. Hans Christian Andersen's heroine longs for a human soul—a timeless yearning that has inspired many retellings.

Or maybe they appeal to our sense of adventure, that innate desire to explore the unknown. Maybe that is why pirates often crop up in mermaid stories. Even before Johnny Depp swaggered onto the big screen as the beloved Captain Jack Sparrow, people have long been fascinated with the freedom and excitement in swashbuckling yarns. Is it a coincidence that both pirates and mermaids inhabit the sea? I think not. The vast waters are very much unexplored, and perhaps this awakens a spirit of exploration inside us, long dormant in today's society.

Mermaids also bring with them a theme of change—of being something different, something unique. They are an enigma, but beautiful and mysterious all the while. Some souls crave this, to be away from the mundane and closer to the miraculous. But yet, these all-powerful creatures still exhibit both emotional and physical vulnerability. They are relatable, and we find it easy to slip into their shoes—er...*flippers*.

Perhaps you, yourself, have your own reasons for loving mermaids, and that is what draws you here. We hope that you will enjoy the pieces found in these pages. Some of them sink to the depths of the ocean and linger in the darkness there while others float along the waves with the sun shining upon their faces. Sometimes these mermaids must make hard choices, fight monsters, or sacrifice a piece of themselves. Sometimes they make friends with pirates; sometimes they find enemies amongst friends. Because of this, we have included a trigger warning page at the back of the book if there are some mermaids whose grottos you may not wish to visit just yet.

For all you intrepid adventurers, we bid you welcome into the deep blue. Beware: sirens lurk here...but so does hope.

—Beka Gremikova and Hannah Carter

Trigger Warnings

Please be advised that there will be spoilers in this list of Trigger Warnings. We have tried to be as thorough as possible, and apologize in advance for any triggers we may have missed.

"A Creature Birthed of Rage": themes of human sacrifice

"Hope is a Dangerous Thing": death of a loved one/parent

"A Sea Full of Stars": Implied contemplation of suicide

"The Mermaid's Soul": themes of human sacrifice, starvation, loss of loved ones

"Ebbing of the Tide": themes of euthanasia, family fractures, and memory loss

"Sea of Sorrow": themes of parental loss, grief, and memory loss

"The Sea's Beloved": themes of human sacrifice

"The Song of the Siren Sea": parental abandonment

"The Day Water Became Wood": death of a loved one, death of self

"A Wish and a Choice": themes of self-sacrifice, death, loss of a loved one, grief

"The Selkie's Gift": themes of implied sexual assault

Please be advised that the following stories have tragic or bitter-sweet endings: "Ebbing of the Tide," "Into the Depths," "Sea of Sorrow," "Hunger," "At Fin's Length," "The Day Water Became Wood," "A Wish and a Choice."

Tears of the Sea

Savannah Jezowski

They say it is an abomination to leave the sea.

In the darkness of the sea caves, the Mer mothers croon that to us while we are still cocooned in our eggs, long before we even know who we are. They tell us that the sea is our realm, that we belong to her and she to us. It is an unbreakable bond, and no one ever truly leaves the sea.

No one wants to.

But I have always been different. I hatched too early and was born with a disfigured fin, my body smaller and weaker than the others. My skin was a mottled white, with only hints of green, while all my brothers and sisters were born in vibrant shades of aqua and turquoise and amber. My mother claims this is why I am unreasonable, why I long for things I shouldn't, why I ask the questions no one else ever thinks to.

You must fight the weakness, LeRae, she told me once as she tucked me and the other hatchlings into our hollows, covering us with seaweed wraps to stave off the chill of the night waters. *You must not go the way of the sand-walkers; they are abominations.*

That night, I dreamed that I swam to the shore, stood up on two legs, and walked away from the sea. Ever since then, I have wondered what would really happen if I tried to leave the sea. No one will tell me; it is an abomination, they say.

I like to go to the coves to hide among the rocks and watch life beyond the water. It is beautiful in its own way, in a sharper, clearer sense. On land, things are not hidden behind aquamarine ripples. The plants do not waft in the currents but are instead stirred in gentle breezes. I like the feel of the wind, but the sun dries out my skin. Here, the sea is almost too warm, the shallow waters heated by the sun.

It is here, in my rocky hideaway, that I first see them: a male and a female. They came from the forest and built a shelter on the beach. During the day, the male fishes in their little boat, his dark skin glistening in the sunlight. At night, they sit on the beach and hold hands. The murmur of their voices and occasional bursts of laughter echo across the gentle swell of the waves.

I long to know what they say to each other. The Mer do not laugh, not often. I asked one of the elder Mer once why that was so, and he said, *Laughter is a foolish thing when there are mouths to feed.*

But the sand-walkers do not live by this code. They work endlessly and often go hungry, but still they laugh. They always laugh.

One day, the male sand-walker brings his boat close to my hiding place. I wait under the water in the shadow of the rocks while he dives into the water to fish. It amazes me that he can swim without fins, but his long legs propel him through the water. He surfaces frequently for air, as he has no gills. My fingers press against the soft row of slits along my throat.

He catches a fish in his mouth and surfaces to toss it into the boat. He does not have much success but persists throughout the day. I watch him until he returns to the shore as the sun lowers in the sky. The water has begun to cool and soothes my sunbaked skin.

So this is where you hide.

I dive into the water at the intrusion into my thoughts. A Mer waits for me deeper down, concealed in the shadows. It is one of the Guardians, Selken. *I should tell your brother where you play, merling.*

You follow me? I dart up to him so that our faces are only inches apart. It is a challenge, but he merely splays his palm across my forehead, the way elders do to the young. It is often a fond gesture, but I find it demeaning. To me, it means that I am young and foolish, and I amuse him. *I do not need following.*

Especially from a Guardian only two hatches beyond me.

Oma may not think so. Selken no longer smiles, the dark sea-weed-green of his eyes filled with troubling thoughts, like stormy water churned up by angry winds.

My heart throbs faintly; I know my older brother would agree with him. They are bonded, sworn friends; they never disagree. *Oma does not need to know everything.*

He shakes his head at my suggestion. I bare my teeth, but I am angrier at myself than him. I swim back up to the surface, knowing it will irk him. To my surprise, he splashes out right onto my rock beside me. I have never seen him out of the water before; his skin is a deep aquamarine, with swirls that are almost pearl and silver. Even in the darkness of the deep water, I could always see his color, but not with the sun glinting off his scales.

He is beautiful. I look down at my arm and rub skin that lacks vibrancy, that's muted and sickish.

I almost fall back into the water when he takes my hand and examines it, rubbing the fingers and the webbing between them, as if he has never seen a hand before. I try to pull away, but he tightens his grip.

"I've been keeping watch over you for some time. You're not like the others." His voice is surprisingly mellow. I find that I like the sound of it.

I turn my face away. It doesn't matter if he alludes to only my sisters or to all the Mer; I don't look like any of them.

"You're going to get hurt, LeRae."

His adamancy causes me to turn my eyes to his. A shudder ripples through me, tightening into a ball in the pit of my stomach. "What do you mean?"

Selken jerks his head toward the shore. "Sand-walkers are dangerous, merling. You shouldn't come here anymore."

"I'm just watching."

The way he looks at me makes me feel as if he can read my heart and see the truth: that I do much more than watch, that I dream about walking on the sand.

"Be careful that your watching does not become your downfall."

His words burden me, but that is something I am used to.

He insists on taking me back to the caves, and I sigh, knowing it will be a hard swim. But to my surprise, he matches pace with me and stops occasionally to point out a fish that he saw that I did not see, or to comment on a reef that looks extraordinarily average. I do not know if I should be flattered or offended. I deliberately pick up the pace.

It is late when we return, and my mother waits for me. Judging by the furrow between her eyes, I know she is upset. As soon as she sees us, her lithe fin propels her toward us through the dark water.

What have you been doing?

Her thoughts are forceful, angry, but laced with relief.

We were together, Selken tells her, matter-of-factly.

Together?

Something in my mother's tone bothers me. Selken is well liked in our pod; I am the last Mer he would ever spend time with willingly. But the way she says "together" means something more than, "We swam home from the cove admiring imaginary fish."

I was at the cove. He made me come home. I watch the truth drain the color from her cheeks. She looks at me, no thoughts connecting us, but I know what she is thinking: I am always a disappointment.

We were at the cove, he admits, scowling at me. *Together.*

I wrinkle my nose at him, knowing he meant to irk me and feeling annoyed. For some reason, my mother snorts. I glance at her, startled by the bubbles dancing from her parted lips and up her delicate cheeks. She seals her lips and jerks her head toward our cave. This means I will hear more later, but not in front of Selken.

I begin to swim away when Selken's thoughts interrupt me. *I would have wished to speak to her father.*

My father is dead, killed many years ago by the striped shark that harasses the coastal waters. There is only one reason why Selken would confess something so personal to my mother, and it is a ludicrous reason.

Oma will hear your words, my mother tells him, casting me a furtive glance I cannot interpret. *We are willing.*

You are willing, I tell her, deliberately blocking Selken from my thoughts. *I am not! This is Oma's doing. I won't be fishbait for my brother.*

Selken is a noble hunter, my mother tells me, *and Oma will give his blessing. This is best, I think.*

Best for who? You put them up to this, I see. You think a noble husband will make me a noble Mer, Mother? When she does not deny the accusation, I know it is the truth. *Why is it so wrong for me to go to the cove? I just like to watch them.*

They are not like us, LeRae. She catches my face in her webbed fingers and peers earnestly into my eyes. *They have turned their backs on the sea; they are the most dangerous adversaries you will ever encounter. I beg you to see reason!*

Sand-walkers are not monsters.

They are more dangerous than monsters. They are betrayers. Selken's thoughts intrude into our conversation. Clearly my mother is feeding him my thoughts, or perhaps I am simply being careless and letting him in. Very well, let him eavesdrop. What he hears will surely make him despise me.

Maybe they are not as bad as we have been told. I think about the sand-walkers on the beach: how they live, how they love, how they laugh.

My mother's face darkens in anger. *You are hopeless!*

See? I turn to Selken, my heart strangely heavy. *It is pointless. I am beyond hope.* I bare my teeth and spin away, swimming as fast as I can toward the cave. In my haste, I misjudge a turn and my damaged fin cannot keep me from smashing into a rock outcropping. I hiss with pain; wounded, angry, I swim to my hollow.

When I wake the next morning, my body aches from the impact. I am grateful my mother still sleeps as I leave the cave. I see Oma and some of the Guardians above me, their bodies silhouetted against the clear water sparkling in the morning sunlight. No doubt they are scanning the early morning waters for hungry predators. He sees me and frowns. Selken has told him of my behavior, I am sure. A lecture will be forthcoming if I do not disappear soon.

I am nearly to the cove when I hear the water stirring behind me. Instincts drive me toward the bottom of the sea, scattering a school of stingrays as I seek shelter on the reef. My heart thunders in my ears as I scan the water for dangers.

It is only me.

I loose a mouthful of exasperated bubbles as Selken's amused thoughts force themselves on me.

He appears above me, unarmed but for a black stone knife sheathed onto his arm. He is clearly not out to hunt. *You are fortunate I am not a shark, merling.*

And you that I am unarmed, I hiss at him, the tiny fins along the curve of my jawline flared in anger. I am sure Oma sent him after me. I ignore him and continue on my way, but I can hear the water stirring as he follows.

As I near the rocks, my skin crawls with unease. The ocean is still and quiet, crystal clear. I can easily see that all around us the seabed is deserted; I scan the waters anxiously. Selken's hand encases my arm in a biting grip.

A shadow passes over us. I flinch and shift closer to him, peering up as the fisherman's boat glides over us from the right, where trees cast long shadows over the sea. Relief floods through me, but then I notice that the bottom of the boat sinks deep into the water—as though it is weighted down.

Something is wrong.

Selken tugs on my arm, clearly indicating that we should leave, but I want to know what is happening. I try to pull away, but he bares his teeth and jerks his head toward the deep water.

Please! Just a moment—

Vibrations ripple through the water. Selken yanks me down to the bottom of the seabed, shielding my body with his. I glance up just as a sand-walker plunges from the boat. A dark red stain mingles with the water and begins to swirl around the motionless body. I stare up into the blank face of my sand-walker.

When I scream into the waves, Selken whips his knife out of the sheath and twists to see what I see. I yank at his arm, screaming for him to stop.

It's my sand-walker!

As one we glance upward, watching as the boat jags away. I slip free while Selken is distracted and rush to the sand-walker. He is heavier than he appears, but I pull him behind the rocks and remove him from the tug of the waves.

No gills. But I feel the faint pulsing of his lifeblood beneath his skin.

The boat heads straight for the beach. For the hut. Selken is screaming at me, his mental barrage hammering against my head.

They are going to kill her.

Somehow, I know this. Perhaps everything the Mer have told me is true; it's monstrous to kill your own. I throw back my head and scream. The sound of the Mer cry reverberates across the water, echoing over the lapping waves, rich and filled with a strength I didn't know I possessed. The sand-walker emerges from the hut, cries out, and disappears into the forest. The men on the boat shout and wave weapons in the air.

Selken yanks me back beneath the waves. *What do you think you are doing?*

They are going to kill her! Even before the thought has fully formed, I am swimming toward the boat. I can hear Selken behind me, feel his fingers grabbing for my fin, but I dart out of his grasp in an awkward pinwheel and angle up toward the boat. Gritting my teeth, I smash into the bottom of the boat full force. Two men topple into the water. I can barely hear their screams over the ringing of my own exploding head. I grab the man nearest me and yank him down to the seabed. He screams and thrashes until I release him. I let him surface and gulp at the air before grabbing him again and dragging him back to the bottom in a flurry of frantic bubbles. I do this twice before he begins to swim frantically for the shore.

Powerful hands grab me from behind. Dark sand-walker hands. They squeeze into the soft flesh of my arms, surely leaving bruises. Selken darts around me and yanks the sand-walker away, killing him with one swift stroke of his knife. Blood erupts into the water, rippling over the both of us.

Horrified, I stroke backward to free myself of the contamination.

The other sand-walkers flee to the shore and disappear into the jungle. I touch my forehead to Selken's hands, acknowledging that he has saved my life, that I am now indebted to him. He says nothing but helps drag my injured sand-walker toward the shore.

"We should leave him here, in the rocks." Selken's voice holds a grim, deadly edge. Our eyes meet, and I realize how worried he truly is.

We both could have met our deaths this day.

"I can't leave him here," I whisper.

Frustration mars Selken's beautiful face as he shoves away and sinks mostly below the water, his seaweed-green eyes churning with anger.

I continue alone, dragging my sand-walker to the beach.

The woman sees us coming and emerges from the jungle, running toward me. As soon as he is in the shallow water, I slither backward, toward the sea. But she cries out to me, dropping to her knees and wrapping her slender dark arms around her beloved.

For the first time, we truly see each other. I know the look in her weeping eyes.

I have seen that look before: in my mother's eyes, when Elder Brother saved her youngest hatchling from the belly of the white shark. We call it the Owing. My mother will forever be in Elder Brother's debt, as I will forever be in Selken's. I see the Owing in the sand-walker's black eyes now as she walks toward me. It would be a dishonor to swim away without giving her the satisfaction of acknowledging her debt. It is the nature of the Owing.

I use my arms to push myself up from the surf and drag my scales through the sand. It is difficult, but I struggle until the surf no longer reaches me. The sun burns into my scales, sizzling as the water drains away and evaporates. I have never experienced such pain as when my scales begin to fall away. By the time I find my feet and try to stand, the pain has left me, replaced by a soothing coolness that wraps around my body.

I am different, but I am still me.

I stagger, wrapped in a mess of seaweed. She thrusts her arms around me before I hit the sand, the words that pour from her lips as foreign to me as the legs that now replace my scales, but somehow I understand her. She points to her sand-walker—the lover, the fisherman—and presses her cheek to mine. I shiver as her warm flood of tears cascades down my cheek and onto my lips. I taste them and shudder with shock as my tongue recognizes the taste of her tears.

Salty like my scales. Salty like the sea. The truth of our kinship will forever change my course.

How can we be enemies when sand-walkers weep the sea?

I return to the water, smiling as the wet sand squishes between my toes. I dive into the surf and feel my legs twine together, once again a mangled fin. I call out to Selken with my thoughts.

You came back, then. His thoughts pelt me—fast, almost incoherent.

I can barely contain my excitement. I see him at last, swimming toward me with slow but powerful strokes. We hover just below the surface with sunlight casting rippling rays around us. His skin is a rainbow of vibrant colors. He stares at me. I can feel his thoughts, rumbling on the edge of my subconscious, like a storm brewing far off on the horizon. He is trying to block them from me, but I can read snatches. He is angry, afraid, relieved.

It's not as we've been told. I have tasted the tears of sand-walkers. They haven't abandoned the sea, Selken. They keep it in their tears.

Selken stares at me, his eyes dark, troubled. At last he raises his hand and splays his palm over my forehead. This time, the gesture feels fond and not demeaning. *You're not like the others, LeRae.*

Is that so bad?

He does not answer me, but his thoughts are less abrasive, no longer hammering at me in frustration. He takes my hands in his, and I think about my sand-walkers, laughing on their beach. *Perhaps, we ought not tell your mother—or Oma—about this,* Selken says at last, his lips lifted at the corners in a hint of amusement.

At first, I am frustrated. I want to tell everyone what I have learned, to prove that I was right all along and that they have all been wrong. But he squeezes my hand and drifts closer, so close I can see nothing but the dark of his eyes.

They are not ready, he whispers to me. His thoughts are gentle, private, and I find myself giving in to his logic. *There will be a time,* he promises.

I hold you to it.

He smiles openly this time, and I find he is much more pleasant when he smiles.

I smile tentatively in return and do not pull my hand from his. *Do you really wish to speak with Oma?* I ask, feeling unusually shy.

He does not answer with thoughts, but his smile and the look in his eyes is answer enough. A school of minnows shimmer nearby. They spiral around us, unafraid, then dart away into a sea of sand-walker tears.

A Creature Birthed of Rage

Lacey R. Scott

Not many people could claim the prestigious title of sacrificial lamb. Then again, not many people were as lucky as *me*.

Three days prior, my life had been a normal one. Well, as normal as one could be when you were stuck with your alcoholic father in a rural fishing village on the edge of the harsh northern sea.

I tossed a chunk of fish innards over the port side of the boat. An offering to the sleek leopard seals that churned the frigid waters, waiting for our castoffs. I wouldn't say I feared the giant beasts. Not like some of the more superstitious villagers, but I definitely held a healthy dose of respect for them.

Slicing through the belly of a fish with a practiced ease, I allowed myself a quick glance at the seals and frowned.

Though solitary by nature, the prospect of an easy meal was too tempting an offer to pass up, so it wasn't uncommon to see a few hover eagerly by the boat. There was Spot, the one with an abnormally large spot on his head; Tin, the runt of the group; and, of course, Tubby, the one with a little more blubber than the rest. Even Scar—a particularly surly female with a nasty jagged scar across her back—had made an appearance today.

And, while I may not have been the most creative when it came to naming the usual seals I'd come to recognize by sight after years working on the fishing vessel, I *could* admit that the unusual number of them circling the boat was unsettling.

For whatever reason, they numbered more than I had ever witnessed before, and *that* was where the problem began. Leopard seals were seen as a bad omen, as many still clung to the old belief that they were the treasured pets of the sea gods. Many believed the creatures to be shapeshifting sirens who were said to lure the wicked and impure to their watery graves. To see one in its shifted form was considered a curse upon you.

"Nara!" Tilliam shouted, pulling my attention back to the matter at hand—fish guts. "Toss this to the devil's beasts."

Though he was the captain's son, Tilliam wasn't in charge of the ship. However, when it came to pecking order, it was common knowledge that I sat at the very bottom. So when he shoved his heavy wooden bucket of waste into my arms—purposefully sloshing the mess on my weather-worn apron—it was in my best interest to obey. It didn't matter that each member of the crew was responsible for disposing of their own fish waste, nor did it matter that I could gut three fish in the time it took for any other man to gut one. The simple truth of the matter was that I wasn't a man and, therefore, would never be seen as an equal in their eyes.

Not in the mood for another black eye, I held my tongue and marched silently to the railing to dump the bucket's contents into the whirling mass of beasts below. There was something mesmerizing about the way their sleek bodies slid through the water like a hot knife through a cold stick of butter, their powerful muscles flexing beneath a thick layer of blubber.

For a moment, the waters roiled in the sea leopards' frenzy, only for the creatures to spook and scatter in the next. Brows drawing together, I searched for the source of their discomfort. There were very few things that posed any real threat to a leopard seal, and even less that would drive them away from a meal.

Something moved beneath the surface, and I found myself leaning forward, squinting to try and get a better view. At first, I thought it was another seal; the pattern on its back was nearly identical. But then it twisted, rising closer to the surface, and as it did, the murky waters cleared just enough for me to make out a face.

The face of a man.

Now, three days later, as I sat bound in a tiny canoe, draped in luxurious furs and practically choking on the stench of all the expensive oils the villagers lathered on me, I cursed my feminine desire to wash the filth from my body. Perhaps had I cared less about smelling like fish, I'd not have headed straight to the bathhouse after work the day I'd seen the man amongst the seals.

Trees were scarce in the tundra, making wood a precious commodity usually reserved for building houses and ships. Our heat source came from coal, pried from the belly of the mountains.

Still, mining wasn't easy work, so coal was never used for frivolous things like warming a bath. Which was why I was eternally grateful our village had access to its very own hot spring—though calling it a bathhouse might have been a touch generous.

The rickety old building that had been erected atop it offered a place to strip before opening to the spring. Separated down the middle by a wooden fence for privacy between the sexes, it was the only place I truly felt at peace. Tucked beneath a blanket of stars, I was lulled into a false sense of security. Muscles lax and tongue loose, I whispered the secrets of what I'd seen in the water that day to the woman I thought was a friend.

It was a mistake I wouldn't have long to lament over, as the next morning rumors rose like the tides, sweeping over the already unsteady sands of the village.

The fishing voyages had grown less fruitful over the past few seasons, and the babes born in the village as of late had been primarily female. All—apparently obvious—signs that we'd somehow angered the gods.

It was nonsense, of course, but there was no convincing them otherwise. Especially once they'd finally found the perfect person to sacrifice. The one who had never quite fit in. The one whose only remaining family would have no problem accepting the monetary rewards given for sending me to my death.

Bitterness sat heavy on my tongue as I thought about my father sitting warm in his new cottage, no longer having to steal from me to buy his ale and, though I knew I shouldn't, a part of me hoped he choked on it.

The horrible thought struck like flint over kindling. The spark igniting and licking away at the chains which bound my most secret thoughts. The ones whispered only in my heart on cold and lonely nights when I'd tucked myself beneath a threadbare blanket after a dinner of cold fish broth and bread that was just a touch too stale. When my mind wondered if that would be the night that my drunken father—the shell of a man he'd been before my mother died—finally met his end, passed out somewhere in a snowbank. The ones that secretly hoped he would.

The ceremonial drums beat from somewhere behind me, growing faint as my boat drifted into the mouth of the cave. Imposing and worn smooth through years of relentless waves, I couldn't help but feel a little like I was being swallowed by some great beast.

Then again, that was sort of the point. To be sacrificed to the sea gods, reduced to nothing more than an atonement for a village still clinging uselessly to the past—the superstitious *morons.*

It was ironic, really. Finding myself tied up and presented like a pretty present to a group of deities I didn't even believe in. I mean, I supposed they could exist. It just seemed highly unlikely that they cared about the ongoings of our pathetic little village.

A twinge went through my shoulders. A reminder of the painful position I was bound in. Kneeling on the hard wood of the canoe, with my arms pulled so tightly behind my back I was beginning to lose feeling in my hands.

The pounding of the drums droned in tandem with the twitch in my eye, apparently intent to annoy me even in my final moments. As I drifted further into the cave, the light of the sun dimmed, giving way to the darkness inside. And I briefly considered praying to those gods. Not to save me, of course. Just to make the infernal noise stop.

Shifting, I tried to ease the pain in my shoulders, only to make the comically large fish, which had been placed on a platter in my lap, slide off. The wooden plate clattered against the floor of the boat, the sound echoing off the stone walls as one beady fish eye stared up at me. Blank and empty, and yet somehow portraying offense at being knocked onto the floor.

"Don't give me that look," I groused, trying not to wonder if my eyes would look like that once I finally succumbed to the elements. "You're *already* dead."

The absurdity of the situation caused a sort of deranged laugh to bubble up in my chest. Laughter I didn't hold back, because honestly, who was going to hear me to care? Aside from the fish, anyway. However, my attitude quickly sobered as the tiny boat rounded a corner, bumping up against the side of the cave, and the light was finally snuffed out entirely.

I let out a shaky breath, eyes searching uselessly in the dark. "What are the odds of surviving this?" I asked the fish, nerves pitching my voice an octave higher than it usually was. "Mine, I mean. Since well, you know..." I trailed off, figuring it was rude to remind the fish of his lack of a pulse twice in as many minutes.

I wasn't usually so chatty, especially not with the dead, but my anxiety was ticking higher with each rapid intake of breath. The darkness pressed down around me until it felt like I was suffocating. Why couldn't they have just killed me? Granted me one final act of kindness for the sacrifice I was never willing to make.

The gentle pull of the tide caused my boat to periodically bump against the cave walls, each jostle a terrifying surprise that threatened to make me lose my balance. Just the thought of tumbling into the icy water, bound and helpless, with nothing but my rapidly numbing legs and layer upon layer of heavy fabric to drag me down, was almost more than I could bear.

I couldn't breathe. Why couldn't I breathe?

As my chest grew tight and my head began to spin, a final sarcastic thought crossed my mind.

At least the stupid drums have finally stopped.

It was the violent shock of being plunged into the frigid water that thrust me back into consciousness. My hazy mind distantly aware that I must have passed out and toppled off the boat. Though I had no time to dwell on it.

The salt stung my eyes as I flailed and thrashed in pitch black water, desperately seeking the surface. By what could only be luck, I came up sputtering, trying to cough up the water I'd accidentally inhaled. My legs kicked frantically to keep me afloat against the heavy furs the villagers had cloaked me in.

A sob built in my throat as my body began to tire. My limbs locked up from the painfully cold sea. This was it. I would die here, my bones picked clean and left to rot at the bottom of a cave.

I should have probably made peace with it, been grateful for the life I'd lived, no matter how short. But instead, as the weight of my clothes pulled me beneath the waves and my lungs started to burn, I could only focus on something dark shifting inside me. The creature who'd broken free of its shackles awakening, its stomach empty and eager to devour all those who had put me here. A creature birthed of rage.

The soft whisper of waves lapping against stone called me back from the darkness. A groan vibrated in my aching throat. Who knew being dead would *hurt* so much? Because it definitely did. My chest burned with each jagged breath. My muscles felt sore and stiff. Even the hard slab of stone beneath me was uncomfortable, with a particularly lumpy piece of rock digging into my lower back.

It took considerable effort to open my eyes, to blink the dryness away and take in my surroundings. Surprise rushed through me at the fact that I could see anything at all. A pale light filtered down through a series of cracks high up in the ceiling. Little particles of dust floated through the beams of daylight that cast unusual shapes on the walls.

I licked my lips, which were cracked and coated in salt, before rolling my head to the side. Then I screamed.

With a speed I wouldn't have thought I was capable of attaining only a few moments prior, I launched myself up, pulse thundering, and stared down into the beady blank stare of a dead fish. And not just any dead fish—*the* dead fish. The one that should most definitely be on the bottom of the sea, no doubt knocked from my canoe when I went overboard. And yet, here it was. Lying on the stone beside me.

"How did you get here?" I asked aloud, taking in the cave again with renewed interest. It was just a small chamber, unassuming save for the little ledge I found myself on. With no discernible entrance or exit—unless it was hidden beneath the waves. "How did *I* get here?"

Glancing down at my hands, I noted the chaffed skin where the rope had been before and, a heartbeat later, registered the fact that I was no longer dressed in the layers of sacrificial furs. I frowned, curious that I felt perfectly warm wearing only my underclothes. Maybe I really *was* dead.

"Did..." I swallowed, my voice dropping to an accusatory whisper. "Did you *undress* me?"

The fish remained unhelpfully silent. Wide-eyed and mouth slightly agape, as if it too were just as baffled as I by the strange turn of events.

Huffing, I went back to examining the room, searching for answers or even an escape.

Assuming this wasn't the afterlife, and I hadn't been sentenced to spend the rest of eternity trapped in a cave with a deceased fish, there had to be a logical way I'd gotten here. Which meant there had to be a logical way for me to get out.

Unfortunately, the weak light that filtered in from above didn't extend past the water's surface, leaving the sea below obscured in inky darkness.

Hesitantly, I scooted closer to the edge of the ledge and dipped my finger into the water. It was *warm.* Pleasant, even. Looking back towards the dome-shaped cavern above, I distantly wondered if perhaps I had drifted into the heart of an ancient volcano. The vents somewhere below, akin to those that heated the bathhouse springs.

I began to right myself when something caught my attention. A shape lurked just beneath the surface, an outline I couldn't quite make out through the distorted ripple of the water and shadows.

Squinting, I leaned forward, my fingers gripping the rocky ledge as I brought my face closer to the water's surface. But despite how I tried, I could only see my own distorted face reflected back up at me—until it moved. And I realized, to my horror, that it wasn't my reflection at all, but the face of someone else—*something* else.

The face of a *man*.

My scream echoed through the cave as I flung myself back, heart leaping to my throat.

The face followed, breaking through the surface with a blade-sharp grin splitting its lips and inhumanly beautiful features.

On instinct, I scrambled back, my hands searching for a weapon as his mouth opened further to reveal razor sharp fangs that glistened in the low light. Latching onto the first thing I could find, I flung it forward with all my strength. It hit my attacker square in the face with a wet *thwack*.

He reared back in shock, and maybe just a touch *scandalized*. Then he looked down to where my weapon—the fish—now lay prone on the stone in front of him. Its glassy gaze somehow conveyed just as much offense as the man's did.

Scowling, he hoisted himself up on the ledge, and all rational thought fled from my mind like proverbial rats from a ship. For there was *nothing* rational about him.

From the waist up, he looked like any other man—if that man were obscenely built, with every inch of his body packed with rippling muscle.

Though pale grey, his skin—or at least the texture—seemed human...until it wasn't. Just below his navel, it began to change, morphing into densely packed fur, much like that of a seal. In fact, as my eyes followed the contours of where his legs *should* be, I realized that's exactly what it was. His lower half was identical to a leopard seal's.

"Is this how all humans repay their saviors?" he asked, his voice rough and gravely like it didn't get used often.

Jerking my gaze away from his...flipper, I met his stare. The back of my neck prickled under his predatory scrutiny. *"You* saved me?" I managed to say in obvious disbelief. "But—but you're a *siren.*"

Before the incident on the fishing vessel, I'd only ever seen them carved into the walls of the temple. The fact that I'd lived to encounter him not once but twice did not bode well in my gut.

"Obviously," he retorted dryly.

Confusion was evident in my voice as I asked, *"Why?"*

"I believe the words you're looking for are, 'thank you,'" he said archly.

"I—I mean, yes. *Thank you,* but shouldn't you be...devouring me?"

He hummed, and a wicked grin cut his lips. "Only if you ask nicely, my delectable little sacrifice."

Taken aback by the salaciousness of his tone, heat crawled up my neck and I sputtered, "I-I thought sirens were evil."

"I didn't claim otherwise," he said easily, using his muscular arms to haul his body closer to mine.

I matched his movements, pressing myself against the cool stone at my back. "Then, why? Why did you save me? Why do something so altruistic?"

Distaste tinged his voice. "The act of saving you was the farthest thing from altruistic, I assure you."

Fear iced over my veins as I tucked my knees against my chest. What could he possibly mean by that? Did sirens like to play with their food? Would he save me only to turn around and torture me? What if—

"I heard your song," he said, effectively cutting off my spiraling train of thought.

I blinked. "My what?"

"Your rage, little sacrifice." He shifted closer. "It cried out to me as you sank, bound and drowning, to the bottom of the sea."

I blinked again, dredging up the memory of the emotions I felt as water burned my lungs and consciousness bled from my mind. It wasn't fear that had crippled my limbs, nor anguish or despair at the injustices served against me. No, it was an all-consuming anger that ripped through me like a raging inferno. A desire to rent those who had wronged me limb from limb.

I shivered the vile thoughts away, even as the rage still pulsed within me like a living thing. Needing to change the subject, I asked the conundrum balancing on the tip of my tongue. "You were there...that day on the boat. Why?"

He idly inspected a claw-tipped hand. "What can I say? I appreciate beauty, and it's not every day you see a tundra rose such as yourself elbows-deep in fish guts."

I scoffed at that. At twenty-seven, I was too old to be considered anything but a spinster. Too lean from a lack of food and weathered by the hardships of life, not once had a man looked my way. Not that I had ever wanted them to. I was far too opinionated to make a good wife. "Do not mock me, siren."

His heavy flipper slapped the water where it draped off the ledge. "Perhaps it's you who mocks me. You'd do well to remember I'm not like those simple-minded fools who clomp around your village like bumbling oxen."

I laughed despite myself at the completely fitting imagery, and a small smirk curled one corner of his mouth. The sound of my laughter seemed to give him confidence, and he inched closer.

"I was...intrigued," he admitted, almost reluctantly. "And even more so when only a few short days later, I see the same woman bound like a present for the gods."

"Is that who you serve?" I asked bitterly. "The gods?"

The siren chuckled, low and deep. "I serve myself, human. Can you say the same?"

Resentment was like a wound left to fester. A life of servitude was all I'd ever known. To my father, the village, but never, *never*, myself.

"I could give you what you want," the siren purred, the roughness of his voice slipping away to something dark and silken. I found myself leaning forward as if trying to capture the words with my own lips. "Make your desire for revenge a reality. Grant you *freedom* you've always longed for."

Fog filled my head, my brain feeling sluggish and thick like syrup. Warning bells sounded in my mind as he closed the distance between us, but they were distant—so far away. "How?"

His thumb brushed beneath my chin; his skin, several degrees colder than a human's, was a welcome respite against my flushed face. "Join me," he murmured, tilting my face so that I couldn't escape his eyes, which were dark pools that seemed to mimic the blackness growing within me. "Follow me into the sea, and I'll give you the power you need to destroy the narrow-minded fools who tried to quench your life."

His words cut through the haze in my mind, and though I blinked away the fog, I didn't pull away. "Join you? You mean for me to become a siren?"

His flippers thumped against the stone floor as if he was unable to contain his excitement. "That is exactly what I mean."

My eyes flitted down to his mouth, to the fangs that poked out and dented his supple lower lip. I swallowed thickly. "How?"

His husky laugh reverberated through the cavern as he pulled away, slipping back into the water with more grace than a creature so large had any right to have. "To become a siren, all you have to do is desire it and join me."

Join him? The lingering fog receded from within me like the tide as I registered his meaning. "In the *water?*"

That wicked grin returned. "Exactly."

Fear was a cool bucket of water on my overheated skin. Was this some sort of a trick? Logically, I knew he'd already had every opportunity to pull me beneath the waves, yet the idea of willingly making myself so vulnerable to him was enough to make my stomach roil. It went against every fiber of instinct I possessed.

"How do I know you won't kill me?"

He laughed, a harsh bark of a thing that held some of his previous gravel. "I never said I wouldn't."

I flinched back. "But..."

"To become a siren, your human self must die. Join me and you can have revenge on all those who wronged you, but make no mistake, little sacrifice. You will forever belong to the sea."

I glanced down at the fish, who still remained unhelpfully silent. And I realized the siren was giving me the *choice.* Perhaps, for the first time in my life, someone was offering me the luxury to choose. The power of it was an intoxicating feeling all its own. It burrowed its way between the slats of my ribs and settled amongst the pulsing darkness that waited there.

Gathering my courage, I met the siren's challenging stare. Then I pushed myself to the edge and slipped into the water.

Strong hands caught me by the waist before my head could sink beneath the waves, and I shivered as my own fingers found purchase on the chilly skin of his broad shoulders.

"You're certain, little sacri—"

"Nara," I corrected him. "My name is Nara."

He smiled, and, while it still held all the same wickedness, I couldn't miss the softening of his eyes. "You can call me Kam."

"Kam," I repeated. A hesitant smile pulled my lips as he drew me into him. In the water, he felt so much bigger, the powerful muscles in his tail keeping us afloat with hardly any effort at all.

So many questions raced through my mind. How would this work? Was this how he came to be? Would it hurt? And yet, amidst the fear of the unknown was a peace that could only be found in the certainty of my choice. *My* choice.

"Are you ready?" he asked, his voice surprisingly serious.

"I—" I swallowed. The dark creature inside me shifted in interest, calling out in song. "Yes. Yes, I'm ready."

His smile was genuine as he dipped his head and pressed his lips against mine. The song inside him, now audible to my own ears, harmonized perfectly with my own as he pulled me down into the sea.

SIREN

RACHEL LAWRENCE

IN THIS WORLD'S DEEPEST places dwells
   A girl who loves to sing
   Composing songs to help her mind
   Make sense of many things
   Sometimes the melodies sink down
   Beyond all others' scope
   And settle underneath her heart
   To buoy up her soft hope
   Sometimes the notes flow outward through
   These waves that amplify
   Their sound to fellow swimmers who
   Reflect her own soul's cry
   Sometimes she shouts into the void
   That is the open air
   Remaining clueless to the change
   Her words inspire there
   She's turned the course of many men
   When lyrics she's employed
   Caused them to crash into the truths
   They've tried hard to avoid

And countless have discovered love
Unable to resist
Jumping headfirst into a sea
Where they can drown in bliss
She doesn't know all she's destroyed
Or the people she's set free
By simply singing tunes that teach
Another way to breathe
She's blind to all the lives she's touched
The havoc she can wreak
By sharing honest words that some
Are too afraid to speak
Some may dismiss her songs for now
But soon they'll have no choice
For someday she will realize
The power of her voice

Hope is a Dangerous Thing

Maseeha Seedat

Hope is a dangerous thing. It can drive a man mad.

My father's words echoed in my mind as I stood at the gates to the port of Cádiz, twisting the emerald ring on my finger.

Well, good thing I'm a woman.

Gulls screeched across the sky. The sun rose on the horizon, rousing the sailors and dockworkers to prepare themselves for the day ahead. Most of the boats would return to the harbor tonight full of fish, others in a few weeks with precious treasures from Constantinople and the Americas.

I, on the other hand, didn't know if we would ever make it back home again.

"Ready to go, Captain Isla?" A hand squeezed my shoulder reassuringly.

I looked up, face-to-face with Ray and his silver-streaked dreadlocks—my first mate, my father's best friend. My fingers drummed against the copper-red hilt of my sword—my mother's, technically, but it was all I had left of her now.

"Hoist the anchor," I said, forcing a smile. Ray had no idea what was to come on the journey ahead. None of the crew did. And I couldn't let them find out. As far as they were concerned, we were going to Tenerife to preserve the trade relations my father had made twenty years ago, a year after my mother died bringing me into this world.

Ray ushered me up the gangplank to *Valka*, hollering orders to the crew as I snuck to my quarters. I placed my satchel on my bed. The bag was empty for now, but I would fill it by the time we reached Tenerife, by the time I abandoned my crew, my ship—my home.

No.

I wasn't *abandoning* them. I would survive Tenerife. I would survive the caves of Don Gaspar.

But the caves had haunted the seas for centuries, their legends claiming an evil spirit roamed in its shadows, that a darkness lived there capable of consuming you whole. If that was true, my chances of returning home alive were almost non-existent.

I strolled to my father's desk in the far corner of my room. I hadn't touched it since he died on our last adventure. All his papers were still scattered—many of them maps filled with his illustrations—and his drawers held every record of his journeys.

No one would search here for my secret.

I opened the top drawer, pulling out a letter with a blood-red wax seal and a stamp from Tenerife. We had journeyed there a few moons ago to rekindle my father's trade connections. That was when I found the letter on my desk.

At first, I assumed it was a record of the new deals we'd made. Those thoughts vanished when I saw the name of the sender on the back.

Valka.

My mother's name.

I rubbed the weathered parchment between my fingers, resisting the urge to reread it even though I knew it by heart. In her cursive hand, my mother detailed how much she missed my father, how much she longed to see me, and how some curse trapped her to the caves of Don Gaspar and Tenerife's waters, waiting for her savior.

Hope is a dangerous thing, my father would say. *It kindles a fire that cannot be doused without killing a little of your soul.*

But the fire had already been sparked within me. The only way to extinguish it was to find her. I had to go to Don Gaspar. I had to survive the caves. If there was even the slightest possibility of rebuilding my family, I had to risk it all.

A lone tear trailed down my cheek.

"Isla, you in here?" Ray called with a knock.

I flicked away the tear and raced to the door. It swung wide open, almost hitting me off my feet.

I had to hide my nerves a lot better.

"I'm here, Ray." I smiled again. "I was on my way to take the wheel."

"All yours, Captain." He bowed theatrically, his dreadlocks dancing in the wind.

I edged past him, trying to walk calmly as his stare burned into my back. The helmsman handed me the wheel with a deep nod; the familiar grain of the wood was comforting against my trembling hands. It felt like home, freedom, and the chance for me to finally steer my own course without my father worrying about his "little girl."

The summer breeze filled *Valka*'s sail and rippled through my red frock coat as I set our course southwest. We would reach Tenerife in one week. I had plenty of time to plan my escape off *Valka*.

Our third night journeying to Tenerife carried a full moon. It wafted in and out of the clouds as the crew drew straws for their watch shifts. I hooked my arm around the rope net I sat in, listening to the gentle melody of the waves lapping against *Valka*'s side. Ray scrambled up the net to join me.

"It's time for us to draw our straws, Captain." He rattled the sticks in his fist, a sly glimmer in his eyes.

Of course. It was my father's tradition to tell legends on the night of the full moon. Either the captain or the first mate had the honor, so it was me against Ray.

I closed my eyes, waving my hands over his fist as I picked out a straw. He did the same, pulling his out with an extravagant flourish.

Mine was shorter.

Ray whooped with delight, hollering to the crew below us, "Oy! Gather round. Time for our captain to share her wisdom. Whether it is wise or foolish, that will be up to interpretation."

The men gathered on crates and barrels around the mainmast as the cook emerged from the galley, a massive pot in his burly arms. Whatever it was, it smelled delicious. Bowls were passed around as I slid down from the nets, my mother's sword swinging in its scabbard at my waist. I took my bowl and stood on a barrel in the center, flicking through the stories in my mind.

Only one stood out.

"All right, all right, save your interpretations for later." The crew fell silent, waiting for me to speak. "Now, this story was first told to me by my father, Captain Adrian. May he rest in peace—"

"May he rest in peace," echoed the crew.

"—and tonight, we'll see if I can live up to his legacy." I cleared my throat, easing my voice into the rhythm and cadence my father had taught me.

"Beyond seven mountain ranges, beyond seven seas," I began, my tone echoing the days of old, "a little girl lived on the coast of Ireland. Now, this little girl loved the ocean, and she spent every spare moment she could muster in a cove hidden in the craggy cliffs of her island.

"'Be careful,' her mother would warn her. 'There are beasts in these waters, and little girls like you are their favorite snack.'"

The crew chuckled at this. Fine, the story was childish, but my father had designed it for the six-year-old I once was. It was meant to be that way.

"One day, the girl sat in the crashing waves, eyes closed, lost in her daydreams of sailing around the world. She was so consumed in her thoughts that she didn't notice the roaring thunder even though there were no clouds. She didn't see the shadow lurking in the waters, getting closer to shore."

Gasps fluttered across the ring, echoing in the silence of the open ocean. A grin crept across my face. The crew always played along with my extravagant bedtime stories.

"The shadow rose out of the water, taking the form of a kelpie, a sea monster that could easily be mistaken for a horse. Its body was dark and slick like oil, its mane made of tangled seaweed.

"But the girl was still lost in her dreams. The beast bent low, loosening its enormous jaw. Its teeth clamped over her foot, and her eyes shot open as it threw her onto its back. The girl screamed for help, struggling against the sticky black fur of the kelpie. No one came.

"The beast dove deeper into the ocean, deeper and deeper, until all she could see was the swirling, twirling mane of her kidnapper. But then she noticed something. Hidden in the seaweed strands, the kelpie had a bridle and razor-edged metal reins draped over its neck."

"The Bane!" the men yelled, just like I did as a child. Every monster had a Bane, something that could be used against it, part of the curse that made them what they were.

"That's right." I grinned. "It was the only way to steer the beast. Even if she cut her hands off in the process, the little girl had to take this chance. She had to get home."

I paused, drawing out the tension. The crew was still, silent.

A deep breath filled my lungs. Moonlight glinted off my emerald ring. "The little girl grabbed the reins, bubbles rushing out of her mouth as she screamed from the pain. The metal sliced into her palms as she forced the kelpie back to shore. The beast had to obey, for the bridle slit into his jaw, spewing a dark liquid through his teeth.

"Once back on shore, the little girl dismounted, still holding the reins. Her blood dripped into the ocean as the kelpie whinnied, black ooze streaking down its charcoal-grey neck. It yanked its head back, wrenching the reins free of the girl's hands, and sped through the crashing waves as fast as it could. The little girl never saw it again, and she lived happily until the end of her days."

That was how I ended my stories.

My father had used his own style. *What was the moral of the story?* he would ask. I always knew the answer. Every story he told me had the same answer.

The greatest weapon against any beast is its own.

I strolled across *Valka*'s deck as the sun rose on the sixth day, my arms trembling even though I tried to stay calm. If the crew felt I was up to something, all of this would be for nothing. The keys to the hull rattled on my belt loop, clattering even more when I shoved them into the lock.

The door creaked open, and I peered through the darkness.

I reached for a bag half-filled with salted beef. No one would find it missing, not when we had about a dozen bags still unopened in the pantry. I crept back to my quarters, locking the door behind me, and strode across the wooden floor until my footsteps made a hollow *thump*. I pulled the floorboard away, revealing a small compartment packed with my stolen goods. A few water skins, an array of food, some alcohol and bandages—everything I could possibly need for Tenerife. I hoped it was enough.

My mind began to wander, trying to picture my mother when I'd save her, when I'd break her curse and bring her back home. My memory conjured up a woman, but I couldn't distinguish her features. Of course I couldn't. She died the day I was born. The only reason I knew my mother's face was the portrait over the fireplace back home in Cádiz.

"Captain?" Ray's voice yanked me out of my daydreams. "Isla? Are you all right?"

I glanced at the red clock hanging on the wall. *Blast it*. I was usually at breakfast by now.

"Coming!" I said, my voice shrill as I kicked the floorboard back into place. I opened the door, barrelling into Ray's chest as he stood there, patiently waiting.

His brows furrowed, concerned. "Isla, what's going on? You cried when we left Cádiz, and now you're all flustered. Is everything all right?"

"Yes!" My cheeks burned red. They had to be as bright as my hair, *at least*. "I haven't been sleeping well. But I'll take it easy today, I promise."

Ray placed his hands on my shoulders, pushing me back into the room. His worried expression turned cold, hard. My heart pounded faster. "Sit," he said. I obeyed as he locked the door behind him.

"Are you okay, Ray?" I tilted my head, trying to turn the tables. "Something's going on."

"Don't even try it," he said, his voice taking on his "serious-father" tone. "Listen, the last promise I made to your father was that

I would keep you safe. How can I honor that vow if you're keeping secrets from me?"

"What secrets?" I squeaked.

"Why are we going to Tenerife again? We just went there."

I crossed my arms defensively. "Because that island has treasures beyond our wildest dreams. My father knew that. We need to maintain the relationships he made and keep the trade running—"

"Isla..." He tapped his foot impatiently. "What's the real reason?"

"That *is* the real reason."

Ray sighed, shaking his head. He walked to my father's desk, pulling open the top drawer.

"Oy, that's captain's property!" I jumped off the bed. "You have no right—"

He pulled out my mother's letter. I froze.

"You're going because of this," he said. "You think she's still alive, don't you?" I was silent. "Don't you?"

I hung my head, defeated. "Yes."

Ray's glare softened. "Of course you do. Your father did the same thing. You're identical."

"My father?" My heart battered against my ribs. "You mean he got a letter like this?"

Ray rummaged around in his pockets until he wrenched out a crinkled piece of parchment. The handwriting, the seal, the stamp—they all matched my letter.

"Why didn't he tell me about it?" I forced myself to breathe. "Why didn't *you* tell me about it?"

"Because this letter destroyed him, Isla. Trust me, you don't want to find what's waiting for you there."

Tears started to pour down my face. Ray pulled out his patch-work hankie, placing it firmly in my hand.

"I know what's there." I sniffled. "My *mother* is there, waiting for me to save her."

"No, she's not." Ray sat me in my father's chair, kneeling so his eyes were level with mine. "Isla, she's dead. I saw her chest still after you were born. I saw them bury her at sea. She can't be—"

"Don't! Don't say it." The flame in my chest burned brighter, refusing to die with Ray's concern.

"Fine, but you can't go," Ray insisted. "You're going to fall into the same trap as your father."

"What trap?"

Ray's gaze dropped to his mud-splattered boots.

"What trap?" I insisted.

"This letter is not from Valka," Ray explained. "It came from a siren who lurks in the caves of Don Gaspar. Your father saw her when he reached the island, and she morphed her appearance, taking the form of the person dearest in his memory: your moth-er." He held my father's letter between his fingers. "She must have slipped this into his bag while he was asleep. By the time I woke up the next morning...he was already on his way to the caves. I couldn't stop him, but *please* let me stop you. Let me save you."

His eyes met mine, and I felt the pain in them, the regret in his glistening tears. I didn't believe him. How could I? Yes, I believed in monsters. Every good sailor did. But Ray never told me about the letter, and now he was creating an elaborate story to keep me from finding my family?

I grabbed my letter back from Ray, stuffing it into my pocket. "Not a word of this to the crew."

He stiffened, glaring at me. "No.... Isla, you can't be serious. You're putting their lives in danger. Your father did the same thing on our last adventure, and look what happened to him."

"You think I don't know that?" I threw the handkerchief in his face. "You think I want to hurt you? I don't have a choice, Ray."

"Yes, you do. This isn't you talking, Isla. It's the siren's magic. The letter, it's cursed. It's tricking your mind."

"Enough lies, Ray. If she's alive, I have to find her!"

Ray's lips set in a firm line, and he bent to pick up his hankie, turning his back on me. He unlocked the door and stood, waiting. "I just realized something," he whispered.

"What?"

He glanced over his shoulder. "We're not the same height."

I rolled my eyes. "So?"

"So...that means we don't have to see eye to eye on everything."

He shut the door firmly.

I stayed in my quarters the whole day, twirling the emerald ring on my finger. Sunlight glinted off the gold band as dusk approached. A knock at the door came from one of the deckhands bringing me a bowl of stew. I wolfed it down greedily.

It would be my last meal before Tenerife.

That night, I didn't sleep. I lay in bed, watching the moonlight flicker across the clock on the wall until, at last, it struck five.

It was time.

I crept out of my quarters, checking if the coast was clear. There was no time to bump into Ray and endure another lecture.

I didn't need to collide with him accidentally. He leaned against my doorframe, his gaze firm on the horizon.

"Where are you going?" Ray asked.

"Nature called," I lied.

He looked me dead in the eye, and it took all my energy not to squirm under his stare. "Oh," he eventually said. "Sorry, I was standing guard here in case you decided to sneak off to the caves."

"I wouldn't dream of doing that, Ray." I bowed my head, hoping he would fall for my bluff. "You were right. This was a stupid idea. I promise I won't go to the caves. Let's use this wasted trip to at least check on our trade in Tenerife, all right?"

Ray nodded, turning back to the horizon. "All right. I'll leave you to your business."

I started walking towards the lavatories at the bow of the ship, quickly turning a corner and out of Ray's sight.

I knew *Valka* like the back of my hand. All her secrets, her hidden passages, all of them were engraved in the creases of my skin. It was easy to reach the galley without being discovered. A warm glow radiated from the coal fire in the back, casting shadows across the tabletops and crates that filled the cramped room. The cook bustled through the mess, chopping slimy carrots in one corner, stewing salted meat in a pot on the stove—a whirling tornado as he prepared breakfast.

He almost tripped over his feet when he saw me in the doorway.

"Captain, I didn't notice you there." He bowed, taking off his hat.

"Don't worry, Cookie. Do you have a minute?"

He guffawed, the motion wobbling his enormous belly. "Of course I do. You were always in the galley as a child, sneaking off with biscuits and the rare strawberry. I couldn't get rid of you then, and I doubt I could get you out of my kitchen now."

Perfect. It was time to use my charms to my advantage.

I sighed, faking relief. "Oh, thank goodness. I really need your help."

"What's the matter, Captain? I'm all yours."

"A few of the lads got bored in the middle of the night, so one decided to show off his knots and unraveled the rope holding the cargo below deck. Now a dozen barrels are rolling about and crashing into the crates, ruining all of our goods from Cádiz. We could use someone with muscles like yours to fix the whole mess."

"Me?" he gasped. "Surely there are younger, stronger men above deck who can help."

"They're not as strong as you, Cookie. Everyone knows you're the toughest man on board."

Cookie puffed out his chest, rolling his shoulders in bravado.

This was too easy.

"You can count on me, Captain," he said. "Keep an eye on the pot, would you?"

"Will do, Cookie. Thank you."

He hurtled down the hallway. By the time he would return, confused by the lack of broken cargo, I would be at the helm like nothing was wrong. He would be busy with breakfast. I had plenty of time to cook up another lie to explain his little trip to the hold.

I peered into the pot. The murky liquid bubbled excitedly, and I lifted the emerald off my ring, revealing a hidden capsule filled with valerian oil. I had bought it back in Cádiz from a healer, claiming I had insomnia. Just a drop of the liquid could put a grown man to sleep in an hour. A whole vial split between thirty men? They wouldn't notice I had left them for Tenerife until they woke up tonight.

The sun started to rise, and I took the helm. It wasn't long before the breakfast bell was rung, and Cookie brought out the stew. Confusion crossed his face as he brought my bowl to me.

"Captain, about the hold...."

"Yes, Cookie?"

"It was sorted by the time I got there."

"Oh. The boys must have cleaned it themselves." I chuckled innocently, placing a spoonful of stew between my lips. I spoke with my mouth full. "This is delicious, by the way. You have to teach me the recipe one day."

Cookie's chest puffed out again. Nothing like complimenting a chef's cooking to make him all warm and fuzzy inside. He rushed back to his pot as I spewed my mouthful of broth back into the bowl. I wouldn't fall victim to my own tricks.

I scanned the deck, making sure every man had at least a sip of the broth. My eyes met Ray's. He slurped a spoonful, scowling at me.

As the sun rose, scattering shimmering diamonds in the ocean, the island of Tenerife loomed ahead. Sunlight trickled through the clouds that smothered the mountain peaks, illuminating little details across the island: the shadows falling down the cliffs, the birds circling the volcano, the waves crashing on the shore.

"Land ho!" yelled a deckhand from the crow's nest. His voice trailed off in a yawn.

We had to dock the ship before everyone fell asleep.

"Ready the anchor!" I ordered. "Ease the sails."

"Yes, Captain!" the crew hollered, leaping into action. Well, they tried to, but the sleeping draught had already taken effect. The helmsman took the wheel from me as I raced to join the men and speed up their sluggish pace. A few hobbled to release the anchor while the deckhands hauled in the sails with gaping yawns.

That's when they started to drop. At first, no one noticed, but more started to pass out across the deck.

We had to dock *now*.

"Release the anchor!" I ordered, and a chain of voices carried my message to the men below. A deep whirring filled the air as they released the anchor, and the chain unwound until it hit the ocean floor. The helmsman carried us a bit farther, nestling the anchor into place before he slumped against the wheel.

I stared at the crew around me, all of them asleep. My plan had worked. All I had to do now was find my mother.

"Isla!"

I knew that voice. I gulped, whirling around. Ray clambered out of the hold; he grasped my shoulders, his firm grip heavier.

"Isla, what did you do?" he whispered, eyes wide.

He should have been asleep by now.

"I'm sorry, Ray, I really am." I shoved his hand off my shoulder, and he stumbled to his knees.

"Isla, don't go... Please, don't." He sank to the floor, his eyes fluttering shut.

I turned him onto his side, brushing the dreadlocks away from his eyes. "I have to," I whispered, and the flame in me burned brighter.

Ray was safe here. They were all safe. If Don Gaspar took a turn for the worse, at least I would be the only one going down. He could still lead the crew and get them all home safely.

Besides, there was a silver lining. Ray would make sure I went down as a legend.

I grabbed my satchel from under the floorboards, draping its strap across my chest, and dropped into the rowboat.

I severed the ropes tethering me to *Valka*.

It was time to see my mother.

The boat scraped against craggy pebbles as I pulled it onto shore. The stones pierced through my boots, but not even this stabbing pain could chip away the flickering hope inside me.

The wilderness of Tenerife was nothing like the ports back home in Cádiz. We didn't have many trees—not to mention the bushes and cacti scattered across the rocky plains of this island. I wandered along the dirt roads to the heart of the isle, to the little valley where the caves rested in their slumber. The locals paid no attention to me. I probably wasn't the first explorer searching for Don Gaspar's caverns.

Around noon, the plains dropped into a canyon; there, shelves of rock formed a path to the babbling waters of the lazy river below. At the base of the canyon, hidden in the shadows, was a gaping dark inlet. The entrance to the caves.

My fingers drummed against my hilt as I descended into the murky waters. Mother probably wouldn't recognize me. I was a newborn the last time we were together. But that didn't mean she couldn't get to know me. I could fill her in on everything. My first sword fight. The day I mastered all my knots. The annual shanty competition with the crew.

It would be like she was never gone.

I jumped the last few feet, and my boots splashed in the algae-ridden river, the spray soaking my clothes. I shook myself dry and ducked into the cool shadows of the cliffs, unsheathing my mother's sword. Maybe now I could finally return it to her.

The cavern mouth was pitch black, darker than the bottom of the sea, like a deep, eternal slumber. A shudder crept through my bones.

Ray had said she was a siren, and this could have been a siren's lair. *But what does he know? I knew* this was my mother. I was going to save her.

Before I could change my mind, I entered the caves, blinking rapidly as my eyes adjusted to the shadowed world before me.

My hope burned brighter, smoldering in my chest, lighting the path ahead. Through the gloom, the dusted sienna rock formed terraces that cascaded from ceiling to floor, each filled with bubbling pools of water. Stalactites hanging from the arches overhead dripped down to the flooded floor, every splash reverberating in the vast, empty space.

The rhythm of my heartbeat pounded in my ears. Hopefully, I could break her curse so she could finally return to civilization.

"Mother?" I called out.

Buffoon. She's never been called Mother in her life.

I cleared my throat. "Valka?"

It was the first time I had said the word without thinking of my majestic ship.

Something splashed in the water a few feet ahead. I gripped my sword tighter. "Valka?" I inched forward.

A light flickered at the back of the cave, casting long, terrifying shadows across the arches. Adrenaline coursed through my veins, setting my blood aflame as I inched closer.

The cave opened into a small chamber, where a thick column with weathered rings held the roof up. Gemstones were scattered in the rockface, glittering in the glow of a nearby campfire. Beside the fire stood a woman, her flaming red hair streaked with gray, permanent wrinkles around her eyes. Could it be? A flimsy seaweed-green dress was wrapped over her body, barely covering the sickly glow of her blotchy skin.

She was there. She was right there.

"Are you—" My breath rattled through my lips. "Are you Valka?"

She nodded, walking over to me.

She's real. My breath caught in my throat as she ran her fingers through my carmine braid. Her hands trailed down to my shoulders, resting there while she stared deep into my eyes. I gulped hard. She was real...

"It's me," I said, praying she remembered. "Isla."

"Isla..." she whispered as if testing the taste of the word in her mouth. She smiled, her teeth still pearly white after all this time. From this angle, they were pointed like daggers. I blinked, and they were normal, human. Maybe it had been a trick of the light.

"How long has it been?" she asked.

"Too long." Tears streaked through my grimy face.

She is real, said the voice in my head, trying to convince my heart.

I ripped the satchel off my chest as Valka pulled me in, wrapping her arms around my shoulders. Her grip tightened, and my sword slipped from my fingers in shock. I inhaled sharply, her musty scent something I never wanted to forget. My head started to spin.

She was *real*.

Then why did this feel so wrong?

Something spat against my hope, threatening to kill the flames just before they rose to their glory.

Doubt.

What if Ray was right? What if she was a siren? A monster bound to its prison and the waters around it.

No. This was my mother. She was right in front of me, holding me in her arms, her wild hair trailing over my shoulders.

I had to test her. I had to prove that she was real or else she would never feel like home to me.

"Do you remember me?" I asked, loosening my embrace, but she held on tighter.

See? I tried to convince myself. *She never wants to let me go.*

"Of course I do," she said.

"Do you remember our home?"

She sat near the fire, pulling me to the ground with her. "How could I forget?"

"Can you tell me about it? Father never went back there after you…left."

She took my hands in hers, her yellowing nails digging into my skin. I winced, wriggling my fingers free of her grip. As soon as we got out of the caves, I was taking her to the best salon in all of Spain. "Well, it's probably changed since then. We used to live in a beautiful city called Barcelona."

I felt a sledgehammer slam into my gut.

"What was it like?" I asked, even though my home was in Cádiz.

She was my mother. She was my *mother*.

"There were forests everywhere," she continued, "as far as the eye could see, almost like the wildlife here in Tenerife. Your father and I built a treehouse in one of the elder trees. We used to go there every summer to get away from the bustling ships."

Forests? The closest forests to Cádiz were a day's hike away at least.

Tears pricked my eyes. She had to be my mother. She just had to. She was all the family I had left in this world. She couldn't be a lie.

"Oh, you're crying," she said, cupping my face in her hands. "Here, let me get some water for you."

I nodded, the fire in my chest sizzling out as she strolled to a spring at the back of the cave. *This can't be happening.*

Valka— No, this was not my mother. Ray had been right.

How had I been so foolish? Of course my mother was dead. Of course it just had to be a siren trying to scrape together its next meal instead of *my mother* waiting for me to rescue her.

None of this was real.

Anger replaced my hope, bubbling deep in my stomach. It twisted itself around inside me, warping my judgment, taking over my every thought and movement.

With her back turned to me, I reached into my boot, pulling out my hidden dagger. The siren turned to face me, and I tucked it into my sleeve.

"Is everything all right?" she asked, handing me a roughly carved wooden dish.

"Everything's fine." I placed the bowl beside me. I couldn't tell if she'd poisoned it. "I just can't believe I found you."

I pulled the siren close to my chest, holding her there with all my strength.

"Isla, darling, you're squeezing a little too tight."

I bit back my tears. *This is not my mother.*

"Isla? Isla, stop it!" The siren hissed furiously, struggling against my grip. Her hands clawed at my spine, ripping through my red coat and burrowing into my skin. I ignored the pain and gripped my dagger, willing my hand to slice the little hollow at the back of her neck.

This is not my mother. She isn't real.

I shut my eyes and bared my teeth. Kill her! Kill her, and it would all be over, and I could go back to Ray, the crew—back to my *Valka*.

But I couldn't. How could I kill someone who looked so much like me, so much like *her*?

My fingers went numb, and the next thing I knew, I was crying into the siren's shoulder, arms limp by my sides. She stopped clawing and instead ran her fingers through my hair to comfort me. With the other hand, she threw my dagger across the room.

"I'm sorry!" I said, and I meant it. "I'm so sorry."

The siren sighed and pulled me in closer. "Well, I've been starving since your father escaped me all those years ago."

Thick black slime oozed through her crimson locks, covering her entire body as she closed her jaw over my shoulder. I winced and shoved her away from me, scrambling for my sword as blood dripped down my arm. The siren slithered across the ground and slammed into my chest.

I landed on my back, bashing my head against a protruding rock.

The world started to spin as black spots clouded my vision. The siren dug her thumb into my shoulder, and a scream escaped my lips. I had never felt pain like this in my entire life. I writhed furiously, reaching for a slab of firewood, for my sword—anything to slam into her skull.

She pinned my arms under her knees as the ooze sizzled away, revealing the beast that trapped me, that had fooled me. *Why had I trusted that letter instead of Ray?* Her large pointed ears towered over her head. Darkness consumed her eyes. Her dagger-like grin glittered in the firelight, dribbling spit onto my face.

My vision swam as her grip tightened over my throat.

This was what hope brought.

This was the end.

Why have I been so foolish?

My eyes fluttered shut. I listened to my pounding heart, my rasping breaths for one last time.

A clatter of stones echoed through the caves, followed by the faint splash of feet in water.

The siren hissed as the splashing came to a stop. A dull *thwack* rang against the rock, trembling the overhanging stalactites.

The siren ripped her hands off my throat and landed to my right, growling furiously. A torrent of stones rained from the cavern roof, and something warm and heavy landed on my lap.

I sputtered, blinking rapidly to clear my darkening vision. Even though it was blurred, I recognized the object on my lap. My satchel.

"Sorry I'm late," laughed a familiar voice. "Someone wanted me to sleep through the party!"

There in the half-light stood Ray, his coat in tatters, sword in hand as he ducked and swerved around the siren. She dove at him and missed, making him chuckle, which only angered the beast further. Her legs merged into a shimmering fishtail—the final step to destroy her human disguise. Ray swung his sword around, bashing the hilt against her head, effortlessly knocking her to the ground. He sat on top of the beast, holding her down firmly by her wrists.

He turned to me, urgency in his gaze. "Isla, you need to find her Bane, now!"

Of course. Her Bane. *The greatest weapon against any beast is its own.*

As the siren clawed at Ray, I dashed around the cave, teetering from the lack of oxygen. The Bane had to be on her, like in the story of the kelpie, or at least near her. I had seen that monster up close. The Bane definitely wasn't on her. It had to be in the cave.

Ray grunted as the siren dug her talons into his leg. "Isla! Any minute now."

"I'm trying!" I coughed and stumbled sideways, bashing into the cavern wall.

A loose rock dislodged itself as I fell to the ground. I clung to the wall, fingers digging into a small crevice, and pushed myself up. Inside the nook, my hand closed over a gleaming dagger; shimmering scales etched into its bone hilt. It had to be her Bane.

"Got it!" I wheezed, and I chucked the dagger to Ray.

He caught it and pinned the siren's arms under his knees. He raised the dagger over his head, knuckles white against the hilt. I shut my eyes, shivering as the squelch of spurting blood echoed through the cavern.

I peeked one eye open. Ray wrenched the Bane free of her throat. He thrust it into her stomach, and the siren's whimpering cries soon faded to silence.

My legs finally gave in, and I collapsed onto my back, my insides shattered into a million pieces. Tears streamed across my sand-ridden face as my mind stretched across the cave, desperately searching for the broken shards of my soul. It reached into the shadows and crevices and rebuilt me until I was whole—almost. I couldn't find all the pieces. Part of me had died with the siren, leaving a hollow emptiness deep in my crux.

Hope is a dangerous thing.

I turned to face the siren. Even in her beast-form, she had red hair, a complexion as pale as the moon. She could have been my mother with a fishtail.

It will be the loose thread that pulls your sanity apart.

"She's not Valka," Ray said. "She tried to kill you."

"Yeah, I can tell," I muttered, pulling off my crimson coat to reveal the bloodstained shirt beneath it. "Can you grab some bandages for me?"

Ray's eyes widened, and he rummaged in my bag as I eased my shirt off my shoulder. He took out the alcohol and bandages, then hesitated. "This might sting a little."

"I know." I needed a distraction from the pain. "How are you awake? You ate the stew."

Ray poured the alcohol over the bandages and sat beside me, reeking of sweat. "Because I knew your father. He used a sleeping draught on me when he went after the siren." He chuckled, rinsing my wound in the alcohol. I screamed, and it echoed across the cave as I squeezed Ray's forearm. "Sorry, kid, I did warn you."

I winced. "Just keep talking."

"Aye, Captain." Ray started to wrap my shoulder in the bandages. "I faked breakfast this morning, just like you, then I pretended to pass out, which I did pretty well if I do say so myself. But once I got to the island, one of the local's bulls broke loose, and guess who the beast decided to go after?" He turned to show me the rips along the back of his jacket. "Destiny really didn't want me to save your life."

My gaze fell to the siren's lifeless body. "I'm sorry I didn't listen to you."

"I'm sorry I didn't lock you in your room." Ray traced his fingers along his sword. "Part of me hoped she would be gone. Your father tried to kill her after her illusion faded, but you know how the stories work. A beast can only be killed with their own Bane. But Adrian couldn't find where the siren hid her dagger, so he tried to kill her with his own sword. Of course she regenerated. I just thought she would have left this dump after all these years."

I sat up, taking out my disheveled braid and layering my hair over my shoulders. "I don't want to be here anymore. Let's go home."

I stood up, but Ray grabbed my hand, pulling me back beside him. I leaned against him, listening to the soothing rhythm of his heart. "Isla, you didn't do anything wrong. You followed your heart, kid. Just listen to me next time so you don't act like a fool." He elbowed me playfully, but I kept my gaze steady on my trembling hands. He squeezed my fingers tight. "You know, you still have me, right? You still have the crew. Cádiz. You have our *Valka*. You still have a family."

I grinned through my tears. "Are you going soft on me, Ray?"

He pushed me off his chest and strode across the room to retrieve his sword. I stood as he handed me my mother's sword— No, it was mine. I was sure of that.

"Of course not, Captain." He kneeled before me, holding the siren's blood-stained dagger. "A token of your victory."

"My victory?" I sputtered a laugh. "I think you slew her while I tried to breathe."

"Let's just say it was you." He winked. "The crew would probably treat you more like our captain and less like your father's little girl after learning you found, spoke to, and 'slew' a siren in one day."

"And if they discover it's a lie? What will happen to my reputation then?"

"Come on. It will be fun!" He pouted like a child.

I couldn't help laughing. "All right, fine, but only for a few days. Then we'll tell them the truth."

"Fine." He rolled his eyes as I tucked the dagger in my belt before looping my arm into his.

Something ancient and familiar bubbled inside me, something I hadn't felt since I found the siren's letter.

I was home, and I'd never doubt that again.

A Sea Full of Stars

Anne J. Hill

The deck is bare of human life other than the pirate pacing and watchkeeping. Only the moon and stars keep him company this night.

The watchkeeper's boots clip across the swaying deck. His hands are clasped behind his back, head tilted high. Waves lap against the side of the ship and rock him to an unheard lullaby. The air tastes far too familiar tonight. Like an old memory personally sent from the ocean to his lips.

It's been years since he got his sea legs, but this feels like his first time traveling the ocean.

Alone. With the stars and moon.

This rugged ship has been through too much in her time, making each footstep creak out in weary pain. The watchkeeper has never bonded with this vessel or the rest of her crew, and guilt rides over him like an unwanted love affair. He's only recently boarded her after the unfortunate events of his past ship. The one he captained and loved selflessly for years—*The Howler*.

Captains are meant to go down with their ships.

He'd jumped his ship. A lover leaving his darling to sink alone in a sea full of death.

And now he stands alone on unfamiliar wood with a crew that isn't his. When he was captain, he would have never been caught pacing the decks in the dead of night. That is not a captain's duty. Not in his mind.

He takes in a sharp breath and swallows it. All he has to do is keep breathing. And for now, pacing. Ignoring the thoughts playing over in his head. The ones that have haunted him for years. Nothing else will pass the time during this night shift.

A good captain always goes down with his ship. If you can find a good captain, he'll strap himself to the mast and dive to the depths with his vessel.

A cloud glides over the moon, stealing his main source of sight. A shiver wafts through the air at the memories. *A good captain wouldn't be ghostly white and praying to be saved. He'd sink, willingly, with a smile.*

His feet refuse to pace anymore, and his hands grip the railing. His toes push up so he can lean over and stare the lethal waves in the face. Images of *The Howler* sinking as he stood safely on an island, half his crew panting on the shoreline, course through his mind. The screaming, the fire, the cannonballs.

He'd fled like the least of them and did nothing to save the rest of his crew or his beautiful vessel.

But now is his chance to join them as he floats over the very spot where *The Howler* once sank.

He teeters over the rail and flirts with death like she is his new lover. Mist sprays his face, promising instant relief if he just jumps into the sea's warm embrace.

Something stirs in the water. Something other than the waves that smack the side of the ship.

"Jump. Join us," a voice whispers from the sea. A smiling woman slowly emerges, her expression assuring warmth and safety. Her fin gracefully flaps under the water.

He rubs his eyes, blinking at the mermaid. Never has he seen such a beautiful creature, with black hair trickling down her bare pale chest and eyes the color of the sea. "Have I gone mad?" he whispers to the beauty.

The merwoman smiles. Her hand reaches up towards him. The ship shifts towards her, and she grabs the wood to pull herself up so they're face to face. She touches his cheek. She is flesh. She is real. Her fingers are smooth against his rough skin.

Knowing something so fantastical exists in his world almost makes him want to ground his feet to the deck and press on, but—

"Come, Silus," the mermaid whispers as she traces the line along his jaw. Water drizzles down her pale cheek and over her lips, and the urge to kiss those lips for an eternity knots itself in his stomach.

She knows his name.

A shiver runs down his spine, and he smiles. Many know his name, but none say it like they know *him* and know the horrors of his past and his choices. As if she can somehow read his soul at first glance.

"Follow me." She slips back into the water and lifts her hand to him. The waves tip the ship sideways so that if he leans out, he can entwine his fingers with hers.

"Yes," he whispers and reaches his hand towards death's open arms.

Jumping off a sinking ship is noble. Smart. Wise.

Abandon all hope, those who board.

Just one more shove, and he'll be consumed by the inviting depths.

Her fingers clasp around his, and he feels himself begin to slip over the edge, his feet coming off the deck.

The clouds part and something else in the dark water catches his eyes. A sparkle.

A star.

He tilts his head and gazes upward to find the moon and stars remaining strong. They dance and flicker—a reality worth living for.

He yanks his hand free of her grip. She seethes, fangs protruding as she lunges towards him. His feet hit solid wood, and the ship straightens to its full height. Her body slams against the ship's side.

He closes his eyes and takes a deep breath. One more step. One more day. He opens his eyes, and the siren is gone, washed away in the sea.

The sea that covers a multitude of sins.

The night slowly drifts away, and then dawn rises. The crew stirs; their voices chirp on deck. A hand lands on his shoulder with a welcoming squeeze, and the captain asks, "All good last night, sailor?"

Silus nods, a smile parting his lips. "All good, Captain."

"Couldn't have slept well without knowing you had your eye on things, Silus." The captain pats his back before turning away, adding, "Job well done."

A surge of renewed hope floods him. He can build a new life on this ship...

And Silus is no longer alone in the sea full of stars.

THE MERMAID'S SOUL

BEKA GREMIKOVA

IT ENDED THE MOMENT Ianthe hesitated.

All around her, the storm raged. Waves battered the shoreline and the wind clawed Ianthe's hair from her scalp. Overhead, clouds roiled and the earth shook as thunder boomed, the vibrations rippling through the ocean. As lightning split the sky, it illuminated the darkness and turned everything a sickly green.

But Ianthe didn't note the buckling waves or hear the wind or feel the hiss of the sea against her skin. All she saw was the pale, drawn face of the man she held; all she heard was the low rattle of his breath; and all she felt was the heaviness of his half-dead body in her arms. Dark curls stuck to his temple as water trickled from the creases in his skin. He seemed as helpless as a newborn calf in the jaws of a wolf.

Did mermaids have souls?

Ianthe didn't think so. None of their lore alluded to the hope of living forever after death—they simply melted into seafoam and melded with the whitecaps, returning to the very waters from whence they'd been born.

So if she killed this human, it wouldn't matter. She had no soul to suffer for it.

But she wanted one. Oh, how she wanted one! Her grip tightened on the man's waist as she fought to keep him afloat. *Humans* had souls, from everything she'd heard and witnessed for herself. Men died, and then their souls went to a Forever-Place, where they lived either in eternal bliss or eternal torment.

Eternal torment was for those who did evil, her mother had told her when Ianthe asked about it years ago.

She bit her lip. Murder was evil. Did killing this human count as murder when humans threatened her existence—when all they ever did was capture her kind and steal their scales for wishes?

Humans had murdered her, too.

And loved you, an inner voice whispered.

She pushed that voice away as the man's eyes fluttered open, startling and blue. Her grip on him slipped, but she managed to snag his tunic before he sank below the surface. Her tail thrashed and flexed as it worked to keep them both afloat. Cradling him close, she tried to decide what to do. He was staring at her, eyes wide—in horror or awe, she could not tell. She hadn't spoken to a person in a long time, but the yearning to find the answers to her questions made her brave. "Can you tell me about souls?" she whispered.

He blinked. "Souls?" he croaked.

She nodded. "How do you get one?"

He frowned. "Why would you want a soul? You're a mermaid—you live for three hundred years!"

And then turn into nothing but seafoam. Even the sea's magic can't protect us from that, she wanted to say, but the youth went on before she could utter a word. "Why would you even ask for one?" he snapped. "So you can murder sailors for eternity?"

His words lashed at her. Desperation seized her limbs. "No! I—I'm not like that! I want—" She broke off.

She wanted to be human again; she wanted to live forever, and she wanted to one day rejoin her mother and father. But how could she expect him to understand? How could she expect him to listen and save her from her sorrows? Nothing she *wanted* would change anything; there was no way to go back. She could only accept her new place in life and survive—and fight against the very humans who had done her wrong.

After all, she was only a weakness to be discarded. Tears trickled down her cheeks, and a sob burst from her lips.

With a raspy cough, the man squirmed in her arms. "You–you're crying." He raised a hand to trace his fingers across her damp cheek. "I didn't know mermaids could cry. I thought they shed scales to show their sorrow."

Ianthe's mouth trembled. "I'm not a real mermaid," she whispered as she bowed her head. She wished she could vanish and wished that it might be true—that perhaps she really was more human than mermaid.

The man laughed—a low, strangled sound that made her wince. "You look real to me! Or am I dead and dreaming?"

"Don't laugh!" She swiped at her eyes and cursed her weakness. Suddenly she wanted very much to kill him, to join her sea-sisters in their quest and drag him down into the depths, forgetting her own humanity and everything she'd left behind. She was doomed anyways.

But the notion was forgotten as he took her hand and met her gaze. "I'm sorry. I shouldn't have laughed. What—or who—are you really?" he asked quietly.

She took a deep breath, inhaling air that hummed with energy and an excitement she felt in every surge of her heart—hope. Perhaps she could be saved. Perhaps she wouldn't be entirely forsaken by the land. Perhaps—just perhaps—there was *some* way the earth would welcome her back. "My name is Ianthe."

The man started in her arms, but when she paused, he urged her to continue. She dove into the past like a mermaid slipping beneath the waves.

I was born different from most other babies in our fishing village. The villagers desired strength in their children—that's how you survived. But while most sickly children died off before the age of four, I held on, stubborn but by no means strong. I was ill most of the time, and every spare morsel my parents could afford went into my mouth.

They told me I had a rich, long-lost uncle who had worked his way to nobility, but they hadn't heard from him in years because of his many travels. They told me one day I would have a home where I could truly get well. But the years passed, and I learned not to take it for granted.

The year I turned sixteen—the year I died—a famine hit our village. The fish weren't biting, and we slowly starved. I remember watching Mother and Father become thinner and thinner as they gave up their food to keep me alive. They shouldn't have both-

ered—they would have been better off without me. At least, that's what the village elders said.

"Why waste good food on a girl that should be dead?" one of them, a bitter old man named Sar, always claimed. He would badger my parents incessantly about it. I think Sar only wanted my food for himself; his wife and child had already died, and he had this odd, crazed light in his eyes.

But the other villagers agreed with him, and after my parents' deaths, there was nobody to protect me. It only took one whisper before the entire village believed me a witch. It wasn't natural that one so ill-looking should live so long, they said, except by the devil's power. But they only believed it because they wanted what little food I had—they wanted to kill me, eat, and then starve some more.

They threw me into the sea. I remember dying—I stopped breathing, and darkness closed over me. I remember panic, sudden peace, and floating upwards towards a shimmering light. But then I was jerked back into the searing currents, and I awoke with a tail, surrounded by the others who had 'rescued' me.

The others say we live a long time. But we don't have souls. We don't go to heaven. And we're supposed to kill any human we can catch.

Ianthe stopped. Perhaps she had gone too far already. The man's eyes were narrow and his lips a tight line. His nostrils flared like those of an angry bull she'd once seen loose in a neighbouring village.

"They murdered you?" he asked softly. "For what little food you had?" His words were more a breath than anything else, as though he could hardly utter them for their cruelty.

She nodded.

"And you…want to kill me?"

She flushed with shame. "Yes. No. I…" Did he hate her? Did he think her a traitor?

She shook herself. Why did she care so much? Humankind had betrayed *her*. Ianthe trembled and clenched her fists. Sobs ripped at her lungs like claws. She'd never been able to cry in front of the other mermaids, had never been able to sort out the feelings twisted within her chest. She'd thought she hated humans because that was how the others saw the world. She'd believed humans hated her because, other than her parents, who else had proved her wrong—and who else *could*?

But this man was smiling sadly at her, void of judgement and without anger. He didn't even seem afraid that she would kill him. Instead, he smoothed the hair from her face and asked if she would take him to shore.

"Why should I?" she asked, suddenly afraid she was dreaming, afraid to surrender and then wake up. The hope she'd clung to just a few moments ago now felt painful. "Why should I trust you?"

"I have no way to prove myself," he said. "I can only tell you that I'm Prince Taren, and I know your uncle. He asked me to search for you on my travels, though I hardly dreamed I'd find you in the sea."

Her throat closed. "Tell me his name," she hissed.

"Odar." The name slipped from Taren's lips so easily, she could well imagine he'd said it a hundred times. "He'd hoped to bring his sister and her entire family to live with him in the city." His gaze flickered downwards, his lips twisting. "We were too late to help your parents, Ianthe...but..." He hesitated. "It may not be too late to bring you home."

May not. So no promise that he could really help her. Her stomach churned. Always so close, yet so far. How could she go home when she was still a mermaid? Rage ripped through her, its sear hotter than the lightning glancing across the clouds.

"How will you bring me home if I'm still a mermaid?" she snapped. She flexed her tail to splash water against his face. The wind shrieked and tugged at her with the will of a killer. She should just drown him.

He shook his head, spray flying from his curls. "There may be a way to change you back," he spluttered as water streamed down his cheeks. "But we must get to shore first."

"And why should I believe you?" The words caught in her throat.

He gazed up at her, his eyes lidded, his breaths turning shallow. "You don't have to believe me, but you have far more to lose than I do."

She licked her lips, which were suddenly as dry as stone.

Taren gave her a sad smile. He felt heavier in her arms, as though his body struggled to hold on to life. "I know you're afraid, Ianthe. But think about your uncle—he wants to meet you more than anything else in the world."

"Even if I'm like this?" She gestured to her glowing scales, and her voice broke. "Even if I'm weak and eat a lot of food?"

Even if the entire world deemed her worthless?

Taren's eyes glistened. "Yes, Ianthe. Even if you're cold and hungry, he loves you."

It sounded too good to be true. Which meant it mostly likely was a lie as beautiful as a mermaid's smile before she drowned you beneath the water. She leaned away from him, and he said, with a quick, urgent note to his voice, "The mermaids don't own you. Their hatred doesn't have to be yours, too."

"What if it's too late?" Tears pricked again, and a few trickled across her cheeks.

His gaze seared her skin. "No mermaid can cry, Ianthe." His voice strengthened. "You have a soul."

She opened her mouth to protest—how could she dare to believe him? how could she dare to hope when it might crush her to pieces?—but he raised a finger to her lips.

"Trust me," he said. "Save me. Then let me try to save you."

The words hung suspended in the air. She wanted to reach out and grab them. Below her, the currents tugged at her tail with whispers of death and depths and drowning. Above her head, gulls screeched as the wind snatched at them and tore out their feathers. She was surrounded by greed and hatred, darkness and fear.

Give in, the sea hissed. *This is what you are now.*

She closed her eyes—and then Taren's fingers brushed her cheek. She opened her eyes again; he watched her, his gaze as bright and calm as sunrise over a gentle sea.

He'd said he would try to save her.

But what if he couldn't?

Kill him, the sea raged. *What good is he if he cannot give you what you want?*

The words stunned her like a pummelling current. They echoed the very sentiments that had doomed her all those years ago.

She wrapped her arms tighter around Taren. Even if he couldn't bring her humanity back, he'd shown her more love than she'd known in a long time. In the few moments she'd held him, he'd reminded her of the love humans could give one another—the love she'd been forced to push aside under the cold, hungry sea.

The love that, she realized, she didn't want to lose sight of, even if she never regained her legs.

"Hold on," she whispered and struck out against the current. The sea hissed and sprayed her face with its stinging fingers. It sucked at her skin and slashed at her scales. *Traitor, traitor*, it snarled. Ianthe shut out its angry words and fought.

What felt like hours later, the storm subsided, and she dragged herself and Taren into shallow water. The sun stroked her hair as she collapsed, Taren gasping beside her. Her lungs heaved with exertion, but she'd never felt more at ease. The waves now were tiny, lapping against her fingers like puppies. The beach sprawled glittering and white before her, dotted with shells and scuttling crabs.

She'd nearly forgotten the beauty she'd left behind in her human life.

She glanced at Taren, who had risen to his hands and knees in the shallows. "Are you well?" she asked.

"Yes," he breathed. His dark curls dangled in his eyes. "Thank you." He tottered to his feet, staggering a few splashing steps before he turned to her. "Are you ready?"

A lump crammed her throat, and she tried to swallow past it as the old fears rose again. The currents tugged at her fins, ready to haul her back into the darkness where she belonged.

But she'd fought the storm and won: she could conquer the fear.

When he gently repeated the question, she nodded.

He bent to pick her up and carried her to where the first grains of sand kissed the waves. Then, placing her down, he stepped back. "Have you ever been on land since your change?"

She stared at him. "Why should I have?"

He only bent his head towards her tail. "I just have a theory. Watch."

So she did, her fingers clenched into the sand.

Her tail sparkled in the soft sunlight that beamed through the clouds. As she stared at her tail, it began to blur, the fine pink veins that curled between each individual scale melting away. The blur seeped through her scales, creeping across the entire lower half of her body. As though her limbs were rejecting the sea's magic—as though they instead remembered the soil from which the first humans had been fashioned.

As though the earth were calling her back to itself.

Then there was pain. Ianthe shuddered, but had no strength to scream. Her lips parted, her agony sliding out in wordless gasps.

After a few more breath-wrenching moments, the pain was gone.

Instead of a tail, two brown legs rested on the sand. A seaweed skirt draped down to her knees. Letting out a sigh of exhaustion, she let her head drop back against the ground. "They're *real*," she murmured. She could feel their heaviness, could feel how they tethered her to the beach.

He knelt beside her, his own eyes wide. "I...I wasn't sure if it would work," he admitted. "You're the first mermaid I've ever met who's actually human. But I thought, if the sea turned you into a mermaid, perhaps the earth would turn you back." He bit his lip.

She wanted to sob. All this time, she could have come back...and she'd never known.

As her head spun, she slowly sat up. Through the dizzying thoughts, one flared bright and clear. "So I can...I can go to my uncle?"

He nodded.

Sunlight fluttered against her face. She basked in its warmth.

"I... I truly have a soul?" she whispered—because she needed one more assurance that the magic had worked. That it had restored both her humanity and all the promises it held. That she could love and be loved; that she could rejoin her parents in a land that never died; that the sea and its anger could not claim her for its own.

Taren stood once more and stretched out his hand. For a moment, she stared at his palm, at the scars and calluses that scored it. Then she grasped his fingers and toddled to her feet like a baby on its first walk into the world. "Do you doubt yourself still, Ianthe?" His voice was soft, prompting.

She bowed her head; her hair, long and dark and slick, slid over her nose. She wanted to chop it all off. "I've just...I've been a mermaid so long." *Too long.* And if being a mermaid had taught her anything, it was that often beauty and light could not be fully trusted.

He reached to wipe away her tears. "But not forever."

No, she realized with a gurgling rush, not forever. She wasn't there anymore, tossed about in a wrathful sea; she was here, holding his hand on a beach as the sun tickled her eyelashes. In the distance, across the rolling green hills, a city beckoned.

She *was* human—that much she knew. And as long as that remained true, perhaps she'd eventually believe she had a soul, too. Perhaps she'd eventually leave the sea's indignant whispers behind entirely, learn to trust and embrace honest beauty when she found it.

For now, she allowed Taren to tug her gently across the sand.

"How far is the city?" she asked as she stumbled over a piece of driftwood.

He raked his fingers through his hair and offered a sheepish smile. "It's...a bit of a long walk."

Another realization struck her—one that made her feel even more unsteady on her legs. She glanced away so he wouldn't see the blush that crept over her cheeks. "I—I'm rather looking forward to it." Such a journey felt like a gift. *He* felt like a gift.

When she dared to look at him again, he was grinning back at her. "So am I."

And then, without hesitation, he stepped forward, leading her away from the sea.

Ebbing of the Tide

Zimri A. Z. Zoran

"Where are we going, *skat*?" Grethe's fins didn't work well anymore, so she braced herself on the young mermaid's arm. She felt as though the short-haired girl at her side was familiar, but she couldn't remember why. She would have liked to address the girl by name, and she felt like she should already know, so the fact that she couldn't recall was frustrating.

"I told you already, *Morfar*, we're going to go somewhere nice! A vacation! You've always worked so hard to make us fit for royalty; you deserve to rest."

Ah, so apparently this girl was her granddaughter, but did she not have six of them? Or was it seven? Which one could this be? What were their names again?

Grethe bit her lip harshly as the lack of memory frustrated her more. If only she had others her age to remind her of these things so the young ones wouldn't cast those pitying eyes upon her, but she couldn't recollect seeing any swimming about the palace.

"Oh, that sounds nice, Maren," she tried, her joy bubbling in the crinkles around her eyes as she remembered a name.

The girl sighed, and Grethe could tell she'd gotten it wrong. "I'm Helena, *Morfar*. Maren has been gone for...a long time."

Gone? Grethe huffed. What did that mean? She hated it when she was treated like a child just because she was old. Maren was such a sweet child. How Grethe wished she could tell her how well she'd grown, how she had her mother's sweet spirit. If Grethe could see Maren again, she could apologize for all the painful things she'd put the child through for the sake of beauty and aristocratic decorum.

Where did Maren go? Did she die? Did she leave? Grethe couldn't seem to remember what had happened. It felt like it was something significant.

Maren...who was Maren again?

Helena patted Grethe's hand. "Don't worry, *Morfar. Far* and your other *barnebarns* have found a wonderful, peaceful place for you! It'll be lovely and warm, and there will be many seashells to decorate your hair!"

Helena brushed her fingers through Grethe's long, luscious locks. "I know how much you love that, and I certainly miss it myself!"

Grethe squinted at the girl. What had happened to her hair? Why was it so short? Did she not know that mermaids couldn't grow their hair back once it was cut? What was her name? "That sounds lovely, *min skat.*"

The girl tensed and her eyes darted elsewhere. She glanced at the soldiers escorting them, but Grethe wasn't sure why. Soldiers always escorted her everywhere. That was simply natural for the dowager queen.

"They're just keeping us safe," Grethe assured. "Don't mind them."

One of the guards let slip a sympathetic look at the girl, and Grethe furrowed her brows. She was definitely missing something. If only she could remember what it was. Perhaps it was one of her son's outlandish "surprises."

Such tomfoolery would never have become so prevalent when the advising elders swam at the king's side. She never did approve of his rash dismissal of them. Speaking wisdom acquired through age and experience should be valued! Though perhaps they desired retirement; but she couldn't seem to recall what became of them.

The girl took Grethe towards the surface slowly, coaxing Grethe's arthritic tail to wave softly with the current. Grethe wondered if she'd ever been wherever the girl was taking her. Did this current feel familiar?

Grethe felt goosebumps trail her skin when they breached the surface. "It's dangerous up here, *skat*! We should return before surface dwellers discover us!"

The girl patted Grethe's hand again. "Don't worry, *Morfar*, no one will ever see us. We're taking you somewhere secret. You'll love it so much!"

Grethe tried to breathe as she let the girl lead her. A few twists and turns landed the party in a beautiful tide pool. The water was warm and the pool was filled with starfish, colorful plants, and shimmering seashells.

Every inch of shore was coated in a layer of seafoam.

Grethe felt goosebumps trail up her arms, but the reason escaped her. Must have been the chill in the air. It was so dreadfully cold up here.

Grethe's guards lapped the entrance to the tide pool, ever vigilant. The girl squeezed Grethe's hand. "Isn't it beautiful, *Morfar*? Come, let's sit on the rocks and I'll put seashells in your hair."

Grethe followed the young woman's lead and eased herself ashore. The girl sat behind her and began to comb through Grethe's long hair with her fingers. Grethe closed her eyes to revel in the familiar feeling.

Yes, this did feel lovely. Nostalgic, somehow.

What was this girl's name again?

She absolutely should know. In the air, the girl smelled so familiar. Family, perhaps?

Grethe sensed the distinct gentle tug of braids being woven into her silver hair and hummed. "That feels so lovely, Helena."

The name felt right on her lips, but it caused the girl's hands to freeze mid-braid, and Grethe worried that she'd gotten it wrong again.

Grethe turned her head and saw the girl's face contorted in a most strange and troubled countenance.

"Turn around, *M-Morfar*, I can't f-finish your braid like this…" the girl stuttered and choked.

Grethe obeyed and breathed the briny air, listening to the rumbling of the waves.

A few minutes, or perhaps a few hours—Grethe wasn't sure—passed, and she opened her eyes to find herself alone in a gorgeous tide pool filled with seafoam. How pretty!

Her hair was plaited in elaborate braids, woven with seashells and pearls. Someone must have done her hair; her hands couldn't do this themselves anymore. Grethe wondered who it had been…

Was she always sitting alone? Grethe fought her memory for some semblance of what she was doing there and found nothing.

She pursed her lips against the frustration, and her fins swished violently in the tide pool. Foam tingled against her scales. What an odd sensation. The froth in the water fizzled on the tips of her tail, and she bent down to scoop up a handful of the swarming seafoam clinging to her fins. She cupped the bubbly substance in her hands and hummed.

"How warm! It reminds me so of Maren, sweet girl. My precious *barnebarn.*"

Grethe held the seafoam close to her heart and smiled. As she looked down at the seafoam in her hands, she was no longer able to tell where her hands stopped and where the seafoam began.

Belly of the Sea

Adella Quick

Oblivious to the danger below
Mouth turned up to a smiling sun
You float on the sea's smooth face
Alone
Salty waves lap over your body
You search the horizon
The stories don't scare you but
They should
Not beautiful, but fearsome
Spiteful, not longing for love
Licking her lips in anticipation
She waits
Dark eyes cut through the murk
Hungrily eyeing her prey
She makes her way closer
Until
She drags you down
The sun's warmth no longer felt
Swallowed beneath the waves

A Heart for the Sea Queen

Erin Artfitch

I stare into the glimmering sea and memorize the fiery horizon before slashing my brush across the canvas. A gentle wave rocks the ship, guiding my brushstroke. The painting is only half-finished by my standards. While it holds an impressive likeness of the oceanic scene before me, it lacks emotion.

A replica without soul or depth.

"A stunning work of art, Odette." My betrothed positions himself into my line of sight, effectively blocking my view of the horizon.

My fingers tighten around the brush. "You are too kind."

"I think you may have erred here." He glances over his shoulder. "Unless you've spotted a dolphin, of course."

"It's a mermaid's tail fin."

"What?" He props his elbows against the polished railing of his family's ship, chuckling. As if what I said was so preposterous that he can't withhold his amusement. The sharp breeze pulls a few silky-black strands from his hair tie. With proud cheekbones, an aquiline nose, and eyes the color of seagrass, he represents the epitome of breeding and high society.

Yet the sight of his handsome face pierces my heart like a harpoon.

"A mermaid. Or, merfolk, really. It could be a male."

"Merfolk?" Diego's lips twist into a mocking smile. "Milady, I did not believe you listened to sailor superstitions."

These superstitions are heralded as fact on my island. As much my family's heritage as the blood running through my veins.

"For decades, our sailors have shared tales of the merfolk frequenting these waters," I say. "We've seen vessels abandoned by their crew. Sailors gone mad by a siren's song."

Only last summer, our family's schooner vanished under mysterious circumstances. That was before I lost— My heart squeezes, and I force my mind away from that line of thought.

"Hogwash." Diego captures a golden curl that rests on my shoulder. My skin crawls as his gaze travels down my dress, halting on any flesh bared to the humid breeze. This evening he looks like a gentleman, adorned in a thin ivory shirt, knee-length breeches, a sapphire waistcoat, and black boots with gleaming buckles. Last night, he looked more like a pirate, drunk with my family's wine.

I turn back to my canvas and define the mermaid's tail with a darker hue of green, making it a prominent, unmistakable feature of my painting. "They say these waters are inhabited by the Sea Queen herself," I continue. "She pulls young men and women into the depths and steals their hearts for eternity."

"What would the Sea Queen want with a few hearts?"

"Sorrow," I say. "The Sea Queen was in love with a human male, only to be betrayed. So she fills her court with desperate, wronged souls. She offers them immortality and beauty—"

"That doesn't sound too bad."

"—in exchange for their eternal servitude."

"Delightful hogwash." His smile is so indulgent that I want to slap it from his face. Finally, he releases my captive curl. "I had no idea you believed such whimsical notions."

Your brother did.

"I imagine there are a number of things I don't know about you," he continues.

"I'm sure—"

"But I will." He captures my hand in his and plucks the paintbrush from my fingers. "Join me in the hull. Our chef is preparing a delicious stew tonight." His gaze rakes over my body, leaving me no doubt as to what he is truly hungry for. Suddenly I am grateful for the crew around us, manning the sails and mopping the deck.

I plaster a polite smile onto my lips. "I was thinking of retiring early. I fear I am still acquiring my sea legs."

A blatant lie, of course. I toddled across the deck of my father's cog before my own nursery.

Diego's lips tighten, and I know he's not fooled. "Then a cup of tea in my quarters." He leans forward and presses a kiss to my hand. For a moment, I can do nothing but stare, struck by the haunting similarities between him and his brother. Then I am horrified by the differences.

Diego's lips are wet and insistent. His brother's were soft and tender. Where Diego's eyes promise a night of passionate caresses and calculated alibis later, the depth of devotion inside his twin's awakened a fire I had not known I possessed.

Yes, fate is cruel.

For cruelty is forcing a girl to marry a boy who shares the face of her one true love but none of his redeeming qualities.

For a heartbeat, I entertain the idea of shoving him off the bloody boat. I smooth my features into a doe-like expression instead. "Sir, I beg your pardon, but meeting in such intimacy—and without my chaperone—would be improper." I press lightly against his chest with my free hand. Not hard enough to offend, but enough that his scent of cloying perfume and rum is out of my nostrils. I want to convince him that my objections come from well-bred sensibilities rather than disdain.

The latter would only entice him more.

His grin is as sharp as a shark's. "My lady, please don't misunderstand my intentions. I only wish to become more acquainted with you."

"I—"

"You and my brother were *well-acquainted* during your betrothal, but we are so different."

I pull my hand from his. "That is a vast understatement." The moment the words escape my lips, I know I have made a grave mistake.

A strange mixture of coldness and heat enters his expression. "Surely you do not still harbor feelings for Tomas."

Hearing his name—even spoken by his brother's vile lips—steals the breath from my lungs and tears the festering wound in my chest wide open.

When my father declared that I was to marry the heir to a powerful family, I accepted my fate without complaint. Even my parents, whose affections burn bright after two decades, were not wed for love. Love matters little when compared to my family's health and continuation. The de Leon family could provide the capital and resources we needed while our island provided the one resource they did not control: sugar cane.

I expected to meet someone spoiled from a life of privilege. But Tomas…he defied every one of those expectations. He possessed a heart as big as his coin purse and passion as bright as the sun.

We spent the early days of our courtship touring the island together, spotting dolphins, exploring waterfalls, and spending countless hours planning our future. We wanted to build a school for the children of our harvesters. Secure our operation for generations.

And our nights? Those were filled with sweet kisses by the jasmine bushes and slow dances under the stars.

"Milady, forgive me. I didn't mean to injure you." Diego's slippery voice pulls me from the bittersweet memories. He leans forward until his breath mingles with my own. "I did not know you would be so affected still. How long has it been? A year?"

I clear my throat. "Eleven months."

Eleven months, three weeks, three days, and eight hours since his ship set sail for the mainland coast. It should've been an easy voyage.

Our merchants discovered the wreckage not even a week later.

"I have been generous with your grieving period."

Generous. The de Leons allowed me six months before sending Tomas' twin to fulfill the contract.

"I grieve for my brother too, Odette. But this partnership need not be beneficial only to our families." Diego's fingertips trail across my collarbone until they meet the laced line of my bodice. His other hand slides behind me. He presses into the small of my back, pulling me flush against his chest. "I can give you things my brother wouldn't dream of. Forget him. Embrace your future with me."

His eyes dare me to either reject or succumb to his advances. The bustling deck hushes, and I feel the stare of a dozen sailors. Even the waves seem to settle, as if the sea itself waits for my response.

Dreams, love, and desire do not exist in these turbulent waters. Only duty.

"Tomas is dead, as is our engagement." My voice sounds as hollow as my heart. "I only look to the future. With you."

The instant I say the words, our ship lurches. My canvas crashes to the floor, splattering a rainbow of colors across the wooden planks. Diego falls, pulling me with him. I drag myself to the railing and scan the open seas. A few fiery-red cumuli billow across the horizon, but there are no thunderheads to account for a sudden gust of wind. No sails from pirate ships.

Then I see it. An iridescent tail fin, disappearing into a rising wave.

"Avast ye! Fins starboard—" The sailor's warning curdles into a scream. A strange sound, similar to a dolphin's whistle, hits my ears. Suddenly sailors to my left and right are falling.

The ship is under attack.

My betrothed finally crawls to his feet. He grips the hilt of his sword, face contorted with panicked rage. Then something flies past me, and he falls too. I gape. His legs are bound by bolas made from woven seaweed and rocks.

"Diego." I start toward him when a big hand encloses my wrist. I spin, fingers curled and nails ready to strike my attacker.

"Odette." The voice that says my name is achingly familiar—and one that I never thought I would hear again.

At first glance, the creature in front of me could be mistaken for a man. His golden skin glows in the dusky sun, speckled with water droplets and seaweed. Black hair tangles above arms powerful enough to break a man's neck. My gaze travels lower, down his muscular abdomen to the fishtail that grips the railing securely.

But that is not why my body goes limp or my lungs forget to breathe.

His eyes are the same. The color of seagrass under sunlight.

"Tomas?"

The shock of him alive—here, on this ship—passes quickly, replaced by an all-consuming joy. *Tomas is alive.* How many prayers have I sent heavenward? How many nights have I yearned to speak to him just one more time?

I take a step toward him, a smile breaking across my face. "I thought you were dead."

I wait for Tomas to mirror my elation. For his arms to open and receive me. Instead, he looks at his brother, still bound on the floor.

"I heard." The warmth in his voice—one of the features that defined him—is gone. What's left is a hauntingly ethereal melody that sends shivers down my spine. Tales from my childhood flood my brain. Lore of sailors following sirens into misty, jagged rocks, desperate to hear more of their song.

Then his actual words process.

He heard.

Stars above. He heard me denounce him. My heart shatters like glass. "Tomas—"

A scream from a sailor draws my attention. Merfolk swarm the vessel, incapacitating the crew with speeds that should be impossible from finned creatures. They wield tridents, sharpened shells, and deadly spiked urchins.

Tomas watches with utter detachment.

"Brother." Diego's voice is high and trembling as he unknots the bolas around his ankles. "How is this possible? They found the wreckage of your ship against the rocks. Bodies—"

I roll my eyes; any simpleton can see that the creature in front of us is not the boy we once knew.

"Your brother is dead," Tomas confirms. There is a slight echo to his voice, reminding me of the way a person's voice might sound underwater. "When I sank into the depths, the Sea Queen found me. She revived me..."

An invisible spider crawls up my spine. *I know this story.*

"...in exchange for my eternal servitude."

Only the sound of the sails flapping against the breeze fill the deck. The eerie silence prickles at my spine. The sailors are either incapacitated or unconscious, but thankfully, I see no grievous injuries.

"Eternal servitude," Diego echoes. "This is madness. Is there no way we can save you from this fate?"

This time flickers of humanity cross Tomas' features. Anger. Retribution. Vengeance. "The Sea Queen will grant me freedom in exchange for an object."

Diego's throat bobs. Hope fills his eyes just as it fills my heart. "Brother, untie me. I will raise the depths of the ocean to get this for you!"

I wonder if Tomas hears the insincerity in his brother's voice, or if he notices how Diego's gaze slides to his abandoned sword, as if he is still contemplating cutting Tomas down.

"It is a heart."

"A heart?" There is disgust in Diego's voice, but my instincts warn that whatever Tomas says next will be much more gruesome.

"She will release me from my service if I bring her the heart of the one closest to mine in life." Finally, he faces me directly, forcing me to bear the full weight of his inhuman gaze. A memory assails me—the soft press of his lips. His chest beating against mine as he held me tenderly in his arms... Those recollections fall flat as the newest memory pushes itself forward. Me, telling Diego that I only look to a future with him.

I want to tell him that I didn't mean it, that my statement came from a sense of duty rather than desire. The ice inside his gaze stops me. An apology, given under duress, will never convince him.

I adjust my definition of cruelty. Cruelty is to be reunited with the boy you love only for him to despise you.

"My heart." I clench the fabric of my bodice, feeling the organ beat like a drum underneath. "You want to give her my heart."

The sun sinks behind the horizon when the tribe of merfolk force us into a rowboat. I sit on the first bench while Diego occupies the rear. Water laps at my ankles, seeping into the hem of my skirt. I shiver, chilled to the bone.

A pair of mermaids, clad only in seashells and seaweed, guard each side. Their pale, gaunt faces gleam like ivory against the moonlight. Scales plate their shoulders like armor, shimmering as they swim in sync. They stare ahead, dark eyes disconcertingly unemotional.

Tomas guides the front of the boat from the water, his powerful tail propelling us forward. My chest pinches painfully, and I immediately regret looking at him. Stars above, he is so beautiful. Somehow the moonlight defines him more than the sun ever could. He looks like a painting come to life. Tiny iridescent scales glint across his flesh and jagged fins protrude from his forearms. The sight of him makes me question my sanity, and I wonder if this entire adventure is merely the elaborate delusion of a grief-stricken artist. I shake my head and dismiss the idea. No mind, however creative, could imagine Tomas like this.

"Why?"

He turns slightly, the only indication that he heard my rough whisper.

"The Tomas I knew would never hurt another soul, even to save himself. This isn't you. The Sea Queen has captured your heart, but she can't steal your soul. You're not wicked like her." I reach for his shoulder.

Tomas deftly moves away. "The Sea Queen is not wicked. She simply is."

Diego cuts me off before I can argue further. "Do not listen to the girl, brother." He throws me a smirk. "She only seeks to save her own life. Yours is worth more than hers."

"You blackguard," I say through gritted teeth. Only an hour ago he slandered his brother.

Diego's eyes narrow, and his grin sharpens. When he opens his mouth again, I tense, ready for the cut of his next insult. Then Tomas slows to a halt, and Diego's response dissolves like sea foam on the beach. Moonlight ripples across the black waters. Sea stacks loom over us, barely visible against the twinkling night sky. They form a semi-circle of jagged rocks protruding from the waters. Fog sweeps across the bottom of the rock formation, but I can still make out the glint of dozens of eyes.

Every pair is focused on our boat.

A host of merfolk rest on every flat area like gulls congregating on a beach. This is a tribunal. A courtroom, and I am the defendant. Suddenly dizzy, I sway backward in my seat and nearly topple over the side of the boat.

A webbed hand steadies me. "It's time." Tomas looks up toward a particularly large rock formation. "The Sea Queen waits."

She sits tall on a stone throne, wearing a crown of seashells, starfish, and pearls. Kelp is braided into her dark hair. Where Tomas's facial features hint at human origins, the Sea Queen's hint at no such thing. She watches me with black eyes too big for her thin, triangular face. Her pointed ears reach to the height of her forehead and are webbed like her hands and tail fin.

I feel the sudden—and insane—urge to paint her. Even facing death, it's impossible not to be captured by her beauty.

She doesn't look at me with malice. Only curiosity.

"Son of the Sea, do you come with the heart you wish to exchange for your own?"

Tomas swims closer to her and gestures at us. "I do." His voice is neutral, but his body is tense. He turns, holding my gaze a moment too long for a soulless being.

My pulse quickens at what I see in his expression.

Sorrow.

Diego must have picked up on it too. "Don't let your feelings sway you, Tomas. There are plenty of women out there. She has three sisters on Isla de Fuerte that probably look just like her."

I shake my head and glance at my betrothed. "Your loyalty is humbling."

Diego shrugs, unrepentant. "He's my brother, love. What do you expect?"

"And the fact that your heart will be safe once the Sea Queen possesses mine has nothing to do with your motives?"

Diego's smile sharpens.

"Brother." Tomas' ghostly voice ripples toward us. He seems to chew on the word, as if it is a term he doesn't fully comprehend.

Diego nods. "Give the Sea Queen her heart, and we'll go back to the mainland together."

Tomas turns from his brother, watching the sweeping waves crash rhythmically against the stacks.

"It's fine." I swallow hard and remind myself that while Tomas might be a shell of the person he once was, the indecision twisting his otherworldly features proves that there may be a shred of humanity inside him. "The Tomas I fell in love with was selfless and good. He would have sacrificed himself for anyone." I give him a smile, letting my love shine through my eyes. I want to envelop him and warm the cold cavity in his chest. "That's the Tomas the world needs. Promise to take care of my family. Secure the island for future generations, just as we planned."

I blink, and he is a breath away from me. He holds a dagger; I recognize his family's coat of arms on the pommel. My chest constricts. He must have had the dagger when the sea devoured him.

"You would sacrifice your heart for mine?" he asks.

I reach out slowly, terrified he will move away. He doesn't. Flames sizzle at my fingertips as I memorize the texture of his skin beneath mine.

"Cruelty is possessing a dead heart while the one you love dies without one." I grab his other hand and pull it to my chest. Water cascades from his palm, soaking my bodice. My breaths come out unevenly and—though it is hard to tell in the darkness—I think his do, too. "Take it. It belongs to you."

Next to me, Diego makes a sound of disgust in his throat. "Tomas, what are you waiting for? Cut out her heart and let's leave this place." He turns to the bare-chested mermaid closest to him. "If you would like to join us, our ship has a newly unoccupied room."

"Do you recognize this dagger, brother?" Tomas' voice is sharp and almost human. It cuts through the silence like an arrow.

Diego pulls his roaming gaze from the mermaid to inspect the knife. "Is that our family crest? It's yours. What of it?"

"Is it? Odette, how did they tell you I died?"

"A—a storm sank your ship."

"A convenient lie. We were attacked."

I gasp. "By who?"

"I barely saw. Man after man fell. When the pirates set the ship aflame, I jumped overboard. A man followed me. He pursued me like a hound from hell, even though the sea would have surely killed me just as easily. Before he drowned, he revealed that he was blood-bound to slay me with his master's blade."

Blood-bound. My breath catches as stories from my childhood pierce through my fearful mind. A blood-bound man is an enchanted, indentured servant, forever chained to his master unless he completes his task exactly as instructed. Only the cruelest—and most desperate—of men invoke this tainted magic. Tomas holds the dagger against the moonlight and slowly turns it upside down. I stare at his family crest, and then something else catches my eye. The initials D.D.L.

Diego de Leon.

Diego sees it too, and for the first time since I met him, his mask of arrogance crumbles. Around us, the merfolk watch like silent spectators of a theatrical production. The Sea Queen's eyes light hungrily.

The Sea Queen, who fills her court with desperate, wronged souls.

"I ask again. Do you recognize this dagger, brother?" Tomas asks.

"That was stolen so long ago..." Diego's excuse falls flat. The truth is written in his trembling hands and shifting eyes.

"You betrayed your own brother," I say, the horror of it dawning on me. "Why? How could you?"

He stole everything from me. From Tomas.

"For months, I wondered the same," Tomas says.

Diego glances at the black waters, as if he is contemplating jumping in to escape his crimes.

"Answer him." The Sea Queen's command is barely a hiss, and yet the magic flowing through it makes my skin tingle.

Diego's face twists as he resists her power. Then the confession bursts from his lips. "Because you did not deserve the charmed life you led. Tomas, the perfect one, destined for greatness. Mother and Father chose you for Isla de Fuerte. To carry on and expand their empire. Never me." Hatred burns through his gaze. "I am the useless twin they write off. Trapped in your shadow, even in death."

He looks at me then, and suddenly his earlier pursuit makes more sense. He couldn't care less about my affections, only taking everything that had once been his brother's.

Tomas swallows and—even as an immortal without a heart—it is obvious how devastated he is. He holds his brother's gaze for a long moment, everything he wants to say and can't—regret, devastation, and love—passing through the distance.

Finally, Tomas turns to me and grasps my hands in his. "I knew my brother planned my death, but that did not cut as badly as the idea that you might have conspired with him."

A knot forms in my throat. "Never. I love you."

"I know." He caresses my face with his webbed hands. "Your Highness, you offered to transfer my service to the heart closest to mine in life. What heart is closer than my own twin's?"

My mouth drops as I begin to understand the full repercussion of Tomas's words.

"I'm your brother!" Diego punches the side of the rowboat, drawing our attention.

"Is it an acceptable trade, my queen?" Tomas asks.

The Sea Queen's eyes glow with deadly retribution. "It is."

"You can't kill me!"

Tomas's brows draw together. "No. That is where you and I differ, brother. You will serve the Sea Queen until you have paid your debt in full."

Diego looks from us to the Sea Queen. "You can't do this. It is cruel!"

Cruelty? The word reverberates across my skin, drawing a bitter laugh out of me. "Cruelty is taking your brother's life to assuage your pride," I say.

His eyes widen as he finally hears my true voice—and the depth of my disdain for him.

Tomas approaches him next, tears glistening in the starlight. "When your ship passed over the seas to Isla de Fuerte, I let you go. I believed you had fallen for Odette and an impassioned heart led you to seek my life." Tomas looks at me. The burning anger in his gaze makes me shudder. Not anger toward me, but *for* me. "But then I saw how you spoke to her. As if she was just another object to possess. I could not watch from the depths while you destroyed her heart."

Warmth fills me at that last part. Tomas never intended to sacrifice me. The surprise attack, his cold indifference—it was all a ruse for his real target: Diego.

Tomas presses his hand to Diego's chest. "Brother, you coveted my life? My inheritance? I give it to you freely." An aquamarine light glows from Tomas' palm and quickly expands through his brother's skin. A gut-wrenching groan escapes from Diego's throat. Tomas clutches his brother to him, comforting, even as he lets out a sharp intake himself. I gape as Tomas slowly becomes more human while gills rip open the side of Diego's neck. Fins slash through his forearms and scales eat away his soft human flesh.

The light disappears abruptly, and Diego flails like a fish out of water.

A mermaid encloses her arms around the fledgling merman, pulling him from the boat just as a long tail replaces his feet. His scream is cut off as the sea swallows him without mercy.

The sound of labored breathing draws me away from the horrific sight. Tomas leans against the side of the boat, struggling to maintain his hold. I gasp and pull at his arm. Slick skin slides against mine. His scales and fins are gone, leaving only seaweed and a dense layer of green algae to cover his exposed flesh.

I tug him into the boat and into my arms. He clutches me as if I am his lifeline. He laughs. It is rich, beautiful, and fills my belly with an answering warmth.

This is Tomas. This is the boy I would gladly die for over and over.

"You're alive," I half-laugh and half-cry.

"So are you." He pulls back, and I am captured by his vibrant green eyes. He looks at me as his twin never did: with absolute devotion and awe, as if he is amazed that I am holding him. I feather his face with kisses, desperate to ease his pain—and convince myself that he is truly well and alive. He tastes like salt and the sea and a hint of jasmine. He smells like home.

He draws me close. So close that there isn't an inch between us. When his lips press against mine, I feel as if my heart has finally come back to life.

And it beats as one with his.

Seaweed & Sirens

Wyn Estelle Owens

On the day the pirate came, the storm arrived first, like a herald of his approach. Thunder cracked open the clouds, sending rain down in torrents back into the sea from whence it rose. Lightning pierced the gloom, filling the sky with blinding brilliance before the darkness crashed back over everything like a breaking wave.

Zelda lay on the soft sand at the bottom of her pool, watching the rain pounding against the water, the surface rippling beneath the barrage. She could hear the thunder all around her, strangely muffled and almost soothing. Deep in her pool, she was safe from the heavens' wrath if the lightning was to somehow strike the pond rather than at the trees on the island. After each flash, little glows sparked all around her, the light-creatures responding to the great flashes in the heavens.

It was beautiful and relaxing, and Zelda could rest. Any ship coming near would be far too busy battling the storm to pay her island any attention. She had nothing to fear.

She tipped her head back, enjoying the light show around and above her, and—

She felt something.

The faintest tug on her hair, a sensation being passed along—someone was nearby. Zelda shot upright, sinking her hands into the weeds all around her, curling her fingers around the stipes and closing her eyes in concentration, trying to figure out what her forest was telling her.

One person—floating—blood—all alone

All alone

Zelda bit her lip, torn with indecision. Madame Gaspara's instructions had been *very* clear. *"There are lots of evil men out there on the sea, men who'll do anything to gain riches— who'll covet either the treasure on this island...or mermaids like us. Ruthless, cruel and violent men, who think only of themselves. Pirates. You must not let* anyone *come here, for your own safety."*

But...

It was only one man. Injured and alone. Surely, Zelda thought, she could protect herself from one wounded man?

Besides, this was hardly different than when her forest brought tell of wounded sea creatures and she had them carried to her island to tend them.

So with a deep breath, and a whispered apology to Madame Gaspara, Zelda rose to the surface, her hair immediately slicking back against her skull. With a heave, she pulled herself onto one of the rocks that rimmed the edge of her pool, wincing slightly at the tug on her head. Then she took a deep breath, twisted her fingers in the strands of her tresses, and sang.

Aekan de Marin was having a bad day. The only upside was that he could report back to his father and say, *"Yes, the crew of the Mafalda has been breaking the King's Articles as you expected and can be considered lawless brigands."*

After all, they had stabbed him and tossed him into the sea along with their illicit cargo in hopes of telling the Pirate King that his son had never reached them and that if their ship were searched, no evidence of their misdeeds would appear.

It wasn't a terrible plan, all told, but it wasn't particularly great, either. Especially because they'd failed to outright kill him. As Aekan's father was fond of saying, while you're still afloat, there's always a chance.

And, thanks to the barrels the crew of the *Mafalda* had tossed overboard, Aekan was still afloat, if bleeding and clinging to a barrel in the middle of the storm.

Hopefully there aren't any sharks nearby.

He shifted his grip on the barrel, pulling himself a little higher and flinching at the sting from his wounded shoulder.

He might still be afloat, but where was he supposed to go now? He couldn't navigate in the middle of a storm without a compass—if a barrel *could* be navigated.

He sighed and leaned his forehead against the wood, wincing as a flash of lightning darted across the clouds. Thunder cracked a moment later.

Then, in the silence left by the thunder, there came the strains of a song.

It was a lovely sound, sweet and rich and full of feeling, somehow managing to rise clearly about the sounds of sea and storm.

Aekan didn't trust it in the slightest. He'd been born on *The Boundless*, the flagship of the Pirate Fleet, and his first steps were taken along the boards of that good ship's deck. He'd been raised hearing the legends and tales of the Great Sea, with its wonders and terrors. He knew what happened when foolish sailors followed a siren's song.

Kicking as hard as he could, he tried to turn his barrel in the opposite direction.

The barrel seemed to have other plans, as it refused to move the way he wanted. Instead, the barrel began to steadily drift *towards* the source of the music.

Aekan let out a hysterical laugh. *Are barrels normally susceptible to sirens or is this one just special?*

Still, siren-susceptible or not, Aekan figured that he stood a better chance with the barrel than without it, so he hung grimly as the music dragged the barrel closer.

Within minutes, a little island came into sight, lit now and again by the bright white arching between the clouds. It looked deceptively simple, but, here and there amidst the waves, Aekan caught glimpses of stark points of rock jutting forth from the deep.

He shuddered and clung all the tighter to the barrel, trying not to think of how many hapless sailors had cast their ships upon those very rocks...and whether or not that was to be his fate, too. He didn't *feel* like the song was enticing him, but maybe that was how it worked. You'd think you were safe and not even realize you'd already been enthralled.

And yet, somehow, his barrel managed to avoid all the rocks, despite the heaving waves. It was almost as if the barrel had a mind of its own—or someone was guiding it skillfully along a safe path to the island.

A few scant minutes later, Aekan's toes dragged into the sand of the shallows, his makeshift craft gently running aground. He slumped against the barrel in relief as he peered up at the island. It rose in a gentle slope above him, covered in thick vegetation, with palms swaying in the rainy winds. He didn't like that he already couldn't see very much with all the plants impeding the already poor visibility; but neither did it appear to be a likely place for a siren to lurk.

Still...once he was on land, he at least wouldn't be in danger of drowning anymore. He dug his feet into the sand and pushed off the barrel—only for something to brush against his ankle.

Aekan was no stranger to seaweed touching him in the shallows, but he'd never had a piece of seaweed wrap itself around his leg before. The next second, there was a sudden *tug*. Aekan's leg was yanked sharply out from under him, and the air whooshed out of his lungs as his back crashed against the sand. Within moments, hundreds of weeds seemed to clutch onto him, and he was moving, carried swiftly through the shallows, the fronds somehow buoying him enough to keep his head above the water.

Aekan tried to kick, to writhe, to *get out*, but the plants only clutched tighter and moved faster, dragging him along. Suddenly, the water splashing against him felt different, not so gritty and salty but clean and fresh, and...were those *trees* above him? Was he on the *island*? What in all the Great Sea—

The singing cut off, and in the same instant the weeds let go, sending Aekan splashing down into the water. In a wild scramble, Aekan staggered to his feet, frantically casting around for something, anything he could use as a weapon—

"Oh! You're awake! I was worried you were unconscious."

Aekan's head shot up, his fingers clenching around the rock he'd grabbed from the streambed below, eyes wildly darting back and forth.

"Here I am!"

There was a large boulder a couple feet in front of him, and a girl's head peeked over the top. He couldn't see much of her features—only a dim shape in the storm's darkness. "Please don't hit me with that rock," she said.

Well. *She* could apparently see *him* rather clearly. Not the most ideal situation. The girl's tone of voice was nervous, however, and it sent a twinge of guilt through his stomach.

He lowered the rock, but he didn't let go; his mother hadn't raised a fool. There were many dangerous things in the sea, and after all he'd been through today, he'd be a brainless idiot to let go of his one advantage.

He missed his sword.

"Who are you, miss?" He peered into the darkness, hoping for a flash of lightning to discern her features.

"Zelda."

Well, that was helpful. What now? "Do you know what brought me here?" He tried his best to keep his tone even, calm, and non-accusing. If she wasn't responsible, he didn't want to get on her bad side, after all. And if she was—

"Yes! My forest did, because I asked it to."

Aekan blinked. Her *what*? "Your...*forest?*"

"My forest!" Zelda's voice had changed, some of the uncertainty vanishing beneath an audible wave of pride and enthusiasm. "All the kelp and seaweed and water plants—they're all my friends, see?" And with that, she hummed a quick few notes, and Aekan felt something brush against his feet.

He looked down and saw the fronds of the weeds lift out of the water and wave at him.

A high-pitched yelp tore from his lips, and he stumbled back, somehow managing to scramble onto the bank and away from the waving weeds.

Giggles cascaded down from above, and Aekan's head snapped back up towards the girl as realization crashed through him like a breaking wave. "Did you—did your plants drag me here? Is that what that was?"

"Yes, I just *told* you—my forest brought you here!" Her voice sounded somewhat exasperated. To be fair, however, while Aekan had seen a lot of mysterious things throughout the sea, he'd never seen a girl control seaweed with her *voice*. For that matter, he'd never seen *anyone* control seaweed whatsoever.

Aekan stared up at her. "...Why?"

"Because! My forest told me you were hurt and all alone." She ducked slightly behind the rock as if to hide. Her voice had dropped from indignation to...some soft, quiet emotion that Aekan couldn't quite discern.

"There's no pain that hurts like being alone," she said, her voice still soft. "So I wanted to help."

"I wouldn't know," Aekan replied, the words falling from his lips with barely half a thought behind them. "I've been surrounded by friends my whole life until today, but...thank you." He grinned slightly, though he doubted she could see it in the dark.

Realization dawned on him that it wasn't quite so dark as it had been a little while before, and neither was the rain pattering down around him. A silence had fallen, the thunder now far away, and the blackness and rain-blindness had begun to lighten steadily into a grayness. If he squinted, he could make out the girl's features: thick, wavy, and wild hair and eyes that gleamed oddly, catching and holding what little light there was to be had.

Zelda smiled, and he could see it now, peeking over the boulder—a flash of sharp, white teeth in the gloaming.

"Of course. I'm glad I could help." She pulled herself up a bit with a wince, resting her chin on her folded arms. "How is your wound? Do you want me to look at it?"

Oh! My wound. Aekan's hand automatically went to his shoulder. He'd completely forgotten all about being stabbed, what with getting abducted by seaweed and everything. Honestly, it was a miracle he hadn't bled ou—

His fingers touched something cold and slimy. There was a mass of weeds wrapped around the wound in his shoulder, clinging as tightly as a bandage. He glanced up to stare wordlessly at Zelda.

She smiled again, sweet and bright. "Well? Do you?"

With a faint sigh and a rueful chuckle, Aekan shook his head. "Thank you. I'd like that."

"All right then, come this way, please!" She disappeared with a faint splashing sound.

Aekan blinked, shook his head again, and started to climb up the slope around the boulder.

He wasn't expecting what he saw when he reached the top. A huge pool nestled on the top of the slope, almost big enough for a ship to float inside. It was clearly deep, and the surface glowed faintly, lit from above by some sort of glowing ore that ringed the pool. The depths were filled with all sorts of plant life, and small organisms glittered here and there—either the scales of fish catching against the soft light from the rocks above or shining in their own luminescence.

And in the middle of it all floated Zelda, and the soft light gleamed off the deep green scales of her long, fishlike tail.

Ah, Aekan thought. *She* was *a siren all along.*

But— He studied her expression: wide eyes and a bright smile—*perhaps not a bad one?*

There were stranger things out there on the waves, after all.

"Why are you standing there?" Zelda said cheerfully and, with a deft flick of her tail, swam over to a large, flat rock that sat just above the surface of the water on the edge of her pool. She patted the stone and smiled. "Come and sit here, please, while I go fetch my supplies."

She floated back a few feet, watching as Aekan carefully sat down upon the rock, his legs dangling into the rain-warmed water. Then, with a flick and a splash, she turned and dove into the depths of the pool.

Aekan stared at the ripples left behind in her wake, bemused. This day certainly hadn't gone according to plan, but, well...

Plans were never his strong point. Mother said he was *far* too much like Father in that case. And, if Zelda was a threat, he wouldn't be much of a match to her, injured as he was. If he tried to run, her plants would only drag him back again. He might as well stay and see this out.

After a few minutes of nothing but the soft hush of the water lapping at the rocks that edged the pool, Zelda's head popped out of the water once more, her arms full of oddments like glass jars and wide clam shells. "I got my supplies, and I'll have your shoulder fixed up soon!" She smiled again.

Aekan noticed her teeth were quite sharp but tried not to let that get to him. Why would she patch him up if she was planning on eating him later? Seemed like a bit of wasted effort.

Of course, he wasn't a siren himself, so he had no idea how they behaved. Still...

He eyed her as she hauled herself up onto the rock next to him, meticulously arranging her armload of objects with a look of concentration on her face.

She didn't *seem* to be malicious.

She set to work, carefully humming to the seaweed wrapped around his shoulder, encouraging the fronds to peel back. She peered and poked at the wound beneath with a frown on her face and then went about sorting through her collection. After a bit, she picked up a clam shell and opened it, scooping out a green-blue paste and smearing it across the wound on his shoulder.

It tingled—a not-unpleasant sensation, but not wholly comfortable either. Rather like having a siren hanging over your shoulder, sharp teeth rather close to your vulnerable neck.

He took the opportunity to observe her, for it was light enough now that he could see the details he had missed in the earlier gloaming. She had rich dark skin like the people from the islands to the south, but her hair...it wasn't like any hair he'd ever seen on a human. It was thick and *green*, like seaweed, and ridiculously long. Its ends trailed off into the depths of the pool, deeper than Aekan could see. With hair that long, Aekan thought, it'd be a wonder if it never tangled in Zelda's seaweed forest.

"You seem rather skilled at this," Aekan finally said when he felt like he could take the silence no longer. "Do you often take in drifting sailors and patch them up?"

Zelda jerked, her eyes flying wide. They were rather nice eyes, a traitorous part of Aekan's mind noted distantly. As wide and black as the depths of the ocean itself and gleaming with a faint sheen in the light of the luminous rocks.

"Oh, no!" She shook her head firmly. "You're the first human I've ever met!"

Aekan blinked. "Really? Never a single human, whatsoever?"

"Oh, well, I've never left the island, you know," she said, beginning to lay some long, broad seaweed...leaves?—Aekan didn't know the term—against his wound. They slapped wetly against his skin but seemed to stick into place. "And this island has a lot of really strong currents and sharp rocks around it. Without knowing the way, any ship would probably crash into the rocks! It's even extremely hard for mermaids like me, or so I've been told." She sent him a shy sideways glance as she worked. "I know the way, though, so I used my forest to bring you along the safe path here!"

One thing stood out the most to Aekan, and he tipped his head to one side, curious. "You've never left the island before?"

She shook her head. "No. Madame Gaspara told me it's very dangerous out there for mermaids like me, especially with—" She suddenly bit her lip, and when she spoke again her voice was somewhat halting. "Well, with...with the pirates. And things."

He couldn't blame Zelda for being worried about pirates. Of course, many of them followed the Articles and were loyal to the rule of the Pirate King—those who protected the peace of the waves, anyways. But there were plenty of lawless brigands out there; *they* cared only for themselves. Aekan certainly knew the dangers a person like Zelda would face from the stories he'd heard growing up. There was a market for things like siren scales and hair, and some fancied keeping such strange and mysterious beings as pets and would pay great amounts to have one. And of course, where there was money, there were also pirates who lacked the scruples to not pursue it.

And yet...

Aekan eyed her thoughtfully. A moment ago, her movements had been practiced and confident, but now her fingers were fumbling with her tools.

He decided not to say anything about his own connection to pirates, though. Not right now, anyway. It could wait.

"I'm impressed, then," he said, shooting her what his mother called his best grin. "You seem rather comfortable with me for someone who's never met a human before."

"Oh, well..." She ducked her head. "You're the first human I've helped, but I've helped lots of other things before! Like dolphins, or seals, or otters—things like that. So..." She gulped, glancing to one side, her cheeks flushing faintly blue. "So I've been pretending you're a seal. Since I don't know how to treat humans."

Aekan blinked. He blinked again. "A *seal*?"

Zelda nodded. "I've never seen one with red fur like your hair, but that just makes you a special seal!"

There was a long moment of silence.

Then Aekan laughed. "I've never seen a red seal either, but if I find one, I'll tell you."

Her eyes widened before she bounced a little in the water. "I'd love that!" She began wrapping a length of seaweed around his shoulder again, and there was a long moment before she spoke again. "If...if you are going to tell me about the red seal, does...does that mean you'll come back and visit?"

Aekan shot her a quick look.

"There's no pain that hurts like being alone. So I wanted to help."

"I think I can visit now and again," he said with a slow grin. "As long as you show me the way each time."

The smile she sent him was so bright he thought the sun had emerged from behind the clouds.

It took a bit of work and several days, but Aekan managed to make a serviceable raft out of some of the trees on the island. Meanwhile, Zelda kept a lookout for ships, since her forest stretched for miles around. On the third day of Aekan's stay on the island, a ship happened to pass nearby, so he dragged the raft onto the beach and prepared to set sail.

"Well," he said as Zelda packed some of her dried seaweed for him to take, just in case. One could never be too careful when the sea was concerned. "Are you going to come down to the beach and see me off?"

Zelda froze halfway through wrapping the seaweed in a leaf, her gaze still fixed on her work. "...I can't."

Her voice was quiet. Aekan frowned. Zelda, he had learned during his three-day stay, was *not* quiet by nature. She was almost always singing or humming or chattering to her forest or the birds or fish—though the birds and fish couldn't understand her like her forest did.

"What's wrong?" he asked.

Zelda slowly set the seaweed down on the rock, letting her hands fall still beside it. After a moment she shook her head, raising her chin and smiling. "Nothing's wrong," she said cheerily. "I just am not able to leave the pool."

Aekan's eyebrows shot up. "Why? Because of the boulder? I can probably help you over that if it's too high—"

"Oh, no, not my boulder." She took a deep breath. "It's my hair, you see."

"Well...it is rather long, I guess."

Zelda chuckled, but it was an odd, gasping, gulping chuckle, and Aekan didn't like the sound of it at all. "It's *very* long, and it's a part of my forest. I can't leave my pool. My hair is bound up into the kelp that grows here, and I can't."

Aekan leaned forward, staring down into the pool. Her hair was green as kelp, that was for sure, and incredibly long, and it had always looked tangled up amongst the long kelp plants. But he'd never seen it hinder her movement before...except apparently, it always had been.

"Then...why don't you just cut it?"

Zelda's eyes immediately went wide. "I can't do that! I've been like this ever since I was born. What if it kills me?" She drew away slightly, wrapping her arms around herself. "Besides, it's my duty to protect this island. It's my home! How can I protect it if I can't hear my forest speak? I can't abandon my duty here!"

"Your duty?" Aekan tipped his head to one side. "To whom?"

"To Madame Gaspara."

The pirate folded his arms across his chest, raising an eyebrow. "And just *who* is Madame Gaspara, anyway? You've mentioned her before."

Zelda's gaze shifted downwards, and she hugged herself tighter. "She's the mermaid who saved my life when I was a baby. She took care of me when my parents abandoned me, and in return I—I guard this island from pirates." She looked up at him, her black eyes pleading. "You see, don't you? I have my duty; I have to repay my debt. Besides...this island is the only home I've ever known!"

Aekan stared at her for a long, long moment in silence. "Even if it's lonely?"

Her eyes widened, but she bit her lip and nodded firmly.

"And...that's why you can't ever leave the island?"

She bit her lip harder but sharply nodded her head.

Aekan eyed her for a moment longer before heaving a sigh. "Well, I guess I'll have to stop by whenever I can and tell you stories of my adventures." When Zelda only blinked at him, he grinned in return sharp and bright, as brilliant as the morning sun dazzling his fiery hair, and winked. "If you can't go out and see the world, I'll just have to bring the world to you."

And with that promise, Aekan left the island, his departure safe-guided by Zelda's song and the forest beneath her command.

Aekan had been gone for a month when Zelda next felt a presence within her forest. For a moment, her heart leapt in excitement—before she realized just who it was.

Madame Gaspara had returned from her treasure hunting.

She was a mermaid, better able to combat the deadly labyrinth of rocks and currents that surrounded the island, but "better able" did not mean "safely." So she, too, let Zelda's forest guide her surely between the dangers to the island's shallows. Once she reached the shallows, Gaspara slipped onto the soft white sand of the beach.

For a moment, her lionfish's tail glimmered wetly in the sunlight, striped with orange and maroon and white, with long, venomous spines emerging in fan shapes from the sides, but then it *shifted* and *changed* and in a blink of an eye, two legs lay upon the sand instead. And with an ease born of long practice, Gaspara slipped to her feet and climbed the island's slope, eel-yellow eyes darting about and examining the surroundings carefully.

Zelda was waiting for her when she reached the pool, sitting obediently on a rock at the edge. Gaspara calmly took a seat on a rock higher above the waterline, crossing her legs and resting her hands elegantly upon her knees.

Zelda eyed Madame Gaspara's legs. After meeting Aekan, and now watching Gaspara stroll towards her, she wondered what it would be like if she could climb out of her pool and touch dry ground, where she too could grow legs.

Then she'd be able to walk side-by-side with Aekan.

"Well, Zelda, how have you been while I was gone? Have you been busy?" Madame Gaspara's voice was a low, throbbing hum that was somehow both pleasant and nerve-wracking to Zelda's ear.

She simply shook her head. "No ships came close, though some debris did wash ashore. I did tend to a wounded seal, but that was really the only thing of note I did since your last visit." Gaspara asked that of her *every* visit, so Zelda knew there was no need to fear that Gaspara had noticed something. Zelda would be fine as long as she made sure to act like she normally did.

Gaspara hummed, her eyes piercing the top of Zelda's head, and she tapped her long, sharp nails against her knee. "So therefore I assume my treasure is still safe within the grotto?"

"Of course," Zelda said. "I know my duty."

"Good, Zelda." Gaspara tossed the word of praise offhandedly, like one tosses breadcrumbs onto a pond. But it was rare enough that Gaspara offered any compliments at all, so Zelda hoped that it meant her guardian had been completely fooled. "I'll go and attend that now. I have a couple new items to add to my collection." With that, Madame Gaspara stood and dove into the pool, her legs transforming into one long tail the instant they completely submerged.

With a few powerful sweeps of her tail, Gaspara slipped through a small passageway in the side of the pool, which led to the hidden grotto where she kept her treasure.

Zelda had never seen Gaspara's hoard clearly herself, for she could only swim so far, but she had caught glimpses of it when Gaspara came out clad in some bright, shiny thing. Sometimes the garment was silver or white as the moon or bright yellow like the sun, and the older mermaid often wore smaller stones all the colors of the rainbow.

They were pretty, truly, but she didn't understand why Gaspara thought so highly of them. They were only stones and things.

Zelda slowly sank down to the bottom of the pool, curling up in the soft sand in the midst of the thickest patch of kelp.

Why would Gaspara spend all her time on the island fawning over rocks and leaving Zelda alone? Gaspara had said to consider her a mother, but Aekan had talked about his mother when he was here. She was a kind woman, brave and gentle, who always had the time for a hug.

Zelda wrapped her arms around herself and curled up, wondering what a hug was. From the way Aekan's voice had sounded, it seemed like a very nice thing.

Aekan kept his word and returned a couple weeks after Madame Gaspara's visit in his own little rowboat. He was in command of a small ship of his own, a gift from his father. Since he'd promised Zelda he'd keep her and her island a secret, he'd ordered his ship, the *Euphoria,* to drop anchor some distance away while he attended to business. He took a rowboat and set off in the direction of the island.

As soon as he was fairly certain he had crossed the boundaries of Zelda's forest, he leaned over the side and shouted, "Ahoy, there! It's me, Aekan! Permission to come ashore?"

There was a moment of silence, wherein an impression of Aekan's message flew through the forest to Zelda's ears and then Zelda's song flew to Aekan's. Within minutes, Aekan was dragging his rowboat ashore, slinging his pack over his shoulder, and climbing up the slope, whistling cheerfully to Zelda's song along the way.

She was waiting for him, propped up on her big boulder, a bright smile on her face as she attempted to hide the strain on her scalp from pulling the weeds to their limits. She didn't quite succeed, so Aekan picked up his steps, trying to reach her as quickly as possible. He skidded to a stop at the edge of the pool, and Zelda sank back into the water with a sigh of relief as he sent his boots flying to one side with a couple deft kicks. Then he plopped down onto his favorite rock, dangled his feet into the cool, clear water, and smiled at Zelda as she popped out in front of him.

"You came back!" she said, and Aekan grinned, holding up his satchel proudly.

"Not only that, I came bearing gifts."

Zelda pulled herself onto the rock next to his, her head tipping to one side. "Gifts?"

"Gifts."

Aekan had been sailing the seas since before he was born; he'd grown up hearing about all the people and creatures that dwelt therein. Sirens, he knew, were hoarders, who delighted in collecting treasure and shiny baubles of all sorts, and Aekan had prepared accordingly.

He set the satchel in his lap and began digging in it. "I wasn't able to find a red seal, so to make up for it, I brought a bunch of souvenirs for you. First—" He pulled out a necklace and dangled it from his fingers, letting it spin slightly to show off the collection of colorful shells and polished stone beads. "I have *this*."

Zelda let out a little gasp, reaching out to touch a particularly pretty shell with swirls dyed in shades of blue, green, and brown. "I've never seen shells like this before."

"The sea they came from is a several months' voyage from here." Aekan winked. "Few currents could have carried them here without a little help." He held out the necklace and raised an eyebrow.

Zelda's cheeks darkened with a deep blue flush, and she nodded her permission.

Carefully, Aekan draped the necklace over her shoulders, fingers brushing against the strange texture of her thick green hair. Once the necklace was arranged, Aekan swiftly drew away and quickly began to dig in his satchel again, trying not to look at Zelda as she stared at the shells she now wore and stroked them gently with admiration.

He pulled out a glass bottle, seaweed green with whorls of a lighter shade. "They make this glass from the sands of a faraway island. I thought you could use it for one of your medicines?"

He held it out, and Zelda took it from him reverently, her eyes wide. She had some glass in her collection, but all of it was eroded by wave and sand, textured and opaque. This was smooth and clear, and it shone rather than glowed in the sunlight.

She clutched it tightly to her, her eyes wide and glimmering, her smile bright as the light reflecting off the bottle. "Thank you."

Aekan felt a surge of triumphant warmth in his chest at having gotten a gift she seemed to like—and at having made her smile like that. "Would you like to hear about the island it comes from?"

"Yes, please!"

It became routine; Aekan would show up every month or so with a bag full of gifts from faraway islands and twice as many tales about distant shores. Tales of dark magic that stole the will, stories of pirate kings falling for selkie maidens, legends of great monsters that lurked in the deep. Mind full of stories, Zelda gathered all her treasures in a chest that her forest had brought her from a sunken ship and hid the chest carefully in a bed of her kelp.

From time to time, she would take out her treasures and look at them: a necklace made of colorful shells from a distant sea, an ornamental knife made of sea-glass, and a collection of small statues of land-creatures, which Aekan had swiftly figured out fascinated her.

She knew her treasures were nothing like those which Gaspara hoarded in her grotto. From the stories Aekan told her, Zelda had begun to understand those sorts of things were desperately wanted and valued out there in the Great Sea, but even so…

Every so often, she would hold her new glass bottles up to the sun so the light could shine through them bright and clear and think that this was a treasure more wonderful than all of Gaspara's metal and jewels.

"You know, Aekan," Zelda said one day, floating on her back as she listened to Aekan weave a yarn about an adventure he'd been on when he was younger, "you've told me about all sorts of different islands, but what island do *you* come from?"

"Me?" Aekan propped his cheek on a fist and grinned. "I don't come from an island; that's why I haven't told you. I was born on a pirate ship."

Zelda shot upright, her eyes wide. "A *pirate* ship?" Her voice was breathless, thin and scared. "How did you escape?"

"…I never had to escape." He hauled himself upright, letting his smile become gentler as he looked at her. "I know you've been told to fear pirates, but let me assure you. There's hardly a safer place out on the waves than on a pirate ship you trust."

"But…" She wrapped her arms around herself, squeezing as if that could set the world aright. "How can you *trust* a ship full of pirates? They're…they're thieves and murderers and… and kidnappers!"

"Truly, there are some brigands out there like that," Aekan said slowly. "But those are only those that don't follow the Articles. Most pirates are brave warriors and adventurers who keep the peace on the seas and protect those who can't protect themselves—who follow the rules of the Pirate King."

"And can the Pirate King be trusted?"

Aekan's gaze was firm and unwavering. "Absolutely."

A sharp tooth bit against Zelda's lip, and her eyes were glimmering with the tears she could not shed, full of confusion and uncertainty. "How can you be *sure*?"

A smile flickered across the man's face, something that seemed rueful and faintly amused. "Well, it was *his* ship I was born on. *The Boundless.*" He leaned back on his hands, tilting his head to one side. "My father's ship."

The water lapped softly against the rocks.

Zelda stared. "Your *father* is the Pirate King?"

His smile grew into a grin, and he made a little bow. "Prince Aekan de Marin of the Grand Pirate Fleet, at your service." His expression turned into something sheepish, and he rubbed the back on his neck. "Sorry about not telling you before; I'm not used to people not knowing that. That's my fault—rather arrogant of me, isn't it?"

"No, it's all right." Her eyes were still wide, but she swam a little closer. "You said you were born on a pirate ship?"

"Yes, on my father's ship, *The Boundless.* It was stormy like on the day you found me, and one of the old salts said to my father, 'Ahh, with a storm like this, that boy'll be trouble.'" He leaned forward, spreading his hands. "And do you know what my father said?"

Breathless, Zelda shook her head.

Aekan's smile grew. "My father *laughed*. 'Of course he will be! Trouble for his enemies. Trouble for those who do evil.' So my father called me Aekan, which means 'trouble.'"

"And that's how you got your name?"

"Yep!" He leaned back again and raised an eyebrow at her. "And how did you get your name, Miss Zelda?"

Zelda was silent. She looked down, twining her fingers nervously into the strands of kelp around her. "I don't know. Madame Gaspara never told me. It's always just been my name."

Aekan hummed thoughtfully. "Well, it's a pretty name." He paused for a moment, in which a blue flush crawled across Zelda's cheeks, before saying hesitantly, "How did you end up on this island, anyway? Madame isn't your mother, is she?"

"Not by blood," Zelda said quietly. "But she did raise me. She took care of me ever since before I hatched. My parents abandoned my egg in this pool and left me all alone."

Aekan kicked slowly, watching the water drag and ripple around his leg. "And...how long have you been able to control your forest?"

"Since I hatched."

His fingers drummed against the stone. "I've heard tell recently...of a certain seaweed called *zeldophyta* that, when eaten, can grant powers very similar to yours. But...it grows far away from here; the waters surrounding this island don't suit it at all." He raised his blue eyes to meet hers. "If that's where your powers came from...it's a miracle you were able to find it and eat it as a baby all alone in your pool."

After that, there wasn't much more to be said. Aekan gave her a pat on the head and a wave as he set off down the hill, promising to return soon.

Zelda was left alone in her pool. She pulled herself as high on the boulder as she could go, feeling the pull and strain of the kelp's grip on her hair, and thought.

She thought of the stories Madame had told her—of the cruel and heartless pirates; of finding her egg alone and abandoned in the pool; how she'd helped Zelda hatch; how Gaspara had taken care of her as a hatchling.

From the way Madame told it, Zelda had been attached to her forest from the moment she wriggled free from her egg. But she never gave a reason *why*.

She hardly ever gave Zelda anything except a word or two of praise, only bestowed when a task was particularly well done. The only things she ever brought for her were garments as Zelda grew—poor garments, hardly anything compared to the things Madame herself wore. She gave Zelda nothing else: not presents, not food, not kindness. Only duty, and cold demands, and fear of the world outside.

Aekan, however...Aekan had given her *everything*. Presents, food, kindness...*answers*. He gave her the world as best he could. If he was a pirate, then what Madame said of them could not be entirely true.

Aekan was warm and bright; Madame was cold and dark. Zelda knew her people were creatures of the sea who lived in the cold, dark depths...but she would much rather swim in the shallows, surrounded by her forest, basking in the warmth of the sun.

Zelda thought about all of these things, and she waited for Aekan to return.

But Madame Gaspara returned first.

"Zelda!"

Madame Gaspara's voice struck like a cold wind, sharp enough to cut to the bone. Zelda startled and slipped off the rock where she'd been sunbathing, shooting down to the depths with a few swift flips of her tail.

When she saw where Madame was, however, Zelda froze, her heart dropping into her stomach. Madame's eyes gleamed as yellow as poison in the gloaming, but Zelda wouldn't meet her guardian's gaze. She could only stare at the necklace of shells that Aekan had brought her, the one from the island of Rolfida, which floated from the tips of Madame's nails as if Gaspara could hardly bear to touch such filth.

Zelda felt heat beginning to build inside her chest, a heat that she wasn't entirely sure was fear or anger.

"What is this?" Madame demanded, piercing as a sea-urchin's spine. But instead of forcing Zelda to cower, they spurred on that heat inside, and words tumbled from her mouth before she could stop them.

"How did I get my powers, Madame?"

Madame paused before her eyes narrowed into slits. "You were born with them, of course."

There was a rush of something—more anger? Sadness? *Relief?*—that swept over Zelda's shoulders, taking away a burden she had never realized she bore. "No. No I wasn't. The zel—" She stumbled over the word, but surged onward anyway, too afraid to lose her momentum in swimming against Madame's current. "The *zel-do-phy-ta* that grants it doesn't grow here. Besides—how can you be *born* with something a weed gives you?"

Madame tipped her head to one side and shrugged elegantly, as if the answer were obvious. "Such a thing can happen...if your mother consumed the *zeldophyta* while preparing to lay your egg, that is."

The heat was coiling further inside her chest, winding tighter and tighter, climbing up her chest towards her throat. "Where did my mother get the...the seaweed?"

There was a long moment of silence. "She stole from me." Madame's voice was high and full of justice, and she looked down her elegant nose at Zelda. "She was caught up in the currents around the island, battered and wounded, but somehow managed to claw her way up the stream and into the pool. I used the zel-dophyta to navigate to the island, and I had some laid out to dry upon the rocks while I ran an errand. She ate these for the weeks she spent in my pool before laying your egg and dying of her wounds. I returned, robbed of my supply and *trapped* on the island, so it was only fair I used *you* to repay your mother's debt. Then you hatched. Within moments your hair latched onto the weeds around you, and I realized you were *useable*. And so you have been. Useful." Her tone dropped as abruptly as an island shelf. "I hope you will remain that way."

Zelda felt her heart hammering, like the sound of rain upon rock. Every other part of her felt numb, her mind swirling in a whirlpool of confusion. Everything she had ever known to be true *wasn't.*

Madame hadn't always been the kindest—but Zelda had at least thought that she *cared.*

Zelda felt her fins shaking, but she gathered her strength and swam back a foot.

If possible, Madame's expression grew colder.

"Tell me where you got all these little...trinkets, and I may be inclined to see you as useful still."

There was nowhere to go; she could only swim so far, leashed to the kelp as she was. So she fled in the only way she was able and closed her mouth tightly.

"I see how it is," Madame said, her tone soaked with disappointment, which might have cut more deeply had she not used that tone so often before. As it was, it only stoked the heat within Zelda's chest. "Then, if you have no desire to be useful, I shall have to take matters into my own hands."

With a powerful stroke of her tail, Madame darted forward, her hands reaching out, claws outspread. Zelda tried to turn and dart away, but cruel fingers snagged her hair and dragged her down, down to the bottom of the pool. Madame fumbled for something within Zelda's treasure chest, and then there was a tearing sound, a sawing sensation pulling against her scalp—

Some primal urge rose within her, dousing the burning anger with fog and ice, and Zelda thrashed her tail, writhing frantically as a fish caught in a trap. She could hear her plants in the back of her mind, murmuring and crying in response to Zelda's terror.

The tension *snapped*—and all of a sudden, for the first time in her life, there was absolute silence.

There's no pain that hurts like being alone, she had told Aekan. She had hated loneliness her whole life, but in one horrible moment, Zelda realized she had never truly been alone—until now.

Now it was silent, and empty, and Zelda was dreadfully, dreadfully alone—and she *screamed*.

She had little resistance left after that. Madame Gaspara hauled her through the passage and into the grotto and dumped her there. Zelda curled on the weed-covered stone, limp as a dead fish, and watched numbly as Madame snatched up a pouch. Gaspara pulled some dark green pieces of seaweed from within and ate them quickly before turning and diving into the passageway, leaving Zelda behind.

The seaweed stirred as she disappeared, fronds reaching up and curling around Zelda's wrists and fins, their grip cold and cruel.

Zelda lay on the floor of the grotto, uncaring of the riches around her, and dragged her fingers through the weeds on the floor and gasped out tearless sobs when she heard nothing.

"Ahoy, Zelda!" Aekan called, leaning over the side of his rowboat. "It's me, Aekan. Permission to come ashore?"

There was a longer moment of silence than usual, and then the song began.

It wasn't, however, *Zelda's* song, and Aekan felt a chill run through his veins at the realization.

He'd been worried this day might come for months, as much as he'd hoped it never would. So he took a deep breath, carefully threaded the sheath of his cutlass through his sash, and let the forest lead his rowboat..

There was always the possibility, of course, that Gaspara would simply drown him before he ever reached the island, but he didn't think that would be the case. She was a careful woman, he surmised, and would want to know how much he knew, and whom he had told, before she did away with him. Otherwise, she would be followed by a gnawing fear for the rest of her days that someone would show up on her island and take her treasure.

A fear she would be wise to have. Aekan was determined to keep his promise until he breathed his last, but when his last breath fled, it wouldn't take his promise with it.

There was a letter in his desk in the captain's cabin on the *Euphoria* with instructions for his first mate to bring to his father in case Aekan disappeared for longer than a month.

The Pirate King wouldn't take kindly to his eldest son's death, and he would be able to rescue Zelda if Aekan wasn't around to do it himself.

He knew he very well might die, but Aekan refused to leave Zelda alone. She hated being alone, after all.

The rowboat ran aground on the sand with a harsh jolt, nearly knocking him out onto the sand below. He clutched the side of the rowboat, barely keeping himself upright, and sat in stunned silence.

His mouth twisted into a grin.

Zelda always landed the boat with ease, slipping it gently onto the sand as smoothly as sliding a tankard along a well-polished bar.

He already suspected that this Gaspara woman was rather pathetic compared to Zelda, and he guessed this was proof.

So Aekan barked out a laugh and swung over the side of the boat. His boots sank into the sand until the surf lapped at his knees. He eyed the now-familiar rise of the island before him, the thick green vegetation obscuring all sight of the top of the hill, and tried to decide what to do.

He pondered this for all of ten seconds before heading straight on up the hill, following the path he always took.

He never was one for plans.

Zelda heard the singing from where she lay in the grotto and stirred. Gaspara had renewed her supply of *zeldophyta* since the days when Zelda's mother had eaten it, and Madame was taking it now. With the strength of the seaweed behind her, Gaspara had kept Zelda in here for days.

Zelda had hardly resisted at first, reeling from the loss of her forest; now she recognized the futility of trying to flee, for Gaspara was always alert.

Instead, Zelda mourned and tried not to think about why she was still alive and what would happen to her.

She suspected that Gaspara wanted to use her still, and—remembering the tales that Aekan had told her, of dark magic and artifacts that stole away will and self—would find some way to force Zelda to protect the island.

So, in the end, she would trade one type of prison for another: one where even the comfort her forest had given her would be stripped away.

And it will happen soon, a thought said at the back of her mind. *Because that singing probably means that Aekan is here.*

He's here, and he doesn't know that it's not me singing him to shore.

Something pinched inside her, and Zelda sat up, staring at the hole leading from the grotto to her pool.

Perhaps...perhaps Gaspara would be far too distracted in guiding Aekan to notice Zelda slipping past the weeds.

She'd saved Aekan once before, after all. It'd be a shame to let her hard work go to waste so soon.

Aekan wasn't entirely sure what he was expecting, but a tall woman lounging atop Zelda's boulder was not it.

She was strikingly beautiful, and he guessed at least a decade or so older than him, somewhere in her thirties—though, of course, she was clearly not human, so Aekan really had no idea how old she might be.

He'd have to ask for Zelda's age, he mused, and stared up at the woman.

She had richly tanned skin, much like his own, and wild hair that started dark and faded to burnt orange at the ends. Her tail was striped with a pattern of maroon, orange and white, with collections of long spines in the shape of fins arrayed on either side and at the tip.

Aekan stiffened, for he recognized a tail like that. So Madama Gaspara was a lionfish mermaid, complete with venomous spines.

Lovely.

"Not quite what you'd expected?" her voice said, a rich throb that grated at his nerves.

Aekan grinned up at her. "Certainly not. Bit of a let down, really. The lass I was planning on visiting is a fair bit prettier'n you, and she sings much sweeter, too."

Her fine features twisted in rage. She stepped down off the rock and sprang forward, like some kind of cat pouncing upon a helpless mouse.

Except, of course, that Aekan was far from helpless. His cutlass leapt from its sheath in a ringing arc, and it clashed against a knife's edge—his heart sank into his boots.

He'd given Zelda that knife.

The woman had a hoard full of valuable treasure, Zelda had said, and she'd still taken what little treasures Zelda had for her own.

Anger surged within him, trying to replace his heart, but he gritted his teeth and forced it back down. He could be angry later; now he had to focus.

Something swiped at him from the side, and he managed to sidestep just in time to avoid the vicious sweep of Gaspara's claws.

He eyed them as he danced back a step, and wondered if they had the same effect as the spines on her tail presumably did. And of course, even without venom, they looked long and sharp enough to do some damage on their own.

Better not let them get me, then.

And the dance began in earnest, furious and deadly—steel, glass and claw whirling and darting about, seeking an opening. It was hard keeping up with Gaspara because Aekan, sadly, had only one sword while Gaspara had her stolen dagger *and* her dratted claws. But he had one advantage: Gaspara clearly had no experience with swordplay.

He parried her knife away and ducked down, feeling the wind of her claws swinging overhead, and a wide grin tugged at his lips. He was a *pirate*, after all. He could fight his way out of this one yet.

Gaspara seemed to recognize this herself, for she paused. Aekan seized the chance for what it was, surging upright and bringing his sword up for a mighty slash—when Gaspara opened her mouth and *screamed*, and it was unlike any noise Aekan had ever heard. His ears burned, his lungs and heart froze, and his limbs turned to stone.

He was still as a statue, able to watch—but only watch—as his enemy stood victoriously before him.

With a triumphant smirk, Gaspara lifted one long clawed finger and dragged it down his forehead, across his eye, and down his cheek. Had he lungs that worked, he might have gasped or screamed, but as it was, he was forced to endure the burning sting and fearsome throb as silently as a stone.

Gaspara laughed in her scream, though Aekan had not the ears to hear, and she raised the sea-glass dagger she had stolen high in the air.

The scream rang out just as Zelda's head broke the surface, and she hastily swiped water from her eyes, her newly shortened hair floating around her in a dark green cloud. She knew the scream for what it was—a siren scream, which would paralyze any hearer that was not of the merfolk. Zelda panicked, and in her fright reached out for instinct; she opened her mouth and sang.

Eating the *zeldophyta* as an adult gave you a measure of control over it. You were not bound to it, however, and your impressions of what the forest had to say were faded and jumbled and blurred. Zelda was different, though she did not know this. The forest had been a part of her in the egg, and while she no longer knew how to hear her beloved seaweed—not with the 'ears' she had used to hear them severed—the forest was still a part of her, and it knew and loved her voice. And when she sang, the plants danced and rose up, winding around Gaspara in a wave of green, snatching at the knife while one long strand coiled around her throat and cut off the scream.

With the end of the scream, Aekan de Marin snapped out of his trance, and with blood streaming down his face, he swung the cutlass with all his might.

Madame Gaspara never sang again.

Zelda did the best she could to help his eye, but, while she could counteract the venom, her medicines and poultices could only do so much. "I'm sorry," she whispered sadly, though Aekan only laughed.

"No need to be sorry; I'll just have to wear an eyepatch." When her face fell further, Aekan did his best to swallow his laughter and cupped her cheek gently with his palm. "In truth, I would much rather make do with two eyes than one, but I'll manage. I'd much rather have you and an eyepatch than have both my eyes and lose you instead."

"Are you sure?" Her voice was a whisper, but her eyes glimmered with hope.

"Sure as the tides," he said and was rewarded with a smile. This emboldened him, and he tried to wink, which sadly fell a tad flat. "Besides, I'm sure Father will be impressed by how pirate-like I look when I see him next."

Zelda gave him a look that indicated she knew he was doing his best to put his best foot forward, but that was all right. He'd take all the time he needed to adjust to this...change...later.

For now there was something else that needed doing. He slid from the top of Zelda's boulder where they both sat and held up a hand.

Zelda stared down at his hand before looking up and capturing his gaze as surely as she'd snatched his heart.

"I've done my best to bring the world to you, Zelda," he said. "Now would you like to go out and see it for yourself?"

A slow smile crossed her face. "Well," she said, and reached out to lay her hand in his. "You never *did* find that red seal."

With her hand resting gently upon his, Zelda slid down the boulder, and, for the first time in her life, set foot upon dry land.

Into the Depths

Kim Chance

THE SQUEAKING WHEELS OF my mop bucket echo across the polished floors as I push it down the empty corridor—but the sound is nothing compared to the booming of my own heart in my ears. The rhythm of it serves as a cadence for my feet, pushing me forward with an urgency that burns through me. My body is a crucible, and every instinct inside of me is buckling under the immeasurable heat, the pull of *her*, and what I'm about to do.

I grip the wooden handle of the mop as I walk even faster, forcing the bucket's rickety wheels to their limits. One of the main laboratories comes into view, the floor-to-ceiling windows polished and clear. I pause for a moment, pretending to inspect the shiny tile for any areas that need cleaning, but actually I sneak a glance into the lab, searching for anyone who might see me—or try to stop me.

It's nearly 3 a.m., and while I typically don't run into anyone during my shifts, the occasional scientist will work late, determined to make some breakthrough in one of their projects. "*Projects,*" I hiss, the word turning to ash on my tongue. Such a benign word—but one that, in here, means death.

I shake my head and huff out a breath, my nostrils flaring. The coast seems to be clear, so I abandon the mop and swipe my access card. The door to the lab clicks as it unlocks and swings open, the cool air greeting me like a slap.

I hurry through the main computer area. Screens fill one wall entirely, and the shelves of vials and beakers are filled with multi-colored, unknown substances. I press farther into the lab, past the cages and the glass enclosures—test subjects #12 and #28 cry out to me, the sharp sounds piercing my heart. But I cannot help them. At least, not tonight.

As much as I want to take a baseball bat to every single one of the enclosures, to free the pitiful creatures within them, I only have one chance. Only one shot to get this right.

And I'm selfish.

So I keep walking, though I press a palm to my chest, acknowledging the ache there and the ones I'm leaving behind.

I don't stop my trek until I've gone deep into the recesses of the lab, into the restricted section that I shouldn't be able to access.

Yet I am.

A simple computer glitch. A single error. A tiny mistake that granted me, the young down-on-his-luck, after-hours janitor access to anywhere in the entire facility.

One small oversight that brought me to *her*.

I'm breathless when I push through the final set of doors. The blue light from the massive tank at the back of the room glows, beckoning me.

Every cell in my body ignites as I hurry forward, my eyes searching the murky water.

She emerges from the shadows and presses her delicate palm against the glass. Her chestnut brown hair floats around her head like a crown, which only makes the vise around my heart tighten.

I place my own palm on the glass, imagining the soft feel of her slender fingers against my own. "Marina." Her name spills from my lips as I press my forehead against the thick pane that separates us.

She mirrors my movement, her own forehead resting opposite mine through the glass. It's as close as we've ever been able to get to one another.

Finn. My Finn. Her voice is crystal clear in my mind. Soft and sweet, but tinged with sorrow.

Always sorrow.

I step back and scan her body, trying not to make it too obvious, but I cannot stop my reaction when I see the fresh lash marks across the exposed skin of her abdomen or the way her emerald green fins droop from the lack of space and fresh salt. Her beautiful long tail is mottled with scars, both old and new, and several patches are completely bald—her beautiful iridescent scales plucked in the name of science.

I'm okay, she tells me, reading my expression. **Today wasn't as bad as usual.** She offers up a small half-smile, but I know the tiny gesture to make me feel better is an effort for her.

Not as bad as usual. The cruelty she's endured—captured from her home and forced into captivity for experimental purposes—makes everything in my vision go red, and I want to throw my head back and scream my fury for the world to hear. But that would only heap more trouble upon her, and that's the last thing I want.

No, the only thing I want for this beautiful creature, who helped free me from the depths of my own sadness, is to return the favor. So I swallow down the rage and smile back.

"Marina, I got it," I breathe, digging into my pocket to pull out a small vial of amber liquid.

After weeks of trying to swipe it without notice, I've finally managed to steal the most essential part of my plan.

Oh Finn, you did it? You really did it?

"Yes." A lump grows thick in my throat. "I swore to you that I wouldn't stop until I got you out of here. And tonight, I intend to do just that."

Marina's face crumples as the weight of my words settles over her. **I thought I was going to die in here. I think I would have if you hadn't found me.**

"Marina," I whisper, closing my eyes for a second. She thinks I'm a hero, some kind of savior. But really, she is the one who saved me.

Six months ago, when I started my job here at the lab, I wasn't a whole person. I hadn't been for nearly two years after a drunk driver ripped my wife and infant son from me in a matter of seconds. My entire world, gone just like that.

I was absolutely *broken.* Shattered into a thousand pieces, a thousand agonizing wounds that would never heal.

Grief is so much like the vast depths of the ocean, so dark and consuming, and I was drowning in it.

Then one night, I walked through a door in the laboratory that I was never supposed to be able to open.

And that night, I found her tank in the back of the lab.

I'll never forget the moment that our eyes met through the glass. She wasn't afraid of me. It was as if she recognized immediately that I wasn't like her captors or the scientists who saw her only as a specimen. She saw something in me, something different. Something worth taking a chance on. And in that moment, she smiled at me. A tentative, soft whisper of a smile that nearly buckled my knees.

Hello.

When she spoke into my mind that first time, the sweet, tinkling sound of her voice felt like a defibrillator, shocking life into the husk of what used to be my heart.

I snuck in to see her every chance I got after that and what started as an unlikely friendship blossomed into something much deeper, a love unlike any I've ever known.

And it was her ability to love, to love *me*, despite the torture she'd endured, that compelled my deadened lungs to breathe for the first time since the night of the accident, since the night I drowned.

She thinks of me as her saving grace, but really, she found *me*—and then she pulled me up from the depths.

I open my eyes and find her gaze again. "I'm not going to let anything hurt you ever again. I promise."

Her lower lip trembles as she nods. **I trust you, Finn.**

With a shaky hand, I reach for the handgun I hid underneath my shirt earlier. "Go to the back of the tank, okay?"

Returning the vial to my pocket for safekeeping, I wait until I'm sure Marina has flattened herself as best she can against the far panel of the tank.

Then, aiming the gun, I fire a round. With each bullet, the glass begins to spiderweb. I fire a final shot directly at the center of the web. The sound shatters both the silence of the lab and the thick panel of glass that separates us.

Water gushes from the massive hole in the tank, and I plant my feet against the pull of the current. In a swirl of color, Marina shoots from the opening, her tail slapping against the heavy stream. I lunge forward and catch her in my arms before she hits the floor.

The combined weight of her body and the gushing water sends us both flying, but I cradle her against me as my back smacks the hard concrete. I don't feel the sharp pain from my landing, only the weight of her body pressed against mine, the softness of her skin beneath my fingertips.

"Are you okay?" I ask, easing us into an upright position with her wrapped safely in my arms.

"Yes," she gasps, her chest heaving. "Thank you," she manages, her panting growing more rapid. "Oh, Finn."

It is the first time I have heard her voice with my ears and not my mind. Her enclosure kept her from surfacing the waters of her prison, so we've always relied on her ability to project her words directly into my thoughts.

But there's no need for that now, and the sound of my name on her lips warms me from the inside out.

I don't have time to dwell on the feeling for long, though. Her tank may have been her prison, but the water within it kept her alive. Without it....

Shoving my hand into my pocket, I wrap my fingers around the vial, thanking the stars that it's still intact.

"Here." I pull the stopper out of the top. "Drink this."

The solution inside the vial is experimental, a work in progress that could either help her or kill her. It's part of the reason why she was captured in the first place—a drug designed to give humans the capability of breathing underwater. However, so far, the scientists on the project have only managed to do the opposite, giving small-er fish specimens the ability of breathing out-of-water in addition to other random side effects. They haven't tested it on Marina yet, or anything else her size. I don't know if the solution will even work on her, and as much as I don't want to trust it to keep her from suffocating to death, we have no other options. We have to at least try. She won't make it more than a few minutes outside her tank if we don't.

Marina tips her head back and allows me to pour the amber liquid down her throat. She swallows, the sound audible as her lungs rattle from the lack of oxygen.

"Finn," she whispers weakly. Her skin is gray, and the heaving of her chest deepens as she tries to draw breath.

"Hold on." I clutch her tighter. "It's going to work." I rock her back and forth, refusing to believe anything else. Everything about tonight hinges on this—this stupid experimental concoction made by the very scientists who captured her. But it has to work.

I *need* it to work.

All I can do is hold her as we wait. "I've got you," I tell her, smoothing back the hair from her cheeks. "Just hold on, okay? Hold on, Marina. Please...just hold on."

If love could will her lungs to breathe, they would inflate instantly. But it can't.

And they don't.

"Please...." I whisper as I press my lips to her forehead. "Please."

She tries to breathe, but there's no air.

There's. no. air.

The seconds drift away, and so does the life within her.

Tick. Tick. Tick.

Gasp...Gasp...Gasp.

Tick.

Gasp.

Tick.

Gasp.

Tears roll down my cheeks as I trace the planes of her face. Tasting the salt from my own tears, I press my forehead against hers and squeeze my eyes shut, praying for a miracle.

Marina tries one more time to draw breath, but there isn't any. No oxygen left to fill her lungs.

She goes utterly still in my arms.

"Marina? Marina, can you hear me?" I shake her lightly. "Marina!"

As much as I am willing her to breathe with every fiber of my being, her chest doesn't lift.

A sob rips from my throat, and down I go again, sinking into those familiar depths once more. This time it's *my* chest that can't find air—water pouring into my lungs as I drown over and over again.

Down I go.

Deeper.

Deeper.

Deeper still....

.

.

.

.

.

.

But then a warm hand presses against my cheek. I jerk upright, my eyes wide.

Marina's eyes find mine, life shining in them, color in her cheeks. Her long tail is gone, replaced by a pair of human legs. Her fins have transformed into delicate human feet. And her lungs—perfectly human lungs, easily taking oxygen from the air.

All I can do is stare at her, my eyes running up and down her body.

It worked. I don't know how and I couldn't explain the transformation if I tried, but I don't need to. All that matters is that it worked.

It really worked.

"You're okay," I choke out. My tears still flow freely as I relish in the feel of her warm skin against mine.

"Thanks to you," she replies softly, her pink lips curling into a smile.

I shake my head. "I thought... I thought..." I can't bring myself to say the words.

"I know." She pulls my head down even closer to hers. "I know."

And then she presses her lips against mine.

For a moment, all I can do is close my eyes and surrender to her touch. But then color explodes inside of me, every shade and hue imaginable, igniting within me like fireworks, flooding my senses to the point of overwhelm.

I was drowning, but now I'm soaring. I've become a seabird, flying high above the water on wings that will never tire and never fail.

Our lips move against each other, feverish and desperate, yet slow and sweet. The taste of her in my mouth, the sugar and salt on my tongue, wipes away any trace of sorrow still lingering within me. Her kiss is like a balm to my broken and weary heart, mending it and making it whole again.

We pull apart, both breathless. I want to stay in this moment forever, but we can't forget where we are. We can't forget that we're not out of this yet.

"Can you stand?" I don't expect her to be able to walk—or better yet, run—but if the solution in the vial has somehow given her that ability, I'll take it.

Marina bites the corner of her lip. "I don't know. Will you help me?"

I press my lips to her forehead in a quick kiss. "Always."

I shift her to the side so that I can stand, unbuttoning my shirt as I do so. I pull it off and drape it over her shoulders. Then I lift her carefully and steady her as she tries to master her wobbly legs.

She tries to find her balance, but two legs are not the same as her powerful tail. Her knees knock, and she starts to fall for the dozenth time. I catch her and hold her tightly.

Frustration lines her face. "I can't do it," she wails, silver tears lining her eyes.

"It's okay," I soothe, scooping her up in my arms. "I've got you."

She hugs my neck and snuggles in close. "My Finn," she breathes against my skin.

I head for the emergency exit. It's the fastest and most direct route out of the building, and there's a stairwell that leads up to the ground floor. The courtyard perimeter sits at the edge of the beach, nestled just before the line of dunes and seagrass. It's a hundred yards or so to the water—to the safety of the sea.

But this next part is the most dangerous aspect of my plan. The door is alarmed, and I haven't figured out a way to disarm it. Though I know the codes for every other security system in the place for my job, the emergency doors operate on an entirely different system run by the local authorities. I have no way of gaining access without raising suspicion. That means we'll only have minutes to make it to the beach before security swarms the place.

I didn't tell Marina about the security system. I didn't want her to worry. And no matter what, I won't let them put her back in that tank.

So I suck down a breath and push open the door.

A shrill alarm rents the air. Marina jumps in my arms, letting out a fearful cry, but I only grip her tighter and run, pushing my body to its very limits.

Time is a cruel master, both slowing down and speeding up as I run, making it impossible to tell if we're making progress or falling behind.

I focus on nothing but the girl in my arms and the path in front of me.

We make it to the ground floor and out into the courtyard. Already the night sky is illuminated with flashing blue light as sirens wail.

Voices call out, demanding me to stop.

I run and run and run; the salt tang of the sea air urges me closer.

I've got you, I've got you, I've got you. My own words echo in my brain with every step, spurning me on as my legs gain speed.

Gunshots ring out, and Marina burrows even closer into me.

"Don't worry." I grunt. "I've got you."

And I do.

More gunshots. *Bam. Bam. Bam!*

I keep running.

Bam!

Running.

One foot and then the next until finally my feet hit sand. It's harder to maintain my speed now, but I keep running. I carry Marina right to the water's edge.

Waves lap at my boots and soak the legs of my pants, but I don't care. I gently lower her into the water. As soon as her toes touch the foamy crest of one of the waves, her human legs begin to glow, shifting back into her glorious iridescent tail, her fins flapping happily and looking healthier than I've ever seen them.

I drop to my knees, happiness bursting through me. I grip her hands. There's so much I want to say, but we're out of time. I can hear the *thump, thump, thump* of boots running across the sand, voices yelling at us to put our hands in the air.

"I wish we had more time," I tell her as I kiss her palms. Never again will I see them pressed against glass. "But you have to go."

"Come with me. Please, Finn, I—" she starts, but the sentence dies in her throat. Her eyes narrow on something just below where I'm gripping her fingertips. "Finn!"

It's then that I feel it. The sharp pain slicing through my lower back. I reach for the spot, my fingers coming away coated in crimson. A ring of blood soaks the fabric of my shirt, spreading almost as fast as the stabbing ache that doubles me over.

"No, no, no!" Marina cries out, trying to hold me upright as I sag towards the sand. The strength and adrenaline that had been coursing through me quickly drains, only to be replaced by fiery agony that holds me in its claws and digs in.

"Go," I gasp out. I don't have to look behind me to know they're still coming. Whatever small window of time we've been granted is closing fast. "You have to go."

Marina cups my face with her hands, leaning over me. Tears and heartache drip from her, making my chest seize. "It's okay," I tell her. "It's better this way."

"I can't leave you," Marina cries. "Not like this."

"You have to."

The voices behind us are getting louder. They'll be here soon.

"Go, please. You have to go."

Marina shakes her head, resolve settling in her features. "No, I can't."

"You have to…" I rasp. The taste of rust coats my tongue. "Please, for me."

Marina sobs brokenly and hangs her head for a moment. But then she presses her lips to mine in a hurried-but-sweet kiss that, for a moment, makes the pain and everything else fade away.

"I love you," she says against my mouth. "Forever."

And I love you. I don't know if I say the words out loud or not, but I can feel them in everything I am, and I know that she feels them too.

"Marina," I whisper as my vision goes dark.

There is one more warm caress on my face, the whisper of two soft lips against mine, and a splash of warm salt water. And then …she's gone.

I wait for my heart to break all over again, for the pain of it to mix with that of my wound and claim me entirely, but there's only gentle peace that wraps around me. Peace so warm and bright that I can't see or feel anything else. All I feel is sweet, sweet relief. No matter what happens to me, Marina is free. Back home where no one can ever hurt her again.

Free.

My cheeks lift into a smile...because finally after all of this time, I think I am free, too.

I take in one last breath and surrender myself to the depths of whatever lies ahead.

.

.

Not drowning this time.

.

.

Soaring.

OUT OF THE SEA

SAVANNAH JEZOWSKI

I RISE; OUT OF the sea I rise,
a specter of the deep,
salt-kissed skin and seaweed hair
and briny fish scales.
I hear the call of canvas sails
snapping wild in the wind,
the stir of oars dipping
in my bed of sea foam.
I see wild souls who do not heed
the warnings of the rocks
and plot their course across
the siren's watery realm.

I sing a song of lost dreams,
of shadows reaching
across the barren seas
to taint the crest of waves
that kiss the barnacled hulls of ships.
I tantalize their senses
on fog-cloaked seas concealed

and draw them deftly to me;
they come, fools reaching for their deaths.
So I sing a song of passion,
of steel fish hooks
and sun-bleached mermaid bones.

Gently I banish their fears,
curl my mists around their eyes,
raise the ghosts of past ships
sunken in my embrace.
Specters haunt the listing deck,
calling their brothers
to join them in my black waters
with the other skeletal ships.
I rise, out of the sea I rise
to sing a sultry song
that beckons all the sailors
to the siren's watery grave.

I sing a song of hatred,
with monsters from the deep;
my song strikes out like thunder
rolling across the waves.
I raise the ships with ghost shrouds
to dance across the seas
as dry-lightning flashes
across the writhing sky.
I sing—terror fills their wild eyes
as their blood begins to freeze.

I drag the ships of sailors
to the fathoms of the deep.

I sing a song of loneliness,
The oceans still and barren,
the ships afraid to leave their moorings
and venture across my waves.
They snared my sisters,
I sank their ships,
but now what remains?
Only mermaid bones and lifeless sails
and memories of regret.
The seas are mine now.
I sink into the waves and wish
we'd chosen more than death.

I rise; out of the sea I rise,
a specter bent on change,
gone the days of sinking ships
and battle tridents.
I hear the call of canvas sails
snapping once again,
and when the sailor falls
I fetch him from my waves.
I sing a song to reconcile
the realms that once waged war.
Can salty seas and salty tears
mend the scars we've made?

Sea of Sorrow

Moriah Chavis

I stare at the diamond-studded noose around my ring finger as the door shuts behind Dylan.

The death of my mermaid life.

Engagement ring, Kiera.

En. Gage. Ment. Ring.

The giddiness washing through me makes me think of our first kiss on a snow-capped mountain—the first time I ever saw snow. The bitter cold was washed away by the warmth that flooded through me as soon as his lips touched mine. I had never felt so alive, not even while swimming next to a pod of orcas or when I landed my first aerial out of the water.

Being with Dylan—falling in love with him—thawed a piece of my heart I didn't realize was frozen. I love living on land because it gave me him. Ever since the night I met him—before I left the sea, during a trip with some friends to test our land legs—he's always struck me as unlike anyone I've encountered in my two hundred years.

"You going to stare at your hand all night, or are you going to turn around and notice me?"

I scream, spinning around and clutching my hand over my heart. "Seas above, Lucas. What are you doing here?"

My childhood best friend leans against the doorway to my mountain apartment's tiny kitchen. The last time we spoke, things didn't end well. We both said things we didn't mean, and my cheeks burn at the memory—the last words I said to him.

I can't live my life under the sea for someone who won't walk on the sand for me.

"Used the key under your mat while you were on your date," he says, snapping me out of the memory. "Came to see you." He shrugs, but he's anything but relaxed, shoulders tight and eyes wary.

"We're not teenagers anymore, Luke. You can't barge in—"

"I'm sorry, Kier. Really, I wouldn't have come—wouldn't have intruded—if it wasn't important." A fist tightens around my heart. We used to be close, and him intruding on my space wouldn't have bothered me. Mermaid memories are longer, and time is different. What happened two decades ago feels like a year to us—to him. But *I'm* not that person anymore.

"You know, this is the human world." I cross my arms. "I could have you arrested for breaking and entering."

His brow furrows, and I know he really does see me as the girl from before. No, the *mermaid* from before. The realization of what he's done hits him, and he opens his mouth, but I wave him off.

"I'm not going to call the cops," I say.

"Cops?"

"Sharkers." I use the word for our police. "The ones around here seem all right. I feel safe."

He nods slowly and turns a lazy circle around the apartment, studying the walls. Pictures of Dylan and me line the middle of a bookcase, blocking a line of novels my boyfr—*fiancé* bought me for my birthday.

"How do you do this?" Lucas picks up a picture, looks at it for a moment, and then sets it back down. "The air here is way too thin." He runs a hand through his golden hair, ash-gray eyes shining.

"You get used to it." It feels like he's stalling, and I clench my fists as I push past him.

He gently grabs my wrist and holds my hand to the lamp in the foyer. "Nice diamond. No pearl, but...."

I yank my hand away, shooting him a glare.

His gaze is locked on the ring. Hurt wafts off him.

"I don't need your permission." I shove him out of my way, unable to face my own decisions.

"What would your father say?"

I spin to face him. "Don't you dare bring—"

"Your mother is sick, Kiera."

I step back as if slapped. "What?"

"That's why I'm here. Your message was clear last time we spoke. I wouldn't be here if it wasn't important." He claims a chair in my kitchen. My mind spins, processing his words. Mama cannot be sick.

She can't. The words coming out of Lucas's mouth can be nothing short of a lie, and I tell him as much.

"You have no right to be here, not after what you said to me the last time we saw each other."

You would really leave this *for the humans? Do you care so little for your family?*

"I didn't mean—"

"Starfish, I know! We both said things we didn't mean, but it hurt," I interrupt. "You told me I didn't care about my family, that I didn't care about you. So why are you here now, hmm? Why are you gracing me with your presence after three years—"

"It's the oil sickness, Kier. A rig busted a few weeks ago, and she and a few of the elders were in the waters—"

"Shut up, Lucas!" I rush at him and stab my finger against his chest. "You shut up right now. My mama is not sick. She can't be."

"I'm sorry. The sickness started a few months ago, and it came so slowly, no one realized..." His words trail off. "No one realized how serious it was until it was obvious it wasn't something she could survive."

"Survive?"

"You know the oil sickness, Kier." He pauses. "She doesn't know I'm here—she wouldn't want to force you to come home. But I thought...maybe you'd want to say goodbye."

Tears burn behind my eyes. He grabs my wrist, pulling me into his lap. My hands splay across his chest; his heart beats steadily under my palms. It reminds me of stolen kisses and broken promises, and I fight the memories swirling in my gut.

I don't love him, not like he loved me, but the memory of those years we spent together is enough to warm my cheeks and raise the hair on the back of my neck.

"Kier—"

"No," I whisper and rest my head on his shoulder. Waves of homesick overcome me—not because of this man, but because of the life I had to toss away to live the one I have now. It's not fair; I know that. This moment with him is just a reminder of my teenage years and bittersweet sorrow. Years I spent with him and my mama beneath the waves. I clench my eyes shut.

How I wish mermaids could cry.

The next day, I visit Dylan at his cubicle.

"Okay, Jules, I gotta go," I tell my aunt on the phone, staring at him and waving the tips of my fingers.

"You sure this is a good idea, Kier? This is what you want?" Aunt Julianna asks.

Yes, I tell myself. "Yes." When I say it out loud, I can almost believe it.

I end the call and walk through the office, eyes trained on Dylan. He offers me a smile before he calls me over. "What a nice surprise!" He takes my hand and presses a kiss to my knuckles.

My cheeks warm at the public display of affection, and I slide into the free chair next to him. Dylan is everything Lucas is not. While Lucas is golden hair and bright gray eyes, Dylan is brown eyes and hair the color of freshly brewed coffee.

I used to imagine a life with Lucas beneath the sea, filled with endless waves and happiness. But when my mother's sister passed without an heir, the crown went to my mother, changing every-thing. The burden of being the next queen rushed toward me like a quickly approaching wave, ready to tug me under. All I could think about was life on land—a life I had never experienced. Especially when I met Dylan, even though being with him was throwing away everything I had ever known.

Merpeople rarely give up their fins willingly, and I can only think of one merperson who reneged her life at sea: my father's sister, Julianna. She gave up her fins for a human, a daughter she had with a man on land. The man loved her for the few years that they had together, and I always dreamed of something like that, whether above or below the waves. When my aunt announced her choice to our family, the look of determination and love on her face knocked the air from my lungs. She didn't need a tail to be complete when a man and the life they had created together were enough. No, they were everything.

Those who choose land over the sea have time to change their minds—five years before they can no longer shift back. Other than myself, there hasn't been another merperson to make that choice since my aunt—and I was only the second in centuries.

Five years. After five years, I would either give up my tie to the sea and relinquish my claim to the crown or return to my family. The weight of the world would quite literally take away my magic. It's only been three years, but I can feel the pressure of the land. My ability to shift has gotten more difficult, and it would take three years under the waves to rebuild my endurance.

I shouldn't even have to contemplate returning. Merpeople have incredibly long lifespans, and the past queen's death was an accident—a fluke.

Which is why my mother cannot be sick. She was supposed to outlive me.

"What are you doing here, Kier?" Dylan's voice breaks through my thoughts. "And since you're here...scone?" He slides a plate toward me, and my mouth waters. Scones are one of the best parts of my life on land. And this one is blueberry. Dylan buys me one every Saturday because he knows they're my favorite—and he never forgets to include fresh syrup from the farmer's market downtown.

He doesn't know that Lucas was the first person who bought me a scone, and every time he buys me one, I think guiltily of the boy I left behind. I have tried to replace the memory with new ones, but with Lucas waiting in the car, it's even more difficult today.

Focus, Kier. Now is not the time to get sentimental over baked goods.

My bags are packed, and after my visit with Dylan, Lucas and I will board a plane and be at the ocean in a few hours. My stomach turns at the realization: I'll be seeing my parents soon.

"I have to go away for a few days." I pick at the scone, unable to taste the sugar and blueberries because of the bitter anxiety on my tongue. "It's my mother. She's...unwell."

His brow furrows as his lips form a question.

"Please," I beg before he can utter a word. "I don't have time to say how sorry I am for not telling you about my parents. Our relationship is...strained, and I didn't—" I stop and take a deep breath. "My mother is sick."

"Kiera, I thought your parents were dead. You just came in here and said you *must* visit them? I didn't know there was anyone to visit." Red blossoms on his cheeks as guilt gnaws my gut.

I grasp his hands. "I know, and I'm sorry—"

He laughs, though the sound is anything but funny as he pulls his hands away. "Are you not even going to invite me to go?"

Sadness sours against my tongue, and I wish again for tears. But my ability to shift still means I can't be fully human. Not yet. I slide the chair closer to him. "I would, but you don't understand—"

He turns away from me, hurt painting his tone when he says, "I think you should go, Kiera. I have to get back to work."

I turn the engagement ring on my finger before going over to him and leaning down for a kiss. He offers me his cheek, and I have to force back the emotion pooling in my belly. I make it to the parking lot without breaking down, but as soon as I slide into my car, a frustrated groan breaks through my lips.

"Kiera—" Lucas starts.

"Shut up," I snap. I fumble with my keys, but Lucas rips them from my hand.

"Give me back my keys, Lucas!"

He jerks them away, grabbing the wheel with his free hand. "What happened in there, Kiera?"

"Can we just go? Please? I need to see my mother."

He studies me for a long moment, finally nodding and relinquishing the keys. We're silent on the way to the airport. Once we're on the plane at the small airport in Asheville, North Carolina, I cover my eyes with a sleep mask and pop in my headphones, drowning out the possibility of conversation. It's after midnight when we reach the coast and check into our hotel. I try calling Dylan, but it goes straight to voicemail. I don't leave a message. I take off my jewelry and store it in the bag he gave me for Christmas last year, my hand feeling lighter without the weight of the diamond.

I walk out of the bathroom in a swim top and cover to find Lucas staring out at the waves from the balcony.

"Are you ready?" I ask.

He glances at me. "You look like yourself again." A smile tugs at the corner of his mouth.

I roll my eyes and make the short trip to the beach with him closely behind. The moon glitters over the waters, and the beach is almost empty. Even the sea turtles have left their nests behind and returned to the ocean.

We wade into the high tide, the sea brushing against my skin like a soft kiss hello. A sigh pushes its way past my lips, and I choose to ignore the chuckle that comes from Lucas. I dive under the water, relishing the feel of my joints as the waves breathe life back into my unused muscles.

It takes longer than the last time I shifted, and a slight pain lances down my spine. I take a deep breath and clear my brain, calling forth the change. The pain slowly fades as the shift twists my joints and ligaments into submission. I glance behind me as my legs disappear and transform into my silver tail. My eyes readjust to the light, and my lungs welcome the water like an old friend.

"It's a long swim to your old queendom of Marmor," Lucas warns. As if I've forgotten—though it *has* been a while. "And a hard swim when you haven't trained. The Triangle always has a storm brewing."

"I'll be fine," I say, and we begin our journey.

He wasn't wrong, and my body gives out way too soon. We stop halfway to the castle to let me pause and rest my fins. Lucas won't meet my gaze; the truth of what has changed about my body is evident. We haven't said anything to each other since we dove beneath the waves. What waits for us screams louder than the silence, my mother's sickness a wedge between us.

Light reaches farther down now that the sun has risen as the underground city comes into view. My breath catches in my throat. Warring emotions build in my belly, and I hover at the edge of the gate, studying the massive palace stretching high into the water at the city's center. The palace is still covered in bright coral and shines with a vibrancy of its own, tendrils of light stretching into the water and down impossibly far. No human has ever seen the castle, and it's in the center of what they refer to as the Bermuda Triangle.

If you want to be a human, you have to stop thinking of them as different from you, I chide myself.

"Are you ready?" Lucas asks.

I turn to look at him, pushing the swaying strands of hair away from my face. My chest burns with the effort of the swim, but I try to force my breathing into a regular pattern, taking in small gulps of water at a time.

"I'm fine." The words are barely above a whisper. "Let's go."

The guards at the gate don't recognize me at first. "Papers?" They stare at Lucas. "You know the law, Lucas—"

"Since when have we needed papers to enter the city?" I ask. "And don't they just ruin the second they get wet?"

At the sound of my voice, the guard to my right focuses on me. He hurriedly bows. "Our apologies, Your Highness. We did not realize—"

"It's a special blend of seaweed—" the other stutters.

"Why do we need papers?" I interrupt them both.

The first guard's face turns a brilliant shade of red. "With your mother's illness, scavengers have tried to infiltrate the city."

"Sirens?" I ask, heart slamming into my ribs.

Which means the queen is truly dying. Sirens are vicious, and they will impede on any territory when they sense a weakness. For them to gain control of Marmor, part of one of the most dangerous spots in the sea—the Bermuda Triangle—would expand their reach. The very Triangle would grow, taking who knows what with it. If sirens are getting past the magic barrier around the city, then my mother's magic is failing. Her body is failing. My limbs grow numb.

The guards both look to Lucas, and he waves his hand as if to say, "Answer her."

"Yes, Princess," the one to my left says.

I let out a puff of air, bubbles spreading around my face and momentarily obscuring my vision. As soon as they clear, I meet Lucas's gaze.

"Are you ready?" he asks.

Throat tight, I manage a stiff nod as we're ushered into the city.

The entire city pauses as I swim through the streets with Lucas at my side. Whispers tug at my fins, but I grit my teeth and keep moving forward.

If I thought the city was quiet at the sight of the long-lost princess, all sound in the palace ceases to exist. The head maid opens the door, her white hair swaying behind her head.

"Princess Kiera," she whispers before bending at her waist in a hurried bow. "We weren't expecting you."

I give her a tight smile. "Lucas was kind enough to tell me of my mother's condition."

Her eyes flash behind me, a disapproving look passing over her features. "I see." She spins around and rushes to grab a passing maid. "Please let the king know she has arrived."

The second maid gapes at me, eyes wide and mouth open. A bubble of air drops from her lips almost comically, like in one of the shows Dylan watches on the weekends. Thinking his name sends a pang of regret through my middle, and I rub the empty spot on my finger.

Diamonds don't belong in the sea.

And neither does Dylan.

"Tell my father I'll be with my mother when you find him." The words come out harsher than I intended as I swim past the second maid.

She doesn't move to stop me, and I glide through the place that used to be my home, haunted by the ghost of my past and the decisions that led me to leave the water.

The boy at the shore with dark eyes and a kind smile waits for me, even now; though he's angry and confused about the choices I've made to cut him out of this part of my life, I know that Dylan will be there when I return. Leaving the water for good means never seeing the people I loved for so much of my life: the woman who gave birth to me and the father who hugged me when I was hurting or broken. To give up the water is to give them up, too.

The thought of Mama causes my fins to ache. She shouldn't be on her deathbed; it doesn't make sense. She's supposed to be in her prime, since one year of a mermaid's life is about twenty years to a human's.

Even after I left the sea to try living as a human, I thought my family would always be there.

There are moments when giving up a dozen lifetimes for one with Dylan is enough. But since the news about Mama, I've questioned what leaving my parents truly means—what choosing him says about the life I will live.

As I break into my parents' bedroom, I don't want to look at my mother on her bed of seaweed.

But I have to.

The sight twists my gut. The broken image of her, eyes closed, chest rising with each shallow breath. At the sound of my approach, her lashes flutter. The bright green of her eyes has been replaced by a milky gray.

"Mama." My voice splits.

"Hey, Angelfish." She holds out her arms.

In two pumps of my fins, I'm in her weakened grasp. She nuzzles her face in my neck, and sadness wells in my chest. I've never seen my mother weak—and certainly never sick. The mermaid in front of me is a stranger. Where her hair used to sway behind her in golden strands, it's now stringy and lifeless, a muted yellow.

"I've missed you so much." I can barely utter the words.

"I've missed you, too," she murmurs as I pull back, and she runs her fingers through my hair. "Tell me everything I've missed."

For the next few hours, the words tumble out of me as I tell her about my life on land and reveal the good and bad parts of leaving this world behind. She wants to know about Dylan, and as soon as I begin, I can't stop.

"You love him," she says afterwards.

"I—"

"I can see it in your eyes. In the way you speak of him. The way you carry yourself when you talk about him."

"I do," I whisper. "I love him so much, I can hardly believe someone could love another person as much as I do him."

"Good." She takes my hand in hers and squeezes it.

Dad comes in and lies down on the bed beside her, patting my arm. "Missed you, Angelfish. Have you had a chance to see my sister?"

"Missed you, too, Dad." I give in to his embrace. "Aunt Julianna and I spend holidays together. It's nice."

It's not this, I think, *but it's family.*

"Tell me again," Mama says. "Tell me about the mountains—what do they look like up close?"

Her curiosity makes me wonder if Mama might have longed for a life she couldn't have, too, one not as heavy as that of an entire queendom on her shoulders. "Up close, you can't tell you're on one, not until you look out and see the others rolling in the distance. The sea seems so far when you're on top of a mountain. It's like an ocean of itself."

"You love it almost as much as you love your Dylan. I'm glad." A smile tugs at her lips, though her eyes shine in the light from the shell lamps.

Does she think I hate the sea now? I shrug. "It's a place, not a home."

"But a place you love." She pats my hand. "I'm glad you went—glad you forced me to let you go. I feel like I'm seeing a part of you I've never met before."

I steer her away from conversation concerning my life on land and talk about her, recalling memories and the best times of my life beneath the waves. Slowly, night grows nearer, and exhaustion weighs heavily on my mother's face. Dad gets up and gives us a moment alone.

"When do you go back?" Mama croaks, her eyes now on the door.

"Soon, but I won't be gone long, Mama." I kiss her nose. "I have to settle everything on land, and then I'll be back."

I don't want to waste any more time away from you, I add silently.

She touches my forehead, and the look in her eyes doesn't sit well in my stomach. It reminds me of a look I've seen in the mirror while contemplating an idea I wasn't willing to share. "Angelfish," she says, "I have loved you from the moment I saw you. Remember that." She leans over to brush her lips against my cheek.

I push down my misgivings and force a smile onto my face, patting her hand. "See you in about a week." I place a kiss on her forehead before swimming out.

I venture into the hall, expecting Lucas to join me so we can start our long journey back to land.

"Lucas," one of Mama's maids says. Lucas floats over to her, and the mermaid whispers something in his ear.

"What—" I begin to say, but I'm cut off.

"The queen beckons!" Lucas calls over his shoulder.

My brows furrow, and I go to follow him, only to be stopped by the guard posted outside. A nervous laugh escapes me. "I can't go in?"

"I'm sorry, princess. The queen requested an audience with Lucas. Alone."

I open my mouth to respond, but the guard locks the door. After about ten minutes, Lucas comes back out. His face is glazed over in concentration, and I swim up to him. "Lucas?"

A mask falls over his features, one that almost looks like his regular smile—except for the troubling glint in his eye. "Ready to leave, Kiera?" he asks, going past me.

I glance back once more, the tug of my impossible choice drawing me to the room shadowed in responsibility. My mother has months left—if that, and I need to return to spend the little time she has left alongside her.

Preparing to say goodbye and training to be a sliver of the queen she's been.

You'll be back next week, I remind myself as I follow the merman I've known my entire life back to the life I must leave behind...no matter how much it breaks my heart.

"Thank you," I whisper as we walk out of the water, back on human legs.

Lucas glances over at me. "It was nothing, Kiera. Your mother wanted to see you, but she would never have asked you to come back. She wants you to live your life, the life *you* want. Even if it is above land."

"Especially because she knows I'm going to do what I think is right?"

He huffs out a small, humorless laugh. "Yeah, especially then. What will you tell your fiancé?"

I straighten my shoulders, fiddling with my ring finger...only to be reminded again that there's no ring. I love Dylan. Everything about him—the way he smiles, how he treats me, the way he sings Christmas music even in January. A part of me struggles with whether or not loving Dylan means I have to love my family less.

Why does it feel like someone is ripping my heart from my chest no matter which decision I make?

"I will give back the ring," I say. "He was upset when we left." I shrug. "I can spin something."

He squints at me a moment before we walk up the beach and back into our hotel room. When I get out of the shower, he sits on the bed, staring blankly at the television.

Worry pierces my gut, and I take a seat next to him. "What did my mother say to you, Lucas?"

He jumps as if he didn't hear me sit beside him. "Private business, Keir. You know how your mom is when it comes to secrets. A queen never reveals all." He pastes a wicked grin on his face and winks. "Rest. We have the hotel for another night."

I'm asleep in moments, ignorant to when he gets out of the shower or climbs into the other bed.

I wake up to the sun streaming in through the curtains. A red sunrise sweeps across the sky, streaked through with orange and pink. I watch it for a few moments before rolling out of bed and getting ready. Lucas stretches awake and disappears into the bathroom. Ten minutes later, he's dressed, and we're on our way to the lobby for breakfast. Lucas picks us out a table in the back corner, far from listening ears and wandering eyes. We eat in silence, Lucas scowling at most of the options the hotel has to offer.

"Nothing is fresh," he says, and a corner of my mouth tugs upward. His gaze flicks toward me. "What?"

"You're not made for this." A smile wiggles its way onto my face.

"Neither are you," he replies, cheeks reddening as he looks back down at his plate.

A flush rises to my cheeks. I do fit here, this version of me. I've adapted—evolved and changed to match my environment. The mermaid I'll have to reintroduce myself to *doesn't* belong here. She prefers salmon over chicken and seaweed over chips. She would rather go for a night swim instead of a stroll through the woods when they first change in the fall.

"Well, I eat bacon now," I tell him and glance toward the breakfast bar. My eyes fall on a heap of baked goods. My heart aches for Dylan; I wonder if he's munching on scones in his office.

"Gonna grab you a plateful?" Lucas asks.

I smile wistfully and sneak over to the bar, placing three scones on my plate.

"Are you meeting with your aunt while you're here?" he asks as soon as I return to our table.

I nod. "I'm going to transfer access to all of my accounts to her. I can keep them open if need be in case of an emergency, but I won't need them. Oh! I forgot napkins, and these can be crumbly." I jump up and grab a handful before coming back to my scones, which are now covered in syrup.

"You remembered," I say, looking down at my plate. I glance up, and the smile in his eyes tells me this particular memory hasn't soured between us.

"We went to that little diner on the pier when you turned sixteen. Human years," he adds before I correct him. My real sixteenth birthday was spent saving survivors of a sinking ship. It's why he took me to the diner.

You gave up your birthday to help others. The least you can do when you look *sixteen is enjoy it a little.*

"The waitress told you the syrup was for the pancakes, and you thought she meant the scones—neither of us knew the names of most human foods then." My chest warms at the memory, and I take a bite. "It's still delicious," I say, but the aftertaste is slightly too sweet, and I take a sip of my orange juice to wash it away.

"I have the hotel room until tomorrow." The water Lucas got sits untouched; being from the sea, the water always tastes strange on land—never enough salt. He fiddles with the brim of his cup. "You can stay in it until you meet with your aunt."

"Thanks, Lucas."

We fall into an uncomfortable silence, our plates empty, the words unable to come. "Kiera—" he begins at the same time I say, "Lucas—"

"It's fine," he says. "Say it."

I reach across the table and touch his hand. "Thank you for not saying anything. You didn't tell me if this was a good decision or a bad one. It's mine, and you haven't said anything about it. So...thank you."

His lips quirk into a grin. "Kiera, I've loved you since the moment I saw you. I want you happy, no matter what that means."

My throat feels thick, and I squeeze his fingers. "I want that for you, too, Lucas."

He laughs, the sound hollow. The hotel dining room dissolves into silence as the remaining guests start to leave their tables and begin their days. My head begins to spin, and I rub my forehead, wincing.

"I'm sorry," Lucas whispers, and my brow furrows. "I couldn't tell you before, but now..." His words trail off. "Now I know you won't remember this. Your mother made me promise, Kier. I didn't want to do it, but—" He stops and shakes his head. "The dying wish of my queen," he finishes in a low voice, "to make her daughter happy."

"What—" I reach for my fork, but my hand can't grasp it. "That's...funny...." My words slur together, and Lucas runs over, catching me before my head hits the table. I glance around the room, noticing for the first time the complete emptiness of the breakfast area—the table in the corner he picked.

"Lucas..." My breaths quicken in panic. Did he drug the syrup?

"I'm sorry, Angelfish," he whispers, taking me into his arms as the world fades to black. "She made the choice she knew you were too stubborn to make, but she wanted you to forget. She made me promise."

I wake to the knock at my hotel door. A steady rhythm pounds against my skull, and I stumble to the entryway, peeking through the peephole before swinging the door wide open.

"Hey, Julianna," I say, brows scrunching together.

My aunt's face turns into a mask of concern, and she pushes her way into the room, cupping my face between her hands. "Are you all right, Kier?" she asks. "What's wrong? Did something happen to your mother?"

The pain in my head dissipates slightly at her words. "What are you talking about?"

She closes the door behind her and moves me to the bed. "Your mother, darling. Is something the matter?"

"Jules... Mama's been gone for three years—Dad longer than that."

A strange look passes over my aunt's face, a mix of horror and understanding. "I can't believe she would do such a thing..." she whispers.

Before I can open my mouth to ask her what's wrong, she goes to the small kitchenette and fills me a plastic cup with water.

"Drink this, Kier," she says.

Her eyes follow my movements as I drink, and I hand her the cup after it's empty.

"Thanks. That helped," I say.

She slowly takes the cup from me, turning away and brushing her hand under her eyes as if drying tears.

"Are you all right?" I ask.

Julianna's gaze jerks back to mine, and I think I must have imagined it. "I'm fine, Kier."

My chest tightens, and I rub it, an unfamiliar ache forming. A burning builds behind my eyes, and I stand and walk to my luggage, hurriedly digging through the bag until I find my phone. I hit my last call, ignoring the missed messages and other notifications.

"Kiera?" Dylan answers, voice hesitant.

A sob breaks through my lips as the tears begin to fall. "Dylan, I miss you." My cheeks are now wet with tears.

"Where are you, babe? What happened?" His voice turns soft and kind. The sound of him getting up from his desk and rushing to grab his things fills my ears.

"I don't know."

Julianna takes the phone from me and whispers to Dylan. I find a spot on the bed, curling into a ball as the absence of something pierces my soul, bringing forth a bitter sadness for a missing piece I can't find.

As soon as she's off the phone, my aunt joins me on the bed. Something wet drips onto the pillow, and I raise a shaking hand up to my face, tracing the tears stuck beneath my eyes. It only makes them come faster. My vision blurs, and I look up at my aunt, unable to form the words for this sadness welling inside me. "Julianna?"

My aunt's eyes glimmer and she wraps me in her arms, soothing me as I cry.

THE SEA'S BELOVED

MARIELLA TAYLOR

RIKKANA IS BORN, AS all creatures are—formed of light and breath and earth. And, as all young maidens do, she grows in grace and beauty in a village by the sea. Each day, she bows her body and places her offerings before the statues of the Four Brothers.

She leaves the small flame of her candle to die out among the others at the feet of the golden statue of Light. She leaves the kiss of her lips against the white alabaster fingers of Brother Breath. For Brother Earth, she brings the fruit of her labor, small leaves or fruits or odds and ends from her garden, and prays beneath his bronze shadow the prayer she was taught from

birth— "May the Brothers grant her a long and happy life beneath the blessing of their gaze"—before they will deliver her to the fourth.

It has been said that Brother Sea knows all and holds all. He consumes the living and drives out their breath, drags them down into unfathomable depths and empty oblivion to Rest. Nothing may appease him; no one may forgo his choosing.

Wives and mothers leave their fearful offerings at the stone feet of Brother Sea. Gifts of hope and penance so that while their men sail upon his waters, the fourth Brother will leave them in peace. They offer him anything, everything—food, cloth, riches, even bones or bits of fish and shells they have hunted from his shores—for no one knows the gift that will kindle the heart of the sea.

No one but Rikkana.

Rikkana recalls days as a child sitting in the sand, watching the village women dig for clams along the beach. Their sticks dug deep gouges in the sand on Brother Earth's surface, Brother Light kissing them away when Brother Sea's tides washed ashore. She recalls her mother's stooped body beneath the weight of the basket strapped to her back, the musky scent of death rising from its contents.

Her hands were small then, her tiny limbs too weak to hold a basket of her own—though that time would come soon enough. But most of all, when Rikkana is wrapped in the warm embrace of those memories, she remembers the ripples on the surface of the water, the ones that no one else could see.

Like glass they were—fractured images of light and dark, forming a watery, grim face—a face that has watched over her from the moment her parents brought her to the sea six days after her birth to sprinkle her with the salt of sea and set sail their pyres of offerings, praying their protections and charms over her tiny soul. Grim features at first, wary and halting. Sharp edges that no man nor child can fathom. But when her mother called to her to return home, Rikkana smiled at that face and waved. And in the days that came, she found that Brother Sea cracked open his maw and smiled back, his slippery waves kissing her ankles as he rushed in to mark the evening.

Now, she has come of age, and she holds a basket of her own. Now, Brother Sea's fingers trace the lines of her legs, and his salty touch presses like stinging kisses along the length of them. The other women dare not voice their jealousy when his gifts wash up at her feet, but they are appeased when she digs for the clams alongside them, digs until her hands split raw and shaking. And at the day's end, when her work is done, they watch with sharp, cold eyes and whisper behind their bleeding, bandaged hands. "What kind of magic is this?" they ask each other. "That the sea has become enraptured by a woman."

"They call me a witch," Rikkana tells him, her voice low, vanishing beneath the crashing of his waves. She seats herself on the edge of that cliff, on the stone they cut his statue from. The jagged edges smoothed by time and salt curve in to hold her as she sinks her feet into the sand. When she closes her eyes and feels the spray of him against her flesh, Rikkana wonders if her prayers and offerings are for naught. She wonders some days if she truly desires the long life for which they all ask.

She opens her eyes to see him come as Brother Light sinks into his horizons. The man-like shape of him builds in the foaming waters. His face cracks with easy smiles, and she imagines the ache in his arms and his breast is the same as hers when he cannot hold her.

Rikkana has never left offerings at the feet of that stone statue, that single-tailed likeness of the Fourth Brother. But here, in this place, amidst the stone from which he was carved, at the heart of the shrine which they have built together, she leaves him her offerings. She cannot feel his arms around her, cannot feel his kiss on her lips or place her own over his heart, but when she opens her mouth to pour her secrets out into his waiting ears, she imagines the beat of his salt-infested heart.

The Fourth Brother has courted her the way the men have courted for centuries, traditions tried and ageless. Four gifts, four offerings, four choices. He courts her with gifts and music and all the love he knows how to give her. He washes food up at her feet—in the form of small fishes with their glittering scales, crabs with their twisted shells, and oysters with their secret treasures. He grants her freedom, in his own way—in the form of his ear, in the form of his patience, in the form of stolen touches. And when she turns her face into the stinging fingers that brush her cheeks, turns her eyes upon him to give him all the warmth she feels in her heart, Rikkana can feel the dark longing in him.

He bequeaths her rings, thousands upon thousands of them, gathered upon his long walks along the ocean floor. Simple bands, rusted with time, encrusted with the ocean's life, bejeweled with his love. One to mark each count his heart beats while he waits there for her. He places them in her hands, at her feet, marking each one with more kisses on her cheeks, her neck, her ankles. Though she has never felt the warm grip of him around her, she begins to leave her prayers at the feet of the other Brothers in her mornings—prayers in the shape of him.

He has courted her, the way the men have courted for centuries, and yet—there is one thing even the feared Fourth Brother cannot give her. It is the way of man, to give a woman the love of his heart and the pillow of it beneath her head. To give her the strength of his body and the hope of love and long life for many future generations. A long life together—before their bodies will be fed at death into the grip of Brother Sea.

But this gift, this fourth one, is a gift her beloved cannot give her—for he cannot leave the water, and beneath it she will not breathe.

Instead, he whispers in her ear a secret, a name. The name laid upon him by his own father millennia ago. The name she offers when her mother asks after the man she wishes to be her husband.

Anapos.

He may not give her his heart, and he may not give her his shelter, his strength, but Brother Sea will give her his tenderness and his secrets if only she will grant him her patience and her faithfulness.

He waits, he tells her, beneath the water for the day she will come to him. He waits, he tells her, and he builds her a monument of stone—a memorial for her death that even the gods themselves would envy. He waits, he promises, kissing her ankles as Rikkana trudges back to the village with tears on her face and screaming in her chest. She loves him, the sea, her Anapos, so deeply—so why can she not have him? Why must she be born a human, born of light and breath and earth, unable to even hold his hand?

As she sinks into her bed and weeps, she pretends not to hear her mother's anxious murmuring. Fervent prayers for her protection certainly—from the sea, from the village, from herself. All these prayers Rikkana watches her lips murmur as her father cocoons his wife against his chest. Her mother falls asleep to the beat of a strong heart beneath her ear while her daughter strains her ears for the labored pounding of the seas on the cliff walls. Oh, to be so lucky. Oh, to have such hope.

Days and weeks and months have passed when she leaves the idol's courtyard with sea-cracked lips and a heavy heart. The Four Brothers have not heard her prayers, she thinks. They have not felt the love, the desperate hopes and whispered dreams she pours out at their feet, though her tears have stained their statues.

She stumbles out from the courtyard into a wasteland of angry faces. And she knows, dear gods, she *knows.* When the men come up those steps for her, she sinks to her knees, Brother Breath drying the tears that stain their tracks upon her face. Laughter comes then, bright and brilliant as Brother Light when he breaks over the morning horizons. She looks up into her father's face as he pityingly binds her hands while others bind her feet.

As her father carries her down the path, followed by that mob of hissing villains with their angry whispers of "Witchling," she rests her head on his shoulder and smiles when Brother Earth catches his sandy essence in her curls. And she has hope, so much hope. So much faith that maybe, perhaps, there is life somewhere beyond this.

They take her there—to the shrine Anapos built for her, to the place she sat and whispered all her secrets, to that place where all his gifts to her are buried—waiting faithfully. Her father stands with her on that precipice while another man adds the millstone to her feet. The weight of it sinking to the sand, holding her there in that moment, sets her heart free, free, free. *Simple, fool, witch,* they'll call her. *Returned to the depths and the devil,* they'll say. But gods, she can't stop—she can't stop smiling, tearful dripping thing that it is.

"I am sorry," her father whispers, pressing a rough kiss against the top of her head. Rikkana gazes over the cliff edge into the fractured, seething gaze of her beloved. Watches him rage beneath the surface of the water, all snarling foam and cracking waves against the cliffside.

"Don't be," she whispers back to her father. "They cannot hurt me any longer."

Then she is falling. Brother Breath's arms skim along her body, slowing her descent. Brother Light and Brother Earth whisper their goodbyes into her ears, and then—then the cold. Icy, shocking cold wraps tightly around her lungs. Brother Breath's essence pulls bubbles from her body as she sinks so, so fast into blackness.

And then it separates, gathers into a face—his face—and strong, supportive arms, skin colored in deep blues and greys and rage. There is no smile when he greets her; she gives up her last breaths to splay her fingers against his cheek, feel the solid plains of him beneath her hand, and whisper his name:

"Anapos."

She feels them.

She feels them around her, in her, with her—even in death. She feels Brother Breath through the gills ruffling against her neck, feels his resurrecting kiss upon her forehead. She feels Brother Light gazing down at her through the murky waters, gifting her his smile. She feels Brother Earth's hands upon her legs, cocooning them in silt and mud, murmuring his charms until all that remains are smooth fins and glittering scales. And she feels the cut of a knife against her chest as her beloved rips out her broken, dying heart and replaces it with his own. A heart that is finally, *finally* hers.

When she opens her eyes, it is to a new dawn, a new age. An age where Brother Sea spares none but his own and snaps all men in his teeth. Her village has been washed away, her people's bodies buried in mounds of earth as far as the eye can see, and she rests there in her beloved's arms, her cheek against his chest. She smiles at the Four Brothers and thanks them in her heart of hearts for their gifts.

Brother Sea sits on his throne, a throne built of stone and salt and bone, his darling queen held in his arms, her head against the empty place in his chest. When she raises her head to look up at him with those emerald eyes that he has so deeply missed, he places his kiss upon her lips and revels in the feel of her—awake and alive and *his*.

He smiles then, threading his fingers through her hair, and whispers, "Welcome, my queen."

Hunger

Julia Skinner

The rippling marsh sucks at my feet as I stagger to the edge of the pond. An almost invisible sheet of water stretches across the land, as if the pond behind me is reaching reaching *reaching* to grasp any soul who dares stray close to the edge of the road ahead.

It *is*, of course.

I rasp a breath, chest thudding in time with the water's feral hunger. A dull, muggy fog blankets the air around the edges of the marsh, clinging to the bowed trees and wisping across the hole-ridden road. Storm clouds rumble above. It is the same kind of wet day as when I first came. Young, sarcastic, a mind full of dares. Back when I was...*more me*. Now I'm more the water. More the hunger. It pounds in my chest—a single, insistent drum.

Wrapping my muddy arms around my stomach, I slosh toward the empty road. There is a faint growl of motor and rubber in the air, the sound of some lonely truck rounding the distant bend. My heartbeat races. *Finally*. Something to feed the water's hunger.

Barely anyone comes past here anymore. Not now that there are so many reports of disappearances, of monsters snatching passengers from their cars.

"They get it wrong," I whisper. The water hisses back, threading through my sopping wet clothes. "We...we don't touch the ones who drive on; we only claim the ones who touch the water."

My friends warned me of the creatures who dwelled within the pond—about the veins of black that twisted beneath their scales, of fish that could walk like men. *"Guess I'll just die, then!"* I laughed, throwing my camera around my neck. It had been a challenge: prove to everyone that the rumors were false or come back with proof that they were true.

Feed me, the water in my veins hisses. *Feed. Feed. Feed.*

I reach the end of the marsh and come to a stop. I am bound here. I cannot touch dry land. None of us can. *Once upon a time you could,* a small voice inside me says. It...feels strange to think of that time. The time before the water sank into my soul and claimed me. I glance upward, toward the dark clouds.

The water within them calls to me, prickling through my skin like thousands of needles.

I stand, frozen, for what feels like a lifetime. Waiting for that rumbling vehicle to pull closer, to satiate the gnawing need in my stomach. At last, a lone pick-up truck with peeling blue paint comes into view, clanking down the overgrown road.

MINE, the water roars in my skull.

The truck pulls to a stop. The door swings open. A man in overalls steps out and stares at me. To his eyes, at least from this far, I am nothing more than a drenched young man. "There are monsters in that lake," he says with a heavy drawl. "You shouldn't be messin' around there, bud."

His tone makes my lip curl. It grates against my spine like all the voices from my past used to.

"Hey, bud!" he barks. "Ya hear? I'm talkin' to ya."

I blink. Above, silent lightning flashes through the downcast sky. "I heard."

"Bad things happen to folks in these parts," he says.

"I guess," I rasp, "I'll just die then."

The man snorts and turns back to his truck. "Right. Have fun with that, stupid."

The first trickle of rain weeps from the sky as he reaches for the door. Thudding. Thudding. *Thudding*.

"No use running, no use hiding," I whisper, and the man pauses, one foot on the floor of his truck. "The water is everywhere."

Everywhere...

Trickling...

Creeping...

ROARING.

"And it's hungry"—I step forward, drawn through the water falling from the sky— "*bud*."

So, so hungry.

The Merwitch

Amber Kirkpatrick

There is an eerie Cajun tale
of a sprite so dark and sinister—
She lurks among wetland roots,
and even gators shake and quiver.
To find her you must at first
brave the mud and the muck;
watch out for crawdad holes,
and green toads springing up.
Beware of the cottonmouth,
With that gaping maw wide and sly,
Gliding through the bayou murk—
you'll pray he slithers by.
But if you survive all that
and call out to her low,
she may rise from shadowed waters,
locked in her spell of woe.
Pocked grey skin of the moon,
and venomous black lips,
hair hard as onyx stones,
tumbled, tossed, and saber-tipped.

Absent are the eyes,
only fathomless holes remain,
which cast deep into your soul—
Your heart will carry a foul stain.
But her siren call is husky,
and no man can demur,
he waits for her embrace
and swampland fire conjure.
For she tastes of wild cherries,
her hands drift in ways unknown—
enticing, alluring, ever pulling
at his heart as it turns to stone.
To drown in brackish waters deep,
with that red-tinted scaly tail
wrapped tight around his body—
dreams of lust he will inhale.
Thus many a man of the south
has found his way to doom...
for it ain't all belles and BBQ, boys—
there's a merwitch in the swampy gloom.

Trashy Romance

Hope Bolinger

Something I never knew about Lake Erie...it apparently has mermaids.

At least, at first glance in the waters, I think it does. A girl with fiery red dreadlocks—and a tail to match—dips and up down the waves. The gooey sand sticks to my feet as I stagger forward and squint to get a better look.

Wind whips my hair. The noise from the Lake Erie beach behind me muffles—the families on towels spreading out picnic arrangements, the longboarders sailing down steep-hilled boardwalks toward the concessions stands below.

Mildewed air attacks my nostrils.

Ugh, of all the states I chose to live in...why Ohio? Now at twenty-one and fresh (and early) out of college, you'd think I'd have gone for at least Michigan, which doesn't have the Great Lake none of the other lakes like to discuss. Erie is the black sheep of the Midwestern bodies of water.

Glittery scales dip up and below the water's surface. I swallow the cinnamony remnants of the granola bar whose wrapper I pocketed in my shorts before I entered the lake. Sunbeams blotch my pale shoulders and turn them pink. Why'd I opt for the yellow polka-dot bikini today like some 60s music cliché?

Her head surfaces; she quirks a dark eyebrow at me. Then her arm pokes through the water, something pinched in her fingertips—a granola bar wrapper. "Did you drop this?" Her voice comes out low like a rumble of thunder. Blue skies etch above us.

I pat my pockets, heat sizzling in my cheeks. This time a sparse cloud has shielded the sun, so I have nothing to blame but my embarrassment. "Uh—yeah, sorry. I'd meant to throw it away. That's why it was in my pocket." My waist has barely ventured too far into the waters, and I didn't think the current was strong enough to yank any litter out of the shorts.

Her chin bobbles up and down in the water. "Uh huh. That's what they all say. How do you think Lake Erie became well known for how much trash it has in it?"

Blonde curls suction themselves to my nose because of the humid day. Unsuccessfully, I attempt to blow this section of hair off with one breath. My hands cup my bony elbows, and everything feels like my entire skeleton has just gotten exposed to this girl. "I said I was sorry. Won't happen again."

This wasn't like me at all. I'd spent years back in high school rallying Earth Day events and insisting the girls in my dorm use the recycling bins out in the hallways. In fact, just this morning, I'd tossed several bags of chips I encountered on the beach into the bins found on the sidewalks. How could I have ended up so careless?

As I reach for the wrapper, she yanks it back and a smile wriggles up her cheeks. Her large fins clap the water behind her. "You wanna try one of these tails on for size?"

Oh, she must be a professional mermaid—ladies who wear neoprene tails and grace the waters of aquariums and corporate parties everywhere.

The coconut sunblock I smeared on my face earlier seeps into my mouth, and I spit out the bitter taste. "Sure. What girl doesn't dream about becoming a mermaid?"

"Naiad, actually." With a sweeping gesture, she motions to a large gray bin offshore. "You'll find some spare tails in there. Think of it as a favor to me since you decided to trash the lake."

A favor? Girl, I'd wear a mermaid tail for fifty bucks if given the chance.

Wading over to the water's edge, I unclip the latch and choose a purple tail for myself. Right before I slip it on, I notice a chip bag floating on the surface of the water. So I return to the waters, pick it up, and toss it in the trash. Then I return to the changing station. I unbutton my shorts to reveal a polka-dot swimsuit bottom. I park in the sand, grimace about the amount of grains chafing my thighs, and shimmy into the tail with some difficulty.

The girl in the red tail treads close to the shoreline. "Need a little help getting into the water?" She quirks her brow again.

I think about the amount of effort it'll take to flop my way into the lake. Glancing over my shoulder, I see a family's eyes burning into me. Yeah, no, I don't want to risk getting embarrassed. "Sure, that would be great. I didn't catch your name."

She extends her hand, long fingers straining toward me. "Annika. And you?"

"Sabrina." I clasp her hand. Something burning hot overtakes my legs. She pulls me into the water, but the cooling effect of the lake does little to calm the sizzling that's happening in my calves and on my neck.

Struggling to tread water, I take in a deep breath and clasp my hand to my neck. Lines have formed on the skin, and something taps my fingertips and recedes.

Gills?

Girl, no, don't be ridiculous. I kick my legs one by one, but find that I can't distinguish the left from the right. In horror, I watch as Annika climbs onto the shore with legs. All of her red scales have vanished.

She salutes me with two fingers. "Thank you for your service."

Naiad 101. This was taught to me ten minutes later—the whole "thank you for your service" part.

1)   Naiads are protectors of lakes and bodies of freshwater.

2)   There had originally been no naiads in Lake Erie.

3)   But after the people trashed the waters, water deities cursed some lake-goers and made them oversee the garbage cleanup.

4)   The only ways to get rid of the curse:

a)   Clean the entire lake.

b)   Pass on your curse to another human by physical contact. They must be wearing one of the mermaid—I mean, naiad—tails from the gray bin.

A male naiad with dark skin and a sharp jawline finds me huddled on the shore that night, clasping my knees—wait, no, I guess just tail—to my chest. I'm holding back sobs until they weigh my ribcage down like stones.

"Rough first day?" He flops beside me. "Name's Murrow, by the way."

I hiccup. "Yeah, my roommate's gonna be freaking out that I'm not back at the apartment." I introduce myself. "How long have you been on Lake Duty, Murrow? And how long does it take to get used to having gills and lungs?" It requires two different types of breathing techniques to operate both, and when the gills surge full of water, it tickles your neck. I don't know if I can get used to that—ever.

Despite living in the lake's waters, he smells nice, sweet. I could get used to a scent like that.

In fact, I won't mind some more one-on-one time with this guy. Maybe we can be cursed for a few weeks to get a couple dates in.

"Let's see." He squints at the moon. "You can lose track of the days, but I do remember enduring winter under there. We hibernate."

A cold shudder ripples up my spine. "You're that bad at passing off the curse to someone else?"

"Nah—" He props his hands on the sand, and I have to fight every temptation to lean into his shoulders. His beautiful baritone voice could mesmerize me forever. "—I refuse to curse people."

Something flutters in my stomach. I focus on digging my fingertips into the sand to avoid his eyes. "Why's that?"

"Because, I figure, this mess in the lake, this mess in the world, is everyone's mess. I think it's easy to say, 'Hey, that soda bottle in the lake is yours.' And I'm pretty sure the naiad who cursed me just planted that on me after she saw me drinking Dr. Pepper—"

Same with Annika. Did she pinch the wrapper out of my shorts like an old-fashioned pickpocketer? Just so she could get out of her lake duty?

"—but it takes all eight billion people in this world to create entire trash continents in our oceans. So I'll stick it out until we clean this lake. I want to know I *personally* picked up and tossed away the last chip wrapper when I get my legs again."

My lips twitch. "That's noble, Murrow. I think I'm with you." Wind sends goosebumps up my arms. "I would feel so guilty, leaving someone else in the lake because I didn't want to deal with this stuff." Peering over my shoulder, I glance at the dark bins on the sidewalk. "Problem, though: it's gonna be hard to throw trash in those if we have to flop up and down the beaches."

A sniggering laugh overtakes him, and his index finger lands under his nose. "Yeah, that's why a lot of us do the trash stuff at night. Most naiads sleep in the lake during the day—hence why people don't talk about mermaid sightings all that much. But if we only do it a few hours in the moonlight, it could take ages."

My front teeth crash into my bottom lip. The sound of water receding from the sand and leaving behind foam plumes fills my eardrums for a moment.

Memories flood back from my Earth Day club in high school. Didn't we do a project where we visited Lake Erie beach? And picked up the trash from the shoreline for two hours?

Then the idea hits me.

"I think I know how to get rid of the curse—without passing it onto someone else."

White teeth show in his brilliant smile, even here, out in the darkness. "I'm all ears."

Murrow and I spray a mother and child with water when we flop our fins the next day.

"Hey, cutie!" I make my voice elevate a few notes. "Have you ever wanted to meet a mermaid?"

The small girl, sporting a rainbow-scaled bathing suit, widens her eyes. She glances up at her mom and tugs on the woman's lace cover-up. "Mom, can I meet the mermaids?" She bobbles up and down. "*Please?*"

"We have something even better!" Murrow gestures at the gray bin. "In there are mermaid tails in all sizes."

Something wriggles in my gut about the fact they have ones for children in there. Did some cruel naiad force a kid to leave school and attend to lake duties?

The mom firms her jaw and folds her arms. "How much money to rent the tails?"

"Fifty bucks—" I start to say, and when she turns to the side, uninterested, I throw up a hand. "*But*. If you fish a piece of trash out of the lake, you get ten minutes for free."

"Ten minutes per piece of trash?" She squints at me. "So if I picked up six pieces, Daisy would get an hour in the lake?"

Everyone knows that look stamped on her face—doubt.

Someone in a longboard, holding a hotdog, skitters past on the boardwalk.

"It's part of a Lake Initiative," Murrow cuts in, and I pass him a grateful glance. "To make Lake Erie cleaner." He leans in, his hand on his mouth, in a I-have-a-secret-to-tell-you-Daisy fashion. "So us mermaids can breathe a little better in these waters. They're really stinky."

True. Last night it took forever for me to get used to the garbage smell that filled my nostrils and gills in the water. The slimy lake bottom did little to ease me into sweet dreams, too.

Daisy giggles and squints up at her mom again. "Puh-lease?"

For a few seconds, the mother doesn't move. Then her face softens. "All right, sweetie, let's get as much trash as we can find out of this lake. I want you to have as long in that tail as possible."

After all, what little girl wouldn't want to be a mermaid for a few hours? Emphasis on the *few* hours.

Although "business" booms at the mermaid tail bin, we don't manage to clear out the lake until a few months into summer. Even a news station swings by a few times to interview us on the shoreline.

And someone sends in a large boat to mine the deepest trashy treasures near the center of the lake, because it would be too dangerous to ask families to venture out that far just for a few moments in the tail.

Not to mention some World War II planes and other impossible-to-heave items rest at the bottom of those waters. So we have to get the aid of some heavy equipment to pull those out.

No wonder the other naiads passed on the curse as quickly as they could, with odds stacked against us like that.

True to his wishes, Murrow does fish out the final item of garbage. Instead of a chip bag, it's a granola bar wrapper.

As he flops onto the shore, legs appear as the scales dissolve. I, too, feel a cold sensation rippling up my calves. Oh, these beauties have returned. Clasping my neck, I gasp. The whistling air of the gills has disappeared.

Human again.

My legs wobble as they stagger onto the sand. I collapse, and it takes both Murrow and myself several hours to regain use of our muscles. Man, did Annika make that look easy. But perhaps she'd only spent a day or two in the waters—not months. Or in the case of Murrow, well over a year.

"Well, Sabrina." Starlight glitters in his eyes as he gazes up at the night sky from the sand. "What now?"

"Maybe we grab food somewhere? Anything beats the raw fish and soggy food people have been leaving in the lake." I chew on my lip.

His white smile flashes. "Sounds like a plan, but—" He pauses. "Let's go to some place with washable dishes. No disposable wrappers."

"Agreed." I lie on the sand and let the grains bite into my now un-gilled neck. "No garbage for a while."

The Song of the Siren Sea

Anna Augustine

The Siren Sea
  It beckons me
  Beyond the safety bay
  Danger far below does call
  Tis led me to my grave.

I shut the door on the sea ballad as I tug the collar of my long black coat up and step out into the oncoming storm, a light drizzle already hanging in the air. The voices of the other men at the pub fade away with every step, and my shoulders relax the more distant they become. The night is crisp and cool, a blessed relief after the stale smell of cheap ale and sweaty sailors that the tavern held. A trickle of water snakes down my back as I move through the dingy streets of Idlewile.

The rain begins to pick up, transitioning from a light caress on my skin to a torrential downpour.

Blast this weather, I curse bitterly as a wagon wheel splashes through a puddle, sending mud splattering over my freshly shined boots. I hate this town. Have hated it since the day I was dumped on its doorstep. It's a reminder of all I've lost, and I don't plan on staying any longer than necessary.

My years here formed who I am now. There are days I wish for more. A place to call home. Someone to greet me when I step off my ship after a long journey.

My ship. I sigh.

That's why I hurry across the cobblestones in the downpour tonight. Soon I reach a part of the city that rivals the tavern with its stench. The putrid odor of waste and refuse stings my nose and coats my tongue with its foulness. I swallow the gag rising in my throat as I step under a low doorframe and into the hovel that my one and only companion calls home.

If you could call it as much.

Kendrick lies sprawled over the dining table, a half-finished tankard of ale clutched in his meaty fist. A snore to rival a giant's echoes through the dank room, and a rat scurries across a plate on the floor.

My last friend in Idlewile. When he's not sailing, he's a stone cold drunk. But the fact that we're landlocked right now is his fault.

Another snore punctuates the air and I shake my head, grabbing the nearest pot and spoon and bringing them together.

"All right, you over-indulgent buffoon!" I bellow loudly, kicking the rat out the door in one quick motion to avoid its teeth. "I'm gone for a week, and you turn into this?"

Kendrick splutters, swiping at the drool stuck to his face. His eyes are still slightly dazed, but he smacks his lips together to wet them as he gazes at me. "Edward. I didn't expect ye back so soon." His heavy brogue is even thicker with the slight drunken slur attached to it.

I cross my arms and lean against the doorframe. "That much is obvious."

He rolls his shoulders, tipping his head left then right. His neck cracks loudly, and he sighs in relief. "Please tell me we're getting out of this hellhole soon. How could ye leave me here for three weeks, Eddie?"

I raise my brow. "I wasn't the one who gambled the ship away." I push off the doorframe and straddle a chair, tossing the pot and spoon to the floor. I lean my chin on my arms and shoot him a glare. "That, my dear friend, was you."

Kendrick mutters something under his breath that would make a lady blush beet red. He returns my glare as he runs a hand through his thick auburn hair. "Well, did ye get it back?"

"For a price. A bounty." I pause, wanting him to ask me about our next errand. Our *fool's errand*. My muscles tense at the very thought.

"Well?" He finally huffs, irritation in the planes of his weather-beaten face. "What's the bounty?"

"A siren."

Silence falls over the room, the chill increasing at the very word. Kendrick's eyes grow quite large, any lingering traces of drunkenness gone. "Ye didn't agree ta that, did you?" he whispers.

"I didn't have a choice."

"But everyone knows that those who go into the Siren Sea never return!"

"Those people aren't me. Edward Burke always returns." I smirk, despite fingers twitching on the back of the chair. "I've beaten the odds before. I'll beat them again."

"Yer luck won't hold out forever."

"We don't have a choice!" I practically holler, pushing away from the chair. "I wasn't the cursed fool who traded the ship!"

Heat rushes my face as my words hang heavy in the air. Kendrick's jaw works up and down for a long moment. Then he stands unsteadily to his feet, swiping the half-finished bottle of rum from the table as he does. "No, but yer the cursed fool who'll be sailin' into the Siren Sea by hisself, 'cause I ain't going there." He takes a swig of booze and stomps into the street.

"Kendrick! Come back!" I call after him. The door thuds with a finality that matches the ache behind my eyes.

"Me and my blasted big mouth." I rough a hand over my face. I can't stand around and wait for him to come back. If I want to keep my ship, then I am just going to have to catch myself a siren.

Watery depths of black and blue,
  Where sirens call for me and you.
  Down to the Siren Sea I'll go,
  And find what awaits me fathoms below.

The blasted sea ballad circles endlessly in my head as I stand aboard my vessel. I somehow managed to hire a crew, although they were a mediocre one at best. The rumors of the Siren Sea—in song, in tale, in truth—were enough to make the stoutest sailor's knees knock together. And my crew was far from brave.

"Ready to shove off, cap'in?" asks Wiggins, my slim, blond-haired first mate, as he chews on a slim piece of wood.

"Aye. Ready the sails!" I call out, leaping up the steps to the helm. "Hoist the gangplank! Make ready for high waters!"

"Aye, aye!" The chorus rings across the deck as the crew springs into action. Nervous laughter and banter blend with curses and grumbles. They all float around me as *The Mermaid*, my precious ship, eases away from the docks and out onto the brilliant blue.

I grip the spokes of the wheel as the sails fill up with the briny sea breeze, which pushes us into the cerulean waves. The freedom of the sea wells up within me, and I fill my lungs with the ocean air.

A pang strikes my heart. Kendrick should be here standing at my side. Not Wiggins. But I shove aside my grief and tighten my grip on the wheel. Kendrick's not here, and I have a bounty to complete.

A few hours later, Wiggins steps towards me, pushing his stocking cap back to wipe at the bead of perspiration on his unusually pale brow. "Cap'in Edward, sir. Now, we means no disrespect, sir. But a few of us be sorta skittery about huntin' for those evil creatures."

Aren't we all.

I, at least, manage to hide it better than most of my crew. I turn and raise a brow at Wiggins. "We're already in high waters. There's no turning back now. The crew knew what they were signing up for; I expect fulfillment of our agreement."

"Aye, sir. It's just...*sirens*, sir." He shivers. The rumors of the sirens—the mutant mermaids of the sea—are whispered in the taverns and shared as horror tales around the fireplaces of families everywhere. I have given little stock to them over the years.

In truth, I believe in mermaids as any good sailor does. They're the guardians of the sea—beautiful, powerful beings who care for the water we tread upon. But the sirens? They are the opposite of mermaids in every way, luring men to their deaths simply because they can. I shake my head.

Wiggins clears his throat. "I just thought to let ye know about the crew's...discomfort, Cap'in." He shifts from side to side, rubbing the back of his sweat-soaked neck.

Are all my crew this agitated? I knew they weren't particularly brave, but I'd thought they were stout enough to face the coming fight. But as I scan the deck again, I notice the wary glances of my men. Their anxiety crackles across the entire ship, almost as strong as the taste of salt in the air. I breathe in measured counts, considering my odds. Mutiny must not be allowed.

"A bonus upon return to shore," I cry out to the men, expecting a cheer at the least. I'm met with dazed expressions instead as a roll of thunder echoes across the blackening waves.

"We're nearing it, cap'in." Wiggins begins twisting his hat to death, his face turning so pale he looks more dead than alive. "Can't you h'er it? Echoin' across the sea? It's *their* sea now, sir."

A flash of lightning is followed by a mighty crack of thunder. I tighten my grip on the wheel as *The Mermaid* climbs a giant wave. The top of the wave seems to touch the clouds for but an instant, bathing my ship in foggy glory. We level, cresting the frothing cap of the surge, before tipping down to ride the swell out.

The wave breaks as if hitting a sandy beach. I loosen my death grip on the wheel, blinking at the absolute stillness of the water all around us. An inky blackness envelopes us, and the sailors hold their lanterns about the deck. They're pinpricks of light reflecting against the uninterrupted surface. Our sails are limp; not a puff of air stirs them. Behind us, the storm still rages, yet not a living thing dares to move on this side of the waters. My men are frozen like statues on the deck. Glazed eyes, open-mouthed...like they're caught in a trance.

Then, slowly, almost as one, they turn starboard. I hear it then: a melodic, serene voice slides over the waves, tickling my ears with its promises of love and life.

Oh, come my pretty sailor.
Come to the ocean floor
And taste the nectar of my love
And live forevermore.

My body lurches toward the voice, feet moving as if they have a will of their own. I know that something is wrong. The stories all say that sirens lie, after all. They feast on men—stupid men who drown beneath the water for the futile hope of love.

Love is a lie. A myth. No one ever really loves. No one truly cares. I learned that ten years ago when I was abandoned by my mother on the streets of Idlewile. She never cared. Why should the sirens?

Yet my heart yearns for their promise. To be cared for and ministered to. I want it. Want it enough to take the plunge.

I'm standing on the edge of the ship. Vaguely, I hear someone screaming, the sounds of splashing to my left and right. Yet my heart soars at the thought of love beyond measure. Lightning flashes across the sky. The ship is frozen in the mirror-like water. The only thing I hear is the haunting promise of the sirens and the rush of blood in my ears. Glancing into the glassy water, I see a face. Gaunt cheeks, white eyes that are locked onto me. Green hair waves in the depths like seaweed in a pond. A black tail matches the twisted fingernails of the siren's hands. She's horrifying. Electrifying. Enticing.

I raise my foot, slowly tipping forward...

Something grabs my shirt, pulling me backward. I tumble to the deck, my head connecting with the hard wood. My eyes clench shut as pain erupts through my skull.

The song cuts off. A hiss floats around me, a venomous, evil sound. Cold dread slithers through my chest, followed by the faintest need to see the source of that hiss.

The ring of a sword being drawn is followed by a heavy string of curses. "Be gone, ye vile creature! No one wants you here no more. You've had your fill, go back to the hell ye spawned from!"

Another hiss sounds, this one chilling my very soul. More curses and the *swish* of steel through the air. Shrieks of anger, a splash, and a roaring explosion. Then heavy, unbroken silence.

"Eddie?"

There is only one person—on land or sea—who dares to call me *Eddie*. His heavy brogue and the smell of brandy that wraps around him is impossible to mistake. I pry my eyelids open, meeting the sparkling blue eyes of Kendrick.

"What are you doing here?" I ask, wondering if I hit my head harder than I thought. Reaching back, I brush my fingers across the knot that's sticky with blood.

"Ya really need to check for stowaways better, Eddie." The insufferable man winks. "But seein' as how I saved yer sorry hide, I'm sure ye'll forgive me." He thumps me on the back, his humor fading. "There's only three of us left, lad."

"Three?" I ask. I glance around the deck. It's empty, save for the few discarded belts with pistols and swords strapped to them—the siren's way of protecting themselves as they dragged the men to their watery graves.

"Where are the sirens?" I ask.

Kendrick points to a barrel set by a post. I squint, my vision hazy from the pain in my head.

"Is that—dynamite? You blew them up?"

"Scared 'em, sure and certain."

I glare at my friend, who is unashamedly grinning. "You're telling me that not only did you smuggle yourself on board, but you brought dangerous explosives on my ship?"

"You're welcome." He pats his pockets, searching for something. He curses and looks over my shoulder. I follow his gaze and see Wiggins with his hands slapped over his ears, his eyes squeezed closed. Kendrick pulls a flask from his jacket pocket and raises it in salute to Wiggins. "There's a wise man."

I blink in astonishment at the weapons, the vague memories of the siren's hold over me haunting. The crew is gone, pulled into the murky depths of the still-as-death ocean. And I would be with them if it weren't for my faithful first mate. "Thank you, Kendrick. You saved my life."

Kendrick waves aside my thanks and downs another long draw of his rum. Wiping his lips with his sleeve and a shake of his head, he eyes me.

"Ask it."

I raise a brow. "Ask what?"

"That question that's stewing in that big head of yours." He grins and takes another swig of his rum.

"How did you not get affected by the siren?"

He reaches into his pocket and draws out two wads of cotton. With another cheeky grin, he thumps my back. "How about we get out of here, Eddie? Before the blasted sirens return with more friends, eh?"

It would mean becoming outlaws. The bounty is still on my head. Still on my ship. But I would be alive. Somehow, that's the more enticing option. "Aye. Let's go."

Clasping my hand, he hauls me to my feet, tightening his grip as he leans in close. "I think we should try being siren slayers."

I raise my brow. "I thought we were escaping from them?"

"Aye, and so we are! This lot, anyways." A conspiratorial glimmer brightens his gaze. "But what's to stop us from findin' more? They lure men to their deaths. What say you and I lure a few of them to theirs?"

I rub my calloused palms together, contemplating his idea. "We'll need a crew."

Kendrick claps his hands once as he strides to Wiggins' side and hauls the scrawny man to his feet. "What about you, man? Want to kill some sirens?"

The twitchy man looks over at us, rubbing his cap over his forehead. "Slay sirens? Are you mad?"

Kendrick chuckles. "Most likely, but what's life without a bit of madness, eh?"

I smile. "I thought you were scared of sirens, Kendrick?"

"Scared?" My friend turns and winks at me. "I'm bloody terrified! But I just fought one off and saved your hide. I suppose we can take on a few more."

I kick my head back and laugh—loud, long, and full of hope. The song of the siren lurks in the back of my mind, but I can hear the lies now. The sirens do not offer love, but I have it. I have it in a faithful friend who would risk everything to protect me. The sirens offer death, but my friend gave me life. I thought I was alone, but I've never been more found.

The tune of the sea ballad rushes me, and I find myself writing a new verse.

And at long last the siren falls
Beneath the icy waves
And now we turn our ship astern,
Away from the siren's grave.
Yet in my heart lies a memory,
Of the siren's whispering song—
Never shall it entice me;
It's buried, dead, and gone.

With that melody teasing my mind, a breeze ripples across the still waters. Cool and fresh, it wipes away the last of the siren's hold. It promises life, hope, and new beginnings.

Wiggins leaps into action to hoist the sails, Kendrick at his heels. I climb up to the wheel, pointing the ship toward the storm that rages behind us. Slowly but steadily, the breeze pushes us forward—toward the raging seas and new adventures.

Of Sea and Starlight

E. A. Hendryx

E-Tren District
City of Remus on planet Sartu

Flarin Mesius had never seen such beautiful—and terrifying—creatures before.

"That's of the Void, that is." Evrah Z'rn elbowed him in the side. "Did ya see that, Flair? You'd think they were tryin' to kill one 'nother."

"I'm watching with both my eyes, aren't I?" In fact, Flarin couldn't take his eyes *off* the sight in front of him.

The Marina proved even better than the neon verts advertised at the spaceport. Concession stands saturated the air with savory scents of seaweed-like burnt ümah and grilled fish, saccharine sweet Gellen pastries, and all the synthol a soldier could buy. The arena itself boasted a ten-story tank filled with bubbling liquid, something close to water but more dense, and teaming with indigenous aquatic plants and marine life. Colorful lights strobed through the dense water and flashed across thousands of faces lining the auditorium seats next to where they sat.

The tank was nothing compared to the actual show stoppers, though. The Loris.

"I heard they'll rip your throat out first chance they get, mate. They hate humans." Evrah shuddered.

"No wonder. We've caged them, haven't we?" Flarin kept his voice low so as not to attract attention, but he'd never been one to enjoy seeing living beings in cages. Even beautiful, water-filled ones.

"I suppose." Evrah wasn't one to rock the boat. "But I hear they mate with human males dumb enough to get close and then toss any male babies ashore since they won't be true Loris. That's vicious."

Flarin had heard that as well, but was it rumor or fact?

"How can somethin' so beautiful be so deadly?" Evrah continued.

Flarin wondered the same thing. The Loris—a race of half-female, half-fish beings with elegant tails and long, flowing hair—were native to the planet Vatalta. The stuff of legends brought to life. Something his Ma would have made up stories about at bedtime.

"I feel better knowin' they're in there and we're here." Evrah's expression hardened with dislike.

Flarin blocked his friend's constant chatter as the scene before him changed from one of mock fights to what he guessed was an underwater stage.

Another school of Loris swam to the front. Each wore jewels and fabric wrapped around their torsos, the ends trailing behind them in the water like visible currents. One specific Loris caught his eye. She was smaller than the others and had long, blonde hair, while a mixture of green, gold, and pearlescent scales covered her tail.

The control-collar that encircled each Loris' throat clearly bothered her more than the others. He watched as she touched it for the third time in less than a minute. Like she wasn't used to wearing it.

Electronic music pumped through the speakers overhead, and the Loris swam into action. They swirled, dove, and flipped to the beat in perfect synchronization, creating a rainbow of colors through the water-like substance.

Bubbles shot up at intervals, adding to the magic of their motion. The music swelled, and emotion stirred inside Flarin as a memory of his sister swept through his mind.

She wore a white dress and danced in a field with her arms up, spinning and twirling to her own inward song. Her girlish laughter echoed from the past...but shattered once the crowd burst into applause.

He swallowed and cleared his throat. As he blinked rapidly, his eyes traveled to the steps where two armed security guards stood. Then to the top of the tank, where metal bars locked the creatures in. Nausea twisted his stomach.

Beauty shouldn't be caged.

"You think it's true they're imported straight from Vatalta despite the embargo on human cargo transport?" he asked.

Evrah shifted toward him, frowning. "Who? Them?" He nodded toward the tank.

"Yeah." Flarin swallowed again. "I heard the commander call it a loophole. Something about them not really being human."

"That ain't human, mate." Evrah shoved a finger toward the water.

His irritation spiked. "They're clearly sentient."

"Maybe, but that don't make them human."

Flarin opened his mouth to argue, but the music changed, and he noticed the Loris with blonde hair touch her collar again. She moved to the side and looked up. He followed the direction of her gaze.

A man stood on the top floor with his arms crossed. Waiting. Guarding.

Flarin watched the Loris as she wove upward behind coral structures and vegetation. Had the man called her back?

She reached the top and broke the surface. It was difficult to see from his vantage, but he leaned to the side and caught sight of another man kneeling down. He wore a dark suit, and something gold flashed over his eye—an ocular implant, perhaps? The next instant, the dark-suited man's hand went to her throat.

Flarin jumped to his feet.

"Where you off to?" Evrah asked.

Flarin's focus shifted to the packed crowd in the colossal stadium. Everywhere people laughed and drank while watching the show. No one else noticed the man and the Loris, all too captivated by the entertainment. Anything to escape their everyday lives on Remus.

But he couldn't just sit there. He had to do something.

"Mate?"

"I'll be back."

Since Evrah had been the one to purchase tickets earlier that day, they were in a section of favorable seats on the fourth level—close to the tank. With the structure reaching ten stories, there was plenty of opportunity for waterfront views, but it also meant Flarin needed to climb six levels. And fast.

He took off at a sprint, attacking three stairs at a time. His quads burned, and his breath came in quick gasps, but this was nothing compared to the training he did as an enlisted soldier for the Alerius Galactic Defense, or AGD.

He huffed a laugh thinking of his roommate. Bricon would have challenged him to go for four stairs at a time. Good was never enough for him; best was always the goal. That's what made him a better soldier than Flarin. Bricon cared. But right now Flarin was thankful for the added motivation as he took the next set of steps without hesitation.

He reached the entrance to the tenth level and stopped. Drawing in deep lungfuls of air, he assessed the situation. There were guards on the other side of the entrance gate marked as a restricted section for VIP guests. Naturally.

With his back to the smooth duraplast wall, Flarin sought the man in the suit and the Loris. A large column blocked his view. Cursing the Void, he spun back to the guards on the other side of the gate. He could easily take them, but getting *through* the locked gate was going to be more challenging.

To the left of the ninth level, a metal screen blocked sight of the E-Tren District's busy streets. It also helped mute the light from the neon verts and bright signage attempting to draw any clientele off the thoroughfare.

He wouldn't have given it a second thought, but Bricon's words rumbled through his subconscious, shifting his perspective.

When you can't go through, go around.

It was crazy. He was crazy for even thinking it. But...

The memory of his sister threatened to surface and steal his focus. He couldn't let it, even if it was part of the reason he considered climbing to the tenth level with no gear.

An image of the Loris' innocent expression pushed him forward. She might be a deadly creature, but she was at the mercy of a violent man. Flarin couldn't ignore that.

He'd made a promise to Tuneya, even if she hadn't lived long enough to hear it.

Flarin would never stand by and let someone suffer.

Never again.

Javrik's meaty fingers closed tightly around Kalyah's neck over the blasted collar. As if zapping her through it hadn't been enough. Her fingers and the tips of her tail fins were still buzzing with numbness from the shock.

"Do you have coral for brains, girl? When I tell you where to go—you go."

She struggled to take in even a whiff of oxygen, but darkness clouded the edge of her vision. When she thought she might actually pass into blackness, he lessened his hold—barely.

"Confused," she croaked.

Anger narrowed his eyes. "You come when you're called. That's the job."

She almost laughed. Job? This wasn't a job. It was a death sentence.

"Sir." One of the guards opened two argentiam-tipped fingers to display a halo. "Master Drvos has changed his request to urgent."

A shiver of fear raced up Kalyah's spine. Drvos d'Quris had requested her? It was too soon. "N-no. Please, not tonight."

"Voids. You'll go, water-scum. Or I'll zap you again on a higher level." Javrik flexed his jaw and tightened the fingers around her throat. He followed the action with a violent shake to prove his point, but it sent the Loltā splashing across his expensive jacket.

"Get your hands off her." A voice like rumbling vulair song caused a shiver to race up Kalyah's spine. The fingers at her neck loosened, but he didn't release her.

The guard whirled around. "How'd you get—"

The young man who spoke like the largest swimming creatures on Vatalta moved faster than the light of stars. The guard was standing one moment, on the ground the next.

"I—what? Who're you?" Javrik growled from where he kneeled in front of her.

"Let. Her. Go." The stranger emphasized each word with a step.

She took in the way the young human stood. Broad shoulders pulled back. The arms at his sides thick with muscle and ready to strike. He radiated power and confidence for one so young. Determination hardened his eyes, and she couldn't help but notice they were the color of the Loltā she swam in.

Javrik stood. "Don't know who you think you are, but you're messing with things beyond your control. Run along before I send you to the Rings."

"I don't think so." He stepped forward, and Javrik pulled out his blast pistol.

By the waters! Now the men were going to fight. So typical of landers.

Kalyah had chosen not to defend herself. She was a prisoner, yes, but only to further her goals, and being sent to Drovs d'Quris, the ruler of Sartu, would have immediately ended any plan she had in place. As she considered the interruption—and the young man behind it—she wondered if this could work to her benefit.

She reached down and plucked a scale from her waist. It stung, but it was a small price to pay. Then, careful to sense the appropriate location for maximum effect, she jabbed the pointed tip into the fleshy part behind Javrik's ankle.

He yelled, but the electronic music blaring through the Marina ate the sound. The next instant, Javrik fell to the floor. Only then did she notice she had the young man's full attention.

"What did you do?" he asked.

"Control the situation. He is merely asleep." She sighed and touched the collar again. This time she took a pin from her hair and unlocked the mechanism in three quick motions. She tossed it to the deck with a clatter. "Well?" Her eyes met his, and she saw a wealth of questions swimming there.

"Well, what? I...was trying to rescue you."

She laughed. "I do not need the help of a human man to save myself."

Her words seemed to impact him like a fin to the chest. He took a step back. Perhaps she had been hasty in her admonishment; he *had* provided a distraction. She had little experience with human males outside of the Marina, but this one had courage and, apparently, skill.

"Forgive me. I mean to say thank you." She shifted her shoulders and took on a humble bearing. "You did me a great service."

He wore suspicion like a garment. While keeping his feet planted wide, the muscles of his forearms twitched in readiness for action.

"Will you lend your hand?" she asked.

He remained grounded like the coral connected to the tank floor.

"Do you not understand?" She knew her words were clear; what was the problem?

"What is it you want from me?"

"To be pulled from the Loltā." She frowned. "Uh, water."

"No. What do you really want?"

By the waters, is he stupid? It would be a shame to waste such handsome genetics on an idiot.

"Will you lift me out?" She spoke slowly this time.

He moved forward, bending to a crouch close to her but still far enough away that she assumed he thought he was out of reach. Little did he know her true power.

"I understand your request. I don't believe you."

She frowned. "That I want out? You saw what Javrik is like. I would very much like to escape."

"You're still lying to me, Loris. The truth, or I turn around and walk out of here." His words were curt and intelligent.

So, not an idiot. Thank the blue for that.

Kalyah needed to swim a fine line. Perhaps some of the truth was necessary here. "Are you trustworthy, human?"

He accepted her challenge. "Fully."

"And how do I know you aren't just saying that?"

"You don't." He didn't flinch.

"What if you are a skin trader looking to take me for your own?"

"I'm a soldier doing what I thought was right." He locked eyes with her as if to convey the conviction of his words.

Stars, but she believed him. "I do need help to escape the Marina. I may have overstated my abilities to be free of Javrik." All true. He nodded. "Your assistance is my only hope for freedom and would be much appreciated." Half true. His help would be useful, but she was resourceful. She offered him what she hoped was a sweet smile.

"Ah." He held up a finger. "You almost made it two full sentences without lying to me, Loris. Goodbye."

He turned, and Kalyah felt the first wave of fear rush over her. Had her smile tipped him off? She'd tried to stroke his ego, but the compliment had landed flat. As she pushed up further from the water, another thought hit her. She would have to leave the Loltā to escape—all the way to the spaceport. She'd never been out for that long. Was it safe to be away from the waters for such a span of time? Had she chosen bravado over common sense?

"Wait." She used her tail to push herself still higher in the water and dove deep for honesty. "I don't need your help to exit the Loltā; I just wanted it."

She expected him to call her out, but he didn't. "The truth. Finally."

She swallowed. Perhaps earlier, when she'd spoken so lightly of needing his aid, she'd actually been more truthful than she realized.

"I will help you on one condition."

"Which is?" She held his blue-eyed gaze and ignored the stirring inside of her.

"I need the truth from you. Always."

Kalyah weighed her options. Leaving the Loltā was one thing. But could she trust him with her means of escaping Sartu?

There was a kindness behind his eyes that she hadn't seen since landing on Sartu. This boy had heart. Perhaps she could use it to her advantage. Besides, agreeing to tell him the truth now only mattered for as long as she was with him.

"I will."

"You'll what?"

"Only speak truth to you."

His lips pursed, no doubt weighting the veracity of her statement. "Deal."

Flarin extended his hand to the girl. She slipped from the—what had she called it?—water and shifted to sit on the duraplast decking.

He saw the change begin immediately at her calves. The scales sank into her skin, dissolving before his eyes. The Loris could turn human? This was something he hadn't known.

As the scales disappeared higher, he quickly averted his gaze and pulled off his plyweave jacket. Extending it back to her, he waited until a light touch rested on his shoulder.

"Thank you," she said.

He turned to face her and gasped. She was taller on land than he'd expected, close to his two meters. Her eyes were an odd shade of light green flecked with silver. They searched his, her expression curious.

"What?" he asked.

"What may I call you?"

"Flarin. Flarin Mesius."

"You are an odd one, Flarin of Mesius."

"Just call me Flarin. Why am I odd?"

"Men count it lucky to see a Loris change—pay much coin for the opportunity—yet you look away?"

"I don't know much about the Loris." Heat creeped up his neck. "But my Ma taught me to respect all women—no matter their species."

"Respect." She repeated the word as if it was foreign on her tongue. "I see."

"And your name?"

"Kalyah of Vatalta. Kalyah is fine."

He dipped his head but felt urgency press him. He could have left—perhaps should have—when she refused to answer him honestly, but now that he had her promise and she had, well, *legs*, it was time to go. "Can you, uh, run?"

Her laugh was as light as Farvis festival bells and made her eyes sparkle. He reminded himself of Evrah's words of caution about the Loris. *They'll rip your throat out first chance they get.* Was she waiting for a chance to devour him? Or were those rumors spread by money-hungry men like the one lying on the floor behind them?

"I can run. Yes."

"Then come on." He took her hand, shocked by the coldness of it.

They took the steps at a fast clip, but he held back his pace, noticing Kalyah was unsteady on her feet. No doubt a symptom of morphing from fish to human.

He frowned. How did that work, anyway?

They reached the fourth level, and he slowed even more. She bumped into him, and a sharp coldness radiated off of her. "Are you...okay?" he asked her.

"In what way?" Her head tilted to the side, blonde hair falling over her shoulder.

"You're freezing."

Her amused smile twisted his gut. As did seeing her bare legs beneath the hemline of his jacket. Even though it reached to her knees, there was plenty of exposed leg to make his pulse tick up. He quickly glanced away.

"A Loris' body rests at a much lower temperature than landers. Fear not—I am well, Flarin."

He took her answer in stride but paused again before going to the next level. "What did you use to take out that jerk up there?"

"Why do you ask?"

"There's a guard." He motioned to the bottom of the stairs, and she followed his gaze.

"Some Loris secrete a natural sedative within our system. I am one such Loris. He will not be harmed, but he will be asleep for hours and have a terrible headache when he wakes up."

"He deserves more." Flarin clenched his jaw. "Do you still have, uh, access to it?"

Her brows drew together. "I am afraid it is not that simple in this form. However…" Her forehead wrinkled in thought. "A kiss could do the trick."

"You're not going to kiss the guard."

"Why not? It is a logical option."

Logical maybe, but forcing her to kiss the guard went against everything he knew to be right. The memory of his sister, forced into a slave-marriage at sixteen, set him against the idea of making Kalyah kiss someone for the sake of their mission. Not to mention that the thought of her kissing the guard caused a hollow ache in his chest. "No. I just wanted a quieter way. I'll handle him." He moved forward, but she gripped his arm.

"You will not allow me to help?"

"I won't stand for anyone to be used like that."

Her eyes widened in surprise, likely at the conviction he heard in his own voice, and a golden glow flashed across her cheeks. What was up with that?

"Come on." He started back down the steps. "Just be ready to run."

Kalyah's legs trembled and refused to move faster. Flarin had taken out the guard with a strike to his neck, but it had drawn attention. They'd escaped the Marina, but as her bare feet slapped against the wet permapave, she knew she couldn't last much longer. It hurt to be in this form, though it was nothing compared to what Javrik would do if he caught her.

They reached the main thoroughfare, and Flarin pulled her into a narrow alleyway shrouded in darkness.

"I'm not sure where to go," he said. She watched as the planes of his face hardened in concentration. "You clearly need to get out of Remus. Probably off Sartu."

Her heart pounded, and she swallowed past the dryness. Could she leave? Her sisters remained locked in a cage and she ran free—her mission had not been successful. It felt like cowardice to go, but it was madness to stay. She would only be captured, punished, and, this time, she'd be sent to d'Quris without hope of escape. Nothing would be gained by her recapture.

"I have a ship." She felt more than saw his reaction. A stiffening of his whole body.

"You...what?"

"I have a ship docked at the spaceport." She licked dry lips.

"A ship? Weren't you traded here?" Flarin ran a hand down his face. "What are you up to, Kalyah?"

"There are answers to your questions, but I do not think now is the time for them. Will you help me get to my ship?"

The sound of thudding boots thundered just beyond the mouth of the alley, and Flarin pulled her against him as he rolled into the darkness of a hidden doorway.

It galled her to know she needed him, but he'd done nothing but help her. He wasn't like the men she'd interacted with at the Marina—wanting only what she refused to give. Ogling her. Trying to touch her. They saw her as property, but he did not.

She felt Flarin's heart pounding against her palm. His body was hot, like the rays of the Alerius sun when you drew near the surface. She'd imagined human heat differently. Thought it would burn to touch or be unpleasant, but as she rested against him in the doorway, she felt nothing but comfort.

This was dangerous thinking.

She had come on this mission to undo what Mother Queen had put into motion. Believed she could make a difference if she uncovered the truth, but the extent of her sisters' slavery was beyond what she'd imagined.

The Loris' queen had entered into a trade agreement that went far past what their law outlined. While Kalyah had been sent on behalf of the investigative branch of the court, she could not stop this alone as she'd once thought.

The commotion on the street passed, but still they remained hidden in the dark. Her limbs started to ache as her body yearned to be back in its natural form. She'd never been gone this long from the Loltā, and her arms and legs weakened by the second. But there were more pressing matters. She could resist the pull for a little while more. She'd have to.

"Flarin." He tensed at her whisper, and she wondered if he still expected danger. "Will you help me?" she asked again.

"Yes." His reply was soft, barely loud enough to hear, but it filled her with relief. They'd reach her ship, and then…

The future stretched out before her in a swath of black unknown. She'd been so sure she could save her people, but that hope was sinking to the depths.

He moved, stepping into the alley and looking left then right. "Come on, Loris. Let's get you to your ship."

They'd made it to a transport shuttle and were headed to the spaceport. It had taken a lot of dodging and triple the time than if they'd gone straight there, but Flarin hadn't wanted to risk anyone following them. He'd managed to get her on board thanks to an overabundance of well-placed creds and a few prayers to the Verse. But it had worked.

Huddling at the back of the transport, Flarin held Kalyah against his chest as if she were asleep. He'd allowed the shuttle attendee to think she was visiting his berth for the night cycle, and the nav-bot wasn't programmed to notice. It was the cameras he worried about.

His unit had been stationed at Sartu for just over half a solar cycle—though it felt like longer—and he knew of Javrik's reach as the right hand of Drvos d'Quris. The ruler of Sartu didn't just own the Marina; he owned the city. If Javrik was doing d'Quris' bidding, he would have access to any resource needed to find Kalyah, assuming she was valuable enough. Flarin didn't know if that was the case, but to be on the safe side he'd had her hide her face with the hood.

About half a planetary hour later, the transport jolted to a stop, and Flarin blinked. He'd been distracted by calculating the best route to her ship, crafting answers for any guards who might stop them, and what he'd tell his buddies if they crossed paths. If being a soldier had taught him anything, it was to have contingencies on top of contingencies.

"Keep your head down. If we see anyone, pretend you're drunk," he murmured.

"Drunk?"

"Just act...tipsy." He frowned. How did you explain alcohol to a woman who was half-fish? "Disoriented."

She nodded, and he saw the attendant at the exit scanning passes. Flarin flashed his permanent one then the temporary card he'd bought off a soldier before boarding, and she waved them by.

They wove through the terminal, ducking holo-verts and dodging Sec-Units. The units would only care if they received an alert, but that could change at any moment.

He checked his visual map via his contacts and saw the dock she'd told him of. It was past the entrance to his military ship, and he couldn't see another way around.

"We're going to be passing my ship's entrance. They may recognize me, so—"

"Flarin!"

He muttered a curse and looked up. "Norr, hey." He flashed his teeth.

"Who you got there?" Norr's wicked smile caused Flarin's free hand to fist. "And does she have a sister?"

Kalyah kept her head down and moaned. Maybe she knew what being drunk was after all. Then she slumped against him. It was a nice addition.

"No, she does *not* have a sister. Bug off, man."

Norr held up his hands. "Sorry, sorry. Just getting bored on guard duty tonight. You know how it is."

He wanted to suggest Norr get back to his duty but held his tongue.

"Have a good night." Norr winked, and Flarin moved past the ship.

Kalyah groaned again and slumped further.

"You can stop acting. We're past the ship entrance."

She didn't respond.

"Kalyah?" Flarin shifted away but her head fell forward. Panic streaked through him, and he reached to cup her cheek.

Her lips were cracked like the ground of the White Desert on Ilyah. Her cheeks looked sunken, and her skin felt warm to the touch. Stars. What was wrong with her?

"Kalyah? What's wrong?"

"L-Loltā..."

His mind cleared. She needed the water she swam in. He hadn't even thought to ask if there was a timeframe she could be without it.

"Is there some on your ship?"

"Yes." Her voice was a whisper.

"I'll get you there." He moved them around the next corner, holding up most of her weight, and then swung her into his arms.

Kalyah's head fell onto his shoulder; she let out a soft moan as his gate jostled her against him, but he couldn't slow. He had no idea how long she could last. He couldn't let her die in his arms.

When he turned the last corner, he realized why she'd docked here. The entire wing was in desperate need of repair. Only half the docks were occupied and the ships that filled those berths were rundown or deca-cycles old. He hoped hers was ready to be fired up and not ancient like most of them.

He saw the dock number and slid to a stop. Slamming a hand against the keypad, he waited. Nothing happened. He pressed the mechanism again. Nothing.

"Key." Kalyah lifted her head before succumbing to the port's artificial gravity.

Like setting down his young niece, he placed Kalyah on the floor and knelt in front of her. "Where's the key, Kal?"

Her eyelids fluttered but didn't open. She tried again to raise her hand, but it fell. "Hair."

Her hair. She'd hidden it there! He leaned forward and gently prodded the mass. There were braids and so many shells and bobbles woven in he almost missed it, but the shiny agentiam key shifted from beneath a shell, and he jumped to his feet.

The doors *whooshed* open, and he picked up Kalyah again, racing into the docked ship.

He looked right and saw the navigation console. Then he turned left; at the end of a narrow hallway, a tank stood, illuminated by a soft blue glow. That was it.

His boots slammed against the duraplast floor toward the tank. There was a small set of stairs, and he carried her to the top. The tank was open, thankfully, and without thought he jumped in with her.

The Loltā sloshed around him. It felt like swimming in liquid gel, but the instant Kalyah's skin touched the water, her feet shifted into fins, and scales crawled up her legs. She rested in his arms, head against his shoulder. Had he been too late?

Then her eyes opened.

"Oh." Her tail flicked through the heavy water, and she pulled back, though not out of his arms.

He reached down to push a strand of hair from her eyes, his fingers trailing against her skin. She was cold to the touch—which, in this case, was a good thing. A sense of overwhelming relief coursed through him. He'd saved her. He'd gotten her to the ship. She was safe.

"Thank you." The golden glow flooded her cheeks again. It drew his attention and seemed to deepen the color. "I...I have never been from the Loltā so long."

"You had me thinking I'd killed you."

Her smile flashed. "Hardly." She moved away from his embrace with a flick of her tail, and he resisted the urge to reach out to her.

Stars. What was he doing?

In one fluid motion, she dove under the surface, reemerging close to him again. The water dripped from her hair, her cheeks, her lips. He watched as they curved into a smile. "You came in the Loltā with me?"

"I guess I wasn't thinking."

"Flarin." She swam closer. The blue lights shimmering through the water cast shadows on her high cheekbones. He hadn't noticed before, but there was the impression of scales near her ears. "You have saved me. Thank you."

He swallowed, fighting the heat in his abdomen at her nearness. "What will you do now?"

Her eyes dropped to the water. "I do not know. There is much I could share, but I will only say the truth." She glanced at him. "I came to save my sisters but must return home empty-handed. The operation is much greater than I first thought—there is no way the Mother Queen can know the extent of d'Quris' evils, or she never would have allowed it. Or so I hope. I...I will have to rethink my strategy."

She was right. He wanted details, but what stuck out to him was obvious. She needed help. The thought tugged at him like the thick water around them, drawing him closer.

"I could help you."

Her eyes widened. "I could not ask—"

"You're not. I'm offering."

Slowly, her shimmering pink lips, refreshed by the Loltā, turned into another smile. "You would do that?"

He took a moment to answer. It would mean leaving his post and paying off his debt with the creds he'd been saving for his own ship. But when he thought of his life in the AGD, it felt empty compared to this. To a rescue mission that would not only change lives, but save them.

"Yes." The word sealed his promise and, as if sensing that, she glided forward.

Her lips alighted on his cheek, a mere flutter before she pulled away. "My sisters and I would be grateful for your help, Flarin of Mesius."

This time, he knew her appreciation was sincere, and it helped solidify his decision. "Then you have it."

Captivity

Megan Dill

the glass cage does not shatter
underneath

the weight of my fists—
my efforts only produce bloody
knuckles and laughs
from the spectators.
they wait—

cameras ready, demanding
tricks and

       f
         l
           i
             p
              s

as if I could actually swim like that

in this
crampedlittletank.
there is no chance of escape.
no way to break
the glass—besides, how could I run away
from here
without legs?

but I continue to PUNCH the walls
until there's blood in the water—
there's an entire ocean out there
waiting for my return

At Fin's Length

J. C. Joiner

THE KRAKEN TIGHTENED ITS tentacles around the middle of my ship. It seemed like with every tentacle my crew cut, another snaked up from the ocean to replace it. Any crew member who had been knocked overboard by the kraken was instantly set upon by the merpeople waiting in the waves below.

"Get the crew to the lifeboats!" I screamed to my first mate over the sounds of cracking hardwood and the desperate cries of my drowning crew. My sword sliced through another tentacle as my breath caught in my chest. I cursed the decision that had driven us from the clutches of the king's guard into the forbidden waters. The king's guard had a policy against hanging female pirates, but the king himself had promised I—Adria McCrae—would be the first. At least my crew would have been spared.

Jenna gave me a tight-lipped nod without an ounce of hope in her eyes. Everything was lost. What the demon merpeople didn't take, the kraken would. Still, with both the kraken and merpeople's attention on destroying the ship, perhaps the rest of my crew could slip away.

I continued to hack at the giant octopus' tentacles as my surviving crew scrambled for the lifeboats. If they were going to have a chance to escape, I would have to take the battle to the merpeople.

Abandoning my futile attempt to dislodge the sea monster, I scrambled down the ladder to the cargo hold. We'd already taken on about a foot of water, so I doubted the gunpowder we'd stolen would do us any good. A keg of lamp oil we'd taken off a merchant caught my eye. Perfect. I hauled it onto my shoulder and struggled to shove it up the ladder to the deck. The ship lurched, and more boards crunched inside the kraken's death hug. With a fierce shove, I managed to get the keg through the hatch and crawled out after it.

Dodging flailing tentacles and splintered boards, I rolled the keg starboard, hoping to distract the attackers from my crew who were trying to lower the lifeboat on the opposite side. I drove my cutlass deep into the lid and let the contents spill out onto the monstrous octopus—and the waiting enemies—below. When the flow was down to a trickle, I grabbed a nearby lantern, smashed the glass on the deck rail, and threw it into the shimmering oil.

"Take that, you bloodthirsty monsters!" I shook my fist at the merfolk in the rising orange light of the spreading flames. Their cries rose, then silenced as they all dove under the water to safety. Even the merfolk's trained kraken began to untangle its tentacles and loosen its grip on my ship.

Too late, I realized one of the slithering tentacles was swinging in my direction. I chopped at one, hacking a length from the end, but two more wiggled into its place. One attempted to take the sword from my hand, but a good swing stopped it in midair. The second tried to coil around my legs. I turned to slice at it with my cutlass, but the impact still threw me overboard into the ocean.

I held my breath as I cut through the flames into the water below. I'd have to stay submerged long enough to swim clear of my own trap. Fortunately it was easier to swim in a pair of leather breeches, linen blouse, and leather vest than in petticoats and skirts, but I still had a very limited time to get to the surface while avoiding enemies that didn't have either restriction.

The full moon was a bright blur on the surface of the dark water, and an easy goal as my lungs began to ache for air. A dark figure circled, bringing me up short as I held my cutlass out in what I hoped was a threatening manner. Not that it'd be much use down here. At first I thought the shadow was one of the kraken's tentacles back to finish what it started, but it slipped into the wavering light cast by the oil burning above and revealed itself as a merman.

Before I could react, the merman caught me by the throat and held his long dagger to my stomach. The heavy leather of my vest wouldn't even serve to slow the blade down. The inhuman creature seemed to be half shadow and half light. His scales reflected the flames as if he himself were made of fire. His red hair flickered in the current like a flame without covering either cold black eye. He was the most horrifying creature I had ever seen.

He was definitely going to kill me.

I released my cutlass and held my head high. My chest burned, and my brain screamed so loudly for air that it was hard to muster any fear of his blade. I was going to die either way. The dagger would be more merciful.

"Are you the queen of the pirates?" His voice was clear and melodic, like a rich baritone speaking in a quiet theater hall.

Humans can't speak underwater, and I was certain if I tried to open my mouth I'd drown immediately, so I merely glared at him and nodded.

He gave a curt nod and shot toward the surface, his hand still clutched tightly around my throat. We broke water a distance from my now-burning ship. He let me go and watched as I gulped air desperately.

"Do not attempt to escape. I can swim farther, faster, and longer than you can."

That was obvious. I was exhausted and breathless already. Treading water was hard enough at the moment. "How many of my crew did you kill, you monster?"

"Your crew was in violation of the Surface-Sea Treaty of our ancestors." The merman frowned and crossed his arms over his chest. "Their lives were forfeit as soon as your ship crossed into our territorial waters. You should be thankful we allowed the small ships you sent out to return to human waters unmolested."

So my crew escaped. I blew out a giddy breath and nearly slipped beneath the surface. An alarmed look crossed the merman's face, and he grabbed my arm to keep me afloat.

"You want me alive. Why?" It couldn't be for any good reason, and my mind was already calculating the easiest way to goad him into killing me.

"Your king has placed a bounty on your head. My young nephew, the prince, was taken as a political prisoner two years ago, and our emperor hopes to exchange you for him."

I laughed out loud—a graceless, barking laugh that seemed to take the merman by surprise. "I doubt they're so eager to hang me that they'll give up a political pawn just to see it happen. If your young prince is even still alive to begin with."

The merman's skin flushed a deeper shade of red, but his face remained expressionless. "Your king has promised my emperor it would be so, and it will be very regrettable indeed for your people if he does not keep his word."

"Yeah, well, everything he does is very regrettable to my people, so that's nothing new." My teeth were chattering, and my legs were beginning to ache from treading water. "But unless you want to exchange a waterlogged corpse for your nephew, you'd better have a better plan than just keeping me here until the king comes out for a stroll."

The merman snorted and shook his head. "There is a cave nearby. It is dry, with enough air for you to breathe but far enough underwater that you cannot escape without my aid. I have been tasked with keeping you there until the exchange can be made. I advise you to take a deep breath."

I barely had time to take his advice before he dove again, swimming faster than before. He guided me with one arm across my back as his powerful tail propelled us deep under the water. Just as I began to feel dizzy from lack of air, we reached the opening of a cave. My head broke the surface with a gasp, and the merman lifted my weak, limp body onto the stone ledge just inside the cave. I lay there for a long time, freezing, half-conscious, and only vaguely aware of the merman working nearby.

Soon, a bright fire burned in a crevasse in the rock wall, warming and lighting the small space as the smoke rose through a high fissure to the surface. The main part of the cave was roughly the size of my ship's cabin, with a smooth, sandy floor and jagged hole in the back that seemed to lead deeper into the cave system. The fire cast flickering shadows on a pile of neatly folded cloths and a basket, but nothing else filled the space.

"You will find food and fresh water here, as well as dry blankets and clothes." He sat at the edge of the rocky platform. "Your kind does not respond well to the cold ocean depths, and I am not a cruel captor."

He was right, of course, and dying of hypothermia did not sound like a pleasant option at the moment.

I summoned the energy to give him a blank stare, finally taking the time to actually notice him. His bottom half was a sleek fishtail covered with deep, blood-red scales flecked with black. His tailfin was wide and faded from the same deep red to a translucent black at the edges where it skimmed the surface of the water. Long, feathery hip fins fluttered in the current to keep him upright in front of me. His top half was nearly human, with heavily defined chest and stomach muscles and thick biceps from swimming. His skin was a reddish-gray, and deep gills looked like cuts between his lower ribs. A spiked dorsal fin ran the whole length of his back, from the nape of his neck to the end of his tail. Sharp, claw-like nails gripped the rocky ledge, and a small, sharp fin ran from the back of his hand to his elbow. His face was angular and grim, with patches of scales fading from his cheekbones to red ear fins far larger than a human's ear.

"I will be at the entrance to the cave." He gestured to the water below him. "If you have any need, you may call me."

"Call you what? Fishbutt?" My wet hair and clothes stuck to me, and I knew this wasn't the time to taunt him, but I couldn't resist.

It was bad enough I didn't have the strength to sit up; I didn't want him thinking that meant I was beaten.

"I am Chinami, captain of the Llyr armies and half-brother to the emperor himself. Either Captain or Chinami will do." A frown flickered across his face as he slipped back into the dark water and disappeared.

I waited until the mermonster was out of sight, then pushed myself up to sit. He was right. I needed to change, eat, and warm up so that I could be ready for my escape attempt. The captain of the fish guard severely underestimated how badly I didn't want to hang. I'd far rather drown in an escape attempt than face the gallows.

I peeled off my soggy clothes—nearly calling to ask the merman if he had a knife to cut off my poorly-thought-through fashion choices—put on the chemise and bloomers he'd left in a neatly folded pile beside the fire, ignored the petticoats and heavy dress, wrapped myself in the coarse blanket, and set into eating the roasted fish and bananas in the basket. Warm, fed, and clothed, I curled up beside the fire to sleep.

The fire still burned when I awoke, and the basket of food had been refilled. None of the things in the cave were of any use to merpeople, and their complete anticipation of my needs seemed to indicate that this cave frequently housed a human prisoner. I'd heard tales of people tortured by the half-human monsters and wondered what my terrifying guard would do to me when he found out our faithless king wasn't interested in trading a valuable political prisoner for the opportunity to hang an embarrassing thorn in his side. Not when he could keep the merprince and let the merpeople get rid of me for him.

I had to escape soon. After rest, fire, and food, I was ready to make my attempt. I just needed a way to distract the merman so I could slip out. How close was he paying attention to me? If he really wanted me alive, he wouldn't let me make the cave uninhabitable. And I'd gamble my last treasure map that he'd be on me the moment I hit the water. I could use both of those to keep him occupied. Everything in the cave that would burn went onto the fire—the basket, the blanket, and the hideous dress he'd left me.

Once the fire grew out of control and smoke billowed into the cave, I dropped my boots into the pool at the edge of the rock ledge. Sure enough, the second boot had barely hit the water when the surface of the pool churned and my guard burst out. With a sharp imprecation under his breath and a glare in my direction, he pulled himself onto the ledge to get a better look at what I'd done.

Careful not to make a splash that might alert him, I lowered myself gently into the pool, took a slow, deep breath, and darted for the exit. Once outside the cave, I shot toward the inky surface, kicking hard with my legs and digging in with my arms. A desperate kick caught my leg on an outcropping rock as I pushed past the cave entrance, drawing a long gash across my calf, but I kept on. He'd discover I was gone soon, and I needed a head start.

A large shadow shot past me, and I bit back a curse. I hadn't expected him to catch up quite *that* fast. The shadow circled back and darted by again, close enough for me to see that it wasn't the right shape for the merman. The wide grin and distinct dorsal fin indicated a different enemy entirely.

Blood streaming from the cut in my leg had attracted a pod of sharks.

A bubble of air escaped my lips as I tried unsuccessfully to scream underwater. There were at least three of them, and I still couldn't tell how far the surface was. Futility filled me like a rock, and even though I was certain I was swimming harder, it seemed like the water had turned to molasses and I was making no progress at all.

In the darkness I glimpsed the biggest shadow rush toward me, mouth open wide to reveal more razor-sharp teeth than I'd found coins in my last treasure chest. I threw up my arms, closed my eyes, and braced myself for the painful attack. My decision to oppose the king's brutality with piracy had put a strain on my relationship with God, but at that moment I was certain no priest had ever prayed more fervently than me.

I heard the impact of one body hitting another, but didn't feel anything. Tentatively, I opened my eyes just in time to see Chinami pull his sword from the shark's throat.

I swam back from the blood swirling in the water as the other two sharks darted past me into the fray. My chest burned from lack of air, but the horror of the bloody scene held me rooted where I was. The second shark floated motionless now, and the sea surrounding them was so red I could no longer distinguish Chinami from the cloudy water. A very human-sounding cry of pain told me he was still there—and not actually winning.

A pang of guilt pricked my heart, but I couldn't really feel too sorry about his fate. Even though Chinami had saved me from the sharks, he was just planning to sell me to be hanged later. I wasn't sure if the winning shark would continue to pursue me or content himself with the dinner he was already surrounded with, so I did the most logical thing I could think of: hurried back to the cave.

By the time my lungs were screaming for air, I realized I had made a grave error. Either I was farther out from the cave than I had realized or the shark attack had gotten me turned around. Whichever it was, I couldn't see the cave—and I wasn't going to make it. My consciousness faltered, and I felt myself beginning to sink when something hit me from behind and propelled me forward.

I gasped and took in water. Panic seized me, and I tried to fight free as my lungs demanded I cough up the water and breathe. A cough and another mouthful of water...and I passed out.

The next thing I knew, I was on my back in the cave, vomiting. By the time my body had expelled all the seawater, my chest and lungs ached and exhaustion seeped into every bone in my body. I lay back on the stone slab, panting for even the smoky air of the cave, and became aware that there was another figure lying still beside me. I sat up and turned to see Chinami on his side facing me, unconscious. His skin was several shades grayer than it had been, and blood flowed from a nasty wound in his tail where a human man's hip would have been.

I caught my lip between my teeth. I'd mended many a wound on my ship, but the thought of helping the monster that held me prisoner irked me. On the other hand, he *had* saved my life three times, and I clearly needed him if I ever planned to leave this cave. I told myself I would help him purely for my own sake—it was certainly not because I'd gotten soft toward mermen—and got to work.

My forgotten vest and leather leggings became bandaging, and the half-burned blanket he'd apparently salvaged from the still-burning fire became a covering to keep him wet, since I assumed fish-men needed water to survive.

Having done all I could, and having offered a desperate prayer for both our survival, I began to explore the cave. I had destroyed all the food, and had no tools to catch more, no access to fresh water, and no dry clothes or blankets to warm me. If I died, he would, too. There was no way they had brought those things through the water, and I already knew the smoke reached the surface. If there wasn't an easy exit, perhaps there was at least a stash of supplies to keep their prisoners alive.

Sure enough, through the hole in the back of the cave was an alcove with a crack that opened to the surface in the high ceiling, beneath which were stacked dried wood, several piles of clothes, and a few baskets. Wondering how a merman got all the dry goods down there, I dragged them out of the alcove into the firelight until I found a pair of boy's breeches, a lady's blouse, another blanket, a cask of water, and some stale bread. I ate, changed, threw some more wood on the fire to keep myself warm, snuggled under the blanket, and fell asleep.

Without sunlight, I had no way of telling how long I slept, but I woke several times just to refresh the fire, check on my patient, and crawl back under the blanket to sleep. My hungry stomach woke me up for good, so I sat beside the fire, chewing half a loaf of dry bread, and watched Chinami sleep.

His color had begun returning to his face, and his bleeding had slowed. I had been careful to keep him wet all night, and I actually thought he might make it. I took a moment to look at him more closely. He didn't look nearly as threatening when he was asleep. His face looked very human, with high cheekbones and a well-defined jawline that was shaded with a shadow of stubble. His fire-red hair was matted to his forehead in gentle waves and nearly hid his otherworldly ears. With the blanket covering his body, I could almost imagine he was a normal human man.

He moaned softly and stirred. With a start, he pushed himself up to half-sitting, favoring his wounded side, and looked around the cave in alarm. His eyes came to rest on me, and his alarm softened to relief.

"No, I didn't attempt to escape again, if that's what you were wondering." I watched the blanket slip off his bare chest and gather around his waist. Suddenly, my mouth felt dry, and my thoughts scrambled. I blamed it on the dry bread and exhaustion and focused my attention on getting a drink from the cask.

"I did warn you that escape would be suicide." His melodic voice scolded absently as he checked the extent of his wound. He frowned even as he nodded. "You did well. One would think you'd cared for merfolk before."

"I have cared for my crew." I shrugged. "You weren't that different, just more...wet."

"That would be one important difference, yes." He threw the blanket aside, flexed his tailfin, and grunted in pain. He tried to slide toward the water, and the grunt became a low cry.

"Maybe you should wait a few more days until you're healed?" I laid my hand on his arm, which felt warm and dry. Probably not a good sign. "I can wet the blanket again."

"Merfolk must return to the sea every day, with rare exceptions." He avoided meeting my eye and scooted closer to the edge, but bumped his hip on the uneven rock and let out a choked sob.

"Let me help." I sighed and crawled out of the blanket toward him. I wasn't about to let my patient die on my watch. I sat beside him, lifted his arm over my shoulders, and helped him slide toward the edge. Once his wound cleared the stone ledge, he dropped the rest of the way into the water and disappeared. When he returned, I helped him back onto the ledge, changed his bandage, and covered him with the damp blanket again to sleep.

"How did you take to being a pirate?" He rolled onto his side to look at me and crooked his arm behind his head like a pillow.

"You think a woman cannot be a pirate?" I bristled as I offered him a piece of smoked fish and half of a loaf of dry bread.

"It's not that." He took the fish, but ignored the bread. "Few pirates I have met would bother to care for an injured enemy."

"I took to piracy when the king took my father's land to build his summer palace. He gave my parents a tiny fraction of the value of the land and drove our family to poverty." I glared at the bread I had crushed to bits in my hand as I remembered the offense. "I determined that I would get the money he owed us one way or another. When he could not catch me, he imprisoned my parents instead. I came back from a raid to find they had died in prison." I shrugged off the painful memories and brushed the crumbs from my hands as if washing away the past. "At that point there was nothing left for me but the sea."

"Your king's cruelty is legendary." Chinami frowned. "Which is why we must find an exchange for my nephew. We already fear what he may have suffered at the monster's hand."

"Do you mean to tell me your emperor is not cruel as well?" I laughed to cover my discomfort at the mention of the hostage exchange.

"Not cruel. Firm and just, serving judgment on those who deserve it." Chinami rolled onto his back and tucked both arms behind his head. "Already our bards have written songs about his noble courage." His steady baritone began to sing softly a grand ballad of bravery, conquest, and justice.

I also lay back on my bed of blankets and savored the dulcet notes of his song until I drifted off to sleep.

We followed this routine for several days. Each day his periods of wakefulness grew longer, and he became more talkative. He also spent more and more time in the water as his health improved. In the evenings, I would share stories of my adventures on the high seas, and he would grace me with songs of the histories of his people. I knew once he reached full strength he would still be tasked with taking me to the king, but blatantly avoided thinking about it by asking him to tell me stories about his family, life under the sea, merfolk legends—basically anything other than my future.

Finally the day came that Chinami was strong enough to report back to the merfolk emperor. He had been pensive and quiet the whole day, only half-listening as I regaled him with the tale of my ship's encounter with a sea serpent. When the story was finished, he reached out his hand to touch the side of my face gently, opened and closed his mouth as if he'd wanted to say something but thought better of it, and slipped into the ocean alone.

He didn't return that night, and the cave seemed silent and lonely without him. I hadn't realized how much I had grown to enjoy his company until he was no longer there. I missed falling asleep to his singing and tossed restlessly the whole night.

A splash woke me the next morning. I sat up to see a red head poking above the surface of the water. Chinami's face was pensive and grim, not unlike the first night I met him. He clearly didn't bring good news. I tossed the blanket aside and scooted to the edge of the ledge, allowing my bare feet to dangle in the water in front of Chinami.

"It is time." His eyes were on my feet rather than my face, and his normally melodic voice was raspy. "The king's ship will pass our borders today, and the emperor has ordered me to deliver you to the king personally."

"The king has promised to hang me."

"I know." Chinami's answer was barely audible.

"If these last few weeks have meant anything to you, I beg you to kill me yourself and be done with it." My voice was low and fierce. "A merciful death at the hand of a friend is far better than the humiliation of a public execution."

He looked at me at last, his eyes wide and his lips downturned. He placed his hands on the ledge on either side of me and pulled himself halfway out of the pool. Rivulets of water streamed between his fins and the deeply etched lines of his muscles as he leaned against the ledge between my knees. I willed myself not to flinch, fully anticipating him to fulfill my request. Using one arm to support himself, he instead leaned closer, gently cupped my chin in his free hand, and pulled me in so that our faces nearly touched.

"I would forfeit my own life before I would lift my hand to harm you." His dark eyes glittered with fear mingled with fierce desire.

I laid my hands on his chest, allowing my fingertips to trace his tight muscles and his gently flaring gills as I wrapped my arms around his waist and threaded my fingers around his dorsal fin. My heart tripped over his nearness, his body pressed against mine, his lips…

His lips brushed mine tentatively, firm and salty with sea water. I parted my lips and lifted my mouth to his. His eyes widened, and his chest heaved with a sharp breath. He slid his hand from my chin to the back of my neck and deepened the kiss.

The kiss broke, leaving me breathless as his lips caressed my jawline and neck. "But what about your nephew? The exchange?" I stumbled over the words, my brain rebelling against my attempt to deny my heart what it wanted.

Chinami pulled back and looked away. "The ransom will be paid. I have spoken to my emperor, and I will take your place as hostage in exchange for my nephew. I am a great warrior, and have led many battles against the human fleets. I am a much more valuable captive than either my nephew or you."

"What? *No.* We established that the king is cruel and hates mer-folk with a vengeance— beyond even his hatred for me." I pushed against his chest and balled a fist to keep from slapping some sense into him. "That's suicide!"

"It is better I die with honor than be forced to choose between my young nephew and my new friend." He ran a hand through his damp hair. "Besides, it may be that your king will have another fate for me. There is no question of yours if I surrender you."

"There has to be another way! Another hostage, or a daring rescue." My mind scrambled for a solution that didn't get one of us killed.

"I *have* tried to come up with an alternative. There simply isn't time." Chinami shook his head. "The exchange must happen tonight."

"What will happen to me?" I asked softly, relaxing in his arms once again, reluctantly submitting to his decision to save my life.

He pulled me closer and rested his forehead against mine. "I would not keep you here trapped like a child's pet, but I also will not return you to your own land unless you wish it. Tell me where you can go to be free, and I will take you there immediately."

"There's an island, not far outside your borders, that is a favorite of pirates. I can find a new crew there and begin again." Excitement thrilled me at the thought of freedom, tainted with bitterness at the cost, and I pressed my lips to his again. His response was more distant, even sorrowful, and I realized this was goodbye. "Thank you, Chinami. For everything. I will not forget you."

"Nor will I forget you." He held me to his chest for a moment longer. "May the bards forever sing of our friendship."

Blood in the Water

AJ Skelly

As I swim to the edge of the reef, I'm met with the chill of the open ocean beyond. Another storm brews. Loose kelp and seaweed toss above me, the rough surface moving the plants torn loose by the last tempest—the one that destroyed our underwater village. Survival means moving on...and crossing the hazardous depths.

Where the great megalodons prowl.

If I fail in my scouting, my entire Mer-pod could be lost.

Meira would be lost.

My heart.

A screech echoes through the water, and my muscles tense from the dorsal along my back all the way to the end of my curved rudder-like tail. Slowly a form emerges through the opaque water. It's a whale. For a moment, the tenseness in my shoulders relaxes. Then the great beast flails. Something is wrong. I smell it before I see the thin trail weeping from its side.

Panic surges through me as I realize the creature has been wounded by a fisherman's harpoon. The behemoth is bleeding.

There is blood in the water.

Now that I've smelled it, the scent of death surrounds me.

With my heart hammering in my chest, I swim back to the village site. Flat rocks, stripped coral, scattered remnants of shells are strewn where once stone and wooden houses sat. No longer a place of safety since the squall destroyed the village, leaving only danger in its wake. It is not safe to cross the open ocean. Not with the blood now present in the water. The great sharks will swarm. Our only hope is to stay hidden among the ruined shoals until the whale has been consumed and the sharks are fat and lazy.

I clutch my spear of sharpened coral between my fingers.

As I near the village, the waters churn. The storm above the ocean's surface grows worse. Coral debris and the driftwood remnants of our homes float in the troubled waters. Tiny grains of sand cling to my hair. Where is the Mer-pod? Where is Meira?

Flashes of memories of the past summer spring to mind as I pass spots we used to roam. The waters were warm as sunlight entered into the darker depths. Meira held my hand as her father gave us permission to court. We twined in and out of the kelp beds, chasing each other, laughing, scales flashing in and out between the heavy green stalks. She let me catch her, and my arms circled about her, bringing her close to my chest.

She surprised me when she leaned in and kissed my cheek. Her eyes twinkled, and I knew I would never love another.

But where is she now?

Wildly, I look for clues. When the current brings a whiff of ink, my heart sinks. I follow the scent to the ledge just beyond where the village used to stand.

I can barely make out the enormous tentacles still waving as the giant squid nurses his wounds. A warrior of the pod must have injured it as they made their escape.

More blood.

Panic claws at me.

The surface waves crash above me, the storm darkening the light that filters into my watery world. A wave slams against the rocks to my right with enough force that I'm swept farther over the ledge.

And then I see them. The whole Mer-pod. My family. Friends. The children. Meira. All swimming as fast as they can against the current into the open sea.

They must have been forced into the exposed water once the giant squid was injured, knowing the scent of blood would bring the creatures of death.

But they don't know about the dying whale. And they're heading straight toward it.

I swim so hard I fear my heart will burst. But I'm not fast enough. When I'm within shouting distance, I call out a warning.

Meira hears me. She turns. I can't make out all her features, but I know her azure eyes will fill with relief to know that I am unharmed. If only she could see the fear in mine.

Vibrations echo in the water below me.

My body freezes. One of the great beasts is swimming up from the depths. My gills stop as I see the nose of the creature materialize below me. The weak light glints off the white of his razor-like teeth. Silvery gray and thrashed with ropy scars, his head, as wide as the body of the whale, emerges from the deep.

He will find the Mer-pod. He will find Meira.

He's three times the size of the injured whale. It's the largest megalodon I've ever seen.

There is no time for anything else.

I must save Meira. I must save my Mer-pod.

A thousand thoughts pound through my brain. The safety of the pod outweighs any other instinct. Meira's safety outweighs everything else. Her shriek pierces the shadowy depths of icy water surrounding me.

Blinking, I catch sight of her green scales, her eyes already locked on me.

I cannot lose her. I will not lose her. We will have more summers. *She* will have more summers.

Without another thought, I take my coral spear and run its sharpened edge over my forearm, spilling my lifeblood into the ocean. I'm momentarily mesmerized as my dark blood swirls in intricate little patterns and whirls around me. With one last look at Meira, I swim upwards, away from my Mer-pod.

I know the instant the great shark smells my blood.

With a palpable burst of excited fury, its speed increases. He's heading straight for me. The massive jaws open. He will easily swallow me whole. I ready my spear. I will not go quietly.

Holding utterly still, I wait, though it's the hardest thing I've ever done. Every instinct is shouting at me to *swim. Swim away. Hide.*

But I don't.

The beast's teeth are the length of my arm. I brace myself.

And then I'm in his mouth.

Just as the massive jaws and throat begin to swallow, before I'm caught in the downward rush of water to the creature's belly, I plunge my spear with all my strength into the upper side of the shark's soft palate.

Hot blood pours down on me as the weight of my body hangs from my weapon. As the shark continues its upward trajectory, my spear tears a heavy cut down the creature's throat and gets stuck in its flesh. I try to take another breath, but there's so much blood that I can't breathe. I will drown in the shark's blood before I'm eaten.

Gasping in the dark cave of the mouth, both my weapon and I are slung loose—dashed side to side as the creature thrashes in pain.

I keep hold of my spear, stabbing again and again, blind, choking on the acrid water.

With a roar that nearly deafens me, the shark opens his giant jaws. Both weak light and fresh ocean water rush in, and I'm able to gasp a breath.

Pushing off the great teeth, I shoot out into the fathomless sea. I pump my tail furiously, taking in great gillfulls of water, trying to rid my system of the shark's stinging blood.

I risk a glance over my shoulder. Terror and relief tingle in my fins. There are two smaller megalodons circling behind, entranced with the smell of the blood emanating from the beast.

I swim to the churning surface and snatch some of the floating seaweed. Tying it off around the cut on my arm, I dive and speed after my Mer-pod, leaving the sharks fighting in their own carnage.

Relief bursts through my scales. At last, I catch the pod, swimming as fast as they can with the young ones and babes. Silent affirmations ripple around us, a brush of hand or fin—words unspoken to leave us undetected but filling my chest with the gratitude of my people.

My eyes search for one Mer only. Meria darts frantically through the swarm of bodies to my side. Her hands cup my face, tail winding around my own as her lips crash hard against mine. For one brief moment, I relax into her embrace and dream of summers yet to come as the world falls away. But as a cold current teases my scales, reality slips back into place. Clasping Meira's hand, I tug her back to the escaping Mer-pod. We dare not stop for a moment longer, but swim on into the darkness with the rest of our kin.

For the moment, we are safe.

The Day Water Became Wood

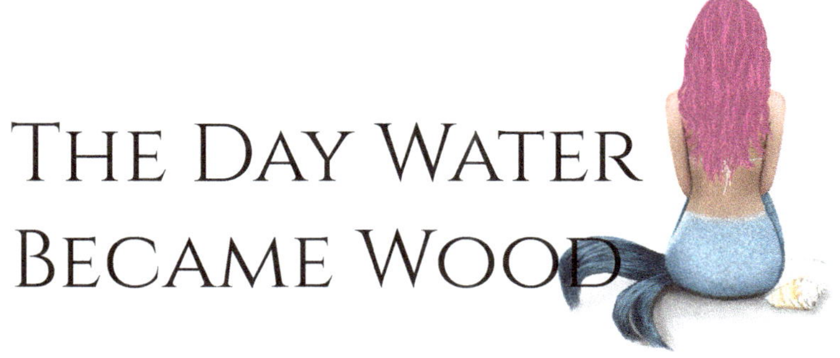

Cassandra Hamm

WAILING ECHOED THROUGH THE salty air, resounding off the cliffs and tearing into the peaceful morning. Naavah gazed at the raft being lowered down, down, down the side of the cliffs by the men who hated her. If she stared hard enough, she could make out the peaceful expression on Coryn's face as he lay on the raft, never to move again. Not in that body, at least.

The priestess's white robes fluttered in the sea breeze like the movement of waves. She intoned, "Be set free from this body of flesh and find life in scales."

The raft touched the ocean's surface. Knives sliced through the ropes. Waves crashed against the rocky face and swamped the raft, hungrily seeking Coryn's lifeless body. The sea would take back what it had given.

"He spent too much time around that enchantress," a nearby woman whispered. Her eyes flicked to Naavah, who stood off to the side, before returning to her companion. Naavah stiffened, though the woman's words shouldn't have surprised her when the villagers sold her their wares at ridiculously high prices and blamed her for infant deaths.

"That's why he got sick," the woman continued. "Had his whole life ahead of him, poor young thing, but no healer can cure a curse."

How dare you. Naavah's mind already formed the spell that would make the woman pay. *I loved him more than life itself.*

"Least he's finally free of her," another woman said. "Even *she* can't control him from the sea."

Naavah's teeth ground against each other. *I will see him again. He is coming back.* She and the rest of the village watched the churning water where Coryn had disappeared, waiting. *He will live again.*

"Look, the heartless mage won't even cry for him. She was just using him."

False! Naavah *wanted* to cry, but her eyes were as dry as sun-bleached bones. The space where he had been was a hollow ache, but she held firm to the thought—*I will see him again. He is coming back.*

She could not shake the knowledge that this was her fault. She had failed to save him.

The priestess bowed her shaved head. "He is returned to the sea."

The sea bubbled and churned. The priestess moaned, her eyes rolling back. Naavah leaned over the side of the cliffs, her heart beating fast.

A head emerged from the sea, covered in hair as white as cresting sea foam.

Naavah called upon the magic in her blood and stepped off the cliff. The air was soft and pliant but solid enough to stand upon.

She lowered herself down, down, down the rocky face, fighting to keep her concentration. But it was so hard when *Coryn* was down there, waiting for her, so close she could already feel the warmth of his skin beneath her fingers—

He looked up as she lowered herself to the rocks. She faltered, staring into icy eyes that had once been dark brown, still set in the same umber skin.

Coryn. Her knees wobbled. *My husband.*

"Naavah," he said, and it was the same voice that had whispered her name against her skin, night after night, while she lay in his arms. Six months of bliss, torn away too soon.

Her eyes moved down his defined chest to what lay below the water. What had once been two strong legs was now one limb covered in iridescent silver scales. Her breath caught. She'd known it would be so, and yet, seeing him this way...

She sat down heavily on the rocks, her hands trembling, her mind unable to work. *He is a merden now. My Coryn is a creature of the ocean.*

Coryn grabbed the rock on which she sat and tried to haul himself up, muscles straining, but his hips stayed firmly below the water. He pushed and pushed at the invisible barrier. She grabbed his hands, slick with water, and pulled, though she knew it was useless.

He let out a strangled groan and let go, sinking back into the ocean. "I can't leave the water. It won't let me."

The magic that made the merden—a deeper magic than she could fathom. One not even she could break. *Or can I?*

A wave crashed over Coryn's head. Naavah jumped back, flinching as spray hit her skin. He shook water from his newly-silver head, smiling. Why was he *smiling?* This was no time for joy.

He eased back onto the rock, his unfamiliar eyes soft as they stared up at her. "I'm glad your face is the first I saw after..."

After the change. She swallowed, eyes flicking down to his tail, back to his face. It was close enough that she could reach out and touch it, but what if his skin felt different now? She wanted to remember him as he *was*, not as this new, seabound creature.

Coryn's hand stretched up, his fingers lightly caressing her jaw. They were cold and slick and ridged, like scales. She flinched back.

Hurt flickered in his eyes as he dropped his hand. "It's just me, Naavah."

But it *wasn't* him. Not really. Not the boy she'd fallen in love with, endured ridicule with, broken the mage code for.

There was a reason mages lived alone. The magic that filled their beings was too potent for a normal human. But Coryn hadn't cared, saying he'd rather live a few days with her than a lifetime alone. They hadn't been married long, but it hadn't mattered. His body couldn't handle the magic inside her.

Now he was gone. *Your fault,* her mind said, louder and more insistent, though she tried to silence it. *You're the reason he's dead.*

"I'll change you back," Naavah said, so softly she barely heard herself over the waves crashing against the rocks.

His forehead creased as he frowned. "That's impossible. Merden magic is much too strong for any mage to break, even one as powerful as you, Naavah."

"But..." Her chest tightened as she gazed at him, powerful and handsome and alien. *Not my Coryn. Not my Coryn.*

She was the reason he'd died. She had to bring him back.

"I know you don't care for the water, but..." Coryn gave her an awkward smile. "You could join me here."

She recoiled.

"Not forever!" He gave a nervous laugh. "Just for a moment. Come in the water with me."

His stare held such longing that she almost jumped in. But the thought of the water all over her skin, closing over her head, dragging her downwards—

She knew it was illogical to think that she would drown if she went in the water. But the ocean was powerful and terrifying––much more powerful than her. And though merden did have a type of magic and immortality, it wasn't *her* magic. It wasn't the power that was as natural to her as breathing, that she could twist and manipulate with a blink. She would be trapped forever in the water she despised.

Never, she thought. *Never.* Not even if it meant being with Coryn forevermore.

"I will be with you again," she said. "But not in the sea."

"Naavah—"

She pressed a finger to his scaly lips. His breath caught as those pale eyes pierced into her soul.

"I will find a way," she said. "I swear it upon my magic."

Naavah didn't know how long she'd stared at the scroll, scouring every spell she'd ever written, every conjuring she'd recorded. Hours? A full month? *Nothing. Nothing. Nothing.*

Turning Coryn back into a human—that was to say, bringing him back to life—was out of the question. Even she would never dare to turn back death. But there *had* to be a way they could be together—a way that didn't involve her giving up her powers and her life.

It's that confounded water. If Coryn weren't trapped in the ocean, things would be so much easier.

Water... Her brow furrowed. What if she could break him *out* of the water somehow? Except that would be rewriting the merden magic, and she didn't dare try that. It would only destroy her.

Her eyes flicked to her windows. On the right was the forest she and Coryn had found solace in while lying in the grass and staring up at the stars. On the left was the village, perched atop the cliffs, and beside that—she knew—the cursed ocean. If only that ocean had never existed.

Long ago, their ancestors had agreed to become merden, protectors of the sea, after they passed, if only the gods would give them favor. It had ended the Sea Plague and granted immortality––but at what cost?

I can't rewrite the magic...but what if I could change the ocean?

Her mind whirred. Altering the fabric of the merden magic would be far too much for a single enchantress, but the ocean itself was separate from the merden curse. It was simply the cage in which the immortal merden found themselves. If she could change the ocean into something else, would it change the merden to land beings?

Naavah scribbled away at her parchment. What would she change the water into? She could dry it up and create a desert, but that sounded terribly unpleasant. What about...another forest? She did love the trees, so peaceful and quiet—they never tried to drown her.

Water into wood. She wrote the words with frenzied excitement. Somehow, she would find a way to turn water into wood. They could build a house there and live in peace. Coryn wouldn't be able to leave the forest, certainly, but he could hold her again.

What about the tail? Frowning, she tapped her quill feather against her cheek. If the ocean became a forest but the merden kept their tails, they'd be rendered helpless in a world not built for them. She'd have to ensure the tails were turned into legs––and their gills into unmarked skin.

So many variables to consider. So many obstacles to overcome. But if anyone could do it, she could.

No clogging, choking water. Just trees and sunlight and beauty.

A soft knock sounded at her door. Startled, she dropped her quill, splattering ink across the parchment.

"Naavah?" The voice was muffled by the wood. "Naavah, my dear girl, are you in there?"

Ivor. Her old mentor. A sorcerer almost as powerful as she. A sorcerer who could help her...or stop her.

"Naavah," he said again.

If she didn't answer, he would grow suspicious. She moved hesitantly toward the door and opened it.

Ivor stood before her, his gray hair as unruly as ever. Her lungs seized at the softness in his eyes.

"My child," he said, raspy and warm, and she nearly threw herself into his arms. "I was so sorry to hear about Coryn's passing."

Naavah swallowed, but still, her eyes stayed dry. Tears were for weaklings and fools. *Heartless,* her mind whispered. *You never really cared about Coryn.*

Lies, all of it. He'd been the beating of her heart, the breath in her lungs. Without him, she had felt as though she was drowning, sinking into the sea, watching others go on without her.

"It must be hard to see him as a merden."

Ivor's detached manner had never irritated her more than in this moment. He'd never understood her bond with Coryn, always attempting to persuade her to stay away from him. When she'd graduated from apprentice to master at eighteen, younger than any previous mage in Valance, he hadn't even attended her wedding.

Only six months with Coryn. She swallowed hard. *Beautiful and brief.*

"But you are young, Naavah," Ivor said. "You will recover from this."

She stiffened. Of all the things she'd expected her former mentor to say, it was not this—minimizing her pain as though it were a minor setback instead of a shattered soul. "I may be young," she said, "but I know I will never find anyone like him again. He was..." *Perfect.*

Ivor's chuckle grated against her already-fragile patience. "There are many more like him, my dear. Don't fret. Though..." His thick eyebrows tugged together like wriggling gray caterpillars. "Perhaps it is time for you to fully embrace the mage code."

Naavah's eyes narrowed. "What are you insinuating, *master?*" She couldn't help the sharp note in her voice.

"Only that we have our rules for a reason. Perhaps if you had not joined yourself with him and spent so much time in his presence, you would not have poisoned his body with magic—"

"How dare you!" She stomped her foot, and the cottage Coryn built for her shuddered. The parchment fluttered off the table and settled against the dirt.

Ivor's wide eyes flicked to the sheets strewn across every available surface, the unwashed clay pots in the kitchen, the untouched food. "My dear girl...please don't tell me you're trying to turn him human. He is part of the sea now, and you cannot change that."

"Of course not," she said. "I know it's impossible."

He wandered closer. She fought the urge to cover up the fallen scroll. He leaned over it, taking in her untidy scrawling. "Water into wood," he murmured. "Hmm."

She didn't like his tone. "Merely some spellwork. I must have *something* to occupy my mind."

"Hmm," he said again.

The air turned thick and icy. *He's going to try to stop me.*

"I will ask you again," Ivor said in a low, dangerous voice. "Do you intend to make him human?"

"I don't." She met his gaze. *Technically true.*

"Then what *do* you intend to do?"

She clenched her jaw.

"Water into wood," he said. "*That* is your plan? To change the sea into a forest?"

She lifted her chin. "And if it is?"

"Seas and skies, Naavah." He grunted, shoving his hands into the wide sleeves of his robe. "You cannot do such a foolhardy thing. I won't allow it."

"You won't allow it?" Naavah snorted. "Ivor, you old fool."

"You're right. What am I thinking? You never listened to a thing I said, even when you were my apprentice." He sighed. "What you wish to do...it is impossible."

"No, it is certainly possible," she said. "The ocean itself is separate from the merden magic. It will not interfere with the ancient magic."

"Perhaps not, but the sea is massive." His arms spread wide, his sleeves drooping low. "The magic needed to change its form...I dare not even think of it."

"You doubt my strength? My mastery of magic? You said I was the most gifted mage you'd ever seen—"

"You are powerful, my dear, especially for one so young." Ivor gazed at her with pity, and she hated him for it. "But even you should not dare to try this. It will destroy you."

She glared at him, breathing hard. "I am already destroyed without him."

"You have more to live for than him." Ivor grabbed her hand. She hissed at the sting of magic and pulled away. "You are just eighteen, Naavah. Coryn would not have wanted you to throw away your life for him. He would want you to live on."

"I'm not throwing away my life!" Naavah's hands shook. She didn't *want* a life without Coryn. Only a few days of it, and she was already cold and hollow. The thought of *not* trying this was like not breathing. *What good is power if I can't use it?* "I'm saving him."

"Being a merden is a beautiful life, Naavah. Do not take that away from him."

Being trapped beneath the sea was *beautiful?* Unable to leave, surrounded by choking, freezing, soulless water? "I'm saving him," she repeated. "But I can't expect *you* to understand attachment. All you care about is the code."

"The code is there for a *reason!*" Ivor shook his gray head. "You selfish girl. Don't you see that this would ruin hundreds of livelihoods? Your actions have far-reaching consequences."

What did she care if the fishermen would be out of work and the sellers would lose their wares? They deserved to know what it felt like to be stripped of everything they loved, to experience the pangs of hunger and want. They deserved to suffer for all they had done to mistreat her just because they couldn't stand the idea of her being powerful.

She waved a hand dismissively. "It's just another sea."

"Just another sea?" Ivor shook his head. "You always were selfish. I thought you might grow out of it, but no. Having this much power at such a young age has gone to your head."

Her jaw tightened. "I'm afraid I must ask you to leave, Ivor."

His eyes stretched wide, his oddly long eyelashes fanning against his wrinkled skin. "You would evict me? Your mentor?"

"You leave me no choice." She exhaled, hating the pain on his face. *He doesn't matter. Only Coryn.* "And you're no longer my mentor, just a foolish old man interfering in matters he doesn't understand."

Ivor's voice broke. "I can't allow you to do this, Naavah. You must understand that."

"Everyone else is against me." She blinked away tears. "Don't you be the same."

"You have done this to yourself." He held out his hands unsteadily.

He would not hurt her. It was against his nature. As unsentimental as the man was, he wouldn't kill her. And she could never kill her former mentor. But she *could* wound. Not with magic––she wanted to save all of that for the spell, which would take an unprecedented amount of power. But she was strong enough. She knew it.

So she grabbed the nearest item—her inkwell––and threw it at Ivor's head. It smashed against his skull with a dull *thud,* spraying ink across his robe. He crumpled. Gasping, she darted toward him. Blood trickled down his forehead from a thin cut, blending with the ink smears.

He's all right, she told herself. *He'll wake up.*

Unable to bear looking at her former mentor any longer, she grabbed the parchment, hurried from her cabin, and started the trek toward the cliffs. All the while, her mind composed the spell so great it could turn water into wood.

I'm coming, Coryn. I'm coming.

Naavah stared out at the great expanse of sea with its white-capped waves, light glinting off the water like precious stones. It was beautiful and terrible, and she knew she should be moved by the sight, but all she wanted was to suck every bit of moisture from it and ensure no one else would be taken captive by these deviously lovely waves. No more gifting their dead to the ocean. Now they would feed a forest.

Naavah lowered herself down the cliffs, careful to use as little magic as possible. She would need every bit of it for what was to come. Balancing precariously on the rocks, she called, "Coryn!"

Gulls shrieked around her as she descended. She flinched at every bit of spray that touched her skin. She'd gone over every bit of the spell, ensuring there were no weaknesses or contradictions. It was solid and sure and perfect, and she had enough energy stored to pull it off. She hoped.

"This will destroy you." Ivor's voice echoed in her head. He hadn't come after her—did that mean he would never wake up? Had she killed him?

No, she couldn't have. It was just a long sleep. That was all. Soon, he'd wake with an aching head and a furious scowl, but he'd forgive her eventually. He'd understand when he saw how she'd beaten the merden magic and found a way around it. She was the greatest mage he'd ever seen—he'd said it himself.

A head emerged from the water. "Naavah!" Coryn's eager expression was a balm to her soul. "You're here! I thought maybe...maybe you didn't want to see me again."

Her breath caught. "Of course I wanted to see you."

"But you've been avoiding me ever since I turned."

It was true; she hadn't been back to the sea since she'd seen him that first time--only a week ago, but those seven days of separation weighed on her heart and mind. Her only thought had been composing the spell that would free him. "But I'm here now."

She smiled. "And I wanted you to see firsthand what I've done for you."

His eyebrows furrowed. "What you've done?"

"I will tear down every barrier between us," Naavah said. "You are my life, my breath, my oxygen, and not even the cursed water can separate us."

His eyes went wide. "Naavah, you can't be serious. The merden magic—"

"I have outwitted the magic." Her voice echoed across the waves. "Today, I will change the sea into a forest, and we will be together forever!"

"Naavah, no!"

But she had already begun the incantation. It felt different than other spells—heavier, more weighty. Almost...wrong. The scent of magic, spicy and cool, choked her. Out of the corner of her eye, she saw Coryn lunging for her and took a step back. He jerked to a halt, caught by the barrier.

Blinking to clear her suddenly unfocused vision, Naavah continued. Energy and power seeped from her body with every syllable. Her knees buckled, thumping against the rocky cliffside. *Just a little more.* Wheezing, she spoke the last words. They hung in the spell-saturated air—and then there was a mighty, deafening roar.

The water dissipated faster than she ever could've believed possible, evaporating and leaving behind barren earth. The coral darkened and sank into the ground, sprouting into thick trunks rife with newly formed leaves. Seaweed thinned into prairie grass. A whale morphed into an enormous gray deer, and a shark shed its cartilage for the thick fur of a wolf. The gulls' plumage turned dark and glossy, their beaks curving wickedly as the seabirds became hawks. And Coryn—

He lay, scratching his tail, scraping off scales, revealing *legs*. Beautiful, human legs— muscular and strong. *It worked! Seas and skies, it worked! Now we can be together again.*

"How...?" His voice was hoarse.

"I...I did it, Coryn." Naavah coughed hard as she gazed around at the bluish-tinted trees and breathed in the spicy magic. The air felt different, broken somehow, but she ignored it. "Now...we can be together."

Coryn stared up at her, his face slack. Her legs buckled. She caught herself on shriveled, bony hands. *What...?* She felt paper-thin, fragile, ready to fall apart.

"Naavah, you're... What *happened* to you?"

"I..." The magic! It had cost too much, just as Ivor had predicted. *No! Not when I'm so close to holding Coryn in my arms again!*

Naavah reached for her husband but nearly fell on her face. Her skin burned, and she saw odd, papery flakes in her peripheral vision––bits of herself melting away.

Coryn took her crumbling face in his hands, gazing at her with horror instead of adoration. It made her feel sick inside. "Why did you do it? I was happy, Naavah."

Happy...in the water? Without *her?* Her heart cracked. *All for nothing...*

"You shouldn't have risked yourself for me," he said. "You should've just come into the water with me! I wouldn't have let you drown."

He wouldn't have. She knew that. She'd always known. But it hadn't been enough. *He* hadn't been enough.

Then it hit her––the mourning––the wailing of things that had been changed into what they were not, torn from their bodies and stuffed into new ones. It sliced into her soul. *Wrong,* they seemed to scream. *This is not how it should be.*

"Naavah, please, hold on!"

But she was crumbling, her body drained of the magic that held it together. She blinked sleepily, her skin on fire. And not even a ritual could save her, could remake her into something magical like Coryn had been remade.

"It was...for you," she whispered through thin lips.

It was like drowning—being sucked into darkness, unable to control her limbs, lungs burning. The last things she saw were Coryn's ice-pale eyes.

A Short-Lived Romance

Megan Dill

A MERMAID FELL IN love with a man,
Unaware of his short lifespan.
He grew old and gray,
Would start to decay,
So she left him before that began.

MERNAIDO!

ABIGAIL FALANGA

"THIS WAS NOT HOW I thought tonight would go!" Steve shouted.

His voice was lost in the roaring wind—along with half the pier and most of the waterfront businesses.

"What?" Sam bellowed from two yards away, wielding a decorative oar like it was his last hope—which maybe it was.

"Meet the girls, have a few drinks, hang out, maybe a nice dinner..." Steve swung his ancient harpoon at a passing object in case it was a sea monster. "Then *this* happens! Just my luck. Every"—the harpoon stuck in what turned out to be a deck chair—"single"—he yanked it free—"date! Just when it looked like I might finally meet someone—catastrophe."

Sam yelled back, "Weren't missing much."

"Well, it would still be better than—"

A zap from a trident brandished by an airborne mermaid interrupted Steve, and he dove for cover.

Greg charged past waving a chainsaw (where'd he found *that*?) at the maelstrom with a garbled war cry.

"Hope we see him again," Sam remarked.

"Shoulda known there's danger seaside—tsunamis, retirees taking pictures, and mer-naidos!"

"Stop whining!" Sam grinned like he was enjoying being sea-soaked, gale-pummeled, and mermaid-bruised. "The night was ruined already, even before the first tornado took out half the restaurant."

Steve couldn't argue. For one thing, his mouth was full of water—and for another, it was true: One drink in, two of the girls had proved loud and snitty, while the other two were no more than makeup-and-filter beauties. Maybe multiple water-tornadoes containing furious, trident-wielding mermaids wreaking destruction on the coastal part of the city had actually improved their night.

A huge military SUV rolled past, and a soldier leaned out to shout: "Clear the area! We're taking it out!"

Steve and Sam sprinted up the street and ducked into the nearest building, which turned out to be a library already sheltering a dripping and anxious clutch of refugees. They were just in time. An explosion rattled the bookshelves, followed by relative peace.

"That's got 'em!" Sam exulted.

"No chance, unfortunately," muttered a man standing near a panoramic window. "The mother-of-all-tornadoes is headed for the school. Just look at her. Bet she's the queen or something."

Steve approached the window and had to admit the mermaid atop the tornado was probably the most beautiful woman he had ever seen—or would've been if she wasn't currently also a rage-monster. A glittering pearl crown graced flowing black-and-sea-green hair, and her shell-clad form was perfect down to the waist (everything below was hidden in mist). Her face was like finely sculpted amber, but twisted in fury and—was he imagining things, or did she look a little terrified? Maybe even desperate.

"Why are they doing this?" Steve wondered, letting the harpoon rest on the soaking carpet.

"Must be ecological revenge," the man at the window said, "for decades of pollution."

Sam snorted. "If so, then why aren't they attacking the factories down the coast? This place can't put out more pollution than *them*. In fact, see how the mermaids are lurching around when they change direction? I don't think they're even *directing* the tornadoes."

"Yes, they look just as scared as they are angry," an old lady wearing a library volunteer badge suggested tremulously. "Maybe they're as much victims of this as any of us."

"They're taking advantage of it, though," window-guy said.

"Yeah..." Sam risked a closer look. "They're angry about something—they *want* something. But what?"

"In old stories," the old lady said, "mermaids want love—companionship—meaning."

Steve stared at the mermaid queen as she brandished her trident even as her shoulders trembled, and a crazy conviction came to him. "Y'know, I think you're right."

He ran for the door before Sam could call him back and tore up the street, round a corner, and toward the wind-lashed school. His pounding heart and legs didn't give him time to think until he skidded to a stop right in front of the tornado.

The mermaid queen raised her trident and poised it, ready to zap him. He recognized something in her beautiful but rageful face: the same disappointment and loneliness he'd felt that very afternoon.

"Truce!" Steve yelled, holding up his hands. "I wanna talk! I think I know why you're here."

"We want nothing from you, human, that you can offer in exchange for your life!" she snarled, the waterspout around and below her whipping into renewed fury.

"What about—love?"

"What is... *love*?"

Steve's brain was starting to work again, screaming that he was too exposed, that he was doing the stupidest thing ever. But he plowed ahead: "It's attraction to beauty and—"

She laughed. "We already have that!"

Well, at least she was laughing at him, right? That meant she might hold off on killing him a little longer. He tried again: "Love is a choice—a commitment to stay together no matter what happens, to always be there for each other, do anything for the other's best."

"But no one ever stays—all are swept away as changefully as these raging waters!" The mermaid's face relaxed into a puzzled frown. "Yet you would remain true to *me*? To never leave? You would *love* me?"

"Yes. But *only*," Steve said firmly, "if you order all your other mernaidoes to back off."

"We have no control over these waterspouts!" she wailed. "They swept us up onto your loathsome land before we could do anything about it, and all we could do was fight off any attacks."

"I think your anger makes the waterspouts worse—look! Yours is already getting smaller."

She looked down, and a smile transformed her face into the soul of brilliance. "You are right! We can be free of this mad water. Very well. If you can agree to leave everything and come with me and never leave my side, I suppose I could...*love* you in return. You *are* quite attractive. I will call to my subjects and tell them to release their anger and so return to the sea."

The queen set a large conch to her lips and blew a strange call.

Her tornado might have been shrinking every second, but it was still strong enough to lift Steve off his feet and up next to her.

"Whoa! Did you say—I'm coming with you?"

"That is what you agreed." She frowned.

"Yes, of course." Steve's mind—and heart—were racing...not least because she was even more stunning up close. "But, uh, I can't breathe underwater."

"You shall transcend!"

"Oh, cool." His brain rebelled, refusing to comprehend everything. He resorted to asking a silly question: "So, uh, I'll be a merman? With a tail and everything?"

"Don't be ridiculous!" She laughed as the tornado whooshed and roared over the angry ocean. "We don't have tails."

The mermaid lifted scaly and colorful toes into view and wriggled them.

Then she grabbed Steve's hand and pulled him toward the water. His stomach dropped at the sudden descent.

At least the city was safe now. But, with his luck in dating, this would *not* end well.

@maxineart

Things of Midnight

Rebekah Isert

"Bjørn."

The voice was quiet, but it snapped me into awareness. I lay there in silence for a moment, listening for some other sound. When there wasn't one, I burrowed further underneath the covers. The late August breeze reached through the open porthole, beneath the blanket, and traced across the back of my neck with frosty fingers. I was cocooned, and there was nothing in the world that could possibly entice me out right now.

"Bjørn, wake up."

The voice was male but still unrecognizable. I kept still, with the hope that whoever it was would go away if I continued to pretend to be asleep.

"Bjørn, wake up. I need your help."

The voice registered. David, one of the newcomers on board the *The North Queen*. An old hand on boats, but new to ours. A decorated war vet—a hero of Dunkirk and Normandy. My new bunkmate. Why would he be waking me up? A drunk sailor? Someone late to report back to the ship? Not that there was much to do in this remote little corner of Canada to keep someone out so late—and it had to be *very* late. Only the troublemakers, wights, and things of midnight would be out now. I didn't move. But they didn't have wights here. Small mercies. Whatever it was, it could either wait until morning or whoever was in trouble could fix it by himself.

Something soft nudged my shoulder. When I didn't respond, he poked me again, harder this time. "I know you're awake. You stopped snoring."

I opened my eyes. It didn't do much good. It was almost pitch-black in the cabin despite the open window. The only glow that I could see came from David's radium-green watch. I blinked a few more times. His silhouette materialized, tall and broad-shouldered.

"What is it?" I growled. I was tired enough that my Norwegian accent, usually minimized as much as I could make it, popped from my lips. People aboard still remembered who Norway had allied with during the war. A war that was not so far removed from peoples' memories. Not that David would care, but it did nothing to improve my mood.

"I need your help," David's soft voice said.

"I heard that. What is it?" I snapped.

The other man hesitated. I hoped it was because of my tone. Maybe he would think better of whatever it was he was thinking and leave me alone. Or just get on with it and tell me what he wanted.

"You gotta come see," he whispered.

I stared at him furiously for a moment, trying to pretend my curiosity wasn't piqued. David wasn't dramatic. If it were only a sailor, he would tell me. If it wasn't that, then... I glared up at him with a vengeance before I realized that he couldn't see my expression. I threw the blanket off of me, and the cold hit me hard with an unsympathetic slap.

"What time is it?" I said. I thought about letting my teeth chatter so David could hear, but I doubted it would do any good.

"A little past two."

My hands paused where they were helping my feet into my boots. "I swear, if this is some kind of a joke—"

"It's not. Please, we don't have much time. Try to be as quiet as you can. We can't wake anyone up."

How I wished that that statement had included me. I finished tying my boots and stood. I grabbed my sweater and yanked it over my head, following it with my toque to protect my ears from the chill. It was August in Churchill, Manitoba. We were just below the Arctic Circle, and it couldn't be more than fifty degrees outside. Like David always said, a man couldn't survive up here without wearing your toque all the time. He certainly believed it—I'd never seen the man without his.

I snatched the waterproof jacket off the wall from where it was hanging by the door. Then, with an effort, I shoved my tired frame into motion and followed my shipmate out the door.

David moved fast, faster than he usually managed to shift his six-foot-two frame around the ship, forcing me to drag my shorter legs along at a much higher velocity than I should have had to before sunrise. That being said, I wasn't far behind him. I managed to keep up with his long stride better and better the more awake I became. I squinted at my companion, his wrinkled forehead and furrowed blond eyebrows faintly illuminated by the night lighting on the ship.

He was worried about something, which worried *me*. David was easygoing and happy. Even over the last couple of days, when we'd had a couple of setbacks with getting our vessel out of dock on time, the Canadian sailor had retained a positive attitude and hadn't seemed to get too worked up about anything.

This was different. A heavy frown sat on his face, and he glanced around as though he was worried that someone would emerge from down below, demanding to know what we were up to.

My stomach churned. What *were* we up to? Would I be held accountable if I didn't know what was going on?

Just as long as it's not drugs or women, I prayed.

We made it to the deck of the ship. Immediately upon exiting the accommodation, the wind, cold and unsympathetic, slammed into us. David didn't seem to notice, looking to ensure I made it through the door before he turned and closed the hatch behind us.

"What's going on?" I demanded.

"Shh. You'll see in a moment."

"Is something wrong with the ship?"

David looked at me, his expression grim. He opened his mouth like he wanted to say something but then closed it. He shook his head. "No Bjørn, it's… I can't explain it. Not in a way that you'll believe me. You're going to have to come see for yourself."

He turned away, heading for the gangway. He walked down it with the same great strides as before. I frowned at his back. What could possibly be off this ship that was unexplainable? It wasn't like there was much up here besides snow, ice, and polar bears—even during the summer like this.

I froze at the top of the gangway. *Stjerner i himmelen*, there wasn't a polar bear out there, was there?

No.

No, it couldn't be. We were trained for that. In case of a polar bear on shore, we had to stay aboard the ship, and if we couldn't drive it away with shouts—if it was even interested in us in the first place—we were given permission to drive it away with guns. David knew this better than most; he was from here, even though I knew he wasn't much for guns—or violence in general. I'd asked him why when he'd first come aboard. He'd given me that small half-smile that I'd seen on more than one ex-servicemen and then shrugged.

"I've seen and done my fair share," he'd said. And that was all he would say.

So what could it *be*, then?

I made it to the bottom of the gangplank, my feet hitting the cement with less noise than I'd anticipated. I twisted my head to the right, the direction that I'd seen David go. I watched him as he walked at the same pace to a small dinghy that was moored to a personnel dock nearby.

Whatever he was after, it was on the water.

I jogged to catch up. I approached him just as he stepped down into the boat. The tickle of curiosity that lay under a thick layer of unease poked at me. I followed suit despite my misgivings, stepping carefully into the boat.

As soon as I was in, David cast off and sat in the stern. His hand paused over the motor for a moment, and then he seemed to think better of it. Instead, he pulled the emergency oars out and handed them to me. "Here. You row, I'll steer."

I locked the oars and began pulling on them. Immediately the dinghy sliced through the water, the only sound the whistling of the wind and the lapping of the waves. It seemed almost wrong to disturb the near-silence, but I couldn't resist.

"How far?" I asked.

David peered out into the darkness. "Not far. Just to *The North Queen's* anchor rode."

The rode? Was it damaged? It seemed unlikely—the chain that held the anchor was enormous and strong. It would take something of massive proportions to damage a structure that big. *Focus.* I turned my mind back to my task of rowing, resisting the urge to look back to try to capture an early glimpse of what we were heading for.

The dinghy was laughably small against the enormous tanker. Even if the *Queen* wasn't an icebreaker, she looked like one, her painted red hull looming above us in the darkness like a giant sea monster about to attack.

"Back oars." David stood up in the boat, a long pole in his hand. I pulled the oars in and watched my shipmate reach into the boat.

When I saw the sharp curve on the end of the polished wood, my mouth opened. "What's with the boathook?"

"Shhh. We don't want to frighten her," he responded, his voice low. David's eyes were focused over my shoulder into the darkness.

"Frighten who?" I turned around in my seat to look for myself. I wasn't prepared for what I saw.

The first thing I noticed was the nets. They were hopelessly tangled around the anchor chain, so tightly bunched that in order to weigh anchor at all, I knew we were going to have to cut all of it away. But that wasn't the only thing I saw.

David had a flashlight in his hand, but for some reason he hadn't turned it on yet. The result was that the only illumination on the rode—and on the thing tied to it—was the dim yellow lights from the harbour.

Its skin was slate-grey, shining like dolphin hide in the yellow light. Wet hair hung down in clumps while its chest heaved up and down with an obvious, panicked effort. I gaped, but David reached out with the boathook, grabbed the chain, and pulled us closer to the anchor and the creature.

"It's okay," he said gently. He spoke softly, his voice low and soothing. "I'm back. I brought someone to help."

The head turned, and I glimpsed its face.

The features on the creature were almost human, except for the eyes. Those *eyes*. Deep, and black as night. There were no discernible irises, as though the black had expanded over the entire white of the eye until there was only darkness.

I cried out, recoiling in shock, and nearly upset the boat in the process.

David dropped low as the small vessel rocked from side to side, grabbed onto the edge, and nearly lost his grip on the boathook. "Bjørn! Bjørn, calm down—it's okay!"

I couldn't stop looking at it. Those haunting eyes. That unnatural skin. And—was that—was that a tail?

"*Himmelen over jorden*, David, what is that thing?" I whispered. I unconsciously brought my arms close to my body as if to protect them.

David looked at the thing, then to me, and then back toward the thing. "She's not a *thing*, Bjørn; she's a mermaid, and she's in trouble."

"A—a what?"

David sighed. He unhooked the boathook, laid it in the bottom of the boat, and then walked toward me. Squatting in front of me, he took my shoulders, and his voice suddenly softened like he was speaking to a little boy instead of a hardened sailor. "A mermaid. Like in the stories. She's caught in the line and can't get out by herself. If she's still exposed to the air when the sun comes out, she's going to die."

She? I looked over his shoulder at the creature. Observing her more closely, she was obviously female, but— "How did you even find her?"

David winced. "I...I heard her."

"You *heard* her?"

David sighed and reached up to pull off his toque. I almost felt like gasping at that in and of itself. I'd never seen him without the cap, and I wasn't prepared for the veritable shock of blond hair that he'd crammed under it. I was even less prepared when I saw the shape of his ears.

"It—you're a—"

"An elf. I'm an elf, Bjørn. And I heard her, and she needs our help. Now, I can't free her by myself. I need you to—"

"You're an elf, David!"

"Yes."

"Like...like...like, an elf!"

"Yes."

I gaped. "Is anyone else on board an elf? Or something? I thought you guys didn't like running water."

"That's a vampire, Bjørn."

"An *elf*, David!"

He pinched the bridge of his nose and then leveled a kind but clearly impatient stare back up at me. "I know, Bjørn. And I'd be happy to talk to you about it, just not right now. Right now, we have someone who needs our help. I need you to hold us close to the rode with the boathook while I get her free—and keep an eye out for her mate. Under no circumstances are you to get into the water, do you hear me? Not even a finger."

I swallowed, looking down into the black, ice-cold water. "Why, what will happen?"

David jammed his toque back onto his head, his smooth skin creased into a frown. "Well, if you're lucky, they'll cut your throat before they eat you."

I stared. "I thought you said she called for help."

"*She* did, yes," David said gruffly. "But mermen are territorial. Worse than the polar bears. They'll tolerate us helping her for now, but the minute we enter their domain, all bets are off. Now, are you going to help?"

I should never have gotten out of bed. But the longer I looked at those deep black eyes, I began to see something there. Fear? The sheer vulnerability of her predicament tugged at me. The exposure. The helplessness. "Yes."

He nodded once. "Good. Grab the boathook. I'll cut her loose. Arms last."

"Arms last?" I asked.

A grim look flashed across David's face. "Well, I imagine that she's hungry after being caught up all night."

My stomach turned itself inside out.

Right.

We maneuvered into position. I grabbed the long pole from David and hooked an enormous link in the anchor rode to pull David into position beside the mermaid. Her head turned, slower than I expected, and I could hear a clicking sound emit from her throat.

"Yes, I'm here," David murmured. "I'm going to cut you loose now, all right?"

She exhaled, a deep *whuff* that came from the base of her lungs. That was apparently a signal to get started, and David reached for the utility knife on his belt, drawing it out slowly.

When David said there was possibly a merman in the water, somewhere in the back of my mind I knew the creature was probably nearby. I'd envisioned it swimming in the harbour, watching closely, but too frightened or wary to interfere.

That made it a complete surprise when something struck the bottom of the boat so hard that I nearly fell into the dark water. Only my grip on the boathook and an impossibly fortunate footing kept me upright and onboard.

"Down!" David commanded me, and we both dropped low, our weight steadying the boat as it rocked furiously from side to side. He looked up at the trapped creature and hissed, "Tell them I'm trying to help you!"

She trilled, and the sound sent shivers down my spine.

David shook his head. "I don't care if they can understand me! It doesn't mean a thing unless it comes from *you*. Tell them I mean you no harm!"

"Them?" I gasped.

David glanced at me, expression grim. "It looks as though there are two of them."

The trilling stopped. The mermaid closed her eyes and took in a deep breath. The water stilled, and for a moment the only rocking of the boat was from the wind. The mermaid opened her mouth and let out a low wailing sound that pierced the air. A sudden peace seemed to pour over me, and my mouth dropped open as I stared at the creature.

David stood and quickly started to cut away at the net, careful to avoid getting too close to the mermaid in the process. I sat, half mesmerized by the sound, suddenly feeling quite relaxed given the circumstances.

I didn't notice that my hands had loosened their grip until the handle of the boathook, still locked around the link of the anchor rode, clattered to the bottom of the ship. I looked down at it, bemused. Then something soft and leathery hit me in the face. I stared at the object, blinking mutely, unmoved. A glove? I glanced up at David, wondering why he would do such a thing.

"Snap out of it!" he barked, holding on tightly to the net to keep us in place. "Pick up the boathook before we lose it!"

Something in the air sharpened, and his words suddenly clicked into place. The heaviness around my limbs—when had that taken hold of me?—dropped away in an instant. My stomach lurched, and my heart sped up as I reached toward the boathook, the handle of which was slowly scraping along the side of the boat as the current twisted us away from the trapped mermaid. Just a few more inches and it would drop into the water. David was our pivot point as he doggedly continued to cut away at the tangled netting, valiantly attempting to keep the boat in the same position by standing as solidly as he could. Just a little closer…

Finally! I caught the boathook, the oak pole smooth under my fingers, just as it reached the edge of the boat and was about to drop over the side. I tightened my grip and towed us back toward the rode as smoothly as I could, trying not to jostle David—who was leaning precariously out of the boat—as I guided the boat back toward the chain.

He had cut a good bit of net away and was now pulling the destroyed mesh into the boat. The seas were getting choppier—or maybe the mermen were getting agitated again. We hadn't been at it that long. Maybe they felt impatient.

I could see them every once in a while, the flash of jet-black scales or horrible, pale faces just near enough to the surface to make themselves known. Worse was the glint of sharp white teeth as one or the other got a little too close to the boat before the creature snarled and dove beneath the water again. My nerves, already as frayed as an old rope, wound tighter and tighter as I watched them circle the boats. Sharks would have been more welcoming.

"How close are we, David?" I couldn't help the tremor in my voice.

"Almost there," David said, his voice distorted. He had the flashlight in his mouth now, shining it on the mermaid. The light guided his careful knife as he cut away with the care of a surgeon at the threads that dug into her skin. There wasn't much left of the netting now. He'd almost freed her torso, and her long grey tail disappeared down into the water. Only her arms were left entangled in the net. "Just a little longer. This part is really tight…"

He made two more cuts, meticulous and purposeful, but on the last, a swell caught the boat. David jerked toward the mermaid, and the flashlight dropped into the bottom of the boat. In the sudden darkness, there was a snap and an unearthly wail.

"I'm sorry! It slipped!" David cried. He shone the light back up onto the mermaid, who still hung suspended by a few scant threads; he whipped the light to her arm where he'd been working. Red. A trickle of blood ran down her skin. David reached into his pocket, frantically grabbing for his handkerchief. The cut didn't look serious, but it ran freely, and before he could staunch the wound, a drop of blood dripped from her hand.

We watched it fall, deep crimson and barely visible in the dim light, toward the water below. The droplet hit the black water, the ripple barely discernible in the wave-tossed surface.

And then the sea exploded.

Something ripped the boathook from my hands, and before I could even take a breath, it flung me from the boat, sending me hurtling head first into the icy cold water. Almost immediately, something struck me in the stomach, hard and unbelievably strong, driving whatever air I had managed to save from my lungs in one painful strike.

Water filled my nose and mouth, and as I struggled to right myself, I was struck again and again. The blows rolled me over and over in the water until I couldn't tell if I was blind, upside down, or about to black out from lack of oxygen. Powerful fingers grabbed me by the ankle, and, before I could so much as look, dragged me sharply downwards. Bubbles streamed past me as we flew through the water, and I could feel my head getting light.

That was when I knew I was going to die.

Curse you, David, I thought with the last of my consciousness. Then I amended my words. *No, curse me. I should never have gotten out of bed.*

The fingers let go of my ankle, flinging me through the water until I hit something hard. The bottom of the harbour? A rock? How was I staying down here? What happened to humans being naturally buoyant?

Who was I kidding? I had no more air to be naturally buoyant with.

I still had my eyes closed. I wanted to open them—something instinctive and primordial in me didn't want to die blind—but I also had no desire to stare down a merman with my last few seconds of life. But why weren't they attacking? Were they waiting until I drowned before they ate me?

I cracked open one eye, expecting to see only blackness.

But there wasn't. There was some sort of light coming from above. The harbour lights? A flashlight? The dim light cast the water in a greyish black, but I could clearly see three figures.

Two were the mermen. One had to be twelve feet long from head to tail with jet-black fins and a haunting, scowling face. The other had darker skin, and, while his tail was also black, there seemed to be some sort of iridescent coating like the shine on fish scales.

It was a pity, I thought, as I looked between the two, that even in my last moments my brain couldn't come up with anything more inventive than those descriptions.

But the last figure... I almost didn't recognize her. Her features were the same, as was the colour of her skin and the hue of her tail, but somehow the mermaid had completely changed. Gone was the clumped hair; her locks now flowed ethereally around her face. The black eyes, once fearful, showed confidence and...compassion?

It was too much. The world was starting to go black again, and not from the lack of air this time. I could feel my head lolling, dropping toward my chest.

Bjørn...

The voice in my head was not my own. It was somewhere between a song and a sigh, floating through my head like a calm sea breeze.

You have saved me, Bjørn. A life for a life; is that not fair? The mermaid took my head in her hands and, placing her lips on mine, filled my screaming lungs with pure, clean air. Then she circled her arms around my chest and tugged on me, sending us both shooting upward with dizzying speed, leaving the scowling mermen behind.

The cold night air was painful as we broke the surface. The stiff breeze took my water-chilled body and froze it almost instantly. I squeezed my eyes shut against the sharp needles of icy wind, but the mermaid's arms remained clasped around me as she hauled me through the water. I gasped, marveling at the superhuman strength in her gentle grip.

"Bjørn!" David's voice was barely audible over the lapping of the waves.

Was he still trying to be quiet? The thought seemed laughable. The mermaid continued to haul me through the water until I felt a different pair of hands grasping at my coat, heaving me bodily from the sea.

I opened my mouth to protest, expecting the dinghy to tip beneath me and send me once again to the ravening beasts below. But it didn't—David's footing was sure, and before I could process anything else, I felt myself being dragged onto something hard and solid, with not even the barest hint of a wave.

I cracked my eyes open. I lay crumpled in a heap on the personnel dock that we'd embarked from. Lifting my head, I scanned the harbour; the wooden dinghy was nowhere to be seen. Nearby, David—also soaked to the skin—squatted on the edge of the pier, whispering to something wet and grey, whose head and shoulders were just out of the water.

A smooth hand reached up toward his face, and I almost cried out a word of warning, only to watch as the long, graceful fingers gently stroked David's cheek. Then the mermaid turned, her dark tail flashing once in the yellow lights of the harbour, and disappeared beneath the black surface.

David stood, watching the choppy water for a moment. I couldn't see his expression, but there was something in his stance that seemed longing. Wistful, even. I didn't blame him. I stared out at the blackness from where I lay, tasting the salt in the air. It promised more than just the sea now.

David turned, shivering in the cold wind, and walked up to me. "You okay?"

I looked down at my waterlogged body. I felt battered and like I'd been through the rotors of a propellor, but miraculously I still had all my own limbs. My skin was unbroken, and, although I felt the beginnings of a nasty bruise on my side, I could tell that my ribs were whole.

I lay back on the wooden pier. I stared up at the cloudy sky, listening to the lapping of the waves, and shook my head disbelievingly. "Never again, David."

David swallowed but nodded. "I understand. I'm sorry, Bjørn." He offered a hand.

I took it, letting him heave me to my feet. "I should never have left my bed," I continued. Both of us shivered violently as we made our way back up the gangplank. I was wet, cold, and in pain. So why did I feel so...good?

He continued to nod, the epitome of graceful regret. "I know. I'm sorry."

"You and your ridiculous, mad, elvish...things."

"I know. I'm sorry."

I sighed and shook my head, thinking of those dark eyes and the sweet tune of her voice... The smallest tickle of pride prickled through me. I looked over at David where he squished along beside me in his sodden clothes. He looked about as good as I felt. I smiled a little and nudged him in the shoulder. "Hey."

"What?"

"Put a word in with the Captain—have him pick the tropics next time."

The Selkie's Gift

Katie Hanna

I've never seen a selkie before.

Everyone knows selkies are a story for children. I'm seventeen, nearly a man, too old to believe in magic. That's what my uncle would say if I told him I saw a selkie…before whipping me for lying. Cormac and the other fishermen would laugh in my face. But I can't deny the proof of my own eyes.

Milky light drips through the low-hanging clouds, casting a shimmer over the beach. Everything gleams: the foam, the pebbles, the shells…and the sealskin spread to dry on a rock.

Even apart from its rich brown sheen and marbled pattern, I know it's a sealskin because I saw a seal crawl onto the beach a few moments ago. But the seal is nowhere in sight.

Instead, a woman unfolds her long limbs to the sun, shaking her wet hair off her shoulders. Her skin glows pink. Her curls are the deep amber of the ocean brine. Filmy silk wraps around her body, a dress of sorts, though nothing like the sturdy woolen dresses the girls in the village wear.

Daft, aye?

If I hadn't watched the seal shift into the woman, I would be calling *myself* daft.

She leans back, her hands planted on the pebbled shore, her eyes fixed on the golden sea. I try to imagine where she's traveled, what she's seen. Does she know what lies beyond the horizon? Does the ocean call to her the way it calls to me?

The nets I'm supposed to be cleaning slide from my fingers, unheeded. Uncle will beat me if I don't finish the job, but I don't care. I never wanted to be a fisherman anyway. I want adventure. Romance. Magic.

When the selkie maiden rises, turning as if to walk farther down the beach, I make up my mind. My voice rings out across the quiet water. "My lady!"

My heart skitters at my own boldness. Blood thumps loudly in my ears.

The maiden whirls to face me. Her filmy gown swirls along with her, floating around her knees. When she catches sight of my fishing boat and nets, her eyes widen.

"I won't hurt you!" I fling out my arms, reaching instinctively across the gap between us. "I promise, my lady!"

Her long legs are already pumping, her feet churning the pebbles. She hurls herself at the rock where her sealskin lies, snatching the skin with both hands.

"Wait! Please!" My shout strains my chest. "I don't want to trap you! Or steal from you!" She dashes for the waves, and I throw a last, desperate cry after her. "I'm not one of...*those men!*"

The woman stills. She stands like a statue at the edge of the surf, her shoulders rigid. Water fizzes around her ankles.

With a deep breath, I take a step toward her. Then another, then another. Shells crunch softly under my bare feet. The woman doesn't move.

In the old stories, human men robbed selkies' skins to trap them into marriage. I don't understand how anyone could be so cruel as to *take* what wasn't freely offered. I understand one thing, though. This selkie maiden has no reason to trust me.

Yet there she stands...

Sunlight reflects off the waves to flash on her skin. Her chest rises and falls as she listens to my approaching footsteps.

My heart thunders louder than ever. I can barely hear my own voice when I speak. "My name is Jamie, my lady."

After a long moment, she turns. She keeps a wary distance between us, clutching her precious sealskin to her breast. But her eyes—round, brown, soft—seem to hold as much curiosity as fear.

I swallow uncomfortably as she studies me. I know I'm not much to look at, with big dark eyes that leap from my pale face like a startled rabbit's. But at least I don't look like my uncle, grim-faced and lantern-jawed.

I hope I don't look like a monster to be feared.

The selkie maiden's lips flutter with a brief smile. "Jamie, aye?"

I wipe my sweaty, nervous palms on my breeches, clearing my throat. I'm only seventeen. I don't know how to talk to women, let alone a maid as beautiful as this. "Aye."

Her smile returns, curving deeper this time. Her warm brown eyes crinkle. "You may call me Síofra."

"Síofra," I repeat, savoring the sweet taste on my tongue. I know it means *elf* or *sprite*, which suits her dancing curls and foaming gown.

"Come." Síofra beckons, mischief twinkling in her gaze. "Walk with me."

I do as I'm told. How could I not? This is the adventure I've always longed for. My legs stretch to keep up with her long strides. She's taller than me, and her limbs move with an easy rhythm that tells of hours of swimming and running.

Síofra leads me toward the big craggy rocks. When we reach them, she spreads her sealskin to dry once more, smoothing it with loving hands. I can't take my eyes off the beautiful swirls of silver-gray and brown umber. The dappled pattern winks at me in the sunlight.

The selkie maiden holds out her hand. "Will you dance with me, Jamie?"

My breath catches. A mad flush races up my neck. I stare at her. She meets my gaze boldly, with only the hint of a rosy blush in her own cheeks.

My face splits in a grin. My pulse hammers like a drum as I reach out in response. "Of course, my lady Síofra."

She clasps my fingers in her soft firm ones, then presses our palms together. Gooseflesh spreads up my arms. My grin widens.

Síofra steps to the side with a graceful swish of her skirt. Recognizing the pattern of an old folk dance, I step to the opposite side. Our palms meet in the middle.

Giggling, the selkie maid sidesteps again. I follow her.

Round, and round, and round, and round...

The only music we need is the lap of waves on the beach and the fluting cries of the distant seabirds. Sun burnishes Síofra's hair, turning it to lustrous copper. My blood flows warm and strong in my veins. I've never felt so alive.

Without warning, Síofra pulls my arm above my head. She spins me with a flick of her strong wrist, the way a village lad might twirl a girl while dancing.

My head whirls with the motion. Air rushes around me, billowing my shirt. I gasp for breath.

At my gasp, I sense Síofra stiffen. She bites her lip, dropping my hand too quickly. I stagger sideways, dizzy, reeling. But a laugh bubbles inside my chest.

The selkie maiden stares at me, eyes round as saucers.

I can't stop laughing, even though my voice is ragged. "You—" That's all I can manage. "*You—*"

Now Síofra begins to laugh too. Not giggling, but truly laughing, high and clear like a silver bell.

We double over, overcome with glee. The shore rings with our mirth. But in the gap where one laugh ends and a fresh one begins, I hear something...

The sharp *clink* of a man's boot dislodging a rock.

My instincts scream danger. I jerk upright, swing around—

Cormac, the strongest, cruelest man in the village, crouches behind us like a hunter ready to spring. He must have crept up while we were lost in the dance. Cormac's orange hair burns like a bonfire. His eyes are fixed on Síofra with a lurid gleam.

A strangled yell escapes me. Síofra spins wildly toward the sound, her face draining white when she sees her attacker.

Cormac rockets to his feet and dashes forward.

I throw myself in his path, my arms and legs flailing. *"Stay away from her!"*

Cormac slams into me, shoving me to the ground. I land hard on my chest, the wind knocked from my lungs. A razor-sharp shell pierces my skin. I yelp.

I raise my head to see Síofra racing like an arrow down the beach, tugging the sealskin over her shoulders. Cormac barrels after her, greedy hands outstretched. But Síofra plunges into the surf, diving under the silver waves.

I spot a brown seal's head bobbing between two whitecaps before it disappears.

Cormac's enraged shout echoes off the rocks. He shakes his fist at the frothy water. "You won't get rid of me so easily!"

"I told you to stay away from her!" I scramble to my feet, blood dripping down my leg. "She doesn't belong to you!"

"Shut up!" Cormac snarls. He pivots on his heel, pelting down the beach, headed for the fishing boat resting on the shore.

My boat.

He's stealing my boat to hunt Síofra down.

Before the thought takes conscious shape, I'm already running. My feet skim the rough ground. My lungs burn. My eyes smart.

It's no use. Cormac, taller and faster, has already reached his goal. He snatches my fishnets, piles them into my boat, and shoves it into the surf. He wades after it, climbing aboard as the water swells to buoy the little craft.

I know what I have to do. Instead of slowing down, I run harder. Sharp pain stabs my chest. Sweat trickles down my neck. But I don't take my eyes off Cormac's orange head, which bobs as the boat rides the waves. He tosses the net over the side, peering hungrily into the ocean.

My running feet hit the water. Foam licks my legs. Salt stings my bleeding wound. As I push forward, the waves climb to my waist. My breeches are soaked, clinging to my skin. I take a deep breath, then plunge in headfirst.

The water closes over me. The cold embraces me. My world is dark, dark, dark…

I thrash my arms, kicking to propel myself forward. I may not be the swiftest runner, but I'm a born swimmer. I'm going to follow that boat. I'm going to stop Cormac. I'm going to save Síofra.

I stay underwater as long as I can so Cormac won't see me. Pent-up pressure strains my chest. As the seconds tick past, my lungs scream for air. At last, I come up gasping. Water streams down my face, blurring my vision. Waves slosh around my neck, scooping a generous helping of ocean into my open mouth. It tastes salty. Bitter. I choke.

There!

The boat sits only a dozen yards from me, rocking precariously on the waves as Cormac leans over the side. He grasps the net, hefting it aboard. He grunts as if it were heavy. As if it were weighed down by…

A brown seal, tangled in the rope webbing, her wet skin flashing sharply in the pale light.

My scream comes out as a choked whisper. "Siofra!"

My arms beat the waves furiously; I swim harder than I ever have before. Cold spray flies in all directions. As I approach, the boat's curved hull looms over me. I clamber over the side, landing with a *thud*.

Cormac twists his head at the sound. His eyes pop in shock, but he doesn't leap to fend me off. His hands are full of curly auburn hair, brutally wrenching it as his victim struggles. *Human* hair.

Síofra has shifted back into a woman. She's fighting hard, though her lower limbs are still meshed in the net. She rams her shoulder against the wooden hull. The boat sways. Cormac grunts, straining to pin her down.

Whipping the fishing knife from my belt, I hurl myself forward.

Skinny and scrawny though I may be, I land like a ton of bricks on Cormac's back. My elbow hooks around his neck. My steel blade jams against his throat.

His chest swells in a gasp.

Hope blooms in Síofra's eyes.

"Monster." I hardly recognize my own voice, stretched taut as a leather cord. "*Take your hands off her.*"

"Jamie, you little shrimp." Cormac tries to laugh, though it's more of a strangled cough. "You'd never have the guts to—"

Without a word, I slice into his skin.

Blood trickles out, staining my blade red. The cut isn't deep enough to kill...just deep enough to make my point.

Cormac yelps. He yanks his hands off Síofra as if her body were scalding hot metal. Before he can react further, I grab him by the armpits, hauling with all my strength. "Síofra! Help me!"

Síofra catches on instantly. She kicks free of the net, dives forward, and links her strong arms under Cormac's knees. Together, we heave him over the side, dumping him in the ocean. As he hits the surface, a giant wave erupts, washing over us. The boat pitches crazily, knocking me into the wooden boards.

"Devils! Witches! Murderers!" Cormac thrashes his arms, swimming away from us as fast as he can. His cries grow fainter, echoing off the quiet sea. "*Murderers...*"

"Oh, Jamie," Síofra whispers as stillness falls once more.

The selkie maiden huddles in the bottom of the boat, her seal-skin crumpled over her knees. Her beautiful face is white.

I nearly tumble on my face in my eagerness to reach her. My nerves are tingling, my movements clumsy as I take her hands. "You're safe, Síofra. He's gone." I squeeze gently, rubbing warmth into the chilled flesh. "You're safe, my lady."

Síofra raises her brown eyes to me. "You drew blood from him, Jamie." Her hushed voice holds wonder. "One of your own kind."

My gaze catches on my knife, its blade mottled with crimson. A tremor runs through me at the memory of my cold hard anger, but there's no shame in it. I know what I did. I'd do it again.

I look squarely at Síofra. "He's not my kind."

"You don't understand, Jamie!" She shakes her head frantically. Wet hair slips to veil her face. "You made an enemy! You can't go home to your village after this!"

Home. The word conjures up a bleak picture…a cold bed, cold porridge, cold silence, and regular whippings when I don't sell enough fish to fill Uncle's pockets. My village is no true home. It's a place I've always longed to leave.

A crooked grin tugs my mouth. "Maybe it's time I went off to seek my fortune."

"Because of me?" Síofra wrings her hands. "This is all my fault! I've cursed you! I never should have come ashore!"

"Don't say that," I murmur.

With cautious fingers, I brush her curls aside. Even soaked with salt water, the auburn waves are soft to the touch. A thrill races through me.

Her cheek is bare now, exposed to the silver ocean light. Hardly daring to breathe, I cup my palm over the smooth curve.

The selkie maid is very still. Her eyes dart to me like the sun peeping from behind a cloud.

"Síofra, you have shown me more kindness today than my village has given me in many months." My thumb strokes her silken cheek. "Your coming was a gift, not a curse."

Pink creeps into her skin. "Jamie," she begins.

"You asked me to dance with you, my lady." My voice trembles, but I steady it with a quick breath. "Can I ask you to kiss me?"

Síofra swallows, licking her lips. "Jamie, you don't understand."

"Don't understand what?"

"Humans and selkies…we're not…" She flushes deeper red. "We're not the same."

"Not the same? Don't be daft!" Hot anger roils through me. "I don't want us to be the same, Síofra! I just want *you!*"

"Aye, you want me *now!* Will you still want me in a year? A month? A week?" Síofra jerks away from my touch, eyes ablaze. "How long until you tire of my wild ways and wish you'd found a meek village lass to do your bidding, like other men?"

"I'll never tire of you!" The fire in me burns higher, hotter, scorching the air between us. *"I'm not one of those men!"*

Silence vibrates as we glare at each other.

It hurts, being angry with Síofra. Tears sting my eyes. My sight goes blurry. Blindly, I reach out.

My palm brushes her smooth cheek as her arm catches my waist, pulling me close.

Relief overwhelms me. I choke on a sob. Síofra's embrace tightens around me. She crushes my nose against her neck. The milky freshness of her skin mingles with the bitter tang of my tears.

"Jamie?" Síofra's frantic voice crowds my ear. "Jamie, what's wrong? Why are you weeping?"

"Nothing's wrong." I wriggle free, beaming at her through my tears. Her face swims in my vision, shining pink and glorious. "Kiss me, my lady."

She does...

Shyly at first, but soon with an eagerness that matches my own. A wildness that speaks to the sea in her blood. She captures me with her sweet lips, claims me with every fresh kiss. My mouth tingles. My pulse throbs. My whole body begs for more. I clasp her neck with urgent fingers, digging deep into her forest of curls.

After all, the sea sings in my veins, too.

The waves lap against the boat, rocking us gently. The cool breeze riffles through my hair.

Too soon, Síofra draws back. Reluctantly, I loosen my hold. She presses her palms to her burning cheeks, a throaty giggle escaping her.

"What did I tell you, Síofra?" My grin threatens to crack my face in two. "Your coming was a gift, not a curse."

With an effort, Síofra collects herself. "This is no time for foolishness, Jamie. We can't stay here!" Her eyes grow wide, earnest. "The other men from the village might find us—"

"I won't let them near you." I slip an arm around her waist.

"I was *going* to say," Síofra pushes on, trying not to laugh as I nuzzle her neck, "I know a secret island where we can be safe."

I kiss her, slow and sure, murmuring my next words into her lips. "Lead the way, my lady."

Deep Blue

Annee Clark

He expected the water to be cold. A cold that would crush every other thought from his mind. The kind that could freeze his lungs into glass and shatter them.

Instead, it was a blanket, wrapping him whole. Able to swallow him up in its silken embrace. It coaxed him to just give in, to let himself be dragged under.

It was the humming, he realized too soon, that lulled him into comfort even in the sea's icy clutches.

A voice like that could make anything bearable.

A siren's song could charm the grim reaper, could stop death in its tracks.

When the siren poked her head above the surface, the humming seemed to tear a path straight to the overboard pirate, skewering him to the spot.

He didn't want it to end.

Their eyes met. Hers, as golden and glittering as the stars above them. Her porcelain skin glistened in the moonlight.

The humming stopped; the pirate returned to himself all at once.

It *was* cold. The bite of it stole the air from his lungs—or maybe that was just the sight of her.

The pirate scrambled for his sword, yanking it from its scabbard, but the water's chill left his bones so heavy.

The weapon slipped from his numb fingers and sank.

He cursed and dipped beneath the water, craning for his blade to no avail. When he surfaced, the siren's lovely face was mere inches from his. He jolted but couldn't force himself to move away.

Beautiful was too dull a word to describe her. Too meager. It spoke nothing of the sharp edges of her, of the way the water bent around her nimble fingers and beaded on her lips. Golden hair spun silver and haloed by the moon as if its divinity bled over the very essence of her.

He couldn't stop staring.

She looked to be around his age, a mere seventeen, though he could have been off. Surely time wouldn't dare touch such an ethereal creature as her.

Above him, his shipmates laughed and jeered, bidding the siren to drown the poor sod who'd dared to defy his crew, as they steered the ship away. Brazenly certain that throwing her a bone, a metaphorical lamb of sacrifice, would keep them safe from the monsters of the deep.

The pirate shivered.

And the siren *smiled*. "You are not built for these waters, human."

Her speaking voice was a song of its own. It rolled over him like the waves at his back. She continued, "Your people cast you overboard like the guts they chum the water with. Does that make me the shark, dear cabin boy?"

The pirate finally had the sense to back away from her in the water, for all the good that might do him. "I do think I'd feel safer if you were a shark, miss," he admitted, voice choked in a salty rasp.

The siren's laughter was musical. She curved in the water, circling. He stole a glance at her tail, sleek and strong and as golden as the sun that pooled within her eyes.

"*Miss*. So formal coming from a human, especially a pirate. Your kind have no manners." He felt her lips brush his ear. "Wouldn't you rather call me a beast? Monster? Mustn't I be a devilish creature for daring to be beautiful, for tempting your kind so?"

The pirate released a shuddering breath. "These are your waters. The ocean, your home. Some might wager that dying at sea is a risk we ocean-lovers take when sailing her deep blue."

She hummed, arcing in the water to face him again, the waves of her hair framing the sculpt of her cheeks like a perfect painting. "Was it worth it?"

For even a moment on the endless, swelling sea, ever chasing the horizon? He didn't have to think. "Aye."

The siren's eyes narrowed. "Was it not but a week ago your lowly crew tried to capture me in your nets? As if the waters are not ours but yours to raid and cull?"

"I..." The cold rendered him stiff and sodden, the fatigue tugging him under a tumbling wave. When his head bobbed above the surface again, his breathing was labored.

The siren's head cocked like that of a curious bird. Her fluid movements carved through the water, closing the distance between them; she rested a hand over his racing heart.

The cabin boy closed his eyes. "Do what you must. I know better than to invade a home without consequence."

A clawed hand gripped his vest, holding him upright in the water when another wave tried to drag him under. Her fingers flexed. "No fight left in the pretty pirate boy? I could drown you."

He smiled slightly. "If I am to die in Deep Blue, I'll count it payment to her for allowing me to travel across her billowing waters."

The siren's eyes flashed. "In what way did you betray your pirate friends for them to abandon you to the likes of me?"

The cabin boy met her glowing gaze. "I freed the fair siren maiden they tried to pluck from the sea. It took them a week to determine it was I who cut the ropes. They thought if I 'fancied you' so much, it'd be only fair if you had me."

When he had first seen the siren heaved from her beloved sea in a tangle of nets, fated to be grounded upon the deck amongst greasy wooden floorboards, his stomach bottomed out. To keep her there would be as deplorable as dragging a star down from the sky to pin it to the sand.

He'd sliced the pulley ropes and watched her escape back into the water.

The siren's eyes narrowed. "You lie."

His teeth began to chatter. All he could focus on was the searing cold immobilizing his limbs. He closed his eyes again. "I do not. If you are going to kill me, please at least sing as you do it, yeah?"

The lyrical noise of the waves crashing and towing was all that broke the sober silence.

Then, the siren began to sing. The pirate allowed the melody to tug him into oblivion, filling his veins with honey and warmth once more.

He woke up on the beach, hours later. The sun was rising, spilling its light across his beloved horizon.

It reminded him of the gold in her eyes.

A Wish and a Choice

Hannah Carter

Whether on land or sea, Lady Ambrosia knew there to be one undisputed fact that remained true: women always had to finish the wars men start.

Lady Ambrosia's inky octopus tentacles slithered across the little white-haired mermaid's form and lifted her chin while she seized on the bottom of the ocean floor. "You failed me," the Sea Witch hissed. "You are my legs and ears on the surface, and you failed. You had three days to kill the king of Iylamor. I think that is more than generous enough."

The mermaid coughed. Green blood drifted out of her mouth, and the tides swept it away. "King Cyrillus didn't do anything wrong. His kingdom is peaceful. And he has a son."

"I didn't ask you to philosophize." A tentacle wrapped around the mermaid's throat and tightened. The chit gasped and clawed at the soft, supple surface. "I told you to assassinate that man, or my magic would kill you."

The mermaid's eyes flickered over to the shelf where the antidote to Lady Ambrosia's poison rested. The red liquid frothed and bubbled inside the corked bottle like a turbulent, crimson sea. "I won't kill an innocent man. My parents may have owed you for the magic you gifted them, but I refuse to be in your servitude if that is what you want as repayment."

"You act as if you have a choice." Lady Ambrosia drew the girl closer. "I already sent another girl to assassinate him, and she's surfacing right now. The king of Iylamor will die regardless of who holds the knife. I've been paid by Briglen's monarch to end the dispute over the sea border, and I always keep my word." Lady Ambrosia plucked a dagger made of cerulean sea glass from the table next to her.

The mermaid choked and writhed. Her fluke knocked over an empty cauldron and the coral stand next to it. A book of spells drifted down, its seaweed pages fluttering in the currents.

The girl's blue eyes burned as if they possessed a fire that would incinerate her mistress. "I don't know what game you're playing, but you're going to get caught." Her voice came out pained; flecks of blood punctuated every syllable. "I hope you choke on your own machinations."

Lady Ambrosia pressed the dagger against the breast of the mermaid. "And *I* hope your sister isn't quite as mouthy as you. She'll be your replacement in my ranks."

The traitor jerked and cried out, unable to move without upsetting her grievous injuries. Ah. So Lady Ambrosia had found the soft underbelly of this white-haired girl. Those fiery eyes widened, and the Sea Witch wondered if a cold rush of fear might extinguish this mer's inner flame.

"No! Don't you *dare* touch Wisteria!" the mermaid hissed.

"Your family still owes me, and you couldn't pay their debt. How sad."

"No!" the girl screeched. She tried to claw at Lady Ambrosia's face, but the Sea Witch shoved the dagger into the mermaid's heart. Her eyes widened, and the water turned emerald around them as rivulets of blood coiled into the tide. The fire in the girl's eyes dulled to a smolder, a single ember holding onto a spark of resentment. "You're a *monster*, Ambrosia."

"No." Lady Ambrosia leaned in until her lips touched the mermaid's ears. "I'm a Sea Witch, love." She yanked her knife out of the girl's chest and set the body free to drift in the water. Even if that hadn't been a fatal blow, the poison in the mer's body would soon do its work. From the darkened corners of the grotto, other girls poked their heads out of crevices, quiet.

"Remember this moment, girls." Lady Ambrosia turned around and stared at each face in turn. "No one can betray me and live to tell the tale."

"Yes, Lady Ambrosia," a few of them murmured. Others bobbed their heads in agreement; a handful watched in horror as the corpse floated away.

"Good. Until your contracts are repaid in full, do your jobs for me and no one will be hurt." With that, the Sea Witch propelled herself out of the grotto and sealed the exit behind her with a spell.

Now, to locate a certain little mermaid.

Lady Ambrosia had gone up to Witch Rock today.

Wisteria held her breath and squeezed her eyes shut for exactly thirty seconds. Her heart echoed inside her ears, but she held on. Logically, she *knew* her little rituals didn't affect the outcome of anything. But the modicum of control they gave her over her tumultuous existence gave her the fortitude to get up every day.

Witch Rock days meant that Lady Ambrosia had a customer. Customers meant assassinations. Hence, the ritual: if Wisteria didn't want to be picked for an assassination today, she had to hold her breath and close her eyes for exactly thirty seconds. After that, she'd be able to suck in another glorious breath of oxygen-rich water.

Twenty-eight, twenty-nine...thirty.

Just in time.

The Sea Witch swam back into the grotto, propelled by her long black octopus tentacles. "Well, girls. This is certainly an interesting turn of events."

Wisteria fingered the edge of a scale on her gold-and-black tail and flicked her fluke back and forth.

"Perhaps some of you remember, about ten years ago, Briglen paid me to assassinate the king of Iylamor. The job was carried through, though one of my girls betrayed me and was killed for it." Lady Ambrosia stopped by the cauldron and flicked the pages of her spellbook.

Oh, no.

Wisteria sucked in a breath. She couldn't close her eyes and risk inciting Lady Ambrosia's wrath, but the rules of her mind said if she couldn't do that, she could hold her breath for forty seconds and it would reinforce the magic. Wisteria wouldn't be chosen.

But she knew all too well about the Iylamor debacle.

Maybe she should hold her breath until her lungs cried out for air, just to be sure.

"Unfortunately, Iylamor did not fall. My client thought the death of their beloved king would crush the little nation's rebellion and give Briglen access to the seaboard. However, Iylamor has proved scrappier than anticipated." Lady Ambrosia emptied a purple vial into the cauldron, and a puff of smoke wafted upward. "Remember my reputation, girls. Women always have to end wars that men start." Her black eyes locked with Wisteria's golden ones. "This is the only war I have failed to end."

Wisteria swallowed. Lady Ambrosia could not fight against the rituals. Everything would be all right. Except... Wisteria's shoulders ached where she'd been tense for so long.

"Iylamor's prince has now come of age and will be crowned king. He is the only son of the former king, and pressure to produce an heir to make sure that the royal line continues has pushed him to make a hasty decision."

Lungs. Burning. Must. Breathe.

Wisteria gave in and gasped—and prayed it wouldn't break the ritual's magic.

"If we can kill him before he finds a wife, then we can eliminate the rest of the royal bloodline. Our client will be able to end this war, and my good reputation will be redeemed." Lady Ambrosia's eyes swept the room. "One of you will infiltrate the ball and attempt to win the prince's heart. When his guard is down, you are to kill him."

The room fell quiet. Wisteria held her breath again. She knew it from her head down to her tailbones: everything hinged on this moment. If she broke the silence, it would be her.

Heartbeats passed. She prayed that small breath she'd taken moments before wouldn't doom her. If she gave in now, it'd be a disaster.

Her lungs screamed: *breathe!*

One quick inhale wouldn't hurt.

She gulped down one frantic grab for air.

"Wisteria," Lady Ambrosia said with a vindictive smile. "This mission is personal for you. After all, your sister refused to kill this prince's father. Because of *her* failure, I had to capture you."

Wisteria whipped her head around. Her white hair drifted around her face and obscured her view of the Sea Witch. "Primrose didn't—" She cut herself off and cursed that one bit of familial love which might have just sealed her fate.

Lady Ambrosia cracked a clam and tossed it into her cauldron. Her hand circled over the concoction, and she began a low incantation. The atmosphere in the room thickened—it was hard to tell if that was because of Wisteria's perception or the magic, though. But every breath felt like an orca whale settling in her lungs.

"You think she didn't do anything wrong? She's the reason you're in this mess, little mermaid." Lady Ambrosia leaned forward. "She'd almost repaid your parents' debts, you know. She almost had her freedom. But she chose to save some poor stranger and sacrifice *you* instead."

Wisteria's cheeks flushed. "But..."

"So I'll tell you what." The Sea Witch's hand stilled, mid-flourish. "If you murder the crown prince, we'll consider your family's debt paid. You'll be free to do whatever you want."

Free.

The word spun in Wisteria's head until she felt dizzy. *Free.* The thought alone tasted sweet on her tongue. She hadn't been free in ten years. Lady Ambrosia controlled when her girls woke, ate, slept. When they could leave the grotto—which only happened when she needed them to kill someone. It had been a decade since Wisteria had seen the sun...

"One last job. Make up for your sister's failure, and I'll consider your debts paid." Lady Ambrosia gestured to the cauldron.

Wisteria's tongue felt heavy. One of the Sea Witch's tentacles snaked its way over and circled her wrist. With one jerk, she stood by Lady Ambrosia's side next to the cauldron.

"You know the rules," her mistress hissed. "This poison will give you legs, but without the antidote, it will kill you in three days. If you fail me, I'll let you die." Her claw-like fingers seized Wisteria's face. "Get him alone by any means, and once you do, you will kill him. Do you understand?"

The ocean stole any tears that Wisteria might have shed. The Sea Witch wasn't offering her a choice on the mission, but if she had, would Wisteria actually say *no* to killing a stranger and gaining her freedom? She'd never been selected for a mission before—what if she never got this opportunity again?

Of course, if she had a *real* choice, she'd pick freedom without anyone's death. But that would never be an option offered to her.

Lady Ambrosia scooped up a ladle of the poisonous potion. The brew tasted sour on Wistera's tongue and burned as she choked it down. The fire only seemed to intensify on its journey; it felt like hot, liquid iron inside her. It didn't just stop at her stomach—it twisted all the way down to the tip of her tail until it split even her scales.

She doubled over and clutched her abdomen. Lady Ambrosia's tentacle tightened around Wisteria's wrist as the Sea Witch rocketed out of the grotto. Up and up they went—if only Wisteria could appreciate the way the water lightened the closer they drew to the surface, the towering coral, the multicolored fish. But she could only cry out as the fire intensified. She'd seen enough of the other girls' transformations to know that she wouldn't die, but apparently, she could creep up to the brink of death and still live.

Her lungs twisted and tightened, too. The oxygen underwater seemed to feel thicker, as though she was drinking it instead of breathing it, and Wisteria held her breath and pretended this was merely a ritual.

The surface inched closer.

They broke through the waves, and Lady Ambrosia tossed Wisteria onto Witch Rock. Wisteria yelped as pebbles scraped her body while she rolled. She crashed into a jutting peak and lay there, disoriented, wishing she could claw the flame out of her body.

Her scales dried up even faster in the sun until the only sign she'd even been a mer at all were the tiny gold-and-black flakes up and down her legs. She'd have to hide those when she entered the palace.

But—Triton, those legs. Wisteria poked them each in turn. She tried to associate each new part with something she was familiar with: the toes were her fluke; maybe she could wiggle them. The knobby knees were awkward. Bending these legs just felt *wrong*.

"Yes, yes. They're a fine pair of legs," Lady Ambrosia snapped. "A fine pair of man-catching legs."

"Men find them attractive?" Wisteria wrinkled her nose. "But...why?"

"You will find there are a lot of strange things people find attractive." Lady Ambrosia cackled, but Wisteria couldn't see why. Her face flushed. She would never survive among these humans.

"Why don't *you* just go? You know more about the land-dwellers than me, and you actually want this boy dead." Wisteria wrapped her arms around herself and shivered.

The Sea Witch clucked her tongue. "Why would I poison myself? Mer aren't supposed to have legs. Whenever you're on land, not only will you have the pain from my magic in you, but every step will be torturous." She snickered. "Why do you think I need slaves like you in the first place?"

Lady Ambrosia turned away, but Wisteria let out a sharp cry. "Wait! Won't I need clothes?" Her voice trembled. She only wore her seaweed-and-seashell corset, but that would dry up if left in the sun for too long.

"Well, darling, I dare say that being naked as a blue fish might be one way to win the prince's heart, but you'd never get past the palace guards." Lady Ambrosia waved her hand. "But don't worry. I'll take care of that. After all, you can't go to the ball without a magnificent gown." The Sea Witch's dark eyes twinkled—an unnerving sight. "I'll go get it for you." She smirked as she dipped lower into the waves. "Just consider me your fairy godmother."

For hours, the sun scorched Wisteria's skin and eyes as she baked on Witch Rock. Not only did the heat pain her, but her first attempts to walk ended in bloodied knees and pebbles in her hands. But eventually, the moon glided into the sky while Wisteria stumbled into the palace. A curl swung into her face, and she tucked it behind her ear. Lady Ambrosia had styled her hair into an elegant updo, secured with starfish, coral, and pearls. A gold-and-black ballgown—one that perfectly matched Wisteria's tail—trailed past her feet and covered the remnants of the scales on her legs.

Wisteria winced with every footfall, though—and not just because mer were not supposed to have legs and every step was like a knife jabbing into her heels. Lady Ambrosia had bequeathed Wisteria with a pair of beautiful sea glass slippers, made for aesthetics—or perhaps some kind of cruel joke—and not for practicality.

A matching dagger pressed against her waist.

Wisteria took to counting the steps to distract herself from the pain she bore in this form, from the pain the mission birthed inside her.

Twenty-eight, twenty-nine...twenty-nine?

Did they not even have the decency to end on thirty?

Wisteria turned around and recounted. No, she'd calculated it correctly. Twenty-nine. An evil, odd number.

Her mission was doomed.

No, she mustn't think like that. The poison still churned inside of her and sent flashes of heat throughout her body. She whirled back around like she wanted to leave her thoughts behind with those odd-numbered steps. Her mission would succeed, and she'd get her freedom, and—

"*Ack!*" Wisteria crashed into a figure and reeled backward—right toward the stairs.

How ironic.

Those blasted evil stairs would spell her doom after all.

"Careful!" The person she'd hit grabbed her wrist and jerked her forward. Wisteria collided with their chest and wrapped her arms around their neck.

"I'm so sorry," she breathed. "The—the steps. They had *twenty-nine...*"

The person chortled, a low, raspy sound, and Wisteria realized for the first time she'd stumbled straight into a boy. "Twenty-nine? Unacceptable. I shall have the palace servants start mixing the concrete immediately."

Wisteria chuckled, but it felt more nervous than sincere.

The boy leaned in closer. She estimated him to be around her age, nineteen or twenty, though he could have been older. "You look anxious. Don't worry; I am, too." He smirked. "I always feel like a fish out of water at these events."

Wisteria swallowed. What ritual did she have in her arsenal to protect her secret? She'd never expected a casual remark to toe so close to the shoreline. "I'm sure I don't know what you mean."

"Don't you?" The boy offered his arm to her, a more formal invitation. "Hmm. Pardon me if I mistook you for someone else. I thought you were the sister of a dear friend of mine." His dark eyes roamed over her hair before he led her inside the large palace doors. "Someone with hair as white as snow and eyes that blazed with a blue fire."

The light of the golden chandelier blinded Wisteria.

Hair as white as snow.

A full orchestra overwhelmed her ears, and the *people*! After growing up in a grotto that had fifteen girls at most, the crowd seemed suffocating.

Eyes that blazed with a blue fire.

The scales on her legs itched.

White hair. Blazing blue eyes.

Wisteria swayed as the marble parquet floor swirled. "...Prim?"

Secured in the boy's office, Wisteria felt a tad better. She sipped the pink punch he'd obtained for her as she studied this stranger in the white-and-gold doublet.

"First, let me introduce myself." He leaned closer and locked his fingers together. "I think it's only fitting you know the name of your target." He grinned, his ivory-colored teeth dazzling against his ebony skin. "I'm Prince Aurelius, but you can call me Ari. I always find introductions help to foster that interpersonal assassin-and-target bond."

Wisteria choked on her drink and spluttered.

Aurelius'—Ari's—smirk deepened. "Ah, so you *do* have a sense of humor. That's good. I'm afraid I'd feel even worse if my murderer was a stick in the mud. Or a stick in the sand, whatever you mermaids prefer." He paused. "I *am* assuming you're a mermaid, after all. I mean, I haven't seen the scales on your legs, but to ask you to flash anything above your ankle might be a little *too* personal."

For the first time, Wisteria made eye contact and let her gaze linger. "How can you be so friendly to a mer that's supposed to kill you?"

"Easy." Ari relaxed against his seat and used his toe to rock back and forth. "Because you're Prim's sister. Wisteria, right? She called you Wish."

It'd been years since anyone had used that nickname. Tears bubbled up in Wisteria's eyes, and she swiped them away. How odd that the ocean didn't do so for her immediately. "Yes, but—"

"But nothing. Prim spoke highly of you. She knew one day you'd probably be sent to land to finish the job she wouldn't do. You have no idea how long I've been looking for you."

Wisteria snorted. As if she didn't keep track of numbers in her head for everything in her life. "Ten years?"

"Ah, well, all right. I suppose you do." Ari chuckled and let his seat *thump* down. "So I'm very sorry if I seemed forward, accosting you right as you entered the ball. We didn't even get a chance to dance or pretend to flirt before you stabbed me. I've robbed you of that chance because I was so eager to meet you."

Wisteria finished her latest count that she'd started while he spoke. "You have an even twelve buttons on your coat, so I suppose that's a point for me hearing you out. Frankly, if you'd had eleven, I probably would have stabbed you right here."

Ari put his hand over his heart. "As you should." He shifted his weight again and tapped his chest. "Listen. I know I'm in no place to ask you not to murder me, but I'd like for you to at least consider a truce. Possibly even an alliance, in Prim's honor."

"You don't—"

Ari held up a hand. "I know. I'm just a human. I don't know anything about what you've been through. But there's someone who did." He stood up and moved to the mahogany desk that sat in the back of the room. For a few seconds, he shuffled papers around until he pulled out a yellowed envelope sealed with red ink. "Before she left, Prim left this note for my father. When he died, it fell to me." Ari crossed the floor to Wisteria and offered it to her. "Her instructions were to give it to you whenever you came to Iylamor."

Wisteria's hand trembled as she reached for the letter. Her heart stuttered. Hidden inside the envelope was the last message her sister ever left for her. Did she dare open it?

She placed her cup on the table in front of her.

Took a deep, steadying breath and held it for ten seconds.

Starving for this one scrap of hope, Wisteria tore into the letter.

Dearest Wish,

I don't know how long has passed between me penning these words and you reading them, but I expect you've grown into a beautiful young woman by now. I suspect I won't get to see it happen, because I'm going to disobey Ambrosia. Even now, I can feel the poison in my stomach, burning me alive. But I'll tell you a secret.

Sometimes you have to make the hard choices.

I know it seems like we haven't had any voice since Mother and Father fell into Ambrosia's debt. I'd like to think they naively didn't know the consequences of their actions. It helps me to focus on the good memories and not the resentment that might turn me bitter. But here we are: slaves to the Sea Witch.

More than likely, you are here to assassinate either King Cyrillus or Prince Ari. The easy thing to do would be to kill them. But they are good people. Friends. They are tired of this senseless war over their seaboard, and they have done nothing to start it. That is why I have chosen to side with them—but the time has come to make your own choice.

Your choices boil down to this: you may obey Ambrosia, kill your target, and return for the antidote. You will live this way. You may even get your freedom. That reward seems just sick and twisted enough for the Sea Witch to propose it.

Or you can try and end this senseless war once and for all. After all...women always have to finish the wars men start. Use your three days to seek peace and face the death of disobedience.

It will not be easy. As I write this, my three days are almost up. I have failed, but I am leaving you all my information to give you a headstart.

Iylamor's fate is in your hands—but so is your own.

For once, do what <u>you</u> believe is right. Not what Ambrosia or myself tells you. All I want is for you to be free to choose.

Love,

Prim

Primrose's careful handwriting blurred as Wisteria drank in each precious quill stroke. If someone offered her Ari's entire castle or these short paragraphs written by Primrose's hand, Wisteria would choose the letter every time. She hugged it to her chest as though that might make the words absorb into her skin and bring life to her numb, aching heart.

Ari leaned over her shoulder. He smelled sweet—a scent she couldn't place, but one so far removed from the sea that it felt comforting. "Will you help Iylamor end the war, Wish?"

She sniffled. Death followed every decision, but at least she could decide who would face that death.

"I will," she whispered. "You have my word."

Ari clasped her shoulder. "And you have my word—as a prince and as a new friend. I promise that I will not let you die. If we fail at the end of this, you can have my life or I'll go down and get the antidote for you. I've done deep dives before; I'm quite skilled. It only seems fair that we have equal things at stake."

"What?" Wisteria whipped around. "No! You can't—why would you—you're a *prince*—"

"So? That's a title. It doesn't give me more worth than you have." Ari propped his hip up on the edge of the table. "You're offering to give up everything for a kingdom that isn't yours. Why can I not make a similar sacrifice?"

"But...but..." Wisteria stammered.

Ari grinned again. "Don't protest. Can't waste any precious time." He reached for her hand. "Ready to see what we've discovered so far?"

Ari's library was better than any figment of Wisteria's imagination. Tall shelves lined every wall, so huge that everyone save a giant would have to use one of the several ladders around the room to reach the top. A huge window stretched from roof to floor, and moonlight wafted in and cast long shadows.

Wisteria gaped at all these new wonders—especially the fireplace. She dared not get too close, but she sat hypnotized by the way the flames danced until Ari shook her shoulder.

"Look. Right here is all our research." Ari gestured to a pile on the table. "Siren songs intrigued Prim. For years, they've been known to start wars or lure people to their deaths. But she wondered if there might be one that would do the opposite. You know—why did siren songs *have* to be evil?"

Wisteria glanced down at a drawing of a mermaid stretched out on a rock. *Lorelei's Song*, the caption read. She picked up a scrap of paper inked with two fearsome mer: *Scylla's Song* under one and *Charybdis' Song* under another.

"I recognize these names." Wisteria tapped the page. "Lady Ambrosia has books about them."

Ari tilted his head. "What do her books say about them?"

"Just that their songs would lure people to their deaths. But they don't look like this." Wisteria traced her finger over their tails. "They look terrifying in her books. More monster than mer. More like..." She swallowed. "Lady Ambrosia. With tentacles."

Ari's eyes lit up, and he tugged another book out of the stack. "Like this, maybe?"

Wisteria bit off a scream. Even more grotesque than the drawing in Lady Ambrosia's collection, this sketch of Scylla no longer had a tail—just over a dozen snakes that writhed from various parts of her body. Instead of teeth, fangs filled her mouth, and she had an unearthly pallor to her skin like a bloated corpse.

"This one was drawn by the author, right before he killed her," Ari said. "Or so the legend goes."

Wisteria turned between the two pictures: one, a mer youth, and the other, a terrifying demon. "So Scylla writes a song, and somehow, shifts from this to that." She tapped each rendition in turn. "But what happened in between?"

Ari gestured to the library. "Welcome to what I've been trying to piece together for years."

Wisteria clucked her tongue. "Well, I guess we better get started, then. We only have until midnight before my legs disappear for the day." She glanced at the grandfather clock. Four hours and seventeen minutes. "And you best talk quickly."

Ari flashed a smile. "That's my specialty."

For four hours, songs and legends blurred before Wisteria's eyes. It seemed every siren of legend had a special song. Songs for whirlpools, songs for seduction, songs for hypnotizing. But not a single tune seemed conducive to their situation.

She rubbed her fingers along her temple and sighed. "What if I hypnotize the whole army?"

Ari yawned. "Can you hypnotize the whole Briglen army at once? I've only read of a siren affecting a few people at most."

"I...don't know. Lady Ambrosia doesn't teach us anything exactly. But she's got lots of books in her grotto." Oddly, Wisteria had never counted them all, so she didn't have an exact tally. "Maybe tonight when I go back I can look."

"Will she be mad if she catches you? It doesn't seem like it takes a lot for her to resort to murder."

Wisteria swallowed. The poison churned inside her, and she put a fist against her middle to steady herself. "I'm a dead girl anyway in two days." Forty-eight hours and fifteen minutes, to be exact.

"I told you. I'm not letting you die." Ari's eyes flickered to her fist. "What's wrong?"

"The poison." Wisteria flinched. "It's nothing."

Ari scowled. "Maybe I should just kill Ambrosia and be done with it. Then I'll get you the antidote, and—"

"And how do you expect to fight underwater? Surrounded by assassins who will kill you with one word from her? And Lady Ambrosia is dangerous in her own right; she just can't come on land." Or more like she *wouldn't*. The thought made Wisteria's cheeks flush. Yes, why *would* the Sea Witch subject herself to pain and poison when she could inflict it upon girls in her debt?

Ari grumbled and leaned back in his seat, his feet propped up on the table. Wisteria could imagine him tilting back too far and crashing to the floor, snapping his neck—

"Fine. But you'll be back tomorrow, right?" Ari's voice broke her out of a dangerous reverie.

"I'll be back until one of us is dead in two days," Wisteria replied.

They bid goodbye a few minutes later, and Wisteria pushed her way through the throng of dancers in the ballroom. The air felt stifling and choked her—so many humans, so little space, even in a grand castle.

Fire spread throughout her body again, but nowhere worse than in her feet; it felt like knives jabbing her with every step as she escaped outside.

She gladly kicked off the dreaded sea glass slippers at the shoreline and stumbled into the foam. The clock in the castle tower pealed. Wisteria felt each gong inside her heart, from one to twelve. Closing her eyes, she gave in to the magic and let it consume her, transforming her back into a mermaid.

She fell face-first into the waves and almost kissed them in relief.

Mer simply were not made to walk on two feet. And that was none more apparent than when she turned around to hide her shoes so no one would steal them.

Blood stained the bottom of the sea glass slippers.

Notes and lyrics filled Wisteria's gaze. She flipped through the weathered pages of *The Mer Hymnal*. This book housed every song she'd read about with Ari for the last two nights, plus more. Songs to poison. Songs to kill. Songs of death, destruction, and tragedy.

Two hundred and five of them, and not a single one could help.

Her own poison churned inside her stomach. Pain seized her, and she dropped to the cavern floor, one hand clinging to the podium where she'd propped the hymnal. Wisteria gasped and squeezed her eyes closed. Numbers swirled in her head—she'd passed the second night of the ball, which meant she had less than twenty-four hours to live.

She couldn't sleep. Couldn't stop. She needed a song of peace, a song of something *nice...*

A tentacle wrapped around Wisteria's waist.

She shrieked as Lady Ambrosia hoisted her upwards. Wisteria flapped her tail and punched at Lady Ambrosia's grasp, but that only made the pressure tighten on her midsection.

"Fighting back? That's not like you, Wisteria." Lady Ambrosia slithered out of the shadows. The glow stones cast eerie reflections on her face. "What are you looking for, dearie?"

"I—I..." Wisteria swallowed. Too many excuses caught inside of her throat until a half-truth spilled out. "I want to write my own song. To...kill Ar—the prince. I'll sing it at the ball, and..." Her voice trailed off, mind unable to formulate anything else.

"No need. You have the knife, don't you?" Lady Ambrosia drew Wisteria closer. Another tentacle wrapped around Wisteria's fluke. Visions of being torn apart fluttered through her head, and she squirmed more.

"But—I'm a mermaid. I want to sing. I want..." A third of Lady Ambrosia's eight tentacles wrapped around Wisteria's throat.

"Don't get a smart head, Wisteria," Lady Ambrosia hissed. "Don't think you can somehow cheat your fate. You are *mine*, and you will do as I say."

Wisteria choked and gagged. If she held her breath, could she survive? The pressure grew tighter, tighter, *tighter*, a noose around her neck.

"You want to sing? Go ahead and give it a try." Lady Ambrosia chuckled. "Here's what no one told me, *dearie*. When a siren sings, she has to give up a part of herself. I used to be like you, with a pretty little tail. But the more I sang, the more I lost." A dark smile flickered across Lady Ambrosia's face. "The more all the sirens of old lost in pursuit of power. Like my mistress, who lost her life when she got a little too ambitious and tried to turn a whole country into seafoam."

Spots danced in Wisteria's vision until Lady Ambrosia dropped her. Wisteria gasped, her hands going to her neck.

How did they write the songs, though? The silent question died on Wisteria's tongue, joined by many others. *Can a siren write a song for good? Can I help people with my voice? What would I have to give up? I don't care about power. I just want to help Ari stop this war. Help him stop you.*

"You have one more day to kill him. I hope your schemes are going well." Lady Ambrosia grasped Wisteria's white hair and dragged her out of the room. "Your life and freedom hang in the balance, my little mermaid."

The sun painted the horizon brilliant hues of pink, orange, and yellow as it set beyond the line of the sea.

What a beautiful day to die.

Wisteria pulled herself from the ocean. She could feel Lady Ambrosia's steely gaze on her back. Did she suspect Wisteria's betrayal? Even if she did, it didn't matter. Wisteria's three days would be up at midnight, and either she or Ari would be dead.

Pulling on the ballgown once more, Wisteria trudged into the palace.

Ari waited inside. "Wish—" His expression fell, and he reached out for her neck. She flinched, though his touch was far more gentle. "What happened?"

"Lady Ambrosia," Wisteria whispered hoarsely. Her eyes dropped. "She caught me snooping."

"You're bruised." Ari tugged her closer—but again, unlike the Sea Witch's gesture from last night, his was tender.

Wisteria sniffed as she rested her head against his chest. They shouldn't do this, not in the ballroom, but how long had it been since someone hugged her? Since Prim was alive—so ten years ago. Ten years since she had had a friend.

"Was she trying to stop you from singing?" Ari asked sharply. "Did you find the song?"

Wisteria shook her head. "No. I didn't find anything."

Ari released her from his hug, but he still held onto her hand as he led her through the throng of people to the library. "We'll think of something. So long as you can sing, so long as you still have your voice, we can do it. I know."

"What can we do? Every famous siren has used their song to murder, and it's transformed them into hideous beasts or killed them. Each legend about them gets worse and worse, and Lady Ambrosia told me last night that the songs corrupt them. Not just their bodies, but their souls as well." Wisteria counted steps as they walked. She needed two for each marble square, and one-hundred-and-four pairs to get to the library. "Even if I kill all your enemies with a powerful song, who's to say I won't just transform into a soulless beast that needs to be murdered?"

"Because…you're you." Ari opened the door for her and pulled out a seat. All their information, the thousands of books, lay open to various pages. "You're sweet and kind and—"

"Doomed." Wisteria took off her slippers. Part of her wanted to throw them in the fire as one final act of rebellion. "And for all we know, Scylla and even Lady Ambrosia might have been wonderful mer before they used their siren songs. Maybe they've just been corrupted by so many murders."

"We still have time." Ari sat down. "Until midnight—"

"What's midnight going to do? There's not enough hours left for us to accomplish anything." Wisteria slammed one of the books shut. "Face it, Ari. I'm doomed. I'm not going to kill you."

"And what good will that do?" Ari snapped. "My father still died even though Prim didn't kill him. Unless we fix this, we're both going to die together."

Wisteria stood up and shoved her seat out from behind her. "You need to run away. Forget Iylamor and save your life."

"You're asking me to abandon my people. To choose myself over them."

"I don't know what else you want!" Wisteria marched over to one of the shelves and read useless spine after useless spine. "We've tried everything. You've had *years*. Every song a siren has ever created has led to death." She curled her fingers up and drove her fist into the wood. "It can't be done. I want to spend my last day making sure that you will be safe."

"So what? You're just going to give up?" Ari stomped closer to her and gripped her shoulders. "We can do it! We're so close—"

"No, we aren't!" Wisteria's fingers itched to touch one more cover. How many had she actually looked at? Had it been an even number? Not that it mattered now. "Give me this one choice, Ari. Please. Ambrosia has taken away my choice, my *voice*, every day of my life. If the only choice I can ever make is whether or not I live or die on my own terms—I won't let her choose when I die. *I* will choose when I die, and for what cause."

Ari withdrew. She glanced at him as he stood by the fireplace, one arm braced on the mantle.

"You can make your choices. I won't stop you." He addressed the flames. "You don't have to look in another book for a siren song."

"I'm sorry. It's—it's for the best." Wisteria sank down to the floor. "We'll get you out of Iylamor, somewhere Lady Ambrosia can't reach."

"I can't do that, though." He lifted his head, and their eyes locked. "I won't abandon my people to face Briglen when they invade. And I won't leave my friends behind."

Wisteria rubbed her forehead. "They can go with you."

"No, they can't." Ari tossed something into the flames that made them crackle. "Not when one of them is set to die in a few hours."

Wisteria jerked her head up. "Wha—*what*? You mean *me*?"

"Who else? I don't make it a habit to go around collecting cursed companions." Ari undid the gilded buttons on his golden vest and tossed it at her. He loosened up the ties on his puffy, fancy shirt next, though he didn't take it off. "And my friend has made her choice. But the thing is, I can make mine, too."

Wisteria's heart thudded. "What—"

But her question went both unheard and unanswered.

"I'm going to get that antidote for you."

"Ari—" Wisteria stood, but the prince had at least two decades of walking experience on her. He darted out of the room before she could even climb to her feet. Still, she hobbled after him, leaving bloodied footprints behind.

She reached the top of the grand staircase and paused. The music swelled as couples danced, all of them oblivious to the impending war, the assassination, Ari's escape.

Wisteria grasped the railing and struggled down the steps, but her hurried pace was too much to handle. Her bloody foot slipped, and her bottom slammed against the marble. Oh—it hurt far worse than a blow like that would have hurt with a tail. She bit her lip and squeezed her eyes shut to hold back the tears.

Ari would die.

It wouldn't matter that she hadn't stabbed him. If he entered the water, entered Lady Ambrosia's turf, the Sea Witch would kill him herself.

Wisteria fled the ballroom, just as Ari had before her. She limped, though, instead of ran, and by the time she reached the shoreline, every part of her ached. She'd left a bloodstained path behind her, an easy target should any of the revelers notice and wonder.

Ari was nowhere to be seen. Just his boots lingered by the shore, still standing even as the tide washed against their toes. It looked like an invisible ghost stood there, glowing in the moonlight.

Four hours until her death. Who knew how many hours until Ari's. What trick would save them now? Holding her breath, counting backward from one hundred? She knew how ridiculous that was, even as her brain longed to latch onto it as a child might hold onto their parent for safety.

Wisteria could only think of one option: she touched her fingers to her lips, kissed them, and placed them against the shoes. She remembered doing the same to her father and mother's coats before they went out—a traditional mer blessing for safety. Back then, rituals had seemed fun, not as desperate as they'd become to her.

Ari would be safe, then. She'd done the ritual, protected him.

Right?

Inhaling deeply, she squirmed out of her dress, crawled into the tide, and let her legs dissolve back into a tail.

She swam off toward Lady Ambrosia's lair.

Blood marred the water before she even came through the mouth of the grotto.

Just inside the cavern, the Sea Witch stood with Ari wrapped in four tentacles. He struggled weakly as blood gushed from a wound on his arm, his face swollen and battered.

But in his hands, he clutched the antidote.

"Ari!" Wisteria screamed as she plunged through her friend's lifeforce.

"Somehow I doubt you sent him down here so that I would have the pleasure of killing him myself," Lady Ambrosia hissed.

"I-I didn't send him down here at all," Wisteria stammered. "He chose to come." Softer, she added, "I told him to run."

Lady Ambrosia scoffed. "You're just like your sister. And I'll be just as glad to be rid of you." She slung Ari and he hit the rock wall and went down, down, down.

How much longer could he hold his breath?

"No, no…" Wisteria darted over, but before she could reach him, Lady Ambrosia's tentacle wrapped around Wisteria's tail. Wisteria screamed as her enslaver jerked her backward.

"I told Briglen that they could attack at the stroke of midnight on the third day. With the prince dead and no heir apparent, Iylamor would be in disarray by then. I do not intend to break this promise." Lady Ambrosia curled another tentacle around Ari's bare ankle and used her other six free ones to propel herself out of the cavern mouth. "I don't think they'll fault me, though, if I offer them the dead prince's body and tell them to attack a few hours earlier."

Wisteria struggled. Beat her fists against Lady Ambrosia. But still, the Sea Witch held on tight. Everything Wisteria did was useless, ineffective—

The sea glass dagger.

Wisteria reached for the dagger attached to her waist. It hadn't been used since Lady Ambrosia first strapped it onto her young assassin, but…

Counting to ten—Wisteria dared not take the time to count higher—she whipped out the weapon and drove it into the tentacle around her fluke.

Lady Ambrosia howled and slowed her ascent. "You little—" Her insult was cut short by another stab. Inky blood filled the waters, but Wisteria writhed free of her bonds. This time, she didn't bother to stab. Quick as a sailfish and just as deadly and pointed, she sliced through the skinniest part of Lady Ambrosia's tentacles. Wisteria severed the one that held Ari and grabbed the now-unconscious prince, their escape hidden amidst the rolling waves of blood.

Faster. Faster. *Faster.*

Lady Ambrosia's howls and curses chased Wisteria to the surface. But the little mermaid crested on a wave and dragged the prince to the shore. As soon as the water was shallow enough, her tail dissolved, leaving her naked in the moonlight once more, save the seaweed corset she wore. She grabbed the blasted ballgown as she passed by it, but she didn't dare put it on until after she and Ari were far enough from the shoreline.

The palace steps—all twenty-nine of them—became their refuge. Wisteria cradled Ari's head and touched his dark, beaten face.

"Ari," she choked out. "Please. Please wake up."

He didn't stir.

"No. No, please. It can't end like this. It just can't." Wisteria shook him a few times, her hysteria mounting inside of her. Her mind struggled to do the math—how long had they been underwater? How long had he been bleeding? How long, how long, how long?

She cradled the injury on his arm, slapped his back, begged, wheedled, thumped his chest.

"Come back!" she screamed when nothing else worked. She could hardly hear her own cries over the growing sounds of the orchestra. Why did they have to play a waltz when their prince lay dying on the palace steps? "Ari, please! I don't want this! *I don't want this!*"

She could almost hear his teasing voice in her head, like they were having another discussion in the library: *then how can you choose differently?*

She didn't have a choice. She couldn't fight death. A siren could only *cause* death with their songs...

Or...

Or maybe all the others had just *chosen* to cause death.

Maybe it was really just as simple as that, if only she'd had faith like Ari all along.

Maybe the answer wasn't in the past, but in the future.

In this moment.

Wisteria opened her mouth and addressed every mer ancestor, every siren—whoever cared enough to listen to a young girl's pleas.

I will give everything for a song of life. A song of healing. Wisteria's Song.

Everything.

Even my voice.

Even my own life.

The first note left Wisteria's mouth. The melody soared, louder than any human singer could achieve, but softer still. Sweeter. Filled with memories of Primrose's love, their parents' care, of hugs and friendly whispers. Wisteria's mind drifted to Ari, to their days and nights in the library. Funny—she'd never gotten to dance with him at the ball, not once.

She imagined what that would have been like and used it to strengthen her song.

The moon glided higher into the sky. The clouds rolled away, but still she sang.

How far away were the Briglen soldiers? Could they hear? Could the people inside the ball hear? What were the limits of a siren song?

She would break them.

I need a song of peace. I need to stop this senseless war. To end the violence in men's hearts.

After all, women always have to finish the wars men start.

She would sing until her voice deserted her, sing until the armies threw down their weapons and went home. She would sing until Ari's eyes opened and met hers once more.

Or, more realistically, she would sing until the poison killed her.

The injury on Ari's arm began to glow.

The skin seemed to stitch itself back together with a golden light. It passed through all of his body, quelled the swelling on his face, and settled in his chest. He gasped and wheezed, his brown eyes fluttering open.

"...Wish...?"

She only smiled. A few tears dripped off her cheeks and onto his, but she couldn't reply.

"Wish..." He sounded hoarse. His eyes widened more, and he jerked. "What time is it? I had it—I had the antidote—"

Did it even matter anymore? She couldn't stop singing. Not until the burning inside her silenced her bones. Ari's skin still glowed, and she didn't want to stop, not until she knew that he would live on, even if she didn't.

People stumbled out of the ballroom. The orchestra had stopped playing, but Wisteria had taken over the music.

"Where is it?" Ari looked at both of his empty hands. He'd been unconscious—maybe even dead—for so long. Wisteria didn't know when he'd lost it or where they could even look.

He shoved away from her and staggered just like she had when she'd been learning to walk.

"Help me!" He turned and addressed the crowd. "Please. There's a red bottle—my friend saved my life, but she's been poisoned. Please help me find the antidote."

A few murmurs went through the crowd. Some people shifted away from her, while others drifted closer to Ari, though hesitantly.

Wisteria's song grew louder as it reached the climax. She tried to shove it farther, prayed that the breeze would carry it to the armies. And, though she couldn't be sure if it was a vision or just a making of her own mind, she could almost see the soldiers as they marched between trees. They halted, turning their faces to the moon.

"Do you hear that?" they whispered to each other. "That song..."

Wisteria could feel the strength in her voice fading, but she couldn't let it die just yet. She imagined herself right there, like one of those feathered creatures—a bird?—on the branches. She would stop their march. She would fill them with love, with understanding. With peace.

"Why are we fighting?"

"Why are we here?"

"Why do we even need this blasted war?"

She smiled and closed her eyes. Now under the waves, down to Lady Ambrosia. The Sea Witch drifted, the whites of her eyesgone red, her wounds bleeding out. She screamed as the music tore at her, and dissonant notes ripped at Wisteria's tune. But they could not kill it. Wisteria turned her attention to the cavern, where the other poor enslaved girls huddled in fear. Wisteria sang louder for them.

They could be free, too. They could sing her song.

They could keep singing it, so that the shores of Iylamor would remain peaceful long after Wisteria died.

Just a few minutes left.

Join me, Wisteria said. *Please.*

"Wisteria?" one hesitant voice asked. Wisteria heard it as if she were in the room with them. "How do we join you?"

Sing. It may require a sacrifice, but I give you a choice. We don't have to suffer under Lady Ambrosia's thumb any longer.

The captured mermaids glanced at each other. Slowly, one of the girls lifted her voice. Then another, then a third.

They created a beautiful harmony that held strong, even when Wisteria's voice wavered.

Her body burned as the poison sank into her bones. Her song faded along with her vision. She rested at the bottom of those twenty-nine steps. Somehow, it felt fitting, to die on an odd number. At least she hadn't been nineteen at her death. Twenty was such a nice, even number.

"Wish!" That was Ari's voice. She could recognize it. Arms held her—were they his?

If they were, he pulled her close to his chest. "Hurry, please! Has anyone found the antidote?"

He sounded choked up.

Did we do it? She tried to ask, but her voice refused to cooperate. It felt like jamming a rock against another rock and expecting the barrier to evaporate.

A few tears dripped onto her skin.

Far off, she heard the other mermaids singing her song.

They could stop Lady Ambrosia. They could reinstate the peace between Iylamor and Briglen.

"You saved my life," Ari whispered.

Wisteria smiled. She had.

What a good choice.

Of Mermaids and Men

Rachel Lawrence

Pay no mind to any man
  Who makes no time to understand
  The secrets that these oceans keep
  Of strength and beauty running deep—
  Who will not take the risk to gaze
  Beneath the surface where you blaze,
  Whose pride is threatened by your light
  And tries to sway you to lose sight
  Of all that you were made to be:
  A creature of complexity.
  The world has plenty of these men,
  But you are rare, my mermaid friend.
  Don't ever change to fit the mold
  Of someone who would rather hold
  You to a standard you've outgrown
  Than hold your hand inside his own
  And seize the chance to come along
  Enraptured by your siren song—

For nothing could be quite as tragic
As muting mystery and magic
To please a heart that will not prize
The treasure that within you lies.
Better to swim alone than with
A man who makes you live a myth.

Acknowledgments

In an anthology of this size, there are many people involved, and we are grateful for each and every one. We'd especially like to thank the following:

- AJ Skelly and Quill & Flame Publishing: AJ, thank you so much for partnering with Hannah and me to help bring this anthology to the world. We appreciate your publishing and business expertise, and your skills with spreadsheets have been a lifesaver as we navigated these editing seas. ;-) It's been wonderful to have you aboard our publishing ship!

- To all the poets, authors, and artists: Thank you for submitting your pieces and working so hard on edits. Thank you for your patience with our many emails and messages. We are so proud of you all and so happy to feature you in this anthology. We hope this has been a pleasant publishing experience for you, and we're so honoured to have gotten to work with you all!

- To Maria Spada (@mspremades on Instagram), our wonderful cover designer. Thank you so much for your tireless efforts and never getting frustrated with our crazy timeline. We appreciate and love your gorgeous design!

• To you, dear reader: Thank you for reading this book—we hope you've found pieces of adventure, of beauty, of catharsis, of challenge, of hope. May you continue to brave the seas of life and know that, despite the horrors, there are good things, too.

• To God, Alpha and Omega, Beginning and End: Thank You for being there in the peaceful lagoons, in the storm-tossed seas, and in the whispering waves. We are forever grateful for Your guidance and love.

About the Contributors

Angela Patera is a self-taught artist whose art has appeared in numerous publications, as well as on the cover of Selenite Press and Penumbra Online. Her art usually draws inspiration from the genres of horror and fantasy, but also from folklore and nature. You can find her on both Twitter and Instagram as: @angela_art13

Rebekah Isert is the author of Whitney nominated *Wednesday's Book* and *Oak and Ivy*. She loves cats, crafts, and food, and enjoys watching jiu-jitsu matches and hockey games.

Zimri A.Z. Zoran. Tea Drinker. Cat Collector. Introvert bordering on absolute hermitude. When he's not partaking in the standard authorial clichés, he's drowning his stories in sarcastic satire and metaphor with a healthy serving of adventure and sometimes a dash of romance. Still a stealthy dabbler to the world of published work, he's currently scheming his inevitable conquest. You can keep up with his world domination and his animal minions using @zimriazz on social media.

Cassandra Hamm is a psychology nerd, jigsaw puzzler, cat mom, and art collector who spends most of her time lost in another realm. Her award-winning work appears in various anthologies, including Havok Publishing's collections, *Warriors Against the Storm*, *Fantasea*, *Sharper Than Thorns*, and *Wither and Bloom*. A mental health advocate with a passion for social justice, she writes about shattered girls finding their way in the world.

Hope Bolinger is an acquisitions editor and the author of 20+ books. Find out more about her at Hopebolinger.com

Katie Hanna is a writer in her spare time and a dreamer all the time. She has a Master's degree in history from the University of Memphis, and puts it to work writing historical fiction and historical fantasy. Katie likes strong women in her adventure stories and Oreos in her ice cream.

Annee Clark is a 21-year-old aspiring author who enjoys reading, writing, and otherwise engaging in the world of fantasy. While she mostly writes flash fiction, she hopes to someday complete a novel or a collection of short stories. She would like to thank her friends in the online writing community for their support and encouragement throughout her journey.

Anne J. Hill is an author who enjoys writing fantasy for all ages. She runs Twenty Hills Publishing with the help of her circus performing best friend, Lara E. Madden.

Savannah Jezowski lives in a drafty farmhouse in southern Michigan with her Knight in Shining Armor and two wee warrior princesses. She specializes in writing fantasy that features strong heroines and tragic heroes who battle to find light in the darkness. Follow her at www.dragonpenpress.com.

Adella Quick is an aspiring author from southern Ontario and is currently working on her first novel. She also enjoys writing poetry in her spare time. You can read more about Adella's writing journey and connect with her on social media by visiting linktr.ee/Adella.Quick

Rachel Lawrence writes from South Carolina, where she lives with her husband, four children, and no pets (despite the kids' constant campaign for one). She processes the world spinning around her and the thoughts swirling within her through stories and poetry. Her favorite poets range from King David to Elizabeth Barrett Browning to Taylor Swift. Her favorite Story is still being written.

Wyn Estelle Owens spent her childhood with her nose in a book and her head in the clouds, daydreaming about epic quests, high seas adventures, and fairytales. No longer a child (on the outside, anyway), she's started to take those daydreams out of the clouds and put them down on paper, hoping to inspire others in the same way.

Kim Chance is a high-school English teacher and an award-winning author of young adult contemporary fantasy novels. For more information about her novels, visit www.kimchanc e.com

Mariella Taylor was raised on fairy lit paths somewhere between the backstreet alleys of Jackson, Mississippi and the jazz infested avenues of New Orleans. She spends her days juggling armfuls of books and trying to reach the top shelves in all the local libraries, and she spends her nights grumbling at her uncooperative characters. Her writing can be found in Whispers From Before: Tales of Myth and Legend, Aphotic Love, and Fool's Honor.

Anna Augustine is the author of The Taletha Love Stories with Quill and Flame Publishing House. She loves telling stories that inspire hope and joy to her readers.

Meaghan Ward is a self-taught, freelance illustrator who strives to capture emotion in every piece she paints and ultimately dreams of creating artwork worth a thousand words. You can find her on Instagram @meaghan.draws and on Youtube @meaghandraws.

An avid reader and a vivid daydreamer, **Megan Dill** loves reading and writing stories, especially the magical kind with imaginary creatures and crazy adventures. You can find her on Instagram @the_bookish_raven.

Erin Artfich loves writing young adult fantasy stories where the villain is every bit as captivating as the hero. When not writing, she is usually exploring the countryside with her husband and two daughters.

E.A. Hendryx is an author and graphic designer living in Indiana with her husband, two dogs, and a cat named Pages. She's a member of SCBWI and ACFW, and writes fiction in multiple genres. She spends more time on Instagram than she probably should and has built a thriving community around her Instagram platform and brand *CreateExploreRead.*

Julia Skinner is a sinner saved by Jesus, story-addict, and ice cream enthusiast. She dwells in a hobbit hole in South Texas, and spends her days wrangling her two mini monsters (aka Mini Australian Shepherds), reading aloud to her siblings, and dreaming up fantastical worlds.

Abigail Falanga writes fantasy and science fiction, and is possibly some kind of fae creature, living in New Mexico with family, books, and wild ambitions. She's released many flash fictions, short stories, a novel, and co-edits the Whitstead Anthologies, and plans to fill libraries with more writing.

Moriah Chavis is the author of *Heart of the Sea*, a YA fantasy coming late summer 2023, and a two-time graduate from the University of South Carolina. She holds a Bachelor's in Liberal Arts and a Master's in Library and Information Science. Now she works as an elementary school librarian, which is perfect since her favorite two activities are reading or writing. Moriah is also known for perusing bookstores attempting to persuade strangers to read her favorite books, oscillating between watching the *Lord of the*

Rings trilogy (her husband's favorite) or *Harry Potter* (hers), and keeping her books from the clutches of her two feisty cats.

Art allows us to reframe the world, see things not as they are but how they could be, create order out of chaos, and inspire ideas that change the way we look at life. From a young age, **Kaitlyn** has been honing creative skills with this goal in mind, focusing on graphic design, flat lay photography, and creative writing. To see more of Kaitlyn's work, visit her website at Kaitlyn-Emery.com or follow her on Instagram under @kaitlyn_scribbling where she is addicted to getting the perfect bookstagram aesthetic!

Maseeha (@sincerelymaseeha) is a full-time student, part-time writer, and secretly a werewolf, but don't tell anyone that. Her writing ranges from the fun and whimsical to the dark and serious, most of the time settling somewhere in the middle.

AJ Skelly is an author, reader, and lover of all things fantasy, medieval, and fairy-tale-romance. And werewolves. She has a serious soft spot for them. Find her completed bestselling series, *The Wolves of Rock Falls*, wherever books are sold.

You can find out more at www.ajskelly.com.

ABOUT THE EDITORS

Hannah Carter is just a girl who loves to dream and write and still wakes up every day hoping to figure out she's secretly a mermaid. Hannah's debut YA fantasy novel, Depths of Atlantis, is out now through SnowRidge Press. Her short stories and award-winning flash fiction pieces have been published in anthologies such as: SnowRidge Press's "Whispers From Before," all of Twenty Hill's anthologies, Havok's "Prismatic"—where she won an Editor's Choice Award—and "Casting Call," as well as other anthologies from Alex Silvius, Effie Joe Stock, and Nightshade Publishing. In 2022, her flash fiction piece, "A Home for Nova,"

won a Realm Award. Hannah also won a competition with her short story, "Lara." In addition to fiction, she also has had over a dozen devotionals published in various magazines, as well as six devotions published in Finding God in Anime Volumes 1 and 2. In her spare time, she's probably either cuddling her cats, drinking tea, reading, or practicing for her imaginary Broadway debut. Connect with her on Instagram at @mermaidhannahwrites.

Beka Gremikova writes folkloric fantasy from her little nook in the Ottawa Valley, Ontario, Canada. When she's not trekking across the globe, she plays video games, dabbles in art, or curls up in a cozy corner with a mystery novel. Her work can be found in various anthologies—including *Tales From the Tower*, *Sharper Than Thorns*, and *Fantasea*—and her indie debut, *The Other Cinderella*, is now available in ebook and paperback from Amazon. Her first full-length book, a collection of fantasy and sci-fi tales currently codenamed Project Dragon, will release with SnowRidge Press in Fall 2023. To keep up with all her writing mayhem, you can sign up for her newsletter at bekagremikova.com, follow her on Instagram

@beka.gremikova, or join her reader group, "Beka's Books," on Facebook.

About the Publisher

Find other Quill & Flame titles at www.quillandflame.com or

@quill.and.flame.publishers on Instagram.

Stay tuned for more short stories as well as feature releases from Quill & Flame Publishing House by signing up for their newsletter.
Join Quill & Flame Book Tours by emailing quillandflamepublis hinghouse@gmail.com.

IF YOU WANT TO READ MORE BOOKS LIKE

Tide & Scale

QUILL & FLAME PUBLISHING HOUSE HAS YOU COVERED

HEAT WITHOUT THE SCORCH

www.quillandflame.com